Mother of the Blue Wolf

Fractured Empire Saga Book Three

Starr Z. Davies

Character Assassin Books

First published in the United States in 2025 by Character Assassin Books an imprint of Starr Z Davies, 1328 Lynn Avenue Altoona, WI 54720 USA. Email: starr@starrzdavies.com

Cover design and typography by Katrina Design
Book layout and design by Starr Z Davies & Atticus software
Maps, glyphs, and illustrations relating to maps by Starr Z Davies & Inkarnate software

www.starrzdavies.com

Contents

To Lori,
for your *very* early enthusiasm for Mandukhai's epic story.

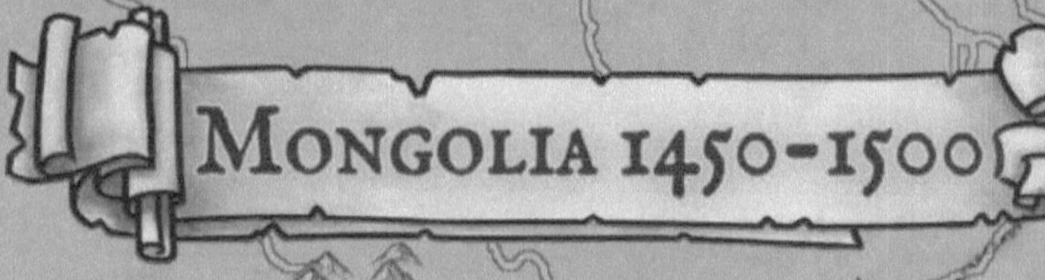

MONGOLIA 1450-1500

OIRAT UYGHUR TERRITORY
KHANGAI MOUNTAINS
ALTAI MOUNTAINS
ZAVKHAN RIVER
TIANSHAN MOUNTAINS
TURFAN
HAMI
GA

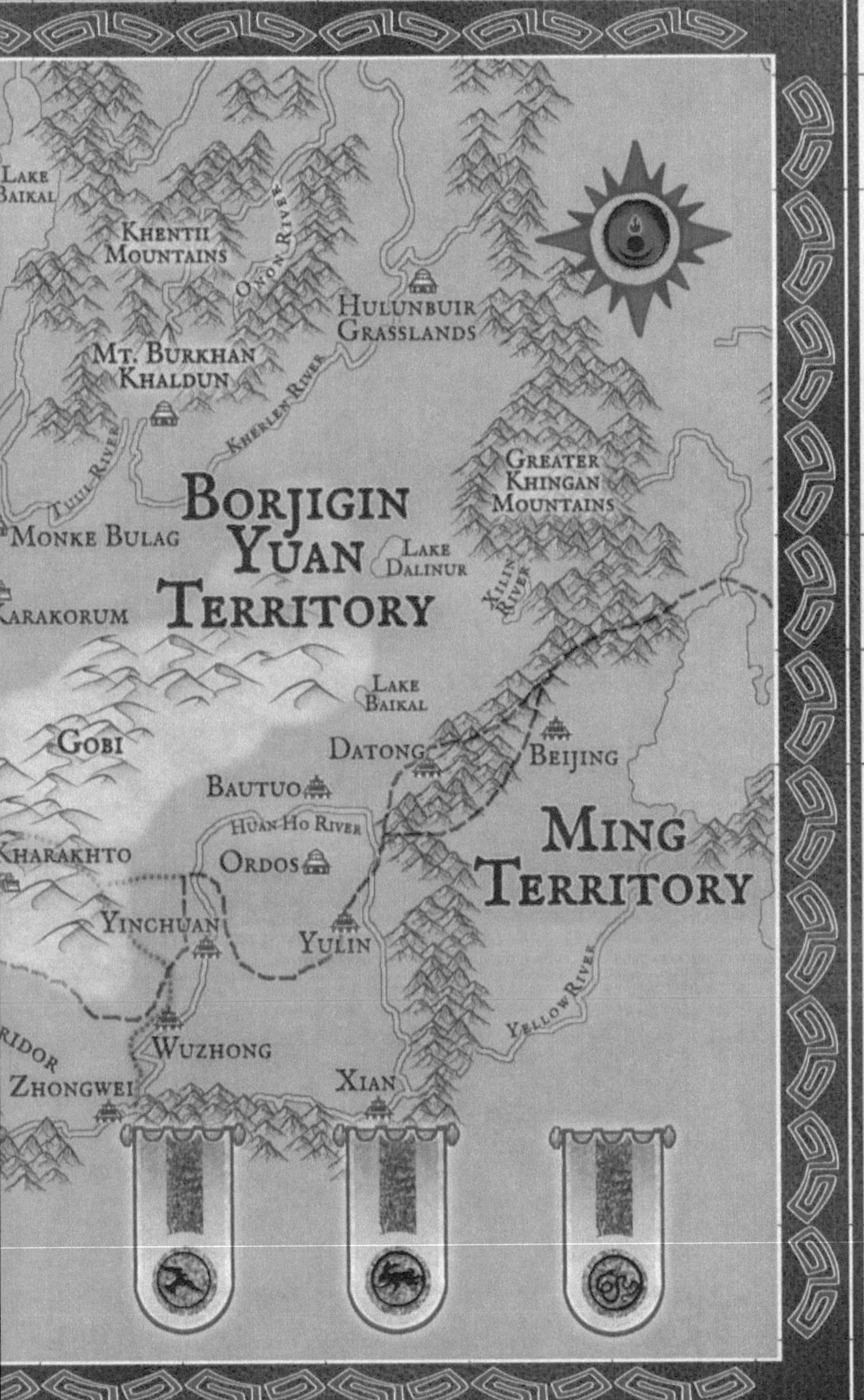

LAKE
BAIKAL
KHENTII
MOUNTAINS
ONON RIVER
HULUNBUIR
GRASSLANDS
MT. BURKHAN
KHALDUN
KHERLEN RIVER
TUUL RIVER
GREATER
KHINGAN
MOUNTAINS
BORJIGIN
YUAN
TERRITORY
MONKE BULAG
LAKE
DALINUR
XILIN RIVER
KARAKORUM
LAKE
BAIKAL
GOBI
DATONG
BEIJING
BAUTUO
HUAN HO RIVER
MING
TERRITORY
KHARAKHTO
ORDOS
YINCHUAN
YULIN
YELLOW RIVER
RIDOR
WUZHONG
ZHONGWEI
XIAN

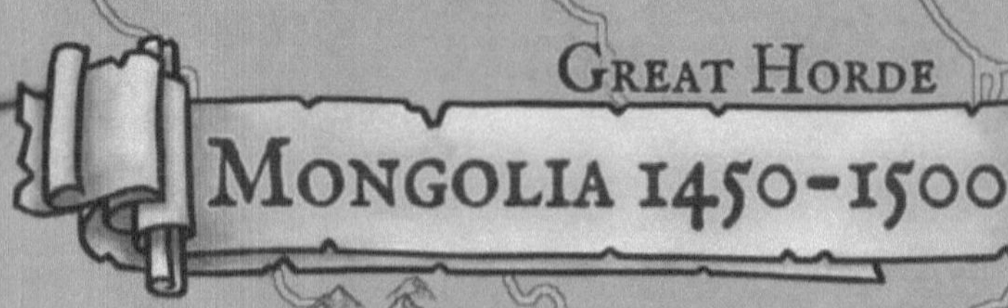

GREAT HORDE
MONGOLIA 1450-1500
OIRAT
UYGHUR

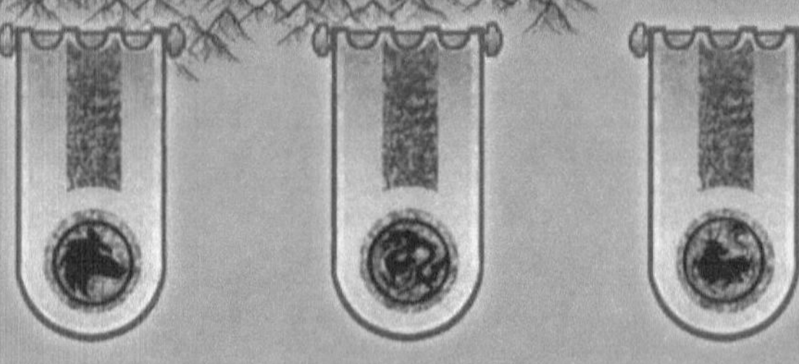

JALAIR
KHORCHIN
& KHARCHIN
JURCHEN
KHORLOD
BORJIGIN
ONGUD
CHAKHAR
ORDOS
MING

ROYAL LINEAGE
THROUGH 1464

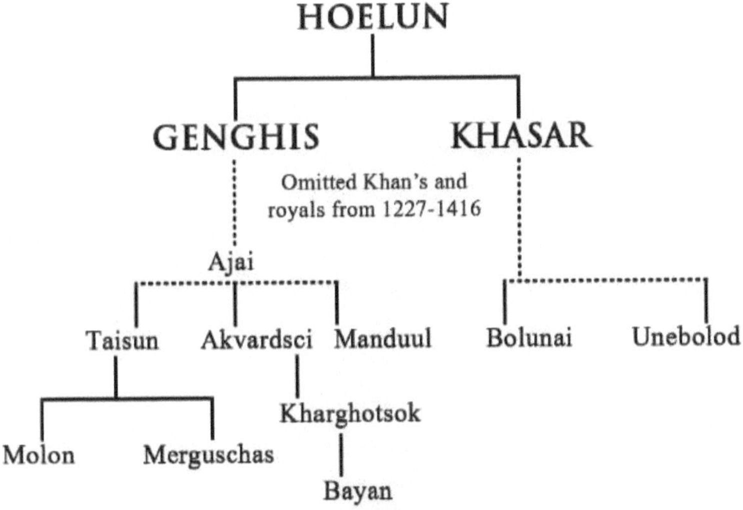

While there are certainly other royals before Ajai, for the purposes of this series, only those after him will be listed to avoid confusion. Esen is not listed on this chart because he does not descend from this royal tree.

Glossary & Pronunciation Guide

airag (eye-rahg) – alcoholic drink made from fermented mare's milk, typically milky in color

arban (ahr-bahn) – unit of ten Mongol warriors

Bankhar (bahn-khahr) – traditional sheepherding dog of the Mongolian steppe; 24-31 inches tall at the shoulder with typically dark brown hair

bariach (bar-ee-ach) – ancient art of bonesetting and therapeutic massage

Biyelgee (bey-eel-geeh) – traditional dance of celebration and community

black airag – stronger version of regular airag with a longer fermentation process, typically clear in color

boal (boh-ahl) – honey wine

bökh (boo-k) – Mongolian style of wrestling where only the feet are allowed to touch the ground or you lose

boqta (bohk-tah) – column-like headdress decorated with beads and silver; the taller the boqta, the more prominent the woman wearing it

buuz (boos) – meat stuffed dumplings

deel (deal) – robe-like wrap worn by the Mongol people, traditionally made of silk, velvet, or woolen felt with ties or silver buttons and belted at the waist with a belt; lined with sheep's wool or fur in the winter

ger (grr) – round, dome-like house made of Birchwood lattice and lathes, then covered in wool felt; known in America as a yurt

gonji (goonj) – a princess

jagan (jah-gahn) – unit of 100 Mongol warriors (or 10 arban)

jinong (gee-nong) – a prince

khatun (ka-toon) – the formal Mongol word for Queen; a title of power

kurultai (kuh-ruhl-tai) – a gathering of tribal lords where they elected the next Great Khan

mingghan (min-ghahn) – unit of 1000 Mongol warriors (or 10 jagan)

orlok (oor-lahk) – field commander of multiple tumens

paiza (pie-zah) – a golden medallion of safe passage, given only to high-ranking officials as a means of protection under the Great Khan

shanaavch (shah-navsh) – headdress made of long strings of beads and bells, typically silver, coral, or turquoise

sulde (sool-duh) – a banner made of colored horse-hair, typically arranged in a circle

toortsog (toort-sogh) – hat made of silk, sometimes with fur or felt lining and a knot of colored tails or feathers at the top; typically worn by noble men

tumen (tyoo-mehn) – regiment of 10,000 Mongol warriors

uni (oo-nee) – a pole made of birch; used as a support beam for the ceiling of a ger

CHARACTERS

Aglaqu (ahg-la-coo) – Ordos Lord

Asha (ah-shah) – Oirat Lord/Paisahan's son

Alayitung (al-eye-ih-toong) – Borjigin commander; Vice Chancellor

Albeq (al-bek) – Tabun khan

Altan (ahl-than) – Lady and commander of the Jalair; Hulun's daughter

Arqai (ar-keye) — Ordos Lord

Arslan (ahr-slahn) – Mandukhai's night guard

Bagasun (ba-ga-soon) – Altan's oldest son

Bagatur (ba-ga-toor) – Kharchin khan

Batsaihan (baht-sahi-han) – Odgerel's father

Bayan Bolkhu Mongke (bay-yahn bohl-koo mohng-kay) – Borjigin prince; last true descendant of Genghis Khan

Berkedai (buhr-ke-dahee) – Khorchin commander; Bayan's guard

Bigirsen (big-er-sehn) – Uyghur warlord; Manduul Khan's Vice Regent; orlok of the southern tumens of the Great Khan

Bolunai (boh-loo-nahee) – Khorchin khan; older brother of Unebolod; descendant of Khasar

Boke (boh-kay) – Borjigin tribe; young leader of Manduul's royal guard

Boragan (bow-ra-gahn) – Ongud Lord; son of Korgiz khan

Borogchin (boh-rohg-chin) – Borjigin princess; niece of Manduul Khan

Burani (bur-ah-nee) – Issama's oldest son with Siker

Chakicha (cha-key-cha) – Tabun Lord; son of Albeq khan

Chenghua (jen-gwa) – Ming Emperor

Chimgee (chim-jee) – Huoshai's mother

Dashai (dah-shy) – man who saves Bayan in the Gobi

Dayan Batu Khan (day-ahn bah-too) – Bayan's long-lost son

Degghar (dehg-ghahr) – Chakhar man; Siker's father

Emeeltorson (em-eel-tor-sun) – Esige/Huoshai's oldest son

Enkh (enk) – Bayan's servant

Esen (eh-sehn) – Oirat Lord and leader; Borjigin Butcher

Esige (eh-seeg-hay) – Borjigin princess; niece of Manduul Khan

Ganzorig (gahn-zor-ig) – Bolunai's youngest son; promised to Odgerel

Genghis Khan (jehn-giss) – First Great Khan of the Mongol Nation; died 1227

Getei (jet-ehee) – Ongud soothsayer

Guden (goo-dehn) – Chakhar khan

Hulun (huh-loon) – Lord of the Jalair

Huoshai (hwoh-shy) – Lord of the Urainkhai

Ibarai (ee-bar-eye) – Ordos Lord/commander

Issama (ee-sah-mah) – Bigirsen's Uyghur advisor

Jaghan (jahg-han) – Jalair tribe; Togochi's wife

Jangi (jahn-jee) – Uyghur warrior; Nemeku's guard

Khadag (kah-dahg) – Uyghur who rescues Batu from Issama

Khasar (kah-sahr) – brother of Genghis; son of Hoelun

Khosoichi (co-soy-chi) – Borjigin shaman; serves Manduul

Khutulun (koo-too-loon) – daughter of Kaidu; warrior princess

Korgiz (koor-gihs) – Ongud khan

Legusi (leg-oo-see) – Ordos khan

Mandukhai (mahn-doo-khahee) – Ongud daughter of a lord; Manduul Khan's second wife

Manduul Khan (mahn-dool) – Oirat-Borjigin ruler of Mongolia; descendent of Genghis Khan

Mendu (mehn-doo) – Khorlod khan

Mingtau (ming-taoo) – Chakhar elder/commander

Mogurkei (mo-gur-kay) – Ordos Lord

Molon Khan (moh-lohn) – 17-year-old Great Khan before Manduul; Manduul's nephew; killed in battle

Nahai (na-hi) – Uyghur commander; Issama's right hand man

Nergui (nair-gooee) – Mandukhai's loyal Ongud guard; murdered by Bayan

Odgerel (ode-ger-el) – Khorchin woman; Unebolod's servant

Odsar (ohd-sahr) – Unebolod's dead wife

Orghana (org-ha-na) – Ordos Lady; Legusi's little sister

Ormeger (or-mee-gr) – Urainkhai commander; Huoshai's cousin

Paisahan (pie-sah-han) – Oirat khan

Qolotai (co-lo-tie) – Issama's third wife

Samur (sah-muhr) – great-great-grandmother of Bayan

Satai (sah-tie) – Lady of the Alaguchid tribe; wife of Unige

Seguse (seg-oo-say) – Uyghur warrior; Borogchin's spy/messenger

Siker (see-kur) – daughter of Degghar; Chakhar girl; Bayan's lover

Soke (soh-kay) – Khorchin commander

Sorkhogtani (sor-kog-ta-nai) – Kublai Khan's mother

Taisun Khan (tahee-soon) – Manduul's older half-brother; killed by Esen

Tayiqu (tay-ick-oo) – Lady of the Urainkhai

Tengghar (tayng-ghahr) – Khorchin lord; Bolunai's son; Unebolod's nephew

Toghon (tohg-hone) – Oirat Lord/commander

Tolokan (toh-low-can) – Urainkhai khan

Toregene (tor-eh-jenay) – Ogedei Khan's wife; empress for five years

Torgus (tohr-gus) – Mandukhai's guard

Torudur (tor-oo-dur) – Togochi's eldest son

Tsetseg (zeht-sehg) – Esen's daughter; Bayan's mother

Togochi (toh-goh-chee) – lord and General of the Khorlod; Manduul's loyal sworn brother (no blood)

Tulugen (too-loo-jen) – Three Guards Lord

Tuya (too-yah) – Mandukhai's Ongud servant

Uingen (oo-in-jen) – Issama's first wife

Unebolod (oo-nuh-boh-lod) – lord of the Khorchin; Manduul's loyal sword brother (no blood); Orlok of the northern tumens of the Great Khan

Unige (oo-nee-kay) – Alyghuchid Lord/leader; Borjigin loyalist; a member of Manduul Khan's council

Wang Yue (wang-you) – Ming Commander

Yaqui (ya-kwee) – Khorlod Lord/commander

Yeke (yeh-keh) – Uyghur daughter of Bigirsen; Manduul Khan's first wife

Yungei (yoon-geh-hee) – Khorchin commander; Bayan's guard

Alyghuchid (al-ee-goo-chid)) – tribe of the northern steppe

Borjigin (bohr-eh-gin) – tribe of the Great Khan Genghis
Chakhar (shah-kahr) – tribe of the southern steppe; Siker's tribe
Great Horde – tribe of the far northern steppe (Russian territory); formerly the Golden Horde
Erkegud (air-ke-goot) – lesser tribe of the Khorlod
Jalair (jah-laheer) – tribe of the northernmost steppe
Kharchin (car-chin) – subtribe of the Khorchin
Khorchin (koor-chin) – tribe of Genghis Khan's younger brother Khasar; Yuan Dynasty ally
Khorlod (koor-lahd) – tribe of the eastern steppe; Togochi's tribe
Oirat (ohee-raht) – collective of four major western tribes who oppose Borjigin rule; commonly called "Four Oirat"
Ongud (ahn-goot) – tribe of the southern steppe; Mandukhai's birth tribe
Ordos (or-dose) – tribe of the southern steppe
Tabun (tah-boon) – lesser tribe of the eastern steppe
Urainkhai (oo-ree-ahng-high) – southern tribe of the steppe
Uyghur (wee-ger) – tribe of the southwestern step; formerly Chagatai Khanate

Locations

Altai Mountains (all-tie) – mountain range cradling Oirat territory
Bautuo (bow-to-oh) – Ming/Mongol city north of the Huang Ho River
Datong (dah-tong) – Ming/Mongol city near the Great Wall
Gansu Corridor (gahn-soo) – corridor between the mountains and rivers leading into China
Greater Khingan Mountains (kin-gahn) – mountain range barring the eastern Mongol border
Hami (hah-mee) – oasis city in the Gobi connecting the far east to the far west
Huang Ho River (wang-ho) – Great Loop river, also known as the Yellow River
Hulunbuir (hoo-loon-boo-eer) – eastern Grasslands of the Khorchin & Kharchin tribes
Khangai Mountains (khan-guy) – mountains west of Mongke Bulag
Karakorum (ka-ra-core-um) – Mongolian sacred capital city
Khentii Mountains (ken-tea) – dominant mountain range in the northern steppe
Kherlen River (curl-ehn) – river of the Mongol steppe

Kokegota (co-keg-oh-ta) – Ming-controlled city

Mongke Bulag (mohng-kay boo-lahg) – Manduul Khan's capital in the Orkhon Valley

Mt. Burkhan Khaldun (bur-khan cahll-dune) – sacred mountain of Genghis in the Khentii mountain range

Ongi River (on-jee) – Small riverbed feeding from Orkhan toward the Gobi

Orkhon Valley (ohrk-hohn) – lush river valley of the Mongol steppe

Tianshan Mountains (tee-ahn-shaan) – mountains dividing Oirat/Uyghur territories

Tohom (too-hom) – red, rocky cliffs at the edge of the Gobi

Turfan (tur-phahn) – city in the former Chagatai khanate

Tuul River (tool) – river branch in heading east out of the Orkhon valley

Wuzhong (woo-zong) – Ming border city on the Huang Ho River

Xilin River (jgee-lyn) – river along the southeastern Mongolian territories

Yinchuan (yin-chwahn) – city bordering the Huang Ho River and Great Wall into the Ordos basin

Yulin (you-lin) – city along the Ming-Mongol border

Zavkhan River (zav-khan) – major river feeding Oirat territory from the Altai mountains

Zhongwei (zong-way) – Ming border city in the Gansu Corridor

MILITARY STRUCTURE

Arban = 10 men

Jagan = 100 men (10 arban)

Mingghan = 1000 men (10 jagan)

Tumen = 10000 men (10 mingghan)

Officer - man in command of a single jagan or arban

Commander - officer in charge of a single mingghan

General - commander in charge of a tumen

Orlok - field marshal in charge of multiple tumens; military strategist

Wolf Mother discovered the Two-legs boy
wounded in a massacred village,
And so she healed him.

Two-legs rode her across the steppe
with no one else to defend him,
And so she protected him.

Abandoned with no one to rear him
Two-legs had only Wolf Mother,
And so she raised him.

As he became a man, Two-legs adored her
and Wolf Mother loved him dearly,
And so she wed him.

And from him, Wolf Mother birthed
ten strapping boys
who would form the Mongol tribes.

~ Tale of the Wolf Mother and the Boy

Heir of Genghis

Mandukhai paced the dais in the gathering tent, back and forth between copper fire pots, as she waited. News of Manduul Khan's death had spread swiftly beyond the heart of the Nation. Keeping such an event secret had only proven possible for so long before Mandukhai could no longer contain the truth. After the tribes surrounding Mongke Bulag had dispersed, word reached the east, south, and west. Now, the Oirat tribes were more active near the borders than ever before. She worried this meant war. Nearly three months had passed since Manduul's funeral and Unebolod's return to Mongke Bulag, which gave the Oirat time to prepare for invasion. They had coveted the title of Great Khan for centuries, and men like Esen had attempted stealing it. Mandukhai knew how that had ended. In revolt and death. Her father had led that revolt. She wanted a more peaceful transition.

Mandukhai had hoped for better support from the Lords regarding her new title of Queen Regent than she had received. Her grasp on the nation slipped little by little each day. Though the Mongol Lords respected her position as was proper, they had made themselves clear. She was not their leader, but a placeholder until *they* selected the next Great Khan. Many of them preferred Unebolod. *I prefer him as well*, she thought.

She and Unebolod had agreed that it was best for her to observe a period of mourning before she would officially accept any offers of marriage—a marriage which would give the man who wed her the strongest claim on the title of Great Khan. Mandukhai appreciated Unebolod's patience, but she knew it would only go so far. He didn't just want her. He wanted the title.

In her vision with Genghis five years ago, he cut Esen's hanging body from a tree and accused him of pretending to be a wolf. Some part of Mandukhai worried that the same fate awaited Unebolod if he took the title before she knew for certain what Batu's fate would be. There could be no doubt for Unebolod to be Great Khan. There could be no heir of Genghis remaining. Only then could Unebolod's path be clear.

Though they flirted with the idea of her officially proclaiming him, she had been careful to avoid the reality of this claim. He could assert himself and try taking the title, citing Manduul naming him next should there be no heirs of Genghis, yet he had not. Not yet.

And there was another heir. Mandukhai sent her Uyghur spy to hunt down the abandoned child months ago. Today, her spy returned to give the full report, but she was certain of one thing.

Batu lived.

The line of Genghis had not died with Manduul and Bayan. If Mandukhai handled this properly, no one would know who Batu was until he came of age.

Unebolod and I can marry, raise Batu, and when the time comes, and he is old enough, we can install him as the next Great Khan. Mandukhai rubbed her hands together, nodding to herself. It would work. It had to. Genghis had told her only he of his bone would have the strength to hold the fractured empire together. Surely that must have meant Batu. *I will tell Unebolod the truth once I am certain Batu will survive.*

She feared for the boy's life. For her plan to work, no one else could know who he truly was. Any man of ambition could kill Bayan's young son to eliminate the boy's rightful claim.

No one in Mongke Bulag doubted Unebolod's ambition. He had set up his ger where Manduul's had stood, a clear signal of his intention. Some nights, the proximity proved a true test of willpower. Mandukhai wanted to go to him.

She paused in her pacing and closed her eyes, hugging her arms against her chest. *I miss having his arms around me.* She wanted to give herself to him as she had years ago—so long ago! However, it would be improper for her to sleep with him until they made their marriage official, and she would not risk any breach of etiquette that might stir anyone's doubt. Unebolod agreed it would be best to wait, but she sensed his tension just as surely as her own whenever they were close to each other.

Today, Unebolod would spend the day with their meager army, training the men for a battle he was certain loomed on the horizon—and perhaps he even looked forward to. The Oirat tribes could attack any day. The tribes were much larger than the meager forces she held together with fish glue and prayers. If the Oirat attacked, they could easily win and steal the khanship. *Genghis, if this is part of your plan, please guide me!*

Genghis had not come to her in another vision. Were it not for her faith in the High Heavens, Mandukhai might have doubted the truth of the promise Genghis made her. That she would birth a pack of wolves to restore the fractured empire.

The door to the gathering tent groaned open. Mandukhai's eyes snapped open, and she turned, relaxing her features in what she hoped was a calm, collected manner. Seguse strode in, unarmed, and stopped in front of the dais. He bowed his head and waited patiently for Mandukhai to speak first.

"I hope you have good news to report, Seguse," Mandukhai said, settling back into her throne atop the dais.

Seguse stood and folded his hands behind his back. "That depends on how you define good, Queen Regent." His weathered face pinched tight. "The boy lives, but barely. He is in the care of one of my fellow Uyghur and his wife."

Mandukhai's stomach churned. She trusted Seguse, who had spied for Borogchin for years. But Uyghur often had prickly loyalties. "Can we trust him?"

Seguse fell silent as he considered this. "I trust him. He doesn't really know who the boy is. Khadag informed me he came across the boy just before Issama's men arrived with orders to capture or kill."

"Did Issama know the boy's parentage?" Mandukhai asked. Issama was now married to the boy's mother. That gave Issama a stronger claim on Batu's life.

"No. Batu lived with an old woman named Bachari, but he was horribly neglected, sickly, and crippled. Issama ordered the ger burned, the old woman killed, and the boy brought to him. It was little more than a means of acquiring her few animals to feed his men."

Mandukhai's nails bit into her palms. "But Issama had no idea?"

"No, Queen Regent. By some stroke of fortune, he did not know at all. Khadag took pity on the boy and smuggled Batu off to his wife, Saichai. She is a gifted healer."

Mandukhai uncurled her fingers and stretched her palm over the carved arms of the chair. Issama had nearly taken the boy. He still could if he ever learned the truth.

"Where is Batu now?" she asked.

"About a hundred miles north of Hami, near the Dragon's Spine of the Gobi," Seguse replied. "I saw Batu with my own eyes. He is not well, Queen Regent—far too ill to make the journey north before spring. He suffers from a sickness of the stomach and ..." Seguse's nose curled ever so slightly in a clear disgust he tried to hide but failed miserably at. "And he has a hunchback-like growth. Saichai said he should have died long ago, and that he's been horribly neglected. She is doing everything she can to heal him. I did not tell them who Batu is, but I expressed your keen interest in his wellbeing. I presume it's safe to assume you will pay them handsomely for their time and financial burden."

Mandukhai nodded. She would pay them in bags of fine silver if it healed Batu and kept him safe.

"I told them as much and pressed the importance of keeping Batu a secret from others," Seguse said. "I reassured Saichai that you would reward her for his safety and healing, but only if he survived and arrived safely in your care this spring. As soon as he is well enough to travel, they will bring him to you."

"You have done well, Seguse," Mandukhai replied. "And as much as I wish I could send you back to ensure Batu's safety, I cannot."

"I am satisfied settling in Mongke Bulag for a time."

"If only. But it is time for you to leave Mongke Bulag."

He drew up to a stiff spine. "Queen Regent?"

"Lord Unebolod has no trust for any man of Uyghur blood," Mandukhai said calmly. "And you are one of the few remaining. However, I do not send you away without purpose. My scouts tell me that the Oirat are moving, possibly against our camp." She refused to call Mongke Bulag a capital any longer. It gave too much permanence to their position and soon they would move on to better pastures. "As a Uyghur, you can infiltrate their position and learn more of their intentions. I cannot have the Oirat kicking up a dust cloud before we have a new Great Khan." When Seguse did not respond, Mandukhai offered a kind smile. "I am promoting you, Seguse, to *jagan* officer. Gather a hundred men capable of carrying out this task with you—Uyghur men, if possible, and men who would be credible as defectors if not Uyghur—and ride west."

Seguse struggled with his smile, but it curled the corner of his lips all the same. "It will be as you command, Queen Regent."

"Do not attack the Oirat, Seguse," she warned. "Your job is to make them believe you have defected to their side. Join them. Serve me well in this, and you will be further rewarded."

Seguse formally thanked Mandukhai and waited for dismissal before leaving her alone once more. She sat back and smiled to herself. Soon, she would have information from deep in Oirat circles to advise her actions further.

Weary, Mandukhai rose and stretched her limbs, then rolled her shoulders. She needed fresh air to fuel her sluggish mind, and so she headed out of the gathering tent.

Mongke Bulag had become a ghost of its former self. Aside from the Borjigin, other tribes had drifted away, no longer tethered to a Great Khan. Only Togochi's Khorlod remained—numbering fewer than ten thousand—and Unebolod's Khorchin dominated the space. Unebolod's presence in Mongke Bulag dwarfed her own. Mandukhai knew that only his love and respect for her kept him from simply seizing control, and she adored him for it all the more.

As she approached her own ger, Mandukhai spotted Unebolod checking the saddle on his mare, tightening the girth strap, and adjusting the blanket. The mare bobbed her head and stomped as Mandukhai approached, which made the leather armor on the mount's chest creak.

Unebolod turned from his task. "I heard you did not rest well again last night," he said.

Mandukhai grimaced. Esige certainly had no trouble sharing anything that was not strictly a secret with him. The girl had so much respect for Unebolod—almost as a daughter would her father. "I am rested as well as I need to be. How is the training going with your men?"

She stopped close enough to feel the heat rolling off his body. As he gazed down at her, he subtly reached for her hand, brushing his fingers over her own and sending a jolt through her body. Such a simple touch. Such an intense response.

Mandukhai's guards lingered nearby, always watching, and she was certain they saw the way Unebolod touched her hand. Yet she did not care. Their job was to guard her, and Unebolod, as they well knew, was no threat. Boke had made a threatening move toward Unebolod shortly after his return to Mongke Bulag, but Mandukhai had dressed Boke down so swiftly and certainly that none of her guards had dared question Unebolod's presence around her again.

"Soke still has the men in the field," he said.

"All of them?"

Unebolod raised a brow at the question but did not answer directly. "Are you aware that Esige has been wrestling my men?"

Mandukhai smothered a smirk. "No. But I imagine she has done well."

Unebolod grimaced. "She has beaten all of them. My men are complaining. It's demoralizing."

"She learned from you," Mandukhai teased, her eyes shining up at him.

He inched closer. "No. I think she gets this stubborn will from you."

"Then I have taught her well."

The tension between the two of them hung in the air like a tangible thing. She wanted to kiss him, or for him to kiss her first. It didn't matter as long as his body pressed against her own. Mandukhai's heart raced. Her stomach tumbled.

Unebolod's throat bobbed, and he stepped back toward his mare. "I should get back out into the field with the men." His fingers reluctantly slid free of hers.

Mandukhai licked her lips. Had the air grown thicker? She watched, breathless, as he swung into the saddle and rode away.

Sensing someone watching her, Mandukhai glanced around.

Odgerel lingered in the doorway of Unebolod's ger. The young woman had arrived in Mongke Bulag with the Khorchin shortly after Unebolod returned. Though he insisted Odgerel only served as his cook, the young woman acted as if she were his wife in so many ways. Too many ways.

The moment Mandukhai met her gaze, Odgerel dropped her own to the ground and bowed only slightly as a show of respect. But the girl clearly did not respect her.

Odgerel was a pretty young woman, and Mandukhai often caught her staring at Unebolod with obvious admiration and desire in her eyes. She had wormed her way into his service during his time away from Mongke Bulag, and though she had not once spoken ill of the Queen Regent, Mandukhai often felt the woman staring at her with sharpened daggers for eyes. Today was no exception.

Mandukhai straightened her back and chin, then strolled back to her own ger. She would not give this girl the satisfaction of knowing how her presence unnerved her. When Mandukhai and Unebolod finally married,

Mandukhai would be sure Odgerel knew her place—or she would be replaced. Mandukhai would not allow a moon-eyed girl to get between her and her future husband. *I need to learn more about this woman,* Mandukhai thought as she entered her home.

Esige bounded toward Mandukhai's ger, her skin warm and flushed with excitement from several bouts of wrestling. At first, the younger men close to her own age had accepted Esige's wrestling challenges, assuming she would lose. How men couldn't learn from their mistakes, Esige would never understand. Some of those men she had been wrestling since they were boys. *And they never win,* she thought as she ducked through the doorway.

The grin on Esige's face stretched so far across her face she could feel the tension in her cheeks and jaw. Today had been different. Kudang, one of the *mingghan* commanders, had challenged her, insisting that if he won, she would speak to Mandukhai about marriage. She, of course, accepted. Kudang had tried so hard, using the skirt of her deel to try and drag her down, only for her to sweep his feet out from under him. He had grabbed her thick braids to bring her close enough to capture her in a neck hold that would have rendered her useless and defeated. Esige had predicted his move, and as he pulled her braids to draw her closer, she punched under his arms, then broke his hold and turned it against him. Only seconds later, he was pinned, face-down, in the dirt with her kneeling on his back.

"They call themselves men," Esige said as she drifted toward the bucket to wash off her hands and face. The tone in her voice made it clear she did not agree with their assessment of themselves.

"Perhaps it's time you let some of them win," Mandukhai mused as she stoked the stove.

Esige snorted. Right. Like that would ever happen. "They will never learn that way."

"Nor will you." Mandukhai's tone was sharper than normal, and disapproval burned in her dark eyes.

Esige stiffened, swiping her damp hands against her clothes. Why was Mandukhai angry with her? "What do I have to learn?"

"That men need to believe they are strong and capable if they are to survive in battle," Mandukhai said with that patient tone that often sounded condescending when she lectured Esige. "Yet your behavior—your constant victory over them—is demoralizing. If they cannot beat a girl, how can they possibly defeat an enemy?"

Esige set her shoulders, cocking her head ever so slightly to the side. "I thought you wanted me to be strong, like Khutulun. I cannot do that if the men don't respect me."

"There is a difference between respect and superiority, Esige."

"Superiority! Shall I offer you a salve for the lip service?" As soon as the words slipped out, Esige wished she could take them back. Especially upon noting the way Mandukhai clenched her hands into fists at her side. *I said too much!*

"I am Queen Regent. It is not the same thing!"

Mandukhai was right, as she often proved to be. On one hand, Esige found it hypocritical that Mandukhai would insist Esige let the men believe they were stronger when Mandukhai herself held more power than any of them. On the other hand, Esige knew that Mandukhai's future—as well as Esige's own—rested on Mandukhai's ability to hold on to that power. Without it, the two of them would be forced into the beds of any Mongol Lords strong enough to overpower them. *All the more reason for me to prove how strong I am now*, she thought.

Despite how she might agree with Mandukhai and regret her words, Esige would never admit it to anyone. Instead, she shrugged as if it didn't matter, then moved toward the butcher block to prepare dinner as if she did not notice Mandukhai's anger.

Behind her back, Esige could hear Mandukhai taking calming breaths. A moment later, Mandukhai joined her, and the two worked in silent tandem as they prepared dinner.

They set the *buuz*—meat-stuffed dumplings—aside to be steamed.

"I would appreciate a bit more respect," Mandukhai whispered.

"How much more respect do you want? I have given you all I have to offer." Esige cleaned the powder from her hands, wiping it on her already dirty deel. "What is really bothering you, Mother?"

Mandukhai's shoulder sagged slightly. Esige had always seen through Mandukhai's words, and Mandukhai often allowed Esige to speak freely, which made this entire conversation a bit startling.

"Unebolod said something about the men complaining," Mandukhai offered. "I'm simply delivering his message."

Esige slumped. "He said that?" She couldn't hide her disappointment. Unebolod was the one who taught her everything she knew about fighting. Now he wanted her to stop? *Because I am a girl and the men can't handle losing to a girl. It's absurd. Strength is strength no matter where it comes from.* But if the men wanted her to fit into their little boxes, she would oblige them until it drove every one of them mad.

"Then I shall become the simpering princess the men need me to be." Her tone dripped with sarcasm. "For the sake of their own egos, I will sacrifice my own on the altar of their shame."

Mandukhai smothered a smirk. "There's a good girl."

Esige rolled her eyes, but inside, Mandukhai's reaction warmed Esige's heart.

Nemeku bounded through the door, giggling up a storm as Mandukhai and Esige stepped back out of his way. Though he was only five, Esige's nephew showed proficiency with bows and riding. Esige adored Nemeku, but sometimes just looking at him reminded her of her sister, murdered by her own husband. *I will see Bigirsen die for it one day*, Esige vowed silently.

"Esige! Esige!" Nemeku danced around her legs like an excited dog. "I taught Torudur to hold a bow today!"

Torudur was Togochi's oldest son, and not yet three years old. Esige was surprised Togochi had not taught his son already.

Mandukhai gaped. "Torudur, Togochi's son? He's barely three. What did Lady Jaghan say?"

Tuya trailed in the door, appearing winded and quite harried, as if she had chased Nemeku all across the capital.

Nemeku scrunched up his face as only an innocent child without a care could do. "She was busy fussing over the baby. I'm going to teach Torudur how to ride next!" The boy's face lit up with certainty and pride.

Babaqai was Togochi's youngest son, almost a year and a half old now, and walking well enough to cause Jaghan trouble.

Mandukhai watched Nemeku, and Esige understood reason for Mandukhai's furrowed brow. Nemeku resembled his father, with his long, narrow face, and a nose that seemed larger each time they looked at it.

They settled into dinner with Nemeku telling grand stories of how he could ride when he was only three, and how Torudur had thought the bow was a funny thing. The boy had dominated the conversation, but as they finished, the food in his stomach slowed him down and Esige noticed how heavy his eyelids had become.

"Tuya, will you please get Nemeku tucked in for the evening? Esige and I will handle this." Mandukhai motioned toward the table.

Tuya bowed, ushering a protesting Nemeku out of the ger. He shared Esige's ger with her. Usually, it was Esige's job to see Nemeku off to bed. Which could only mean one thing.

Esige placed a hand on her hip. "You only send her to do my tasks when you need something else from me."

Mandukhai nodded. "I do. I need you to learn as much as you can about Odgerel."

Odgerel. Unebolod's ridiculously pretty servant. Esige chortled. "Is that green I see on your face?"

Though Mandukhai had not said as much, Esige could tell that her Mother had feelings for Unebolod. She had for a long time, though she thought she hid them well. For Esige, seeing Unebolod and Mandukhai together would be a best-case scenario—like her long-separated parents finally coming together.

Mandukhai scooped up a few of the dishes. "I am not jealous."

Sure you aren't.

"What is there to be jealous of?" Mandukhai asked with an innocence that was clearly forced. "But taking on a servant like her seems out of character for him. I want to know what happened and who she is."

"So the rumors *are* true," Esige said as she joined Mandukhai in clearing the table. "You intend to accept his bid. You never wanted him to marry my sister, did you?"

Mandukhai nearly dropped her dishes, poorly fumbling to recover. "I absolutely did. But it has been years, Esige, and a lot has changed since she left."

Esige wanted to believe Mandukhai, that she truly wanted to see Borogchin married to Unebolod. She had no reason not to believe her. Except for the rumors that Mandukhai and Unebolod had secretly been amorous all along. So much from those days made little sense to Esige anymore.

"Changed," Esige said flatly. Her dinner churned in her stomach. "You mean like her husband murdering her?" Esige spit the words out like a foul taste.

Mandukhai tensed, watching Esige from the corner of her eyes. What was she thinking?

"I have not agreed to accept any man yet," Mandukhai said. "But at this moment, Unebolod has the strongest claim, and is certainly the most popular among many of the Mongol Lords. I just want to be sure he does not have a spy in his midst."

Esige frowned, not convinced, but she nodded. "I will ask around. But you should talk to Boke, too."

Mandukhai's brows shot up her forehead sharply. "Why him?"

Esige rolled her eyes. She had always given Mandukhai credit for being incredibly intelligent and observant, but sometimes she missed things that should be so obvious.

"Because he has been staring at her since the moment she arrived in Mongke Bulag," Esige said, gazing curiously at Mandukhai. "You really haven't noticed?"

Mandukhai perked up ever so slightly. "Does Odgerel return his interest?"

Esige pursed her lips in thought. The few times she had watched Odgerel, the woman never once glanced at Boke—and certainly not while Unebolod was around. *Of course all the women love Unebolod. He's amazing.* She shook her head. "I don't believe so."

Mandukhai's shoulders drooped a little. No doubt it would have been a relief if Odgerel had been interested in Boke. Instead, Mandukhai had noticed what Esige had.

Odgerel had eyes set on Unebolod, and if the woman's family status was right, she could make a move and attempt stealing Unebolod away from Mandukhai.

If this brings Mandukhai and Unebolod together, I will hunt down everything I possibly can about Odgerel, Esige decided. But her instincts warned her to be careful.

CHAPTER TWO

Transitions of Power

Bigirsen paced with thundering steps in his meeting room as Issama entered. The sandstone walls of the palace Bigirsen had claimed in Hami offered relief in the summer and protection against bitter winds in the winter. Today, a fire roared in the massive hearth of the large chamber to burn away the chill in the spring air. Servants cowered in corners, attempting to remain invisible until needed. No one wanted to face the Vice Regent's wrath inadvertently. Issama's only fear of Bigirsen was that the other man would discover his secret designs.

Issama hated being so far from Mongke Bulag when Manduul's life hung in the balance. How could he enact his plan to seize control if he was not there to storm the gathering tent and claim or kill the queen? He needed to return before it was too late. Yet something in Bigirsen's countenance concerned Issama even more. What could have worked him into such a frenzy?

Bigirsen's expression was as dark and ominous as a thundercloud that settled over the wide meeting room. Few places in Hami offered so much space, but Bigirsen had made good use of this small palace. His wives and guards lived within this meager palace, along with his children. He had given Issama use of one wing for himself and his wives. The Hami palace was hardly grand, but it stood above the rest of the small oasis and offered views of the desert on one side and the Tianshan Mountains on the other.

The meeting room doors on the western wall opened to a striking balcony view of the mountains—but not today. Spring winds from the mountains would be too bitter to chase away even with a blazing hearth fire.

In his fist, Bigirsen clenched a piece of parchment that wrinkled between his fingers. The moment Issama entered, Bigirsen waved the parchment fist in the air wildly.

"She refuses to return my son and summons me to her at the festival!" Bigirsen raged. "Me!" He spit on the floor, sneering in a rage. "Who does she think she is to command me?"

Issama folded his hands patiently in front of him and kept his tone calm and even. "Whom do you speak of?"

Bigirsen strode toward him and thrust the parchment against Issama's chest, knocking the breath out of Issama in the process. Without a word, Bigirsen resumed his pacing.

Issama smoothed the parchment out over his chest, watching Bigirsen curiously until he raised the parchment to read the message. His stomach sank. It had happened. Manduul Khan was dead, and Mandukhai had been named Queen Regent until a new Khan was selected at *kurultai*, by order of Manduul. Issama's breath caught. How long had it been since Manduul died? Weeks at least, for the message to reach him. Perhaps months.

And if they knew, Unebolod would know as well. Issama had to sweep in and seize control of Mongke Bulag before Unebolod returned or he would lose his chance forever. *It could be too late already. And I'm trapped in this forsaken place with this lunatic*, he thought bitterly. Everything he had worked for would come crashing down if he could not return to Mongke Bulag immediately.

"If this is Manduul's last command, we cannot ignore her summons," Issama said carefully. Perhaps he could use this as an excuse to leave immediately. Would the Oirat make their move without him? He had an agreement with Paisahan khan, leader of the Oirat. But Paisahan often proved self-serving. Would he betray his promise to Issama to wait for Issama's signal before he attacked? If Paisahan thought it benefitted him, he would likely make his own move for power.

Bigirsen froze with his back as stiff as a tree trunk, facing away from Issama. His broad shoulders heaved with deep breaths of anger. Then Bigirsen clenched both hands into white-knuckled fists at his sides. He didn't turn to face Issama as he spoke in a low, dangerous voice. "She took my son, and now she tries to take my power? I have worked too hard to hand my power over to a woman. And I certainly will not answer to *her*."

He shook his head, making his braided tails wave across his shoulders. "No. I have a message for her. One she will not soon forget."

Before Issama could ask for details, Bigirsen stormed past him, barking out orders to his commander and for the guards to bring in the messenger. Issama's heart leaped into his throat. Just one act of Bigirsen's rage could undo all of Issama's hard work. Ever since Bigirsen killed Borogchin, he had slowly come unhinged. This last stroke could be his undoing. Issama wanted to take power from Bigirsen, but not at the cost of their men. He needed them.

Hustling forward, Issama rushed to Bigirsen's side as two of Bigirsen's personal guards dragged the messenger into the meeting room. Bigirsen kicked the messenger in the back of the legs so that the young man fell to his knees. He raised his sword high over the messenger's neck. Issama panicked and snatched Bigirsen's forearm before he could swing a death blow.

"Wait!" Issama hissed. "You cannot kill him."

Bigirsen scowled at Issama, yanking his arm free. "I can, and I will. And then I will send his head back to her in response. She does not rule over me and she cannot keep me from my son."

Issama glanced at the men around them. Bigirsen's anger had clearly caused some uncertainty. While the men tried to mask it, Issama had become skilled at reading faces.

He edged Bigirsen away from Mandukhai's messenger, as well as the other men, and lowered his voice so only Bigirsen could hear him. "I agree with you on both counts. But if Manduul has given her regency until *kurultai*, you would declare war on her and risk your own allies turning against you with this act. Then she will use Nemeku against you. It's too risky."

Issama knew he had to play into what Bigirsen really wanted. Nemeku. The khanship. It would be the only way to get through to Bigirsen and make him see this act was a poor decision. He glanced at the men who watched the two of them. Mandukhai's messenger was pale-faced but curious.

"Let her think she has won this battle, so you can defeat her at the next," Issama whispered urgently. "Allow me to take men and return in answer to her summons, as a show of faith, and I will be sure she knows you could not disengage completely with the Ming. Then I can also rescue your son from her clutches and bring him back where he belongs. And when the time for *kurultai* comes, and it will come soon, you will be ready to seize control with a half-Borjigin son in your control. At that point, you can do whatever you wish with her. Personally."

Slowly, Bigirsen lowered his sword as he considered the proposal. All Issama could do was hope that Bigirsen would see reason. Of course, by the time they reached *kurultai*, it would be too late for Bigirsen. Issama would be in the position of power instead.

"I am Vice Regent still." Bigirsen sounded more like an angry child than a man in control of anything.

"I know."

"I am Lord of the western Mongols, and the southern tribes are in my control."

Issama had spent years smuggling control of the southern Mongols away from Bigirsen in secret. It was the entire reason Issama had suggested Bayan travel south three years ago. The Ming had disappointed him by failing to capture Bayan, and the Chakhar had lost their nerve to abandon the Golden Prince as Mingtau had promised. As usual, Issama could only trust his own men to finish anything.

Instead of correcting Bigirsen regarding who controlled the south, Issama nodded. "And there is no longer a true descendant of Genghis. Which means any man who has the overwhelming majority of support—as you do—will have no trouble claiming that title justly and lawfully. Nemeku will only strengthen your claim. You are Lord of the West. Unebolod is Lord of the East. And she is the key to the rule over the Nation. Unebolod already has her trust, and you do not. Do this," he waved toward the messenger, "and you will seal your fate."

Bigirsen took a few deep breaths that made his shoulders lurch. Esen had killed Borjigin nobles and seized control without *kurultai*. His grab for power had resulted in a vast divide among the tribes that had ended with a revolt and his death. They could not afford to repeat the mistakes of Esen's past now. Issama held his breath as he waited for Bigirsen to respond.

At long last, Bigirsen slid his sword into his belt. "Fine. But I will not give her any of my men. Send word that we honor Manduul Khan's decision and will meet her at *kurultai* when the time comes, in exchange for Nemeku. Right now, we cannot afford to disengage with the Ming. They are in a transition of power and we need to capitalize on that weakness."

Issama let out a breath of relief and grinned. He would return to Mongke Bulag. "Your will, my Lord. Where will you go next?"

Bigirsen stared at the south as if he could see his destination from where he stood. "We will move south with our reinforcements and push our way into the Ordos basin and the Gansu Corridor while the Ming are weak. We will do what Genghis himself could not. And when we do, it won't matter who claims the title at *kurultai*. The Nation will follow me, believing I have divine right."

Issama froze. "We?"

"Yes, Issama," Bigirsen turned toward him slowly. His gaze clearly dared Issama to challenge him. "You are worth as much as a thousand men. I will not send you into her arms."

No, this was not the plan. He needed to go! Issama had promised the Ming he would leave them alone in exchange for capturing Bayan. However, the Ming had failed to uphold their end. What came next would be their own fault.

"I'm honored by your faith," he said evenly.

"Go compose the message," Bigirsen ordered. He stalked toward the messenger, nudging the kneeling man with the toe of his boot. "Send it back with this spy."

Issama bowed and hustled away from Bigirsen, leaving the messenger in his hands and hoping Bigirsen would keep a level head. Without realizing it, Mandukhai had delivered herself into the jaws of a lion. Perhaps he could not return, but he could offer Mandukhai something he knew she wanted—Bigirsen's head. He would only ask for one favor in exchange. He grinned to himself as he headed toward his office to compose the message.

He who controlled the Queen Regent, controlled the respect of the men at *kurultai*. But it would not be Bigirsen who held that control.

Unebolod leaned back in his seat—the closest to the dais—and watched as Mandukhai directed men and women around the gathering tent. Watching her command the room with so much confidence only stoked the fire burning within him. He understood why they waited, but each passing day made that wait even more difficult. Had they not waited long enough already? Six years had passed since she had first arrived in Mongke Bulag. Six years since he had first laid eyes on her and she immediately had stolen his heart. Six years waiting for Manduul to die so they could be together.

Months had passed since they had burned Manduul's body, and still they waited. *This is inevitable. Why are we still waiting?*

Mandukhai had whipped Mongke Bulag into a frenzy of activity. For the first time since Manduul had first set up his ger, they would abandon this area for greener pastures and the festival—days of horse races, archery contests, wrestling, foot races, and gambling. All the tribes would come together in unity—or at least, that was Mandukhai's hope. When was the last time they had even celebrated? Unebolod could not recall a single festival since Taisun Khan's death decades ago, and Unebolod had been too young to take part.

"I have to ask again," Unebolod said, loud enough to draw Mandukhai's attention. "Why are we not doing this in Karakorum? The land is flatter and better for races."

"It's too close to the Oirat," Mandukhai said with a sigh of exasperation.

She had given up wearing her *boqta* except on strictly formal affairs and often let her hair hang down now. Unebolod enjoyed this change. It made her appear younger and freer.

"I have reports they are agitated," she said.

"Isn't the entire point of this to gather the tribes to install a new Great Khan?" Unebolod asked, leaning forward and resting his arms on his knees. "We do that in Karakorum."

"Genghis did not," Mandukhai said as she sauntered toward him. "He stood on the slopes of Mount Burkhan Khaldun where all the tribes could see him, and they took their oath as one."

Unebolod sat back in his seat as Mandukhai kneeled in front of him. His gaze flitted around the gathering tent, but everyone appeared too busy with their own tasks to notice the two of them. Mandukhai's hands rested tenderly on his knees. He suppressed the urge to kick everyone else out and throw caution to the wind—waiting be damned.

"We will ensure the strength of the next Great Khan on the very same slopes," she said softly, but with a fire of certainty burning in her dark eyes. His pulse raced under that fierce gaze. "And from there, we will restore the fractured empire. A smooth transition of power is necessary."

Mandukhai reached up and brushed her hand over the scar across his cheekbone, as if his face were a visible reminder of that fracture. In some ways, it was. Bigirsen had given him that scar. Soon enough, they would end up facing off again. He couldn't wait to kill Bigirsen.

Unebolod pressed his face into her touch, then captured her hand and pressed it to his lips. The skin was soft, just as he remembered it. These servants had gotten used to small signs of affection between the two of them. Touching hands. Familiar motions. No one ever said anything. Everyone in Mongke Bulag preferred Unebolod as the next Great Khan anyway. They all simply waited for Mandukhai to make her announcement official.

"I'm tired of waiting," he said under his breath, so no one else moving around the gathering tent could hear him.

Mandukhai smiled sadly. "I know. As am I. But what are a few more weeks after so many years?"

"Torture."

She smirked, then rose to her feet. Unebolod hated when she pulled away.

"And necessity," she said as she continued her tasks.

Unebolod grumbled under his breath as he left her to her work. He hated how right she was—how right she always was. Manduul had been wise to leave the management of the tribes in her capable hands. Mandukhai worked like a master potter, molding the clay into position, seeing what the lump would become when no one else could. He admired her for it. Would he be so capable in her position?

As he stepped outside, Unebolod drank in the cool spring air. The chill of winter still clung to the breeze, but in a few short weeks, it would blow away and the heat of summer would be upon them. And in that summer heat, he would stand before the khans of the tribes at *kurultai* and take their oaths as the next Great Khan. Then, he and Mandukhai would at last share a ger.

Mongke Bulag burst at the seams with activity as families packed up their possessions on carts. In the morning, they would break down the gers and head to Mount Burkhan Khaldun. Everyone knew Unebolod would be the next Great Khan, and as he moved toward his ger, those who passed nearby bowed their heads to him respectfully. Unebolod walked taller than he ever had before. His patience had been tested dozens of times over the years, but it had paid off. Manduul had made his preference known, and Mandukhai clearly favored Unebolod. Only Bigirsen would stand against him. *And I will crush him as soon as* kurultai *is over*, Unebolod thought as he reached for his door.

"Brother!" Togochi called, jogging over from his own ger several yards away.

Unebolod paused as Togochi sidestepped Esige on some urgent special mission from Mandukhai, most likely. Outside Togochi's ger, his wife Jaghan gave instructions to a servant while she nursed their newborn daughter. Two sons and a daughter in four years. *Soon I will have sons of my own*, Unebolod thought, and it warmed him.

"Where's the fire, Togochi?" Unebolod asked, offering a rare smile to the Khorlod Lord.

"Hopefully in your own hearth," Togochi teased, grinning like a fool. "Has she said anything yet?"

Unebolod shifted, his lighter mood slipping. He knew what Togochi meant. Mandukhai had not given Unebolod any sort of formal agreement to their union and her selection, and it was making some of the Lords restless despite how much she clearly favored Unebolod. If Unebolod could just get her to agree formally, it would make the transition smoother. He could not understand why she held back with half-promises. They would be together. She had said as much. He simply shook his head in answer to Togochi's question.

Togochi frowned, glancing at the gathering tent, then placed a hand on Unebolod's shoulder. "Well, we both know how she feels about you. I'm sure it won't be long now, with *kurultai* looming closer."

"Has your wife heard anything?" Unebolod asked, glancing past Togochi to where Jaghan disappeared into their ger.

"Not exactly," Togochi said. "Just that she knows how strongly Mandukhai feels for you."

The words should have comforted Unebolod, but they had the opposite effect. This was inevitable. It had always been inevitable.

So why did she hesitate?

Togochi eyed his eldest son, Torudur, as the toddler played with the knucklebones. Torudur did not yet know how to play the game, but the pieces seemed to fascinate him. Togochi only hoped the boy wouldn't try to eat any of the small bones.

Jaghan rose from the dinner table and glided to the washbasin. Only the bare essentials remained inside their ger. The rest had been packed up for tomorrow's journey.

"Let me help you," Togochi said, preparing to rise.

"I can handle it," Jaghan said, waving him off.

Instead of arguing with her, Togochi checked on little Babaqai as the younger boy slept on a mat on the floor. It never ceased to amazing Togochi how smooth and innocent a child's face could be in sleep. When was the last time he slept so peacefully? Years, probably.

Togochi was often quick with jokes around others, but he used those jokes as a mask. *No good comes from showing your fear to others*, his father had taught him. But his father had also been one of the Lords responsible for Molon Khan's imprisonment when Togochi was just a boy. To hold a Borjigin prince captive was the furthest from loyalty to Genghis Togochi could ever imagine. The Khorlod had fallen on ill fates while Molon was in their possession: a famine that killed thousands, a battle that claimed even more, fires and disease. It had taken the Khorlod leaders far too long to realize they had angered the High Heavens by holding Molon prisoner as they had.

Togochi dedicated his life to righting the wrongs the men before him had incurred. He swore to serve the Borjigin heirs above all else. Now, for the first time in his young life, Togochi felt utterly lost. Without a Borjigin heir to obey, he did not know what purpose he served. The best he could offer was to carry out Manduul's dying wish; to follow Mandukhai until a new Great Khan was elected at *kurultai*. But then what?

Part of the reason Togochi had bonded himself so firmly to Unebolod had been the striking similarities in their pasts. While Togochi's tribe had imprisoned and mistreated Molon before he became Great Khan, Unebolod's tribe had held Bayan captive as well—though Bayan had not been a prisoner as Molon had been. Unebolod swore to follow the Borjigin heirs as surely as Togochi had. That likeness and vow had by some unspoken agreement made the two men brothers.

But Manduul was dead. Bayan was dead. The line of Genghis was dead.

"Breathe, Togochi," Jaghan said, resting a hand on his shoulder.

Togochi jumped, then drew in a deep breath as he realized he had been holding little air in his lungs.

"You are under too much stress," Jaghan said.

He patted her hand. "It will get worse before it gets better. He is worried, and I don't blame him. I just don't understand. Why won't she name Unebolod if she already knows she will choose him? She is leaving the door open for any man bold enough to stake his claim."

Jaghan shook her head and smiled sweetly at him. "She has her reasons, but she loves him. And like you, she is also under too much stress."

"What reasons?"

Jaghan waved the question off. "I will speak with her, but I'm not sure what good it will do."

Did his wife know something he didn't? Togochi wished she would talk to him. He had made a promise to serve and protect Mandukhai, but he couldn't do that if he didn't understand what was happening. He also knew his wife well enough to know that no amount of prying would loosen her tongue. She would keep her secret—assuming she had one in the first place.

Togochi took her hand and pressed it to his lips. "You are more than I deserve."

She smirked. "And you had better remember that until the day you die."

"I don't need to remember," Togochi teased back. "You will remind me even in the grave."

Despite his teasing, he knew he would never forget. Jaghan was one of the most remarkable women he had ever known. Delicate yet firm. Demure yet untamed. He adored her. Hopefully Unebolod and Mandukhai would finally find their happiness together as well. They had certainly wanted it long enough.

A shadow fell across Esige's face as the ger flap closed in front of her, plunging her into the darkness outside. Tracking down the truth about Odgerel had proven an interesting challenge, but not impossible. What she uncovered, however, had left a pit of dread in her stomach.

I have to tell Mandukhai before it's too late.

Esige pulled her braided hair over her shoulder and rushed across what remained of the massive camp.

CHAPTER THREE

Inevitable Surrender

Mandukhai's bones ached as she returned to her ger at the end of the day. No wonder Manduul constantly appeared run down. Even organizing something as simple as breaking up this camp—which seemed to have rooted in place—took all the energy she had within her. *I'm hardly twenty-two*, she thought bitterly, *far too young to be in such pain.*

Jaghan stood as Mandukhai entered. The sight of her friend startled Mandukhai, and she pressed a hand against her suddenly pounding heart.

"Jaghan, what are you doing here?" Mandukhai asked, relaxing her shoulders.

"I came to check on your well-being, Mandukhai," Jaghan responded, pouring a cup of tea.

Mandukhai sank down on the edge of her bed and slipped off her boots. "Tired, but otherwise fine. Thank you." She accepted the offered drink and took a careful sip.

"Tomorrow we ride for Mount Burkhan Khaldun, then you can finally have what you have been waiting all this time for," Jaghan said, smirking at her. "You will have a whole new reason to be so exhausted."

For two years, Jaghan had kept Mandukhai's secret—that she had loved Unebolod from her first days in Mongke Bulag. She had accidentally shared the truth with Jaghan one drunken, jealous night. For a while, she had worried Jaghan would tell Togochi or Manduul, but the other woman had kept her secret. It formed a bond of trust and mutual respect between them.

Resisting Unebolod these past few weeks had taken all of Mandukhai's willpower—especially with Odgerel always lingering around him. But Mandukhai never doubted his love for her. Unebolod had given her a promise more than a year ago that he would wait for her. Mandukhai understood how important his word was to him. He would never give in to Odgerel, no matter what the girl did. Mandukhai counted on his patience.

"I don't see why the two of you insist on waiting," Jaghan said, as she settled on a bench with her own tea. "No one would question his validity if you shared his bed a little early. You are only putting off the inevitable surrender. Everyone already expects it."

Everyone? Mandukhai was not sure why that put a foul taste in her mouth, as if Manduul had not placed this decision in her hands. Just the expectation that she would simply hand herself and the Nation over to Unebolod shot a rod of stiffness down her spine. She loved him, but she had a duty to uphold as surely as he did. Manduul trusted her to handle the transition smoothly, though she knew no one would ever see it that way. Everyone saw Unebolod's takeover as inevitable, even if it would be by her own choice. It felt like she had no power over her own life.

Jaghan frowned, then glanced at the door to be sure it was closed. She leaned forward and whispered conspiratorially. "It's the boy, isn't it?"

Mandukhai's heart stopped. Jaghan had been with her when Siker confessed she had a son with Bayan. Jaghan swore never to speak a word to another soul—including Togochi. How much longer would Jaghan hold her tongue?

"No," Mandukhai replied, setting down her cup. "Not exactly. I have already decided what to do with him, should he survive." Mandukhai had not shared with even Jaghan the news of the boy's near-death experience with Issama's men, or how he was currently being treated for multiple ailments. While Jaghan knew Batu had existed in time, she did not know that he still lived. Barely.

"Then what?" Jaghan pressed.

Mandukhai wanted to tell Jaghan the truth, but she did not know how far Jaghan's trust could go. Besides, until she knew if Batu would survive, and she had a chance to tell Unebolod the truth, she could tell no one else.

"I would rather not have people assume that, because I am a woman, I have no right or say in any of this, that I should just give myself to him." The words came out a touch more sharply than she had intended. Exhaustion had frayed her nerves. "I apologize, Jaghan. But I feel as if no one takes what

I am doing seriously. They are just all waiting for ... for the *inevitable*." She spit the last word out, echoing Jaghan's own word.

"I did not mean to hurt your feelings, Mandukhai. I simply thought this is what you wanted."

Mandukhai sighed. "It is. But it is also starting to feel a lot like my betrothal to Manduul, like something that is completely out of my control."

Jaghan rose and glided toward Mandukhai. The other woman's movements were fluid. Without a child weighing her down, Jaghan was quite a graceful woman. She settled beside Mandukhai and took her hand.

"There is a big different between your marriage to Manduul and a marriage to Unebolod," Jaghan said, her voice soothing. "One you disliked. The other you love. Whether the fate of the Nation is your choice or not, the fate of your heart was determined long ago by you."

Mandukhai nodded, but she took little comfort from the words. Particularly because Jaghan's mention of the fate of the Nation only reminded Mandukhai of her vision of Genghis. Like Manduul, Genghis placed the fate of the Nation in her hands.

The door opened and Esige slipped in, closing the door with her back to Mandukhai. "Mother, I know who she is!"

Esige spun around and halted when she spotted Jaghan seated beside Mandukhai. The girl appeared uncertain if she should continue.

"Is everything all right, Mother?" Esige asked, examining with her critical eye the way Jaghan comforted Mandukhai.

"Fine," Mandukhai said.

"Who *who* is?" Jaghan asked, frowning at Esige.

Mandukhai pulled away from Jaghan as she realized what Esige referred to. Her heart pounded against her ribs. Mandukhai's stomach revolted against her, churning in a wild mass as her heart beat in her throat.

"Well then, don't keep me in suspense," Mandukhai said, hardly able to breathe the words.

Esige began pacing the ger. Not a good sign at all. Mandukhai watched the girl's agitated movements as she explained the trail she had followed through the Khorchin tribe to the man Odgerel claimed to be her brother. "Except he isn't her brother," Esige finished.

"What?" Mandukhai's eyes widened.

"I asked around, targeting people who knew him, and confirmed it myself." Esige stopped and spun on her heel to face Mandukhai. "The man she claims to be her brother actually served her father."

Served her ...? Mandukhai's hands began shaking violently. No matter how hard she tried, she could not swallow the lump that grew in her throat.

Esige barreled onward. "Naturally, I had to know who her father was and did some more digging. Her father was Lord Batsaihan, one of the highest officials under Bolunai khan. She had been promised to Lord Ganzorig, Bolunai's youngest son. But they all died in the explosion. They told me the story about how she had died as well, and what a tragedy the whole thing was. No one seemed to realize she was the same girl and the servant tried protecting her identity, feeding into the lie."

"Is her name truly Odgerel?" Jaghan asked, placing her hand once more on Mandukhai's arm to offer reassurance. The offer felt stale to Mandukhai. The world spun. How could Unebolod *not* know who she was?

Esige nodded.

Unless Unebolod *did* know who she was and held her aside until he had secured Mandukhai and the khanship. The Queen Regent and a Khorchin high Lady would make two powerful wives. *He wouldn't do that to me ... would he?* She wanted to trust him, to have faith in him. But the very first bit of advice Unebolod had ever given Mandukhai was to be careful who to trust. Everyone wanted something. And he had always wanted the khanship. His feelings for her may have been genuine, but perhaps he was more like other men than she had thought. A Khan would need many wives. Unebolod would wait for her, then take another. Did Odgerel know this? Was that why she hated Mandukhai, because she could not be the first wife? Mandukhai despised where her thoughts went.

This girl who posed as a simple servant was one of the highest-ranking Ladies of the Khorchin tribe. There could no longer be any doubt in Mandukhai's mind. Odgerel was after one thing—to be the wife of the next Great Khan.

Esige crouched in front of Mandukhai, placing her hands on Mandukhai's knees. "Mother?" She frowned. "He would never betray you."

Mandukhai raised her tremulous gaze to meet Esige's, her vision blurred by tears. "Wouldn't he? Because that is the very first thing he ever warned me of."

"That was years ago," Jaghan replied, rubbing Mandukhai's back. "So much has changed since then, not the least of which is the way you feel for each other."

His voice seeped into her mind. *You consume me.* Mandukhai squeezed her eyes shut and fought to steady her breathing. Nevertheless, his words echoed in her ears. *You have taken me, a mighty warrior, and reduced me to a love-struck boy*. He had been so sincere at that moment, but how much of it was an act to get him to this moment? *I am at your mercy*, he had said. But had he ever been? *Everyone wants something for themselves, Mandukhai, and you may not be prepared to pay the price.* Was this part of that price? He wanted the khanship. She had known that long ago.

Mandukhai scrubbed the heels of her palms against her eyes and let out a shuddering breath as she opened her eyes.

Jaghan chewed her lip in thought, then stood and seized Mandukhai's hand, yanking her to her feet. "Put an end to this now."

"He must have known, Jaghan," Mandukhai said. How could he *not* know a young woman of such high noble birth? "What if others know as well? What if they are mocking me behind my back?"

Jaghan grimaced, then seized Mandukhai's shoulders and shoved her toward the door. "Then show them how wrong they are. Show him how you truly feel. Now. Before she can make her move."

Mandukhai stumbled forward a few steps. "What if they have already...?" The words fell away from her lips.

Esige snorted. "That, we can be certain, has not happened. Yet. People love to share gossip, and no one believed anything had happened. He was cold and distant with her all the way to Mongke Bulag."

"Go show her who you are," Jaghan said.

The two shuffled forward, forcing Mandukhai toward the door. And once more, Mandukhai felt her own decisions removed from her power.

Mandukhai paused at the door to collect herself before pushing out into the fading sunset. She *would* show Odgerel who she was. And the girl would eat dirt if she did not show proper respect to her Queen Regent.

Unebolod sank down on his bed with a grunt of relief, toeing off his boots onto the floor. Odgerel rushed over to retrieve his boots and clean them for tomorrow's ride. The way she bent to pick them up accentuated her wide hips, and he knew she did this to get his attention. He wished he could say he had grown immune to her obvious bid for attention, but the longer he waited for Mandukhai, the harder it became to ignore this woman moving around his ger. He closed his eyes to block her out, propping his hands behind his head. To clear his mind, he focused on his breathing and on the journey ahead.

To prepare for the morning and a quick departure, everyone had packed up all but the essentials. Tomorrow, it would only take an hour or two for the families of Mongke Bulag to break down the gers and begin the trek northeast.

Something brushed his arm. Unebolod's eyes shot open to find Odgerel leaning close over him. Her hair tickled his forearm as she pulled the blanket over him.

"I thought you had fallen asleep," she whispered. "I didn't mean to startle you."

Unebolod realized he had grabbed her arm when he opened his eyes, and he released his grip. "It's fine, but I think I can handle tucking myself in. Thanks anyway."

She flinched, rubbing at her arm as she stepped away. His grip had been too tight, and guilt twisted his gut.

"Did I hurt you?" he asked.

She shook her head. "My brother has done far worse."

Her brother. One of these days, Unebolod would have to track down this brother of hers and make an example of him. He would not tolerate unnecessary abuse when he became Great Khan.

"I'm sorry."

Odgerel waved off his apology.

"Let me see it," he said, sitting up.

"Really, I'm fine," she insisted, but he could see the red mark on her arm.

He sat up and held out a hand. Odgerel studied the offered hand a moment before she sighed and edged closer to the bed and placed her wrist in his hand. He gently shifted her arm around to inspect the damage, but the redness on her skin had already faded.

A muffled voice rose in anger outside. He recognized that voice anywhere. As Mandukhai threw the door open, he dropped Odgerel's arm, his throat tightening. This could not look good.

Odgerel took a few steps back, bowing to Mandukhai.

Unebolod gaped at Mandukhai, jumping to his feet. "What are you doing here?" Crossing his threshold symbolized an agreement. A joining. This was a massive risk.

Mandukhai froze inside the doorway, taking in the scene with such an angry, harsh glare that he wondered just how this *did* look to her.

"You are dismissed, girl," Mandukhai snapped.

Odgerel raised her gaze but didn't move. "I will go when my Lord khan dismisses me."

Unebolod almost laughed, but any mirth died in his throat the moment he saw the fury in Mandukhai's eyes. She looked ready to rip Odgerel's head clean off her body.

"You will go when your *Queen Regent* tells you to go," Mandukhai said, lowering her voice to a dangerous pitch.

To her credit, as insane as she was, Odgerel raised her chin almost defiantly at Mandukhai. *What are you doing, girl?* Unebolod thought.

"Get out!" Mandukhai roared.

Odgerel turned to him, as if waiting for him to confirm the command. Suddenly, none of this was amusing any longer. He wanted her to go, but if he told her to do so, Mandukhai would only be more incensed. She needed to obey Mandukhai's command. Yet her gaze did not shift from him. He gave a subtle nod, hoping Mandukhai would not notice.

Odgerel strode toward the exit, but Mandukhai barred the door with her arm.

"No." Mandukhai stared Odgerel down. "You leave when *I* tell you to."

Odgerel froze in her tracks, glancing at him from the corner of her eyes, begging him for help. Unebolod could not, for the life of him, understand what was happening here. Mandukhai was jealous? But she had never acted like this before, and Odgerel was only a servant, not a threat to her in any way.

Mandukhai leaned toward Odgerel and said something under her breath into the girl's ear. Odgerel's spine stiffened as if someone had shoved a pole straight down her back. When Mandukhai pulled away and left the doorway open, Odgerel remained frozen in place.

"Mandukhai, what is this all about?" Unebolod asked.

She swayed toward him, and had he not been bewildered by the exchange a moment ago, he might have been sorely tempted to capture her in his arms. "Did you know already who she is?"

Unebolod opened his mouth to respond, but observed the way Odgerel trembled. Her reaction killed any protests he might have. He *didn't* know who she was. The girl had shown up on his threshold like all the other girls, with the same sad story about her father and how she had nowhere else to go. He hadn't even questioned it, and his mind had been so singularly focused on returning to Mandukhai he hadn't thought any further about it. Not even when Odgerel had made obvious advances on him. Should he have thought more about who she was? Unebolod shot a questioning gaze at Odgerel, but she dipped her head, unable to match his gaze.

"Her father was Lord Batsaihan," Mandukhai said, and the anger in her tone smoothed out. "She was promised to your youngest nephew."

Unebolod's blood turned cold. *Lady* Odgerel. This girl was a noble.

"But everyone said she had died in the same explosion, that she was with Ganzorig when the gunpowder exploded ..." Unebolod was not sure if he felt angry that Odgerel had lied to him, betrayed because he had trusted her, or afraid of what others thought might have happened with her. Did no one else know who she was? How had no one told him before? Unebolod had never met her before, having spent years away from Hulunbuir, but he had known her father. *She was there the day I arrived*, he realized. Unebolod had not seen her face that day. Only her back as Ganzorig flirted with her.

Now, as he studied her, he could see some resemblances to her father. Particularly the way she held herself. She had always seemed confident to him, something women not of noble birth rarely showed to Lords, if ever. But worse yet, the realization that she had also been relentless.

All those times she tried to entice me... Unebolod knew that, had he given in just once, this girl would be tethered to him forever. Perhaps above Mandukhai. *No wonder she is angry.* Unebolod was thankful for the vow he had given Mandukhai before he left for Hulunbuir. Had he not promised to wait for her, he would have given in to his own desires long ago. And if Odgerel had conceived a child, as a noblewoman, with him as the next Great Khan, her own child would be favored over any he had with Mandukhai.

The way Mandukhai studied his reaction clarified that she doubted him. It cut deeply, but he understood her pain. After all this time, after all their promises, she worried he had strayed, as men often did.

Odgerel had created doubt between them where it had never existed before. Unebolod's anger slowly heated his blood. He would not lose the khanship, or Mandukhai, because of this girl.

"Get her out of here," he growled. "And don't run, girl. I expect my men to find you in the morning."

Tears welled in Odgerel's eyes, but he had no sympathy for her this time. She had entered his ger and toyed with his emotions. Unebolod adopted a stony mask as he met her gaze, then turned his attention to Mandukhai, now standing before him. She waved Odgerel out with evident satisfaction.

Mandukhai slid her hands around his arm, peering up at him. Unebolod cupped Mandukhai's cheek in his palm. He had hoped to see love or desire in those dark eyes. Instead, she appeared uncertain.

"Nothing happened. I give you my word," he reassured her.

Mandukhai pressed her cheek into his hand. "I believe you."

Unebolod needed to be completely honest with her to mend whatever damage might have been done. "I won't lie and say she did not tempt me more than once. It's been so long, Mandukhai."

All the anger melted off of her, and she pressed closer to him. "It has been so long."

The warmth of Mandukhai's body against his own sent his body into reaction mode. His lips parted. His skin tingled as her hands brushed against the front of his deel. He was certain she could feel his heart pounding with desire. Unebolod did not remember putting his arms around her, yet he felt the curve of her spine against his palms.

"You..." He swallowed the lump in his throat. "You should go. Before..."

Mandukhai rose to her toes and pressed a kiss against his lips. He wanted to resist, to stop, to honor their tenuous agreement. But once the gates of his desire had opened, there was no way he could hold it back. Instead of pulling away, Unebolod's muscles locked him in place. Even if this was a new level of torture, he could not pull away if he had tried with all his might. He needed her in every sense of the word. He was always hers. That had never been in question.

Perhaps this would be the only time the two of them could be together until after the ceremony. It would be weeks before he could kiss or touch her like this again. Unebolod refused to let go. Her lips parted, and he matched her welcome with an eager groan of delight. The moment their tongues touched, all the pent-up passion exploded through him. They grasped at each other, unrestrained, uninhibited. He peeled her deel loose around her shoulders, tearing his lips from hers to devour every inch of exposed flesh along her jaw, neck, shoulders.

Mandukhai yanked his belt away, ripping at the ties holding his deel closed. She breathed his name, and the sound stoked the fire burning in him. Unebolod shook off his own deel, consumed by the passion, knowing there would be no way to stop now.

They edged toward the bed, all lips and touches. Mandukhai's hands slid along his spine, and a shot of lightning ran through his very core. No longer hindered by the barrier of their clothes, her soft, smooth skin brushed against him. Mandukhai's gaze fell on him, flushed with desire.

"I was always yours," he whispered.

Mandukhai slid her hand into his and pulled him down on top of her. In moments, they lost themselves in explosive desire, suppressed for far too long. Unebolod held Mandukhai through all the peaks and valleys of passion. Even when the passion had been spent, he refused to let go, afraid that it would be too long before he could touch her like that again.

Any doubt Mandukhai had harbored before entering Unebolod's ger vanished as the flame of their desire consumed them. *I was always yours*, he had said, and those words warmed her even as the cool air chilled the sweat clinging to her skin. His arms remained firmly wrapped around her despite the gentle rise and fall of his chest as he slumbered.

Jaghan was right. While it did not determine the course of a nation, this night confirmed the deeply seeded love in her heart. There could never be another man for her. It had always been him, just as he had always been hers.

Mandukhai smiled and closed her eyes, listening to his steady, strong heartbeat as she rested her head against his chest. Until *kurultai*, this could not happen again. But she could wait a few more weeks now that she had given herself this moment in time.

This had always been inevitable.

CHAPTER FOUR

Through the Orange Haze

Mandukhai propped her chin on Unebolod's chest, studying every angle of his face in a way she had never done before. The strong, angular line of his jaw. The way his upper lip seemed to sink back beneath his facial hair. The sharpness of his cheekbones. Two little crests of skin formed valleys between his eyes toward the bridge of his nose. She loved every detail.

The fingers of one of his hands trailed along her spine as the other hand rested against her arm. Neither of them spoke as they lay together. Waves of passion had consumed the night, banked by slumber until desire woke them once more. Mandukhai had never lain in his arms for so long before, always aware of the danger of his embrace. Now, no one could stop them. Manduul would not kill them. No one would report them. For the first time in her life, Mandukhai truly felt free to do what she wished and choose whomever she chose. It brought a small smile to her lips.

The wolf dawn approached. Mandukhai saw the subtle shift of hues from black to deep blue through the smoke hole. As hard as they might try to cling to this night, the sun would still rise and steal their moment away.

"I did not sleep nearly enough for the ride ahead," Unebolod noted. His chest rumbled as he sighed. "I fear I may never sleep again with you in my bed."

Mandukhai giggled. When was the last time she had laughed? She could not recall. "Then I am doing something wrong."

He smirked, sliding his hand up into her hair and pulling her closer. "Or very right."

Unebolod's lips brushed against hers. Somehow, his kiss contained just as much explosive desire as that first one had. Mandukhai thought her heart would burst from all the love she bore for him. How had she ever doubted him? *Odgerel*, Mandukhai thought, and all the desire shifted into anger. She pulled back, pressing her forehead against his shoulder.

"What is it?" he asked, once more running his hands freely over her skin.

"Her."

He lifted her chin, and his dark eyes pierced her soul. "I told you. Nothing happened. Nothing will happen."

"I'm not sure she will accept that," Mandukhai replied.

"She doesn't have a say in the matter. I will figure out what to do with her after the sun rises. Right now, I would rather figure out what to do with you."

Mandukhai jerked back a few inches. *He* intended to be the one to decide how to punish Odgerel? His hands fell back, but he still did not let go. He hadn't let go all night.

"*You* will decide?" Mandukhai's jaw twitched. Her fingers dug into his chest as anger heated her words. "Unebolod, she disobeyed *me*. I am Queen Regent, not some common woman."

Unebolod appeared amused, which only stoked Mandukhai's anger. Why was he amused by this?

"Mandukhai, don't let your jealousy cloud your judgment," he said. "She is from my tribe, and I will deal with it."

Mandukhai's brows shot up her forehead. She sat up. For the first time all night, his hands fell away from her skin, and her skin turned frigid without his touch. But her anger still warmed her.

"Is this how it will be, then?" she asked sharply, pushing him aside so she could reach the edge of the bed without climbing over him. He would surely pull her into his arms again if she did that, and Mandukhai was uncertain that, even angry, she could ever resist him.

"Why are you irritated with me?" Unebolod propped himself up on his arms, adopting a bewildered expression. He reached for her, but Mandukhai swatted his hand away.

"Because you may as well have slapped me with your cock to prove you are a man and I am not," she snapped.

"If that is what you prefer, I'm more than happy to oblige," he joked.

Mandukhai turned her furious glare at him. He shrank back. Did he really think so little of her? She had thought he was different, that he at least respected her position, unlike most of the other men in the camp.

This judgment was *hers* to make. Odgerel had lied to him, which deserved punishment, but she had disrespected Mandukhai in open defiance.

Unebolod studied her as she glared at him, obviously perplexed. Then he sighed and all the potential humor in him slid away. "You are right," he admitted. "You are Queen Regent, and it is within your right to determine how to deal with her. I just worry that you will let your jealousy guide you toward a poor decision."

"And you think so little of my ability to form judgment," she said. Mandukhai spotted her deel on the floor and leaned forward to grab it.

Unebolod grasped her hand, stopping her from gathering her clothing to dress. "Don't put words in my mouth. You know exactly what I think of your wisdom." He grasped her arm just firmly enough that she could not pull away as he leaned toward her. Maybe she didn't want to pull away. His lips brushed her shoulder. Then he swept her hair away from her neck, leaving a blazing trail of kisses along her skin.

"And if you become Great Khan, will you dismiss me so easily?" she asked, leaning into his touch despite her anger.

This time, he jerked back, his hard eyes locking on hers. "*If?*" The harshness of his tone sent a chill down her spine.

"You know what I mean," Mandukhai replied.

Unebolod slid his hand off her back, sitting up straighter. Anger made the scar across his eye and cheekbone more severe. "Do I? Because you have still not given me a formal agreement. And now you say 'if'. What *should* I think?"

Mandukhai realized that he assumed, based on their history, that she would simply hand control of the Nation over to him. But she could not make such a decision with her heart.

"This is what Manduul wanted," he reminded her.

"In the absence of a Borjigin heir, yes, I know," Mandukhai sighed. Should she tell him the truth? If Batu did not survive Saichai's treatments, it would cause Unebolod pain for no reason. Deep down, Mandukhai knew this boy was the entire reason she had not given Unebolod the agreement he wanted. She worried about Genghis' warning over the future of the Nation. *Only he of my bone will have the might to hold it.* No. She could not tell Unebolod yet.

Mandukhai dipped her chin against her chest. "It makes me feel like a prize. Like little more than a queen for a Khan."

The warmth of his body once more pressed against her back, then he leaned his forehead against her temple. "You are far more than a prize queen." His breath rolled down her cheek. "I promise I will never dismiss you the way Manduul did. I know the kind of woman you are, and I would be a fool to ignore that."

Mandukhai turned to meet his gaze, and his lips captured hers. She was powerless to pull away again. Once more, they fell back on the bed and let the fire consume them.

As the passion died down, and their moans and cries of pleasure no longer pierced the air, something else penetrated the sanctuary of Unebolod's ger. Mandukhai's chest heaved as she felt the rumble, then heard the cries. Before she could speak, Unebolod withdrew from her, dressing faster than she had ever seen anyone dress before.

"Unebolod ..." Mandukhai reached for her clothes to dress as well. By the time her deel was over her shoulders, he was already at the door with his bow and sword.

"Stay here," he said as he jerked open the door.

Mandukhai didn't protest.

Unebolod disappeared into the darkness beyond the ger, slamming the door shut behind him. She heard his commands clearly. "Stay. Protect the Queen Regent."

Those last four words would confirm what everyone already suspected. She had given herself to him. *What have I done?*

The panic at that thought vanished the moment she smelled smoke through the opening in the roof.

Mandukhai jumped to her feet and rushed toward the door. Esige and Nemeku were out there! She threw open the door only to confirm what she already knew.

Mongke Bulag was burning.

All the bliss of the night vanished the moment Unebolod stepped out his door and saw the light from the fires burning on the western edge of Mongke Bulag. He shed the skin of a man of passion and adopted the cold warrior's face as he rushed toward Togochi, who lingered near Mandukhai's ger.

"Where is Mandukhai?" Togochi asked.

"Safe," Unebolod said. "What happened?"

"I'm not sure yet, but the horns of watch never sounded," Togochi replied.

Unebolod understood what that meant. They were under attack, and whoever it was had killed the men on watch. Probably the scouts as well.

One of Unebolod's servants approached with the reins of his mount.

"I was looking for Mandukhai," Togochi said as he climbed into his own saddle. "Where is she?"

"Rally the men and have them fan out in all directions until we can determine the extent of the attack," Unebolod commanded, ignoring his question. "Concentrate the heaviest forces in the west."

Togochi reached over and seized Unebolod's arm. "Answer me!"

Unebolod yanked his arm away and turned his mare west. "Settle down. She's safe in my ger."

Togochi raised a brow. "All night?"

"Is now the time for this?" Unebolod snapped. "You take the north. Soke will take the south. We will leave Alayitung behind with enough men to help put out those fires."

Unebolod did not wait for confirmation before he raced west, where the fires rose into the sky. Screams pierced the air. The thunder of hooves rumbled from all directions, making it impossible to discern where the attack originated or where it was headed. Men ducked out of his mare's path and swiftly mounted their own horses to follow him without command. They rarely needed command for such attacks. Every one of them understood the danger and would follow him.

Secure the camp, route the attackers, he thought as he readied his bow for battle.

The scent of burning felt permeated the air. Women and children ducked for cover in gers and under carts laden with possessions, ready for the ride they were supposed to begin today. Despite the rumble of thousands of hooves against the ground in all directions, Unebolod could hear no telltale signs of battle, such as the clash of swords or whistle of arrows.

Mandukhai strode out of Unebolod's ger only to be blocked by her own guards. None of them budged. In the far west, Mandukhai watched the flames cast an orange glow on the horizon. Who would attack?

"Go back inside, Queen Regent," Arslan said. "It's the safest place for you right now. We will guard the ger."

"I will go where I am needed!" Mandukhai snapped, pushing past him.

Arslan seized her arm and pulled her back, nudging her toward Unebolod's door. "Apologies, my Lady, but Lord Unebolod has ordered us to see to your safety. This is the best place for you to be."

Mandukhai yanked her arm free of his grasp, pulled her knife from her belt. She thrust the point against his chin. "Touch me like that again, Arslan, and it will be the last thing you do. You answer to me, not to him. He is not Great Khan. I am Queen Regent. Now step aside, follow me if you must, but do not dare to stop me again!"

For a moment, no one to move. Arslan gave a small incline of his head in agreement, careful not to cut himself on her knife. Mandukhai tucked it away in her belt and marched past them toward the gathering tent. The guards closed in around her like a shield.

Hopefully, Esige would have the sense to take Nemeku to the gathering tent.

Smoke drifted into camp from the west, creating a thin haze. Warriors hustled around on foot, darting around to carry out commands, though who gave those commands Mandukhai did not know. As she reached the gathering tent, a surge of women rushed out the door, accompanied by an *arban* of ten men. Mandukhai sidestepped with a swish of her deel to avoid being trampled.

The inside of the gathering tent had already transformed into an impressive hub of activity. How long had this attack been underway before she and Unebolod took notice?

Alayitung's shoulders relaxed slightly as he spotted Mandukhai approaching him.

"What is happening, General?" Mandukhai asked, glancing at the women and a handful of men who moved with a clear purpose.

"We aren't certain yet," Alayitung reported. The creases in his face put his worry on display. "Fires started on the western border. No warning was sounded. Lord Unebolod has taken most of the men and rode out to investigate."

Jaghan hustled over, her hair in disarray. The infant girl was slung to her chest, and she clung to the hands of both of her sons, dragging them toward where Mandukhai stood.

"Mandukhai, are we under attack?" she asked as she settled the boys near the dais with some toys. "Togochi rode off with his men as if we were."

"I don't know. Where are Nemeku and Esige?" Mandukhai asked. Dread spread through her chest.

Alayitung waved toward the door. "She went to help organize a group of women to put out the fires. She dropped the boy off in the corner there with the other kids."

"Boke," Mandukhai called. The guard jogged over. "Go find Esige and protect her. Take Torgus along with you. If anything happens to her, I will hold you personally responsible. Is that clear?"

"Yes, Queen Regent," Boke and Torgus said in unison.

Mandukhai nodded in satisfaction as the two rushed out of the gathering tent to follow her orders. She turned to Alayitung. "Until we know more, we need to gather all the elderly and the children who cannot help here in the gathering tent. Alayitung, I want you to organize a ring of warriors to protect this location." As she gave her orders, Mandukhai shuffled toward the children's section of the gathering tent.

A dozen young children were gathered together as older girls attempted distracting the children from the chaos around them. Mandukhai's gaze swept the group. Everything slowed. The air grew thick. Panic made her hands tremble.

"Nemeku?" Mandukhai asked the group, but she knew already.

Nemeku wasn't among them.

Chapter Five

Queen for a Khan

By the time Unebolod reached the line of burning gers on the western edge of camp, smoke filled the air, obscuring his vision. More than a thousand of his men were now at his side. He commanded them to spread out between the gers and seek signs of anyone who did not belong in Mongke Bulag and encourage the rest to travel toward the center of camp, where it would be safer.

Despite the thrill of battle, Unebolod's heartbeat remained steady, his breathing even. He held an arrow on the string of his bow as he guided his mount with his knees but would not draw until necessary.

As he rounded a burning ger, Unebolod spotted a line of women working tirelessly to retrieve buckets of water to put out the flames and prevent the spread. A few dared to move toward patches of burning grass with cloth to smother the flames. Esige bustled among the women, her bow strapped over her shoulder as she organized the entire operation with a regal bearing that reminded him of Mandukhai. He galloped toward her.

"Esige! What are you doing?" he demanded.

"Same as you, I suspect," she replied, hauling a roll of felt off a wagon.

"It isn't safe. Go home."

Esige dropped the felt beside one woman and turned to his mare, smacking her flank and making her lurch. "You first!"

Unebolod maintained control of his mount. Arguing with her right now would be pointless. He commanded ten men to stay and protect the women, then wheeled his mare toward the milling mass of shadows on the western horizon, accentuated by the shifting hues of blue as the wolf dawn began in earnest.

An army.

He raised the horn around his neck to his lips and sounded the alarm. Soke and Togochi would know to come to him here. Then, they would route this army ... or destroy it.

Could this be Bigirsen attacking to get his son back? It was a coward's move to attack in the dark while the camp slumbered, and Bigirsen had never struck Mandukhai as a coward. But amidst the chaos in the gathering tent, it would have been all too easy to smuggle Nemeku out. Her heart sank. If Nemeku fell into his father's hands, Bigirsen could attempt using his son to strengthen his bid at *kurultai*. She could not allow that to happen.

"Organize the woman and children, Jaghan," Mandukhai commanded as she rushed past them toward the door. "Alayitung, protect the women and children."

"Where are you going?" the General called after her.

Mandukhai motioned for Arslan and the rest of her guards to follow. "Nemeku is missing!" She darted out of the gathering tent with her five guards.

Before she went too far, Mandukhai stopped at her ger to retrieve her bow and quiver. She would not be surprised, and she would not hide while Nemeku was missing. The weapon felt familiar in her hand. As she hooked the quiver on her belt, Mandukhai noticed the overturned clay jar she kept the extra sweet curds in. Nemeku had a weakness for curds. She moved to the jar to investigate and noticed a trail of crumbs. Mandukhai followed the trail to the door, praying it would lead her to the boy.

The trail moved around the back of her ger, spotty and trampled by feet, but just enough had been left behind for her to follow.

As she wove toward the east between gers, Mandukhai noted how few men remained in this part of camp. Women and children darted from this ger to that one, gathering supplies to use or herding children out. A few cowered under a nearby cart. Mandukhai stopped only long enough to talk them out of their hiding places and encourage them all to collect in the gathering tent where Jaghan should have been organizing everyone. She asked after Nemeku, but no one had an answer.

The rally horn sounded once. Twice.

Mandukhai spun in a circle to pinpoint the direction. The horn sounded once more, a sure sign that an army had been spotted.

Would Bigirsen use an army as a distraction? Uncertainty rooted her in place.

"We should go back to the gathering tent so Lord Unebolod and Lady Esige know where to find us," Arslan suggested.

Mandukhai knew better. They would not come looking for her. Not until the battle was over ... for better or worse.

Shadows moved between two ger. Then three. Four. Mandukhai turned, swiftly realizing they were surrounded as the warriors stepped out of the shadows, bows raised.

"Lower your weapons!" Mandukhai commanded.

The attacking men laughed, and the sound curdled her stomach.

Arslan and her guards abandoned to command to get her horse and instead formed a defensive ring around Mandukhai, bows drawn.

"That's her," one man said.

Mandukhai cursed herself for not readying her own bow. A mistake she would never make again.

"Where is Nemeku?" she demanded.

"Who?" the man asked.

Her stomach sank. Before she could lift her own weapon, the whistle of arrows filled the air, flying in both directions. The surrounding ring closed tighter as two of her men were hit. Neither fell. Mandukhai struggled to see past the wall of bodies around her, but could see nothing more than the backs of their black armor.

One of her men pitched forward. For just a moment, Mandukhai saw the men who attacked. They had far more dead but still outnumbered her guards three to one. The narrow gap in her circle closed, guarded now by only four bodies. They edged toward a nearby ger, forcing her to shuffle along with them. *They are herding me inside!* Who lived here? It was so close to her own. General Alayitung's family? Her arrival would cost them dearly. *Hopefully no one is there right now.*

Arrows continued to whistle through the air in all directions. Another of her guards fell, spinning from the impact of an arrow in his eye. He died before he hit the ground.

Unebolod rode at the head of the army, a vast line of men as far as he could see in either direction. He had still not identified the attacking army, but it was safe to assume it would be Oirat. They already stirred near the border toward the west.

Horns sounded commands up and down the line, echoing his own sharp blasts. As the men rode hard toward the western horizon, Unebolod watched the dust cloud kicked up by the force they pursued.

He squinted through the haze of dust and dim light of the wolf dawn to identify what this force intended. Why attack Mongke Bulag only to turn and run the moment Unebolod pursued them? Was this a diversion? And if so, to what purpose? *At least I left men back to protect the camp*, he thought. It gave him the freedom to pursue these aggressors without worry.

Soke's southern forces had already swung around wide to meet up with Unebolod's. The Khorchin commander nudged his mount close to Unebolod. "My Lord khan, we should turn back."

Unebolod glanced at Soke. "How many did we leave to protect the camp?"

"As many as we could spare, but not enough if they circle back," Soke said. He spit dust out of his mouth. Soot from the smoke covered Soke's face. Did Unebolod's look the same?

Unebolod nodded and slowed his pace. His horsemen matched his pace without command. Soke was right. If this army circled back to Mongke Bulag with them always on the back of their primary force, the camp would be virtually defenseless, even with Alayitung protecting it.

"Send word north to Togochi," Unebolod commanded. "He will take his men back to block the south and east. They can't attack from the north with the mountains and forest blocking their path. Not without giving themselves away. To be sure, you will take your force north and sweep away any who might flee in that direction." Unebolod also hoped the crisscrossing patterns would make his forces appear in a state of disarray, allowing him more time to take them by surprise.

Soke guided his mount up the line toward where Togochi commanded his men. Unebolod kept his gaze forward, searching out signs that the dust cloud had shifted in either direction.

In less than a minute, Togochi's thousands of horsemen broke away the south, toward Mongke Bulag.

In a footrace, there would be no way to catch up to the men who fled his army. The horses would be evenly matched. One advantage he had was that he knew this land far better than the enemy. Heading straight west would lead the army into a wall of mountains they would have to scale. But if they turned south, there would be a passage through the Khangai Mountains ... right into the heart of Oirat territory. This would be their target.

Unebolod yanked his reins and sounded the command horn. As one, the line of his army followed his lead. He would cut them off at the pass, or he would force them to stand and fight.

Esige paused to catch her breath, wiping her sleeve over her forehead to mop up the sheen of endless sweat. It beaded on her scalp and made her hair stringier each time she brushed her stray hairs back from her face. The fires were dying down now, and her back ached from the lifting and dumping of buckets of water or moving heavy felts to smother flames on the ground. Boke and Torgus had arrived a few minutes ago, attempting to escort her back to the gathering tent. Esige had refused. If the other women could be there to fight the fires, she would be as well. Mandukhai would understand. She would have to.

"I'm perfectly safe with you two loitering in my shadow," Esige had insisted.

Movement from the corner of her eyes caught her attention. Esige dropped to her knees and snatched her bow, as well as an arrow from the quiver. In seconds, she had an arrow drawn, aiming it under a cart where she saw the movement.

In a huff, she released the tension and slid the arrow back in the quiver. "Nemeku, what are you doing here? You should be waiting in the gathering tent with the other children."

Tears streaked his face, and he clung to something in his fist. Esige eased toward him, reaching a hand out.

Nemeku wormed his way out from under the cart and threw his arms around her neck. "I wanna be with you," he whimpered.

Esige folded her arms around his five-year-old frame and rubbed his back. "It's okay. But we should get you back where you are safe. Mandukhai will be worried sick."

She knew the moment she returned to the gathering tent, no one would let her leave again. But she couldn't do her duty out here if she worried about Nemeku the entire time.

Arslan grunted as another arrow thumped into his armor. Mandukhai hated using him as a shield, but only one other guard remained. The ger door pressed against her back.

"Go inside," Arslan hissed under his breath. "We will hold them off as long as we can. Cut the felt and slip out the back, then run. Don't stop until you reach the gathering tent."

Mandukhai wanted to protest but knew there was no point. Arslan's purpose was to protect her. He would die fighting off these men. They outnumbered her two remaining guards, five to one.

"Go with the spirit of Tengri," Mandukhai said, offering the only final prayer she could in this dire moment.

Arslan fired his last arrow and drew his sword as Mandukhai ducked inside.

The ger was blissfully empty. With only the bed and stove, it seemed a barren thing. Mandukhai breathed a sigh of relief. She had been worried that her appearance in the ger would lead to the death of whoever occupied it. If this was Alayitung's ger, as she suspected—it was so hard to tell in the chaos—his family would already be with him in the gathering tent.

Mandukhai rushed to the back wall. She cut the straps holding the lattice in place using her hunting knife, then sawed through the layers of felt, praying to the High Heavens to watch over her. The sounds of fighting diminished outside, and she knew time was wearing thin. She would not get far if she did not get out of here soon.

At last, her knife punched through the rest of the way. Mandukhai turned sideways to slip through the narrow gap.

Cool air slammed into her lungs but did nothing for her pounding heart.

Rough hands seized her arms from behind, and Mandukhai screamed, twisting to break free from the firm grip. The hilt of a sword rammed into her back, sending Mandukhai sprawling on her knees. The sudden jerking motion wrenched at her arms, still held firm by her attacker.

As the attacker edged closer, she recognized his Oirat colors immediately. Mandukhai spit in his face as he crouched in front of her. She yanked at the hands holding her as they bound her wrists together behind her back.

The leader sneered, wiping away the spit on his cheek. "He warned me you were spirited. I'll have to break that before you reach him."

"Who do you serve?" Mandukhai demanded. Had Bigirsen sent these men to capture both her and his son? *Where is Nemeku?*

"You will see soon enough." He pulled out a felt sack poked with holes.

"What do you want?" she asked.

"A queen for a Khan," he replied, then slipped the sack over her head.

A *Bankhar* dog leaped from the shadows, sinking its teeth into the meaty flesh of one of her captor's arms. The man screamed and let go of Mandukhai. She attempted fleeing, but hardly managed more than a step before blinding pain shot through her skull. Mandukhai blinked. The dog yelped and fell to the ground. Someone yanked the sack tight over her head. The last thing she saw before being plunged into darkness was the dog. Not just any dog. She identified the color pattern around the dog's nose.

Kilgor. Unebolod's dog.

Another hammer against her skull plunged her into unconsciousness.

CHAPTER SIX

Routes

ORDOS TERRITORY – LATE SPRING – 1470

Issama waited inside Bigirsen's ger for the Ordos khan to join them. The invitation had been sent at sunrise, and for the next hour, Bigirsen had paced and barked orders at servants in clear agitation. Fury burned at Bigirsen's neck and created deep lines in his aging face. Guards were posted all around the ger, a clear sign of Bigirsen's dominance.

Word of Legusi khan's approach came moments earlier, and Bigirsen settled into the only seat. All the fury and agitation that had dominated his every move for the past hour melted away. The man who sat on a stack of saddles was all confident and as calm as Issama had ever seen. Even the red color faded from Bigirsen's face. The vein that minutes ago had been throbbing in Bigirsen's neck steadied. The absolute command he had over his own emotions at this moment was unlike anything Issama had witnessed before. Bigirsen had prepared to play a game with Legusi, and Issama had not yet puzzled out what it might be.

The stove flickered with fiery life, open to the room. Everything else had been removed. Only Persian rugs, the stack of saddles Bigirsen straddled, and the stove remained.

Issama had not questioned Bigirsen's decision to have his possessions removed, yet he could not fathom the reasoning behind it. He certainly would not ask while the older man had been pulsing with pent-up, violent rage. *He is coming undone because of that woman,* he thought.

Ever since Mandukhai had sent the message summoning Bigirsen, he had inched closer to the edge. How long until he finally threw himself off? *If he ever learns of the message I sent to her, he will take my head without blinking,* Issama thought, folding his hands as he assumed his position, standing behind Bigirsen.

The Uyghur warlord had not shared today's plans with Issama. One moment Bigirsen had been prepared to plunge into Ming territory while the new emperor took over; the next, he had turned the Uyghur army east, deep into Ordos territory. Issama had questioned him, but Bigirsen had responded so harshly Issama hadn't dared ask again.

Only one logical explanation emerged. If they were to fight the Ming, they would need the support of the Ordos tribes. Support that just a year ago had belonged to the Golden Prince. Now, that vacuum of space needed to be filled. Bigirsen would be a logical selection. The Ordos tribes numbered over a hundred thousand warriors. If Bigirsen could take complete control of that, he would be nearly unstoppable. Or so Issama assumed.

The door to the ger stood open, awaiting Lord Legusi's arrival. Dogs barked outside, followed a moment later by a long shadow over the doorway. Then the young Ordos khan ducked into the ger, offering Bigirsen a half-scowl as he bowed respectfully, but without deference.

Legusi was a tall young man, but his shoulders were narrow compared to most of his own guards. His sharp, dark eyes swept the ger critically with what Issama knew from experience would be a man worried about potential danger. He had aligned himself with the Golden Prince despite Bigirsen's previous subjugation of the Ordos tribes under Legusi's father. *He is wise to look for hidden danger.*

Bigirsen rested casually on the stack of saddles, arms on his thighs, staring at Legusi with cold, impassive eyes. But he did not speak. Issama took his cue and maintained a calm, collected composure.

Legusi straightened while two of his men entered, standing at his back without weapons. That detail must have chaffed at them. Relinquishing a weapon never settled well with Lords or their guards. It left them open to attack. Bigirsen wouldn't be that foolish. Not when he invited Legusi to his ger. The reflection of flames from the open stove flickered off Legusi's polished leather and iron-plated armor.

The silence in the ger grew thick as each man waited for the other to speak first. Bigirsen used this tactic often. He would either dominate the conversation immediately, showing he meant business and had other matters to attend, or he would wait and let the silence fester like an open wound—a display of his control. Men would often squirm before breaking first. Dozens of times, Issama watched Bigirsen use this tactic to get men to condemn themselves. The air would grow thick with fear until the other man would finally break down and admit his crime, begging for mercy he must have known he would never receive.

Legusi did not crack under the pressure. He held his chin high, jaw clamped shut. Issama did not know how long they all stood like that. Seconds? Minutes? With so much tension hanging in the air, it became impossible to tell. *Someone needs to speak first*, Issama thought as his own patience wore thin. If his patience waned, surely Bigirsen's did as well. After the rage he had been in earlier, there was no way he would be calm right now.

"This has been most illuminating, Lord Bigirsen," Legusi said at last, then turned for the door.

Guards stepped in the way, blocking their exit. Lord Legusi's men reached for their weapons, only to remember they had none.

"Running so soon, Legusi?" Bigirsen asked. His voice was soft, but the hard edge made his anger clear. He controlled this situation. "Perhaps Lord Aglaqu would be more interested in what I have to say."

Lord Legusi turned to face Bigirsen, his long mustache quivering with indignation. "Aglaqu is a snake. And we have not even begun."

Bigirsen's smile was wolfish. "Indeed, we have not."

Lord Legusi huffed. "Don't waste my time."

"Do you recall the words your father spoke to me all those years ago?" Bigirsen asked casually, though there was nothing casual about his posture. He hunched like a predatory cat prepared to pounce.

Lord Legusi stiffened as if someone had shoved a pole down his spine.

Bigirsen smirked. "You do." His gaze narrowed. "Then why, Legusi khan, have you abandoned that oath?"

Issama's pulse quickened. Legusi's father had been khan of the Ordos tribes for decades before he died of fever two years ago. Legusi was barely old enough to take over at the time. Even now, at nineteen, he was young for a tribal khan of so many. The only oath Issama could assume Bigirsen referred to had been when Legusi's father had vowed to follow and obey Bigirsen's commands. Yet if Legusi did not agree with the oath, Bigirsen had come all this way to start a war with the Ordos tribes. *He can't be that foolish. War with the Ordos could align them with Mandukhai and turn all of the Mongol tribes against the Uyghur. Even with the support of the Oirat, we wouldn't stand a chance.*

"I am not my father," Legusi said, but his air of arrogance could not mask the fear in his voice.

"That much is evident," Bigirsen spat, not bothering to hide his disgust. "At least he knew his place. But you have sided with this false queen, haven't you?"

Legusi opened his mouth to respond, but Bigirsen held up a hand sharply, cutting him off. In a slow, deliberate motion, Bigirsen reached down under one saddle and retrieved a flat metal disk. Firelight caught on it, gleaming like death. Issama squinted at it momentarily, identifying the sharpened piece of armor.

"Manduul Khan has placed her in charge of the Nation until the new Great Khan is selected," Legusi said, his gaze fixed on the disk. "She is not a false queen."

"Manduul Khan is dead, as is his Golden Prince," Bigirsen snapped. "Your oath to that boy died with him."

Lord Legusi raised his chin stubbornly. "My oath is to this Nation."

"Your oath is to me!" Bigirsen roared, clenching the disk hard enough to turn his knuckles white.

Issama was pleased not to be the only man in the ger to flinch.

"He followed the prince as well," Legusi replied, his voice shaking as he waved a trembling hand toward Issama.

"He worked on my orders," Bigirsen said. "Everything he does serves me, unlike you. Issama's loyalty is not in question."

It took great effort for Issama to suppress his delight at that. Bigirsen did not know what Issama was planning. Was Bigirsen's statement the truth? Had Issama pulled the wool over Bigirsen's eyes so he did not suspect? *I would be dead already if he knew even a fraction of it*, Issama reassured himself.

"Tell me, Legusi," Bigirsen said, twisting the metal disk so it caught in the light. "Have you heard the tale of how Genghis Khan conquered the Olkhonud who betrayed him?"

Legusi paled considerably, edging away from the open stove.

Bigirsen surged to his feet, causing Legusi's unarmed guards to move forward. But Bigirsen did not strike. Issama watched as he instead toyed with the young khan, heating the edge of the iron disk over the open stove.

Issama had to admit, this was a stroke of genius—or the act of a madman. Unless Bigirsen intended to kill the young khan.

As the iron heated, Bigirsen watched Legusi expectantly. "Well?"

Legusi swallowed so hard Issama could hear it from the back of the ger. "H-he pulled a piece of plate off of his armor and cut the khan's throat with it."

Bigirsen grinned and laughed with such malevolence that even Issama's skin crawled. "He cut the khan's throat with it," he agreed, nodding. "Brutal, but effective." He lifted the iron and examined the hot, sharp edge. "Now, young khan, will you follow this false queen and risk the same fate, or will you kneel before me now and give over control of your tribes to me so we can finish what Genghis could not?"

Issama watched in fascination as Legusi's entire body trembled before Bigirsen. Legusi's knees gave out, choosing his fate for him. Bigirsen dropped the sharpened metal disk on the rug in front of Legusi, as if challenging him to pick it up and strike out at him. The young khan's gaze fell on the disk. He squeezed his eyes shut.

"I give you gers, horses, salt, and blood," Legusi said, reciting the oath reserved for khans.

"No, my boy," Bigirsen said. He took Legusi's chin in his hand and tilted the young khan's face up to meet his gaze. "You give me your title."

Issama gasped, unable to contain his shock. One could not simply steal a title of lesser khan like this. The Ordos would never agree to it. No one would. Only a Great Khan could give or take such titles. Bigirsen seriously overstepped his rights.

Yet if Bigirsen succeeded, he could control the votes at *kurultai*, and he could not put his own name forward unless he was a High Lord or khan of a tribe. He was currently neither. If Legusi relinquished his title to Bigirsen, it would give Bigirsen the lawful right to claim the title of Great Khan. This could undo all of Issama's careful planning. He had spent years gaining the trust of High Lords and lesser khans to encourage *them* to put his name forward, since he could not do so himself. Bigirsen could rip all of that away from him if he succeeded in his own designs. *I have underestimated you,* Issama thought. *I will not do so again. Mandukhai must be my key.*

One of Legusi's guards chose this moment to decide enough was enough. He lunged forward, reaching for the iron disk on the floor. Bigirsen wrenched a knife from his belt and jammed it up through the guard's chin, through his mouth, and into his brain. In a smooth motion, he yanked it out.

Lord Legusi squawked, and his remaining guard leaped into action, grabbing the young khan and hurling him toward the door. The guard kept his back to the khan like a shield. Bigirsen jumped forward, seizing the guard's head and yanking it back. He jerked the knife across the guard's throat.

Issama watched the death helplessly. None of Bigirsen's guards moved. This act of violence went against the Guest Rights extended to Legusi and his men. Legusi would have every right now to kill Bigirsen with no repercussions. Issama debated whether now would be the moment to kill Bigirsen and forge this alliance. But all the Uyghur guards in the ger were loyal to Bigirsen. With both of Legusi's guards dead, Issama and Legusi alone would not be enough to kill Bigirsen as well as the guards both inside and outside the ger.

Issama also knew he could not stand by and do nothing as this happened. Bigirsen was in a foul mood, and that knife could just as easily turn on him. Instead, he remained in his position and gave a sharp whistle. The dogs outside lunged at the doorway, forcing Legusi back into Bigirsen's waiting arms.

"This is an abomination!" Legusi snapped.

Bigirsen placed his large hand on Legusi's head and forced the young khan to his knees. "No, Legusi. She is an abomination. And I will see her festering wound carved out of the Mongol flesh if I have to cut it out one weak Lord at a time." He raised his bloody knife to Legusi's throat.

"You have it!" Legusi blurted. "The Ordos are yours."

"Good boy," Bigirsen snarled. He called toward the door. "Nahai!"

Issama's second-in-command ducked in, taking in the scene with little more than a raised brow. Nahai was one of the only men Issama trusted.

"See that Lord Legusi is comfortable until his Lords and commanders are gathered," Bigirsen said. He removed the knife from Legusi's throat and wiped the blood off on the young khan's deel. "Then he will announce the relinquishment of his title to me."

Nahai bowed, grabbing Legusi roughly by the arm and yanked him out the door.

Issama understood why Bigirsen had changed course. Conquering the Ordos would cut off Mandukhai from any routes toward the southwest completely. Her only allies would belong to Unebolod in the east. Without the wealth of the Silk Route and the plentiful herds from the Oirat, Mandukhai and Unebolod had nothing to offer their allies.

He means to finish what he started eight years ago, Issama realized. If Bigirsen could re-take control of the southern tribes, they could sweep into Ming territory with only Unebolod's allies at their backs, instead of the entire Mongol Nation. Without these tribes, Mandukhai would lose power, and Unebolod would lose *kurultai*. But Bigirsen's methods would earn him more enemies than allies. *You cannot put humps on a horse and call it a camel*, Issama thought. *It will fool no one.*

Bigirsen would never truly be Great Khan if he stole the title this way. *The enemy of my enemy shall become my ally.*

The sun had fully risen into the wide blue sky by the time Togochi returned to Mongke Bulag. Sweat made the silk beneath his armor stick to his skin and chaff as he rode. He had left his second-in-command, Yaqui, in charge of the Khorlod warriors so that he could check back in with Mandukhai. He worried about the reason for this attack. Why would the invaders not ride into the camp and kill as many as they could? He couldn't understand why they instead lit fires and rode off.

Hopefully she will have more answers by now, he thought as he dismounted outside the gathering tent. A servant came to collect his horse.

Togochi strode into the tent. The inside of the gathering tent burst at the seams with women, children, and men too old to fight. Everyone appeared haggard from the events of the early morning. Some had singed or blackened clothing. Others were covered in sweat or dirt. Everyone had been doing something amidst the chaos.

He spotted his wife surrounded by other Ladies. Their infant daughter was strapped to her chest in a sling. He breathed a sigh of relief upon seeing her. At least his wife was well.

He strode up beside Jaghan and kissed her cheek. "Where is Mandukhai?" he asked, scanning the gathering tent. He had expected to see her perched in her seat on the dais, directing everyone. Instead, he could not spot her at all. But there were at least a hundred people packed inside the tent walls, if not more.

"She went to find Nemeku," Jaghan said. "He disappeared."

Togochi's stomach dropped. He knew Mandukhai worried Bigirsen would come for his son. Had that been the purpose of this attack? Did Bigirsen get his hands on the boy at last? While it was his son, and Bigirsen had rights, Togochi also understood that Nemeku was the son of a Borjigin princess. Without an heir of Genghis, that bloodline would have merit.

Esige strolled into the gathering tent. The girl's clothes were covered in soot, and her face was blackened from the smoke. She had been out fighting fires. But that was not what made Togochi's stomach suddenly churn in a sickening mass.

Nemeku clung to Esige as she carried him into the gathering tent with Boke and Torgus on their heels.

"Mandukhai?" Togochi asked Esige, inquiring if the girl knew anything.

Esige frowned and glanced at the dais, just as he had done upon entering. "I thought she would be here."

"She went looking for Nemeku," Jaghan said, eyeing the trembling little boy in Esige's arms.

Togochi glared at Boke, whose face paled considerably. If anything happened to Mandukhai, Boke would be held responsible.

"I want every available man searching this camp for the Queen Regent immediately!" Togochi shouted. Every muscle in his body suddenly coiled up tightly. "Jaghan, Esige, you will *stay here* and watch over the women and children." He put all the extra stress on his command that he could.

The two of them only nodded.

Togochi grabbed Alayitung's arm and dragged the Borjigin General out with him. If Unebolod returned and they did not find Mandukhai yet, he would burn everything to the ground to search for her.

Togochi had to search everywhere before Unebolod came back. *Please let her be fighting a fire somewhere*, he pleaded to Tengri.

Altai-Khangai Mountain Pass – Late Spring – 1470

It had taken considerable effort to skirt around the fleeing army, but Unebolod had directed his remaining men with expert ease. The enemy army clearly had been headed for the wide-open expanse of land leading into Oirat territory, leaving him no doubt any longer just who they were. The Oirat had probably attacked Mongke Bulag assuming it would be weak without a Great Khan. Unebolod was pleased to prove them wrong.

When the Oirat forces rode toward the open hills, they had sounded an alarm the moment they spotted Unebolod's forces. Like a great wheel, the enemy force had pivoted away and headed south. The Khorchin flank had been prepared for this maneuver, and Unebolod's line swung like a deadly hook from the south, giving the Oirat only two means of escape: back to Mongke Bulag, or through the mountain pass to the northwest.

Unebolod grinned as he kicked his mount into action. Arrows flew, the familiar whistle of them in the breeze feeding into his growing energy. His men were well drilled in such combat, even if they had not used these skills for some time. He had not let them grow rusty over the years, training them and running drills regularly. With no command, they knew to leap into action the moment their khan set the charge, firing right alongside him.

The pulse of battle invigorated Unebolod, shedding his bottled-up tension along with the years he felt had crept up on him since arriving in Mongke Bulag. This sensation of calm logic, battle heat, and the thrill of the chase was something he would grow used to once he became Great Khan.

The sun rose into the sky at Unebolod's back, warming his skin as surely as his blood warmed the rest of his body. He loosed another arrow, watching as an Oirat tumbled from the saddle. The gap shrank between the forces as the thunder of thousands of hooves shook the earth.

For more than a mile, Unebolod's army pursued the Oirat, slowly closing the gap as the mountains loomed closer. The Oirat would make for the pass. Unebolod's pulse quickened. He had sent a thousand of his own men to block the pass, under Soke's command.

Shouts in the distance rose into the air, alongside the bleating of Oirat horns as they attempted to change formation. *They met the rest of my men,* Unebolod thought with satisfaction.

Even from a distance, he could see the churning mass of Oirat probing for a means of escape. But the Khorchin army pinned them in. A *mingghan* of a thousand men blocked the pass, firing on the Oirat with deadly accuracy as Unebolod's remaining two thousand formed a bowl around them until the two sides met and closed in a massive ring around the Oirat.

The circle closed quickly, pinching off the Oirat from any hopes of breaking through the lines. The Khorchin army raced in circles around them, raining death down as their horses kicked up dust to obstruct the enemy from clear lines of sight. Unebolod breathed carefully to avoid sucking in dirt, taking aim with practiced ease and firing in that blissful moment when hooves left the earth. Oirat bodies littered the ground as their numbers depleted. In no time, Unebolod's men had whittled the Oirat down to a handful of men. Those warriors were ripped from their saddles. Khorchin men tore away all weapons, throwing them in a pile out of Oirat reach.

Unebolod hopped off his mare, resting a hand on his hip as the remaining Oirat kneeled with their fingers laced behind their heads. He scanned the battlefield, frowning as he did a quick calculation in his head.

Perhaps only a thousand Oirat in total—alive and dead. That could not have been their entire force. "Where is the rest of your army?" he asked, pacing in front of the dozen remaining men.

To the last man, all the Oirat lifted their heads high in defiance. Unebolod knew this could not be all of them. Only a thousand against a camp full of Khorchin, Khorlod, and Borjigin warriors? They could not have hoped to win.

At a motion from Unebolod, one of his men seized an Oirat warrior by the hair and dragged him in front of the line. With one mighty, swift swing of his sword, the Khorchin warrior hacked off the Oirat's arm. The scream that pierced the air did not faze Unebolod. Instead, he turned to the rest of the Oirat.

"There are worse fates than death," Unebolod said coldly. "Where is the rest of your army?"

One of the Oirat hooted like a madman, and the manic amusement on his face made Unebolod's stomach sink.

"You will never be Great Khan, Khorchin scum," the Oirat chortled. Mad laughter filled the air. "He has taken all and left you with dust."

He? Who could this madman be referring to? Bigirsen, perhaps? Paisahan was the Oirat khan. Had this been his plan? The rest of the Oirat offered grim yet arrogant smirks. All of their eyes shined with the realization that death loomed in their future. Yet none of them truly seemed afraid of their fate. Instead, something far worse revealed itself to Unebolod. Victory.

They kneeled on a battlefield of defeat with the arrogant pride that only came with battle triumph.

Unebolod's heart stopped. The world around him tilted. *He has taken all and left you with dust.* He had routed them and been routed in return.

This was a trick, he realized with certainty, spinning toward the eastern horizon. Fury pulsed in his veins, punctuated by the mad cackling of one of their captors. *I let them lure me out!* He felt his skin mottling as he clenched a sword in his white-knuckled fist. His nostrils flared as he strained to control the rage growing inside him. A growl crept up his throat. He dropped the sword, lunging at the madman. Unebolod wrapped his hands around the man's throat and squeezed.

As he felt the flesh beneath his fingers, then the bones of the throat and neck, Unebolod's vision narrowed. His pulse pounded in his ears, drumming out a hard, steady rhythm of rage. The madman scratched at Unebolod's wrists, but he hardly noticed anything more than the fury burning through him and the redness of the man's face.

Unebolod bared his teeth as he tightened his grip. Something crunched under his hands. The madman fell limp.

Unebolod dropped the body, gasping for breath as if he had just broken the surface of a river. His warriors watched him with intense curiosity. "Kill them all." Staggering a few steps to the side as if drunk on *airag*, he turned toward Mongke Bulag, now miles away.

Toward Mandukhai.

CHAPTER SEVEN

Losing Ground

MONGKE BULAG – 1470

Togochi stood in the center of the clearing, his feet planted in the earth as he took in the scene around him. Dozens of dead Oirat littered the ground, as well as a handful of Mandukhai's guards. A heaviness settled into his limbs and exhaustion made his shoulders sag. Togochi crossed his arms over his chest to keep from rubbing at his eyes. How could he be so tired so early in the day?

The men who examined the surrounding scene gave Togochi wide berth, sensing his somberness. It was rare for Togochi to be so glum. Generally, he sought the light in even the darkest moments. But so much had gone so horribly wrong these past few months. He found little humor left inside. And now this. There could be little doubt about what had happened here.

The Oirat attack had been a ruse to distract their forces. They snuck into camp, killed Mandukhai's guards, and took her. Unebolod would be well beyond furious when he returned to this news. He would be wild, inconsolable ... and ready to kill.

But Togochi knew Mandukhai. She would not want war over this. She would want justice. It was a fine line, but it existed. Unebolod would be unable to see that line.

I have to keep him from crossing it, Togochi thought as he stalked toward the ger where Arslan's dead body guarded the door.

The men had not questioned Unebolod's sudden leap into action. He had simply shouted to ride back like the wind for the queen as he had jumped into his saddle. Now, they closed the gap of miles at dangerous speeds, leaving the dead Oirat behind.

Unebolod raced across the steppe as if the god of death himself rode on his heels. With each thump of the hooves, he whipped his mare faster until she reached her peak speed. It still felt far too slow for his needs. *Please let her be safe in my ger,* he prayed, leaning closer to his mare's neck. But he knew better. Mandukhai would never stay put while he ran off to defend the camp. Unebolod's heart hammered against his ribs and drummed in his ears, nearly as loud as the thump of thousands of hooves at his back.

Smoke continued billowing from the smoldering remains of Mongke Bulag, but the fires had been extinguished. The warriors dismounted as they reached camp, but Unebolod did not break his pace as he darted through the maze of gers toward his own. He shouted for men and women to clear the way ahead of him. But if they were unfortunate enough to remain in his path, Unebolod did not slow or dodge aside. He continued at dangerous speeds until he reached his ger. His mare bucked when he yanked the reins hard. He jumped off her back and dropped the reins.

Unebolod's vision narrowed as he stared at the open door of his ger. All the air in his lungs was knocked out, as if someone had punched him in the gut. *No. No, not now.* Trembling, he edged toward the open door, each step stiff with fear. Had they kidnapped her? He couldn't accept that. Not yet. She could be anywhere. He knew she wouldn't be here. Yet he couldn't help the panic swallowing him whole.

The inside of his ger had fallen dark with no one to stoke the fire in the stove. A quick sweep of the nearly empty space revealed no sign of struggle. Mandukhai certainly would not have gone without a fight.

Desperate to find her elsewhere—anywhere!—he broke from his stupor and ran to her door, which also stood open. Her bow and quiver were missing from their place beside the door. *Curse you, woman! Why can't you do what you're told?* The gathering tent. It had been bustling with activity as he raced past. Maybe she was there.

"Unebolod!"

He rushed out the door to find Esige approaching from behind Mandukhai's ger. Boke followed close on her heels. Unebolod's gaze swept past them, expecting Mandukhai to stroll around the ger with them.

But she did not come.

"Where is she, Boke?" Unebolod asked.

"It isn't his fault," Esige said.

Once more, the ground dropped out from beneath his feet. He took several deep breaths, tempering his anger and terror, then swiftly closed the gap between them. Esige's words only confirmed Unebolod's worst fear. Mandukhai was gone. *No. She can't be.* Unebolod seized the collar of Boke's armor, baring his teeth and leaning closer.

"Where is she?" Unebolod growled.

Somehow, Esige wedged herself between the two men, sliding under Unebolod's arm and pushing him back. His grip did not relent.

"She ordered him to find me!" Esige snapped. "If you want to blame anyone, blame me!"

Unebolod wanted to pummel Boke, to throw his fists into the other man's face until nothing remained to distinguish him. His entire body trembled with white-hot fury. Boke was the head of Mandukhai's guard. He was supposed to protect her.

"Where is she?" Unebolod asked once more, unable to form any other words. His voice shook, revealing his fear to anyone around them.

"Unebolod," a familiar voice called from behind him. "You need to see this."

Trembling, worried about what he needed to see, or what it could mean, Unebolod released Boke. Yet as he let go, he felt as if he let go of Mandukhai herself. When he spun around, Togochi waved behind her ger.

Each step weighed Unebolod down as if there were stones attached to his feet. He followed Togochi around Mandukhai's ger, then further east. Pain clenched his chest, lungs, and throat. Mandukhai was gone. Not only could he lose *kurultai*, but he had lost the woman he loved. With each heavy step, his knees threatened to give out. They continued east, and the path between gers seemed to stretch on for miles, though he knew it had not been far.

Togochi stopped near a ger beside a small clearing nearly a quarter-mile from Mandukhai's ger. Bodies littered the ground, peppered with arrows or sliced wide open. Flies buzzed around already. Unebolod became hyper-aware of what he was looking at. Oirat men ... and Mandukhai's guards.

More than a dozen bodies lay dead in the blood-soaked packed earth. Near the door to a ger, Arslan lay like a barricade, his lifeless eyes staring at the Eternal Blue Sky. Unebolod's skin suddenly turned clammy, despite the sweat rolling down his forehead. Still, he clung to hope that she would be inside, unable to accept that she might be gone, despite all the evidence pointing toward her capture.

He edged toward the door and reached for Arslan to haul the body aside. "Don't bother," Togochi said. "She slipped out the back."

Unebolod froze, spinning around as if Mandukhai would step out of the air and glide toward him. Instead, he watched as Togochi reached out a hand. One of Togochi's men stepped forward, holding out a bow.

Mandukhai's bow.

Every muscle in Unebolod's body coiled tight. He opened his mouth, trying to form the words he dared not utter aloud.

She is gone.

"Kilgor must have attempted defending her." Togochi's eyes shimmered with sympathy Unebolod did not want. "I'm sorry, Unebolod. They killed your dog."

All of this had been a trick to lure the men away from Mongke Bulag so they could slip in and claim what they had truly come for. Any man who could seize control of the Queen Regent had the best position to become the next Great Khan.

The Oirat intended to steal *kurultai.*

Mandukhai woke to a pulsing headache. Darkness filtered through some unknown tunnel. Movements jostled her stomach, and the stench of sweat and blood filled her nose. She blinked against the darkness and moved to reach for the throbbing ache in her head. But her wrists were bound together. Focusing on the tunnel of light, Mandukhai fought to understand what was happening, giving the ropes binding her wrists one more experimental tug.

The attack. The Oirat. *A queen for a Khan,* the Oirat man had said.

Mandukhai squeezed her eyes closed as her stomach roiled. *Don't cry. Don't cry. Think!* There had to be a way to escape. Unebolod would come for her. She only needed to delay these men, slow their pace.

Mandukhai opened her eyes, realizing that the tunnel of light was a hole in the bag they had placed over her head. The ribbon of bright light told her the sun was up. How long had she been unconscious? How far had they come already?

The Oirat had attacked the camp, drawn out her forces, and snuck in to capture her while the men were distracted. Mandukhai hated how brilliant the plan had been, and how it had apparently worked. But if there was one thing she knew for certain, it was that Unebolod would tear the Oirat apart to find her.

Each movement jostled her stomach, and Mandukhai realized they were riding with her body slung over the back of a horse. Testing her luck, Mandukhai carefully shimmied her body, praying no one could see her. With any luck, they would assume she remained unconscious. Nothing bound her to the horse's back. Mandukhai held her breath, waiting to see if one of the men would call out. No call came.

If they made camp, Mandukhai knew exactly what these men would do to her. She had to slow them down, buy time, or escape before nightfall.

If she managed to slide off the horse, she risked being trampled. But would that fate be worse than what these men would do to her?

Steeling her nerves, Mandukhai risked injury, throwing her body off the horse. Her back hit the ground with a thump that raised alarms. Only a narrow ribbon of sight was visible through the hole in the bag over her head. Not nearly enough for her to know what surrounded her. Before they could stop her, Mandukhai bolted to her feet and ran, breathing hard in the sack. She had no idea which way she was going—toward or away from them. The stench of her stale breath slammed back into her face, intensifying the heat.

A shadow fell across her path. Mandukhai shifted course only to hit the solid body of a horse. She spun around, but the motion was too much for her throbbing head. Mandukhai stumbled. Rough hands seized her, yanking her up over a shoulder. The world spun, despite the sack over her face.

"Please, I'm going to be sick," she whimpered. It was not a lie. The increased spinning made her insides twist with nausea.

A slap on her backside stung, shocking her out of the urge to vomit. She yelped.

"Keep quiet until we get there," one man said.

"I can think of a few ways to keep her quiet," another said, and Mandukhai heard the implication crystal clear in his tone.

The comment roused several chuckles from the others.

Too many of them. There were too many of them. She could not tell from the sound of their laughter exactly how many men were with her, but it was more than the two who spoke, for certain.

Mandukhai kicked to break from the man carrying her. Instead of putting her back on the horse, he pressed her back down onto the unforgiving ground. Her head rebounded off the dirt, and she moaned in pain.

"Stay there like a good little woman," one of them said.

Terror seized Mandukhai. Surely they would not do this now. She rolled over, crawling away, hating herself for allowing hot tears to roll down her cheeks.

A hand clamped down on her arms, yanking back with so much force she had no choice but to sit back on her knees.

"Oh, this one needs to be broken," one of them said from directly in front of her. Rough hands groped at her chest.

Mandukhai whimpered. *I am not a helpless woman,* she thought. She slammed her head forward, cracking the skull of the man in front of her.

"Bitch!" He cried out, falling back. At least his hands no longer touched her.

Despite the sack over her head, a strong backhand slammed across Mandukhai's face, making her head pulse and her vision turned to blinding bright light. She squirmed pitifully, realizing she lay on her side on the ground now.

"Enough! She belongs to Paisahan khan," one man barked.

"She's already used," another man said. "He won't never know."

Mandukhai choked back a sob. Her entire head felt like it might split in half. How had matters come to this? She knew full well what would happen once they delivered her to Paisahan khan. He would try to plant his seed to stake his claim.

She could not wait for Unebolod to rescue her. Mandukhai had to find her own way to escape. And if she couldn't escape, Mandukhai had to come up with some way to talk Paisahan out of this horrible plan.

Mongke Bulag

Unebolod paced outside of his ger. Everyone else had packed up their gers. Only his remained. How could they pack up and prepare to leave without their queen? It reeked of abandonment. Unebolod would not abandon Mandukhai. Never again. That first time, after losing their child, had been too much for him. Abandoning her again would destroy him.

Odgerel lingered nearby. They had not spoken since last night when he had kicked her out of his ger. At some point, he would have to deal with her. Right now, he had more pressing matters to attend to.

Esige rushed toward Unebolod's ger with a small squad of boys still too young to fight. "The cart is over there," she said, motioning to the east of Unebolod's ger. "The faster you work, the better."

Unebolod stiffened, glaring at the boys so fiercely they froze, hardly daring to blink.

"We have to pack everything, Unebolod," Esige said with calm patience. She sounded so much like Mandukhai it made his heart ache. "There is nothing more we can do for her until the scouts come back, but we can still carry forward with her plans."

"You expect me to travel to Mount Burkhan Khaldun now?" he asked incredulously.

Esige snorted and rolled her eyes. "No. But that does not mean the rest of the people cannot head there. We can collect her and meet with them faster that way."

"I don't think you understand what is happening, Esige," Unebolod said, stalking toward her. "Without her, there is no *kurultai*. The Oirat have declared war."

Esige raised her chin and somehow, despite being a full head shorter than him, appeared as if she looked down at him. "She was right." Her lips thinned. She composed herself so much like Mandukhai it was like looking at her reflection in this girl. "I'm disappointed in you. I thought you were different."

Unebolod flinched as if she had slapped him. "What?"

"Take your men. Start your war. And when she comes back to us—and she will come back to us, because she is far too fierce to be cowed by something like this—she will not thank you for declaring war on the Oirat before the time was right." Esige shooed the boys toward his ger briskly. "The carts will head to Mount Burkhan Khaldun with enough men to protect them. The rest of your army you can keep behind to launch your war. But I would suggest you speak with your generals before volunteering *their* men."

Unebolod was too stunned to speak as Esige nodded at the boys, who worked quickly, already removing all the straps holding the walls to his ger. She turned on her heel and marched away, disappearing into a mass of bustling bodies.

All around him, Mongke Bulag had vanished. The emptiness reminded him far too much of Mandukhai's absence. Esige was right, although it chaffed at him to admit as much. Mandukhai would be furious with him for declaring war on the Oirat. He only needed to rescue her from their clutches and get her to Mount Burkhan Khaldun. Then he would be Great Khan, and the Oirat would burn.

Unebolod strode away from his ger as the walls crashed to the ground and the boys set to work folding the lattice. Hours had passed since he had returned. Every moment put her further from his grasp. Soke's men were already gone to scout and track before he had returned with his own men. How could they have nothing to report yet?

Togochi lifted one of his young sons into a basket tied behind Jaghan's saddle. The oldest was still too young to ride, and he complained from his place in the cart. As Unebolod approached, Togochi soothed his oldest. Jaghan glanced past Togochi at Unebolod, holding her daughter in a strap against her chest; it would be easier to feed her without stopping this way. She nodded subtly toward Unebolod as she murmured something to her husband.

Togochi turned to face Unebolod, all the fatherly pride washing away with a cold warrior's face. "I was just coming to find you."

"Do you have word yet?" Unebolod asked.

"A moment ago, one of Soke's men returned, saying they found a trail," Togochi said. "Northwest."

Unebolod breathed a sigh of relief. "Assemble your men on the northern training grounds. We leave immediately."

Jaghan tensed, averting her gaze from the conversation as her face paled.

"No." Togochi's one word was like a hammer against Unebolod's chest.

"What do you mean, no?" Unebolod snapped.

Togochi raised his chin and squared his shoulders. "Before anything, I need to make something clear to you. Unebolod, brother, I respect you like no other man, but you have no command over me. I am just as much a leader in this camp as you. But for one difference."

Unebolod reeled, but before he got in a word, Togochi pushed on.

"I swore an oath to Lady Mandukhai the moment Manduul died," Togochi said. "I answer to the Queen Regent, and no one else. Make no mistake. I am your brother still, and when we reach *kurultai*, you know you will have my full support. But until that day, you have no right to direct me."

"I am *orlok*," Unebolod snapped. "I direct all the *tumens*."

Togochi shook his head. "You are too hot right now, Unebolod. Think clearly."

Unebolod could not handle this. Not on top of everything else this horrible day had wrought. Togochi chose *this* moment to abandon him? Togochi knew how he felt about Mandukhai. He knew how Unebolod wanted to be Great Khan, how he worked for this most of his life. Togochi had always been a younger brother to Unebolod, but it had never occurred to him that his brother would act like this.

"You will not join me then?" Unebolod asked, hoping his voice didn't shake. "If you are sworn to her, it's your duty to go after her as much as it is mine. Perhaps more."

"I did not say I would not come along," Togochi said, resting his hand on his sword. "Only that you have no command over me. I follow her. I have left most of my men to protect the families, but a small contingent of them will ride. With me."

Unebolod wanted to punch Togochi in his smug face. But Togochi had never been smug. He had always been calm, honest, and even. Time was wasting as they argued the finer points. Right now, he just wanted as many men as he could gather to rescue her.

"Someone needs to be left in charge of these people," he said.

"I think Esige has matters in hand," Togochi said, striding away from his family after brushing a kiss over Jaghan's hand. "And my wife will help however she can."

"Let's gather our men, then," Unebolod said, lengthening his stride, eager for a fight. "Together."

"Together, brother." Togochi nodded.

CHAPTER EIGHT

Prize to No Man

Mandukhai sat high and proud atop her horse, despite the ropes tying her wrists to the saddle and the fact that they had tied the reins of her mount to another horse like a pack animal. Her chin held high, she maintained a quiet dignity, ignoring the way her hair tangled in a matted mass against her skull where they had knocked her out. The blood had dried, stiffening her hair so that every time she moved her head, she could feel it press and crunch against her.

When they forced her onto this horse, Mandukhai had insisted they remove the felt sack from her head so she could breathe and not worry about vomiting inside of it. The sun proved particularly harsh today, and Mandukhai squinted to lessen the pain it created in her head. The light increased the pain throbbing behind her eyes. Their blow had done some sort of damage. Every movement made her stomach lurch. They had ridden for some time now at a fairly casual jaunt. Mandukhai didn't dare measure the placement of the sun in the sky—her eyes would never allow it—but she felt its warmth move over her body as the day passed.

Once they made camp, she worried about what would happen. Their urgent need for haste was all that had kept them at bay earlier in the day.

A scout raced up to the lead mount—the man in charge, she was sure—and relayed a message. Mandukhai strained in her saddle to hear, but could only catch one word. The rest had been too quiet for her to discern. But that one word offered her some hope.

"... south."

Mandukhai had ridden for miles from Mongke Bulag on Dust's back before—often with Unebolod, Togochi, or her personal guards. She was familiar enough with the surrounding terrain to know they traveled through the Orkhon Valley, even if she could not pinpoint precisely where they were. Ten miles away, perhaps more? Mandukhai was certain, based on how the sun rose and fell against her skin, that they traveled west—likely toward Oirat territory. The only thing south that might warrant a message would be her own trackers ... or her army, as small as it might be.

Summer would be upon them swiftly. The heat and dry air already turned her throat to sand. Mandukhai swallowed to work up saliva, but found the task more of a challenge than she had expected.

"I need water," she said, her voice cracking. "I'm parched."

The leader glanced back at her with a hard scowl, but no one moved toward her. Mandukhai stiffened her back as her anger simmered.

"Your khan will not be pleased if I die of dehydration before we reach him," she said sharply.

"You won't die," the leader said. Then he called to his men over his shoulder. "Pick up the pace or we cannot make camp for the night."

Before Mandukhai could protest, he kicked his horse into a gallop and the rest of the party followed—including the man leading her mount. Only ten men escorted her, but she had spotted dozens more moving around in the distance, and as many more relaying messages back and forth.

Mandukhai saw her situation with striking clarity. She had only two options. First, she could use her wiles to talk her way out of this. But if these men were staunch Oirat, that may not help her. The second option was to slow these men down long enough for her army to catch up ... or escape.

Her only chance of escape was to steal a weapon from one of these men, cut the ropes binding her, and ride as hard as she could straight southeast. Not good odds.

Darkness would provide her with the most cover, and she would need a bow in addition to a knife to pick off any riders who might spot or follow her. *I will be a prize to no man,* she thought as she leaned toward her mount. The way these men spoke earlier, Mandukhai knew they would not keep themselves off of her before she reached their khan. If they made camp, they would force themselves on her. She could not bear the idea. What Manduul had done to her would be nothing compared to what these men would do.

The world lurched and Mandukhai closed her eyes, focused on staying in the saddle. She began tugging lightly at the ropes to loosen them as much as possible around her wrists, working at the binding to attempt freeing even one finger. Just one at a time would do. No matter what happened next, Mandukhai needed her hands free.

Mandukhai could not reach the Oirat khan. *I would rather die trying to escape than reach their territory.* She would rather die trying to escape than risk them setting up camp with her for the night.

Unebolod was far from pleased with how long it took the men to assemble, and even less so with their numbers. Togochi had sent most of his *tumen* with the families headed northeast, along with all the Borjigin warriors who—much to his irritation—had answered to Togochi's command and not his own. When had this shift in power happened? When had Togochi earned the right over him, the *orlok*, to make commands?

This left Unebolod with a little over ten thousand men. Enough to rescue her ... if they reached her before she reached Oirat territory. If not, Unebolod would have to devise a new plan to stop the Oirat khan from laying hands on her. *I will cut off his cock and shove it down his own throat if he touches her*, Unebolod thought, grimacing as the wind lashed at his face.

Boke rode alongside Unebolod as they raced northwest across the Orkhon Valley. The tension between the two of them had grown thick in the moments before they had mounted. Unebolod could not help blaming Boke for Mandukhai's capture. Boke was young and strong—one of the strongest men in Mongke Bulag. He should have been there to protect Mandukhai instead of searching for Esige. He should have stopped these Oirat scum from touching her at all. When this was over, Unebolod would see Boke punished for his failure.

Unebolod glanced at the sky. Well past mid-day. What would those men do to Mandukhai if they stopped to make camp? *I won't stop riding until I find her*, he thought. He would ride to the edge of the world and back, dragging Oirat heads behind him if that was what it took. For now, he could only hope that she was as strong as she acted. Mandukhai would need to be the dragon.

Trees blurred past. Horses splashed across rivers and streams without slowing their pace. Warriors rode at Unebolod's flanks like men ready to conquer the world. The Oirat would feel them coming before they saw the dust cloud from the horses. There would be no surprising them. Unebolod had no intention of sneaking up on them. He planned on charging his warriors right through the Oirat lines, killing every one of them until Mandukhai was once more at his side. Their pace was fast across the rolling hills, but the mounts could handle the charge for miles before they would need to change to fresh ones.

One of Soke's scouts raced toward Unebolod, shifting to match pace and shouting over the thunder of thousands of hooves. "We are gaining on them, my Lord," the scout reported. "We have already killed three of their tails."

Unebolod leaned closer to his mare's neck. "How many?"

The scout just shook his head. They were not close enough yet to know what sort of force the Oirat had with them.

I'm coming, Mandukhai.

The ropes binding Mandukhai's wrists had loosened significantly. The moment she worked her thumb past the rope on one hand, she nearly released a cry of relief, hardly suppressing her glee to avoid arousing suspicion. Once she had her thumb out, she carefully worked her fingers free as well. If she could get one of these men close enough to take their weapon, perhaps alone, she could attempt her escape.

"I have not eaten or had a drop to drink all day!" Mandukhai shouted at the leader. "And I need to relieve myself."

"Do it from the saddle," he called back.

Mandukhai grimaced, tightening her knees against her horse. If they would not stop, she would make her horse stop herself.

"I am a queen," she replied. "I deserve a little more dignity if your khan seeks my favor."

"I don't think it's your favor he seeks," one man laughed.

The leader grumbled and called them to a halt. Mandukhai held the ropes around her wrists so he could not see her free hands. He ordered one of his men to help her. The Oirat warrior smirked as he dismounted and marched over. He was older, but not old. Perhaps in his mid-thirties. As he untied her from the saddle, his gaze swept over her with an interest that made her skin crawl. Then his calloused hands grasped her waist and yanked her from the saddle, right up against him as he roughly planted her feet on the ground.

"Let's go, my *queen*," he sneered, tugging on the ropes she held at her wrists.

The two of them marched away from the rest—all the while, the watchful leader kept his gaze glued to her. They stopped beside a tree and the warrior crossed his arms, smirking.

"Need help?" he asked. He edged closer, sliding his hand up her deel.

"A little dignity and privacy would help," she snapped, stepping back to remove his groping hand. "Regardless of what you might think, your khan intends to make me his wife, which means when this is over, you will answer to me. You might want to reconsider how you treat me right now."

He snorted. "You assume Paisahan will give you any power like Manduul did. He won't." He stalked closer, forcing her to step back until her back pressed against the tree. He pressed his body against hers, once more sliding his hand up the deel. He pulled at the waist of her trousers. "Your only value to him is right between your legs."

"Is she done yet?" the leader called out from the other side of the tree.

His gaze flicked toward the men waiting as his fingers slid into her trousers. "Not yet."

Mandukhai slammed her knee up between his legs, ripping his knife from his belt as he yelped in pain. She drove the knife into his neck and twisted, then yanked it out, shoving him away from her. His hand ripped out of her trousers as he pressed desperately against his gushing neck, eyes wide in shock.

Mandukhai glanced around the tree. Another of the warriors approached, calling after his comrade. Mandukhai waited until he drew around the tree, staring at his friend in alarm. She lunged forward, slicing his arm to break his grip on the reins. Then she reached up and yanked him from the saddle, driving the knife into his heart before he could react. The horse whinnied, stepping back.

A shout called out from the others. Mandukhai leaped into the vacant saddle and kicked the horse deeper into the sparsely scattered trees, away from the men pursuing her. Arrows hammered into the trees as she raced past. Mandukhai's bloody hand slipped on the bow hooked on the saddle, and she fumbled at first to draw an arrow.

Lord Tengri, guide me.

Behind her, the leader barked orders. Mandukhai leaned low to the horse's neck as she glanced in their direction to see how far behind they were. She only had a few seconds of a head start and hoped the forest would protect her. She yanked the reins to turn the horse southeast, toward her own approaching army—at least she prayed they were approaching.

Turning in her saddle, she aimed as Unebolod had taught her. The arrow flew as the hooves left the ground, striking the leader's mount in the neck and sending it crashing into the ground.

The rest of the men spun to give chase. One by one, she fired her arrows. A few struck mounts but didn't fell them. One warrior carried on with an arrow sticking out of his shoulder. But Mandukhai would not have enough arrows to stop them all. They would not kill her. They needed her alive. But that did not mean she would be uninjured, or that they would not kill her horse to slow her down. Without a mount, Mandukhai would never escape.

Another scout reported to Unebolod that they were within two miles of a line of Oirat warriors. Unebolod had grinned at the news, eager to kill. Each death would bring him closer to her, and to vengeance. And when she was in his arms again, Unebolod would clearly make his claim so there could never be a doubt again. Mandukhai was his. She always had been. And he would be Great Khan.

He called for his lines to spread out and slow pace. This would reduce the sound of horses approaching and dust that would give away their approach. If the Oirat had spread out to form a wall, it meant they were making a stand to give Mandukhai more ground between them. They were meant to slow Unebolod down, and it grated on his nerves. In response, he ordered his line to form up as long as possible. Hopefully, they would have the superior force and his men could close in on the Oirat from all sides, forcing them back ... or killing them all.

Oirat milled in a long line in the distance, facing their direction. There would be no taking the force by surprise, which suited Unebolod. He didn't need surprise. He had righteous anger on his side.

Oirat lines were shored up with half as many men as Unebolod commanded. His men increased speed, readying bows for attack. The Oirat launched into action as well. The two armies raced toward each other at dangerous speeds. The moment bows were within range, arrows darkened the sky in both directions. Unebolod raised his shield and ducked to avoid an arrow that shot straight at his head. It skipped off the shield, grazed his helmet, and soared away. He ground his teeth and snarled, firing at the swiftly approaching Oirat line.

Three hundred yards.

At his side, Boke fired arrows like a man possessed. One. Two. Three. Four. All before the Oirat returned the volley. Unebolod hoped the man's aim was accurate, or it would be a waste of arrows.

An arrow hammered Unebolod's helmet, throwing him off balance. He tightened his legs on the mare to keep from falling.

Two hundred yards.

Unebolod raised the horn to his lips and sent out three quick blasts to signal their next maneuver. Instantly, his men shifted direction, kicking up a torrent of dust as they created a churning mass of horsemen. Confused, the Oirat slowed their gallop.

One hundred yards.

Dust clouded the air. Unebolod maintained steady focus. His men had their orders. Soke would see them carried out to the last man. All ten thousand of Unebolod's warriors had kicked up dust to mask their maneuver from the Oirat. Now, they formed a tight, arrow-tip formation with his *jagan* of a hundred lancers at the point.

Fifty yards.

By the time the dust cleared enough for the Oirat to see how the battlefield had changed, it was too late. Their lines were too spread out, weakening their defense against Unebolod's mass of men.

The lancers crashed through the weakened Oirat wall, taking out men and horses with no mercy. Oirat horns sounded to change position, but they had no time. The damage was done. Unebolod's arrow-tip formation had smashed through, just as he had expected. Once the lancers were through the line, the swordsmen on the outer edges of the formation hacked at any unfortunate enough to move too close.

As the swordsmen kept the Oirat away from the breach in their own line, Unebolod, Boke, and Togochi led a mass of warriors through the gap in the Oirat defenses, boiling out on the back of the Oirat line in a ram-horn formation. Once more, dust filled the air as half of Unebolod's men circled back along the line to create smaller arrow-tip formations and attack again.

But Unebolod did not turn back. With Boke and Togochi at his side, along with the other half of his force, Unebolod raced west, away from the Oirat, whose heads would roll. Unebolod had a queen to rescue.

Soke would manage the rest of the Oirat.

Mandukhai had never loathed lacking armor as much as she did at this moment, racing away from her captors with her back turned. The layers of silk would certainly help, but they would not stop an arrow on their own. Attempting to make herself as small of a target as possible, she leaned toward her horse as tight as she dared. The rhythm of her mount seemed to hammer in tandem with her own racing heartbeat.

And they were closing in on her. *If I had Dust, they would never catch me*, she thought bitterly, daring to glance back.

An arrow soared through the air, then struck her horse in the flank. It squealed, but Mandukhai pressed her legs tighter and kicked, firming her grip. Blood flowed from the cuts on her wrists, mingling with the blood of the dead men. Her muscles strained. She clenched the reins, holding on for dear life.

Another arrow whizzed past her head, slamming into the horse's neck inches from her face. Mandukhai yelped. The horse cried out and bucked. Mandukhai's heart jumped into her throat as she nearly fell from the saddle. When its hooves hit the ground again, she slipped to the side. She squeezed her legs so tight against the horse that pain lanced through her muscles and into her back.

She could not escape. They had too many arrows. Her horse would never make it out of range. But if she could reach the rocky bluff fifteen yards away, she could make a stand and attempt picking them off.

Mandukhai glanced back once more. Another arrow struck her horse in the neck. It whinnied, lurched, then tumbled sideways. Mandukhai threw herself from the saddle to avoid being crushed under the horse's weight. At this speed, hitting the ground proved a painful experience. Mandukhai attempted to control the fall, to tuck and roll, but her shoulder slammed against the earth. She cried out as pain lanced outward, burning from her shoulder. And without her arm to stop her, Mandukhai's head struck the ground, plunging her into instant darkness.

Dust swirled around a battlefield as warriors fought in a ring around Mandukhai. She blinked to clear her vision. A shadowy, bulking figure loomed over her. "Remember, always, who your heart belongs to, daughter of the dragon, queen of the wolves," Genghis said, holding out a hand to her. "The power of the wolf pulses through you. Now get up."

Mandukhai heard the thump of boots around her. Her head ached as if her skull had split open and bled out on the ground beneath her. No matter how hard she tried, Mandukhai could not force her eyes open.

"She isn't worth this trouble," a man said from somewhere nearby. The blood pumping in her ears muffled his voice. "Let him take the title without her."

"We don't have enough power to do it without her," another said as they wrapped something around her wrist. "And if she officially declares alignment with Unebolod, this is over before it starts. Paisahan needs her. Now help me get her bound back up. The Khorchin are nearly on us."

Mandukhai's heart leaped. Her men were close. Every second she could stall would be precious.

"Then why are you bandaging her wrists?" one man asked.

Someone walked around her head. Mandukhai attempted opening her eyes, but again could not.

"So she doesn't bleed out on the way!"

Mandukhai steadied her breathing, allowing them to think she remained unconscious on the ground. Her shoulder pulsed in pain. She must have dislocated it in the fall. But the pain in her shoulder was nothing compared to the drums of death thumping in her head.

Something brushed her stomach. A whisper of cloth. Mandukhai cracked her eyes open. For a moment, the dying sunlight was blinding. After a moment, she saw the shadow of a man looming over her. *The power of the wolf pulses through you,* Genghis had said. *Now get up.* Mandukhai swallowed the vomit climbing up her throat.

He dropped one of her wrists to seize the other.

Sunlight caught on the knife tucked in his belt through her narrow vision. Mandukhai focused on her breathing, summoning the strength of Genghis. Then she snatched the knife from his belt and rammed it into his neck. By the time she had twisted the blade, the rest of the men had seized her.

Hands grabbed at her arms, pinning them down as the dead man slumped beside her. Mandukhai squirmed, every part of her body screaming in agony. She tugged, yanked, pushed, clawed at the men holding her down, but it did no good. Someone leaned too close to her face. She bit down as hard as she could on whatever flesh she could reach, ripping off part of his ear with her teeth. He jerked back, shouting and cursing her.

"Hold her steady," another man commanded as he climbed over her. His face loomed close, but she could do more than spit at him. He swiped it away and backhanded her cheek, snarling a black-toothed grimace of hate. "It's time you learn who the stronger sex is. Your dead husband should have broken you from this willfulness long ago."

Mandukhai's gaze darted around at the men surrounding her, fighting against their iron grip in any way she could, desperate to find the leader who had been that voice of reason. Then she saw him dead on the ground. She had killed their leader, and he had been all that had kept them under control before. *Tengri help me!* she prayed desperately.

In an irrevocable act to protect herself from what would come, Mandukhai closed her eyes again and hastily constructed a mental wall, locking all of her pain and fear behind it.

The Oirat force remained miles behind Unebolod as he raced onward. Five scouts had attempted racing away the moment they spotted him and his *mingghans*. Someone swiftly dispatched each of them with an arrow through the head or neck. With the bulk of the Oirat forces behind him, Unebolod was confident they would meet little resistance. None of his men reported any hidden warriors waiting for them to pass. Clearly, the Oirat believed they would stop whatever men came for Mandukhai with their wall tactic. A smirk twitched up the corner of Unebolod's mouth. Good. He could not wait to prove them wrong.

The northern edges of the Khangai Mountains kept pace with them to the south of their position, reminding him that the Oirat had not gotten far enough. A northern pass through the mountains would allow the Oirat a means of escape into their own territory, but Unebolod did not think they were close enough to reach it. Not before his warriors crashed down on them. How many would guard Mandukhai?

Soon enough, he had his answer. In the distance, he spotted a small fist of men—perhaps only seven or eight of them—all on the ground over what appeared to be an animal. With his warriors out for blood, no one was safe. Any man ahead of them would be Oirat. The first arrows took out five of the men.

Then he realized, in horror, that it was not an animal on the ground. Mandukhai lay there, limp and bleeding.

The sixth man died from another arrow.

Terror climbed down Unebolod's spine. Was she alive? What had they done to her?

"The last one is mine!" he called out, then sounded the horn for his men to spread out and search the area.

Boke reached the last man before Unebolod, leaping from his horse and nimbly landing on his feet as he ran toward the last Oirat, who stared at them in terror. Unebolod growled. Boke was Mandukhai's man to command, and not his own. Boke snatched the man by the collar, yanking him away from her with enough force to instantly turn the Oirat's face red and make his eyes bulge.

Unebolod jumped from his saddle and rushed toward the two men, yanking out his sword. Boke wrapped his other hand in the Oirat warrior's hair, yanking him up and exposing his neck. The man clawed at Boke's grip, but was no match for the guard. Unebolod knew he should get answers, but rage turned his vision red the moment he realized the man's stiff cock hung free of his trousers and deel. All logic vanished.

The Oirat's eyes widened, but Unebolod's sword moved before he could react, slicing the cock clean off. Togochi called out for him to stop, but hatred clogged his senses. As the Oirat screamed, Unebolod snatched the appendage off the ground and rammed it down the man's throat, cutting off the shrieks of agony.

"Your khan is next," Unebolod snarled coldly. He heaved his sword at the man's neck. The body crumbled to the ground as Boke raised the head high in the air.

Unebolod's shoulders heaved with ragged breaths. He turned to check on Mandukhai. Her entire body trembled violently, but she pulled herself to her feet, swatting away any offers of assistance. Unebolod's tunnel vision faded as he took in the stunned expressions of everyone around them.

A few steps behind Mandukhai, Togochi glared at him.

Unebolod inched toward Mandukhai, his heart shattering at the empty expression on her face. He raised a bloody hand toward her, releasing his dripping sword onto the ground. He swallowed the lump lodged in his throat. "Did he ...?"

Mandukhai's voice was as blank as her face. "No."

Unebolod wanted to believe her, but the evidence told him otherwise. Instead, he played along. Perhaps she was saving face in front of the men. He sagged his shoulders in relief and closed the gap. "I was so anxious."

He stopped in front of her, and for just a moment, he thought he caught a flicker of something in her eyes. Gratitude, perhaps? But she did not match his gaze for long before her own dropped away. Her skin paled as she took in the death around her. Unebolod reached out to take her hand.

Mandukhai jerked away from his touch, shaking her head ever so slightly. "Thank you for riding to my rescue, but I'm fine."

His heart lurched. Mandukhai was not fine. Her clothes were ripped and covered in blood. He was not sure if it was hers or the Oirats'. She had been through something terrible either way. He could not let this happen again. It was no longer just a matter of becoming Great Khan. It was a matter of her own safety.

"I think it's time we make the claim official," Unebolod said. "So no other ambitious men can try this again."

Mandukhai squared her shoulders, hands clenched in fists at her sides. "I am a prize for no man."

Unebolod stood rooted in place, stunned. No man. Surely she didn't mean no man ever. Surely she didn't mean him.

"Mandukhai—"

"No man."

How had a day that began with them so blissfully as one ended with this chasm now between them?

Mandukhai turned to Togochi. "Get me a horse. We ride for Mount Burkhan Khaldun."

Chapter Nine

The Whole Khan

The sun had set by the time Mandukhai was mounted and ready to ride. They rode north along the bank of the Orkhon River, out of Oirat territory, toward a path that would make for an easier ride to Mount Burkhan Khaldun. She was eager to put as much distance between herself and that cursed place as possible before stopping for the night.

As she rode, Mandukhai held her back straight and her chin high. Surrounded by warriors she led, they could not see Mandukhai as weak. Unebolod had insisted they make camp and wait for the rest of their warriors to join them, but Mandukhai had refused to remain in that place a moment longer. At first, she feared the men would listen to him. Much to her surprise—and his dismay—the surrounding men were Togochi's to command. Togochi seemed eager to listen to her. Or perhaps to make it clear to Unebolod that he was not in command.

The agony on Unebolod's face when she had refused to allow him to "claim" her should have had some effect on Mandukhai. Instead, she felt empty ... and strangely liberated. Manduul had possessed her. Paisahan had intended the same. Unebolod was different, and she knew that, but he didn't seem to understand her need to be in control of her own destiny. Even if she wanted him, she needed him to acknowledge her freedom to make this choice. Instead, he had tried forcing his claim, which only amplified the sense that he did not understand what she knew for certain.

She would never *belong* to any man ever again.

Until he could understand that Mandukhai could not be with him either. This realization fueled her with icy determination to see that the future of the Nation fell only into the most secure hands. If that ended up being Unebolod, all the better. But his inability to control his rage had been terrifying. The pure fury had seemed to engorge his muscles and inflame his hate. The visage had cast a specter of doubt she could not shake.

Unebolod had distanced himself from Mandukhai, silently stewing near the back of their group, far enough that she could not sense him, but still close enough that she knew he watched over her. They would have to discuss what had happened, but she did not want to do that in front of their men. It had to be a private conversation.

Boke rode close at Mandukhai's side, ever vigilant. The only words he uttered since his arrival on the rescue mission had been simply "yes, Queen Regent" whenever she gave commands. Mandukhai assumed her capture had shamed him, but she did not blame him for what had happened. She had sent him to find Esige. What came next had not been his fault. None of them could have known this had been the Oirat plan all along.

They rode for miles. Every muscle and bone in Mandukhai's body pulsed with pain as if a fire burned her from the inside out. Riding in the saddle proved painful, but she gave no complaint. No one could know the truth about what had happened to her. Ever.

Thankfully, the darkness made it easier for her to open her eyes, though she could not turn her head or everything would begin spinning and sickness would rise up her throat. Togochi had carefully reset her dislocated shoulder, and most of the pain was gone now, but she still felt it throbbing in protest with each jostling of the horse.

A scout raced over and reported to Unebolod, but Mandukhai did not dare turn her head to gauge his reaction. Such a motion would inflict nausea again. Instead, she waited for Togochi to ride up beside her.

"We have traveled almost thirty miles," he reported. "The scouts report no one else within at least that many more in all directions. You need rest, Mandukhai. I will set up extra men on watch across short shifts to reduce the chance of anyone nodding off. But I would advise we stop for the night."

The last thing she wanted was to stop. Mandukhai would ride to the end of the earth if it meant moving further from the Oirat. But the men had ridden hard to find her, and they had fought bravely against their enemy. They had earned the right to sleep.

"And you need to speak with Unebolod," Togochi added, eyeing her sideways.

Her heart sank. She knew she needed to speak with him, but if Togochi noticed, that meant this situation was worse than she had thought. "I just need time to process everything that has happened, Togochi. I will talk to him. When I'm ready. And when we have space to speak alone."

"You know he doesn't see you as a prize," Togochi added.

Mandukhai appreciated Togochi's need to mend what he saw as broken, as he often did, but she could not tell him the truth. She was not even sure she could tell Unebolod. She needed to change the subject.

"What of the men left with Soke?" Mandukhai asked, hating how weak her voice sounded. Each word was like a hammer to her head, and her stomach roiled in revolt.

"Soke has defeated the remaining Oirat," Togochi said. "The few Oirat who survived escaped into the mountains with their tails between their legs."

Mandukhai fought to swallow the sickness rising in her throat. "Very well," she croaked, yanking on the reins. Her horse halted, prancing beneath her. The saddle had become incredibly painful. "I want Soke's men to follow on our flank in case of another attack."

Togochi stopped as well, glancing over his shoulder and frowning. Uncertainty rolled off of him.

"Speak," Mandukhai sighed.

"The men with us are Khorlod warriors," Togochi said. "They will follow the command I give."

Mandukhai understood perfectly well what Togochi implied. Soke and his men were Khorchin. And Unebolod was acting stubborn. But above even Unebolod's right to command the Khorchin, Mandukhai had a right to them all. Surely Unebolod would not be so stubborn that he would refuse her.

"Then be sure they know the command comes from their Queen Regent," she replied coolly.

Togochi grimaced, then turned his mount and rode toward Unebolod. Something had transpired between those two men after her capture. Some unspoken tension lingered.

Boke had already dismounted and stood beside Mandukhai's horse. She resented his presence as if she could not get herself out of the saddle. But as she attempted swinging her leg over, Mandukhai's head spun wildly. She lost her balance. As much as she loathed the implication, she was grateful when his massive arms caught her and eased her to the ground. Still, his touch, no matter how innocent, sent a shock of fear through her. Boke released her slowly, making sure that she was steady before letting go completely. Mandukhai swayed but didn't fall. She edged a step away from him.

In quick time, her small band of warriors established a perimeter and set up camp where the Orkhon and Tuul Rivers split. They were perhaps fifty to one hundred miles due north of Mongke Bulag—or what had been Mongke Bulag. That place no longer existed. Togochi had reassured Mandukhai that the rest of the families were guarded and en route to Mount Burkhan Khaldun under Esige and Jaghan's guidance. In all likelihood, Mandukhai and her warriors would reach their rendezvous before the families.

Boke and Togochi had gone to some trouble to strip blankets from horses and create a makeshift tent for Mandukhai beside the river, against the trunk of a young birch tree. They had constructed some of those horse blankets into walls, while others created a bed and pillow for her to rest on. While the men were used to sleeping under the stars, Mandukhai had never done so.

"I don't need a tent," Mandukhai protested as Togochi held one blanket aside for her to enter.

"You need peace and privacy, Mandukhai," Togochi said calmly. "Boke, Unebolod, and I will be outside at all times. We will not leave." Though he did not say it, the "again" was implied well enough.

Mandukhai hated being hidden behind a curtain, but she knew deep down that Togochi was right. After everything she had suffered this day, Mandukhai needed to not be surrounded by men—even if there would be no escaping them.

The moment Mandukhai stepped through, Togochi release the blanket and she was plunged into the dark loneliness of the tent. Mandukhai settled on the blankets gingerly, aware of the bruising and wounds all over her body—and the gash on her head which had stopped bleeding but left her hair matted to her head. Her clothes were torn but not in tatters and covered in blood as well. She was certain she would never sleep again, but the moment she rested her head against the roll of blankets, the exhaustion slammed into her.

A voice welcomed her into dreams, warm, comforting, and familiar. It folded around her like a protective shield. The voice of Genghis Khan.

Unebolod's sleep had been restless, and he tossed and turned. The blanket wall around Mandukhai felt like an actual wall rising between them. He woke in the morning, aching all over and lamenting how drastically one day had changed everything. *I am a prize to no man*, she had said, and those words had been as good as a dagger to his heart. Did she truly think so little of him to think he saw her as a prize? For the past six years, Mandukhai had been his breath. *No man.* Those words had ripped that breath from his lungs. He checked the saddle on his mare to be sure she was ready to ride.

I need to speak with her. She needs to know she is far more to me than some prize. Unebolod strode away from his horse.

Mandukhai's tent had been taken down, and a group of warriors had waded in the shallows of the river, holding the blankets high and averting their gazes. Water splashed on the other side. Unebolod stopped on the bank of the river, waiting. Boke scowled at him as if concerned Unebolod might do something to Mandukhai. *What is wrong with everyone?* But Unebolod had his own bone to pick with Boke. When they reached Mount Burkhan Khaldun, he would insist on Boke's demotion.

Togochi strode up beside Unebolod, putting his back to the river and facing Unebolod. "Don't push her," he said, keeping his voice low so Mandukhai would not overhear. "She needs time to process what has happened to her."

"She needs to know I don't see her as a prize," Unebolod said, then swallowed a lump that leaped into his throat. "You know I don't."

"I know. And she knows. Just let her get there on her own. We don't know what happened to her, and she needs some time to sort through this."

Togochi was likely correct. Unebolod just worried about how long it would take her. Would it be in time for *kurultai*?

"She said nothing had happened yet," Unebolod replied, but as he spoke the words, they felt stale, like a lie.

"Perhaps it's the truth, but if it isn't, she may never tell us. You know that."

Unebolod grimaced and nodded. "I no longer understand her."

Togochi snorted. "Did you ever?"

Unebolod's shoulders tensed. There had been a time when he knew her mind, her heart, her desires. When had that changed?

He could not discuss this any longer. "You do realize we need to talk about what happened between us in Mongke Bulag. As *orlok*—"

"What are you *orlok* of, exactly, Unebolod?" Togochi asked sharply. "Didn't Manduul give that position away? Who has given it back to you since then?"

Unebolod clenched his hands into fists, but as usual, Togochi spoke the blunt truth. Unebolod was not *orlok*. He was not Great Khan. He was no more powerful than Togochi. *Yet.* He turned his attention back to the river. His grasp on everything was slipping through his fingers.

The warriors in the water edged toward the bank but angled away from the two of them. It didn't help the sinking sensation in Unebolod's gut. Mandukhai had said that the Oirat had not had a chance to force themselves on her, but had she lied to hide her shame? Togochi was right. She would never tell them the truth.

Unebolod watched as Boke slid his hand through the blankets, giving Mandukhai a washed deel without looking. A moment later, she called for the men to pack the blankets and ready the horses. As the wall of horse blankets around her dropped and the warriors stalked off, only Boke remained with her—always glued to her side. *Where was that dedication yesterday?*

The sun seemed to make her skin glow. Mandukhai leaned forward and twisted her long hair tight, squeezing out the water. She winced, then reached a trembling hand back to touch her head. Unebolod took a step toward her, but Togochi seized his arm. The two men locked gazes. Unebolod was ready to wrench Togochi's hand away and shove him off, but he noticed the warning in Togochi's eyes. Unebolod hesitated.

Boke stepped around Mandukhai, gingerly parting her hair to inspect the damage. Unebolod struggled to hear what they said to each other, but they kept their voices too quiet to catch more than a word here or there. Not enough to understand much more than Mandukhai's dismissal as she began braiding her hair. Watching her made Unebolod ache all over. He wanted to hold her, to help her. He wanted to be the one who cared for her. Why would she not allow it?

With a huff of frustration, he yanked his arm from Togochi and stormed away. For ten years, he had waited patiently for this moment, this opportunity to become Great Khan. For six years, he had waited patiently for Manduul to die so he could be with Mandukhai. There was no longer a reason to wait. For either.

Unebolod would fix this and get what he wanted.

Esige sat on her stallion, staring north. In just a few days, they would pass through the edge of the gap between rivers and arrive at Mount Burkhan Khaldun. Would Mandukhai meet her there? Had Unebolod and Togochi caught up and rescued her? What would happen to Esige if Mandukhai did not return?

Another horse drew up beside her. Esige groaned inwardly as she realized it was Dawa. *He is relentless*, she thought. How many times did she have to beat him before he came to terms with the truth? Esige had no genuine interest in the Jalair commander.

Dawa was young for his position, only eighteen. His hair hung in looping braids over his shoulders, and his deel was, as always, impressively free of wrinkles and sweat stains that often marked out warriors. Dawa's father was a Jalair Lord, and one of the highest-ranked, at that. But neither man had any claim on the Jalair khan title. Lady Altan still clung to that.

"What will you do if she doesn't return?" Dawa asked.

"She will." Esige said the words with far more vehemence than she intended, as if trying to convince herself more than him.

"You will need a husband to protect you," Dawa said.

She snorted, glaring at him. "The day you beat me in *any* match is the day I will agree you are strong enough to protect me, Dawa. So far, I think I am more capable of protecting myself than any *husband* could ever be."

Dawa sneered. "Women have their place, and men have their own." His hungry, arrogant gaze swept over her.

Esige yanked the reins to turn her stallion, forcing his own mount to shuffle away. "She will be there."

She has to be there, Esige thought desperately as she rode toward the carts loaded with family goods. Esige knew she could only hold the men at bay for so long. For she was a rabbit, and they were wolves on the hunt. How did Mandukhai do this for so long?

Mount Burkhan Khaldun – 1470

A week after the rescue, Mandukhai rode at the center of her line to the tip of the Kherlen River, at the base of Mount Burkhan Khaldun. Wide open grasslands offered plentiful feeding for herds, nestled in the embrace of the great mountain range as if by the arms of the earth mother herself. This place held sacred significance. After suffering defeat at the hands of the Merkit, Genghis had fled to this mountain. It was here Genghis had survived certain death and submitted himself to the will of his god, Lord Tengri. And later, Genghis had proclaimed this place sacred, holy land.

It would be here that they would choose the next Great Khan to reignite the flame of the great Mongol empire.

Mandukhai had taken great care to select this location, despite pushback from the Lords of the tribes, who felt Karakorum was a more traditional place. But their next Khan would not be like every other. He would be the future promised to her by Genghis. A Khan of the whole people. And when she renamed him, there would no longer be any doubt. He would be Dayan Khan.

The Whole Khan.

With this new Khan, she would restore the fractured empire, just as Genghis had promised.

Mandukhai gazed at the mountain. Wind churned around her as the warriors set up camp and created scouting patrols. It swirled the skirt of her deel around her legs as if encouraging her toward the mountain. A small smile curled the corners of her lips. Mandukhai allowed the breeze to guide her, certain the spirits were speaking to her again.

After only a few steps, Togochi marched in front of her, bowing with his fist over his heart. Mandukhai cocked her head at him, pausing her step.

"*Khatun*, I just received word that the families will arrive by sunset," Togochi said.

Khatun. Over the past few days, more and more of the men had called her by this name. When had it first begun? It warmed her heart. Being given such a title without demanding it surely was a sign of the respect these men had for her. Something had changed. But what?

"That was quick," Mandukhai said. The very air around her drew Mandukhai to the slopes of Mount Burkhan Khaldun again, and she struggled to resist.

Togochi smirked. "Apparently Lady Esige drove them quite hard to cover ground once she heard you would meet her here."

Mandukhai nodded. "Thank you, Togochi. I'm sure you are excited to see your family."

"It would be a lie to deny it," he replied. "We organized your men in patrols, along with several volunteers from the Khorchin."

Volunteers. Mandukhai's shoulders tensed. Unebolod did not seem to understand that those were also her men and not his.

"I don't mean to push you," Togochi said. "But at some point, you two will have to talk. It will only get worse the longer you delay."

She said nothing, well aware that she had to speak to Unebolod about all of this, but not yet ready to handle the conversation. Every time she thought about talking to him, she pictured his blood-covered armor ramming the dismembered appendage down the Oirat's throat; the way his shoulders bunched in a rage. It terrified her, if she was honest.

Togochi drew in a steady breath, then let it out slowly. "If I may speak freely?"

Mandukhai quirked an eyebrow at him. "When have you not?"

"You must know he does not think you are a prize," Togochi said.

The words sliced into her heart, and Mandukhai steeled herself against the memories of that horrific day as they threatened to overtake her. She wanted to speak, to defend herself, but could not bring herself to move a muscle.

"I have watched him agonize over your marriage to Manduul for years," Togochi continued. "Imagine spending six years of your life watching him with another woman, yearning for it to be you instead. Still, he waited. He refused other women because his heart belonged to you. You know as well as I do he is not like other men."

Having the truth laid bare at her feet broke through the wall Mandukhai had struggled to hold up these past few days. Her legs grew weak. Her heart hammered against her ribs. Heat flooded her face. Togochi was right. Unebolod was different. It was part of what drew her to him.

Mandukhai licked her lips and let out a shuddering breath. "He stole my heart long ago."

Togochi nodded. "Then why are you holding back?"

Tears welled in Mandukhai's eyes. She squeezed them shut to stem the flow and center herself. Her gaze met Togochi's. "Because the fate of the Nation cannot be guided by the whims of my heart."

"Manduul said—"

"I know precisely what he said!" Mandukhai snapped.

Togochi's face flushed, making Mandukhai feel guilty about her outburst. But she had sworn an oath to the Lords the day she announced Manduul's death, that she would carry out his final wishes for the sake and safety of the entire Mongol Nation. No matter what she wanted, Mandukhai knew she had to find out if Batu would reach her alive before she could accept Unebolod. And he would have to accept that their reign together would be brief. That, she knew, was the hardest part to sell.

"Togochi, you made an oath to Manduul, and to me. I need you to trust that I know what I am doing. A great burden has been placed on my shoulders, and I do not take it lightly. If I do not handle the selection of our next Great Khan carefully, it could end in war. None of us want that."

"Of course, *Khatun*." Togochi bowed again, then strode away.

Mandukhai watched him leave as a great weight pressed against her heart. She needed to speak with Unebolod. But what would she tell him?

Once more, Mandukhai turned her gaze to the sacred mountain, calling on the strength and will of the spirits to guide her.

CHAPTER TEN

Proposals

The moon shone brightly over the red dirt ground as Issama's mount trotted toward the Chakhar camp. He spent the better part of the day attempting to reason with Bigirsen, but the man was further detached from reality than Issama would dare speak aloud. The men sensed it as well. Bigirsen was coming undone, cracking under pressure triggered by years of careful planning crumbling apart. No words could assuage Bigirsen's anger. He had seized control of the Ordos tribes. Tomorrow, he planned on doing the same to the Chakhar.

Issama knew this would end in battle. Guden khan was not the sort of man to give up his position to any but the Great Khan himself—a position Bigirsen seemed determined to steal. *And thus, Esen fell,* Issama thought, recalling all he had learned about Esen's attempt at seizing control years ago. Esen had nearly succeeded until he killed the Borjigin royals. *But there are no Borjigin royals to support any longer.*

Issama prayed Mandukhai had received his offer. While she was likely to reject him personally, he hoped his promise would at least tempt her to consider him. In exchange for her support at *kurultai*, he would destroy Bigirsen. *Unless he does it to himself before then*, Issama mused, not at all disappointed with that prospect.

The further into recklessness Bigirsen slipped, the more his men turned to Issama for leadership. Issama had been careful to step wisely around this growing power so that Bigirsen would not notice. Having his head cut off before he could take control would accomplish nothing.

After Bigirsen had stolen the title of Ordos khan from Lord Legusi, Issama had spotted his first opportunity to sow discord among Bigirsen's men. Issama had met with Legusi in private weeks later, and his petition had been simple but dangerous. Wait for Issama's signal, help him overthrow and kill Bigirsen. Then Legusi would have his title back. The young Lord had been apprehensive, worried it was a trap, but Siker—of all people—had convinced Legusi that soon the Chakhar would support Issama as well. Between the strength of the Ordos and the Chakhar, Bigirsen would have nowhere to turn.

Issama glanced at his wife as they rode through the moonlight. Of the three women, Siker had quickly become his favorite, though he was sure to have his servant keep a close watch on her. He could not afford another willful woman undermining his plans. Siker would make a great queen. He had not dared to tell her she might have to share that position with Mandukhai as well. Siker had already asserted her dominance over his other two wives.

"Why are you staring at me like that?" Siker asked, keeping her voice low, though no one except Nahai—Issama's trusted second-in-command—was anywhere around in the darkness.

"Just musing about our future," Issama replied, glancing at her belly.

In three months, he would have his second child. The first had been with his third wife, who had become pregnant almost immediately. Their daughter had been born only weeks ago. With any luck, Siker would give him a son. It would certainly help her position once he removed Bigirsen after Mandukhai accepted his offer. His son would be the heir to the nation.

"I doubt you think of anything else," Siker said.

Nahai chortled from where he rode at Issama's side. As Issama's plans had expanded, he'd had little choice but to enlist the help of someone he could trust. Unfortunately, he trusted no one. But Nahai was as close as Issama would ever get to trusting another man. Nahai hated Bigirsen. Issama had spent years working with Nahai even before he joined Bigirsen's ranks. Nahai was in his twenties as well, close in age to Issama, and of low birth, just like Issama. The two had bonded over a mutual dislike of Bigirsen once they joined the Uyghur forces. Nahai also understood that Issama was far more intelligent and cunning, and deferred to Issama's judgment in most things. All Issama had to offer was a promise of an elevated position—and an end to the man Nahai hated more than any other.

Issama scowled at Nahai's amusement, which only amplified Nahai's laughter.

"She has a point, my Lord," Nahai said. "In all my years, I have never known a man who thinks so much about his future. It's a perpetual state of being for you."

"And look where it has gotten me." Issama gazed ahead, watching the Chakhar camp as they approached. Guden khan expected him. "I was an orphan with nothing when I began."

"And now you have the world," Nahai remarked.

"No." Issama spotted the approaching Chakhar escort. "But I will. Soon. And the two of you will be right there with me."

They maintained a steady trot so as not to alarm the escort Guden khan sent to greet him. As the warriors identified Issama—and clearly recognized Siker—he noted the way they eyed Issama's weapons.

"They are only meant to protect my wife as we make this midnight journey," Issama reassured them.

The warriors nodded, then formed a ring around the three of them and escorted them into the Chakhar camp to Guden khan's ger. Without being asked, Issama dismounted and removed his weapons from his belt, securing them to his mount. Nahai followed his lead. To Issama's surprise—and amusement—Siker pulled a knife from her own belt and wedged it between the saddle and horse blanket.

Issama ducked through the doorway into Guden's ger first. "My Lord khan," Issama said respectfully, bowing to Guden.

"Nice to see you again, Vice Chancellor, though it is a bit worrisome." Guden motioned to a bench for Issama to sit.

For a moment, Issama hesitated. Why was it worrisome?

The ger was much like any other. A fire burned in the stove to provide light, but it made the inside of the ger feel like a sauna. Sweat pricked at his forehead as Issama sank down on the bench. Nahai joined him. Siker stepped delicately toward the bench, and Issama offered his hand to help her ease down.

Guden's brows shot up. "So it is true, then. You are married?"

Issama puffed up, smothering a satisfied smile. "It is. Manduul Khan blessed our union before he passed."

"And how is this third husband treating you, Lady Siker?" Guden asked.

"Much better than the last, my Lord," Siker replied demurely. "Though that would not require much effort."

"You would speak ill of our dead prince?" Guden's distaste for Siker's blasé attitude toward Bayan surprised Issama, but he kept his features smooth.

"He was no prince when he died," Siker said.

"He will always be a prince," Guden said. "One act will not change that."

"I believe it was more than one." Siker's voice heated with anger. Bayan's betrayal had lit a fire of hate deep inside her.

"Guden khan, if I may," Issama interrupted before matters could spiral out of control. "We have urgent business to discuss, and we must return before the wolf dawn."

Siker had never loved Bayan, and her bitterness toward him only grew once she reached Mongke Bulag. Issama knew all of this. She would tongue-whip any who attempted boosting Bayan's name. It had never been an issue among the Uyghur. It would be here.

Guden sneered, but Issama knew it had nothing to do with their previous conversation. "I will not give my title to Bigirsen. I *cannot*. It's disgraceful. He can kill me, but another will rise in my place. And another. Your Lord will have no choice but to kill us all. And when he does, there will be no title for him to claim. Chakhar will not bend to the will of a usurper."

Issama had counted on this reaction. Guden khan was a strong-willed leader who clung to tradition. But Issama had come with a clear purpose. "That is understandable, Lord Guden, but I should warn you, Bigirsen is coming unraveled. He would gladly wipe out the Chakhar just to prove his point."

"What point would that be?" Guden asked.

"That no one is more powerful than him."

Guden's chin quivered in rage as silence settled over the ger.

Siker stirred, placing a hand over her belly and rubbing it in circles. "My Lord, we did not come to coax you into giving in," she said, breaking the silence. Issama suppressed a proud smile. The two of them had discussed how to handle this meeting extensively. "We came to make you a better offer. I am from this tribe, and I will not see Bigirsen destroy it in folly. I am loyal first to my husband, second to the Chakhar."

Her dulcet voice seemed to ease Guden's anger.

Issama would normally leave his wives out of these matters, but her association with this tribe benefited him. He wanted Guden khan to know, beyond a doubt, that Issama respected her enough to bring her to such an important meeting. And enough to let her speak. Unfortunately, that also meant after tonight Siker would know of the offer Issama sent to Mandukhai.

"As she said, Bigirsen is bent on destroying any in his path," Issama said carefully. "He intends to rob the title of Great Khan by stealing all the lesser khan titles so no one can oppose him."

"Someone will always oppose him," Guden said. "Lady Mandukhai is Queen Regent, and I hear she is showing favor to the Khorchin khan. Manduul Khan named Lord Unebolod in the absence of a Borjigin heir."

"We have never been in such a unique situation before," Issama said. "A Borjigin heir has always been lingering somewhere in the shadows. But thanks to Esen, none remain. Mandukhai may be Queen Regent by Manduul Khan's command, but it is the Lords of the Nation who will decide who is Great Khan. Not her."

"That does not change the facts," Guden said. "Unebolod has enough support to win *kurultai*. And with her backing, no one will oppose him."

"Bigirsen will." Issama's statement hung in the air like smoke, smothering their arguments and suffocating any doubt that there would be war over this title.

"This continues to sound like a threat," Guden replied at last.

Siker had already declared her loyalty to Issama in front of her old khan. Hopefully, Issama's next argument would not make her speak out of turn.

"You are correct." Issama nodded. "Unebolod currently has her support. He has for some time, as I understand it. But Mandukhai is also a woman of reason. I know her well. Better than most, I would wager. She will take this appointment seriously. And while the Lords of the Nation will decide its future, she still holds sway over several of them—Lords critical to a successful bid at *kurultai*. I think Manduul knew this, which was why he placed this in her hands. I have already struck a deal with the Ordos Lords. I bring the same offer to you. Allow Bigirsen to *believe* he has defeated you. Smother him with false loyalty and he will not question it. Then, when Mandukhai accepts my offer, we will kill him."

Guden fell into stunned silence. Every muscle in his aging body tensed so visibly Issama could not have missed it had he tried. Siker eyed Issama from the corner of her eyes, frowning ever so slightly.

"What trickery is this?" Guden asked at last. "I should take you at your word, hand over my people to a usurper on the word of his most trusted man? Do you think me a fool?"

Issama shook his head. "Quite the opposite, Guden khan."

"And what offer am I supposed to believe you have made to Lady Man-dukhai that would make her pull her support from Unebolod?" Guden's voice adopted a sharp edge.

"The one thing I know she has wanted since her first day in Mongke Bulag," Issama said coolly. "Bigirsen's head."

Guden snorted. "What is to keep her from taking that offer, then giving the title to Unebolod still?"

Issama straightened, folding his hands in his lap. Siker would give him an earful for this later, he was certain. "Because the only way she will get his head will be if she accepts my proposal and makes me Great Khan."

Siker gasped sharply, glaring at Issama. But she would either accept that this would be the way, or he would teach her who was in charge of this relationship. And if she could not accept it, once she birthed his son, he would kill her. Issama would certainly hate to lose a woman like her, though. She was wise in all the right places, and servile in all the rest. A perfect partner.

Guden stared Issama down as if he waited for some lie to reveal itself. Issama maintained his calm patience.

"What makes you believe her desire for his head is strong enough to marry you?" Guden asked at last.

Siker grimaced, putting these pieces together for Guden. "Because she loved and cared for one of Manduul's nieces. Then Bigirsen stole the princess in marriage and later killed her. Lady Mandukhai is a vengeful woman." Siker's eyes narrowed as she glared at her husband. "She would do just about anything to ensure his downfall."

Issama nodded to her in gratitude. It would be easier for Guden to swallow this revelation from a woman who had once shared the court with Mandukhai than it would from him. Women talked, and Siker had learned quite a bit about the Great Khan's court during her time in Mongke Bulag.

Guden considered Issama's offer, the minutes growing longer. "My peo-ple will never accept him."

"Then I suggest you spend this evening preparing them," Issama said, hope blooming in his chest.

Guden gulped, then glanced warily at Nahai. "Who is this? Why is *he* here?"

"Nahai has joined us so you know who I trust as my second-in-com-mand. It will be hard to know whom to trust in the weeks to come, save those in this ger. You will receive orders only from us when the time comes. Trust no one else."

"Not even the Ordos Lords?" Guden asked. His brows climbed his forehead.

"It is best that we keep the chain of trust and command simple," Issama pointed out. "Should anything go awry, it is best if you do not know the extent of our network of allies. The more people who know the names of everyone involved, the more danger we are all in. One weak link and everything comes undone. Nahai is not weak. He has sworn an oath to me above Bigirsen, and his eternal soul will be destroyed if he breaks that oath."

Guden examined Nahai, then nodded. "I will do my best to prepare my men, but I cannot promise they will understand. This could still end in war."

Issama had little choice but to agree. After Bigirsen's treatment of Legusi and his men, not everyone would so easily bow to Bigirsen—especially if their khan could not explain why.

CHAPTER ELEVEN

A Great Burden

MOUNT BURKHAN KHALDUN – EARLY SUMMER 1470

Mandukhai held out open arms as Esige flew toward her. Esige hardly felt the ground beneath her feet in her haste. She flung her arms around Mandukhai, throwing her mother off balance. For a moment, the two embraced, and it was the most reassuring moment Esige could ever recall. She had worried that she would never see Mandukhai again, but had refused to voice this concern to anyone else.

As Esige drew back, she noted the way Mandukhai's face contorted ever so slightly in pain. Immediately, Esige's gaze swept over Mandukhai, taking in the cuts on her Mother's face, the bruises along her neck and wrist, and the rips in Mandukhai's deel. Anger pulsed through Esige. What had they done to Mandukhai?

"Are you well?" Esige asked.

Mandukhai smiled affectionately. "I will heal. I am just relieved you are okay."

"I'm sorry, Mother," Esige said. Her voice trembled. "It's my fault. If Boke had been with you and I had not left Nemeku—"

"Hush." Mandukhai stroked Esige's hair, reminding Esige of all the times Mandukhai had comforted her as a little girl, after Borogchin had been carted off with Bigirsen. "They may have found us all the same. But instead of just me, they would have had you as well, and I would hate to think of what they would have done to you."

Esige's face burned with hate. "I would have killed any who tried." Had they forced themselves on Mandukhai? Surely not. Not if their khan had wanted her to bolster his claim on the khanship.

Mandukhai's laugh was light, lilting. "With what? Your hands? It was not so easy as that, believe me. I tried." Mandukhai released her hold on Esige and glanced past her toward the carts. Men and women already worked at constructing gers. "Where *is* Nemeku?"

"With Lady Jaghan," Esige said, turning to watch as Mandukhai's ger was the first to be erected. "He insisted on riding with them to protect her and the children."

Mandukhai smiled. A curious response.

Esige's eyes swept the sacred mountain in the distance. "So this is it," she breathed. "We will have a new Great Khan soon." She could not wait to see Unebolod and Mandukhai together at last.

"Soon," Mandukhai agreed. "But first, we must wait for the other tribes to arrive. Then the festivities will begin."

Esige bounced up on her toes with excitement. The festival would last for days, featuring horse and foot races, archery, and wrestling. She wanted so badly to take part, but Mandukhai had already refused to allow it. Women did not participate, and certainly not princesses. But Esige did not want to be a princess.

Still, if she could not participate in the official events, that did not mean she couldn't still find a few new challengers.

In less than an hour, Mandukhai's ger was erected, and a troop of boys who elbowed each other to be close to Esige had hauled in the furnishings. She allowed the girl to make her tea as they waited for Esige and Nemeku's ger to be constructed. As Esige began mixing the tea leaves, Mandukhai moved to her chest and dug around until she found what she was looking for. A small pouch of mugwort.

Tears blurred Mandukhai's vision as she kneeled before the massive chest. Her heart ached, but nearly as much as the rest of her body. Mandukhai blinked back the tears and closed the chest, then settled on the edge of her bed as Esige handed her the tea. When the girl turned away to check on Nemeku, Mandukhai mixed in a pinch of mugwort.

She raised the cup to her lips. A lump swelled in her throat, making her fear she would be unable to swallow the drink. If her night with Unebolod had produced any children, this would undo the pregnancy. But how could she know? Mandukhai forced down the lump. *I cannot know where the child came from. I cannot risk it.* She cooled the tea and took a generous drink. There were no other options. She would always wonder. So would Unebolod. This had been the undoing of Genghis's eldest son, too. She could not repeat the same mistake.

Boke ducked in, announcing that Esige's ger was ready.

"You two should go get settled for the night," Mandukhai told Esige.

"Are you sure you should be alone?" Esige asked, reaching for Nemeku's hand.

"I must speak to Unebolod and need a moment to prepare."

Esige smiled coyly as she ushered Nemeku out with her. Mandukhai did not correct her. He would not be pleased tonight. Unebolod wanted her to accept his offer formally, which would put him in a position to win *kurultai*. But after what had happened to her, the idea of allowing any man to touch her made her stomach writhe in terror. How long would Unebolod be willing to wait? How long would she need him to? Mandukhai could not imagine sharing his bed would be any more enjoyable than sitting on the sun.

Mandukhai finished her tea in one gulp, then crossed the ger to pull out the red lacquer box from her chest. It was the same box Manduul's final commands had been in. Now, it held offers she could not ignore. The Oirat had attempted forcing her into submission. Other Lords had not been so aggressive. Several had sent her generous proposals she could never accept.

Mandukhai opened the lid, pulling out the top paper. Her reading skills had improved in the years since she had arrived at court. For the hundredth time, she read the offer from Issama. It had seemed a ridiculous thing. How could she ever give the khanship to a man not of pure Mongol heritage? *Genghis would never forgive me*, she thought.

But Issama had also promised that she would not have to perform as a wife unless she chose to do so. It would be on her terms. She could not give Issama the khanship, and she knew as much, but that offer to maintain her own freedom to choose what she did with her body certainly held an appeal that the other offers lacked. *I have three wives*, he had written. *And they are more than eager to share my bed.*

The offer to kill Bigirsen had been the biggest temptation. While the other Lords who had made proposals were true leaders of the Mongol Nation, they could not offer the one thing she had wanted since Bigirsen had stolen Borogchin away. His head. Still, she knew she could not accept.

Unebolod would never bow to a Uyghur. She could never do so either. Mandukhai turned to the stove and dropped Issama's offer into the flames. Unebolod could never know.

Even the Ming had sent her an offer. Submit the Nation to Chinese rule, and she would want for nothing. Mandukhai could live out her days in luxury, however she saw fit. The implication that she would be a prisoner to their court had not been stated outright, but she had certainly read it between the lines. She had rejected this offer outright, though had not sent word. If the Ming used her rejection as an excuse to declare war, the Mongol Nation would fall before a new Great Khan could take control. *When I declare the new Great Khan, the Ming will know.*

Someone cleared his throat from the doorway. Mandukhai dropped the rest of the papers back in the box and snapped the lid shut before spinning around to see Unebolod standing in the doorway.

"May I?" he asked, motioning inside.

Since Manduul's death, Unebolod had not asked permission to enter. Nor had she required him to ask. This change unsettled her.

Mandukhai nodded. Her stomach twisted in knots, and the air suddenly felt thick.

He entered, leaving the door open as a sign he would do nothing without her permission. He did not move inside far before standing straight and lacing his hands behind his back.

"You summoned me?" he asked.

Mandukhai licked her dry lips and motioned for him to sit. He remained statue still.

For days, Mandukhai had run through this conversation in her mind, trying to come up with the right words, the perfect explanation that would allow her to never tell him the whole truth of what had happened to her. Now, with him standing in front of her, those words flew from her mind like birds from a tree. She loved him, but now feared him.

"I ... I appreciate that you have given me space to recover," she said, cursing the tremor in her voice. "It cannot have been easy for you."

"You know I would never hurt you." His arms twitched, but he made no move toward her. Mandukhai knew he wanted to hold her, and she appreciated his restraint. "And you have never been a prize to me."

Please don't make this harder, she thought desperately. He would not understand her hesitation if she didn't tell him what those men had done. But she couldn't allow those memories to surface either, or she might lose her grip on her own sanity. She fought to keep her emotions in check, and it didn't help that he eyed her suspiciously.

"You know my heart is yours," Mandukhai said, fighting to say the words as if someone's hands wrapped around her throat. "It has been for years."

"Then what is the problem, Mandukhai? What have I done wrong? Why will you not let me help you? Why won't you just do what we both know you will do eventually?"

Those words were like a fist over her heart. Tears burned her eyes, and she fought to hold them back. Unebolod shuffled forward half a step, then paused. She could not tell him about Batu until she knew the boy's fate for certain. It would only hurt him.

"Manduul has placed a great burden on my shoulders," she croaked. "I cannot make such a decision in haste."

"Haste?" Unebolod recoiled, spitting the word. "This has hardly been in haste. We have planned this for years!"

The sudden anger made Mandukhai's insides shrivel up. She reflexively shrank back, scrubbing away rogue tears. "Don't shout at me." Her voice sounded so small, even to her own ears.

Unebolod's jaw twitched, and his shoulders took on a dangerous slope, which only reminded her of Manduul when he had forced himself on her years ago. Her heart pulsed in her throat. *I don't want to fear him!*

"I have waited years for this," Unebolod growled. "Manduul declared me an heir. I don't understand why you hesitate. I thought we had an understanding."

The assumption was clear. Unebolod assumed that, by winning her over, he would win this title. Again, it made her feel like a prize. *Should I tell him about the vision now? It could help him understand some of my conflict.*

Before she could speak, he continued, lowering his voice a pitch. "What do you want from me, Mandukhai? If I have not yet given it, I will." He edged toward her slowly with each word, and it made her heart hammer rapidly against her ribs. "Do you want my heart? You have it. Do you want my oath? I gave it, but I can give it again if you doubt me."

Mandukhai retreated, fighting to keep her entire body from trembling in fear. She had never known fear of him before, but a fury burned in him. She witnessed the outcome of his rage when he killed that Oirat. Would it spill over here? Would he force his claim? She hated doubting him.

"Do you want me to promise to respect you always?" he snapped. "Because I always have."

Mandukhai couldn't breathe. Fear had taken hold and chased away all reason. He stalked toward her like a predator with each word, forcing her to back away. Her back bumped into the altar along the north wall. *He wouldn't force his will, would he?*

"Shall I also give you my men, my breath, my life?" Unebolod stood close. So close the heat from his body burned through Mandukhai's deel and into her skin. She wanted to retreat, flee, escape. "Do you want my honor? I have nearly lost it for you before. If you require that sacrifice, I give it."

"No." The word was but a breath from her lips. Mandukhai attempted summoning more words, but all she could do was stare at him with wide eyes as her skin turned clammy and her palms sweated.

Unebolod's expression softened as he slid his hand along her neck, cupping her face. Mandukhai flinched away, emitting an involuntary whimper. Just his touch brought the pain from the attack to the surface. The absolute terror that had seized her body and soul. Everything spun, making Unebolod's wounded expression almost macabre.

"Do you *fear* me?" The words relayed the sheer agony of his emotions. It broke the dam holding back her tears, and she cried, trembling violently against him with nowhere to escape.

"What did they do to you, Mandukhai?" Unebolod asked, stepping away and dropping his hands as if reading her mind.

She wanted to tell him, but couldn't bring the truth to the surface. It was too horrible a thing to relive. Mandukhai squeezed her eyes closed in a lame attempt to stop the tears, hating herself for being so weak, for doubting him, for her complete inability to say anything at all.

"I would never hurt you," he said with a tenderness that forced her to face him. Unebolod's brows knitted together, his mouth down-turned. "If this is about you needing control over yourself, that's fine. I can accept that. If you need space until the time comes to accept my proposal, you have it. I have waited this long. I can wait a little longer."

Once more, she tried to speak. She opened her mouth, but her mind was full of only fear of any man touching her in any intimate way, and her words stopped in her throat.

"If another man tries this sort of thing again, I will not wait any longer," he said. "Until then, I am yours. As I have always been."

Unebolod reached up to brush away her tears, then seemed to think better of it and snapped his hand back. He spun about, marching out of the ger.

All the strength remaining in Mandukhai's body gave out the moment the door closed behind him. She crumbled to the floor and wept.

Chapter Twelve

A Broken Soul

U nebolod rode the defensive perimeter he and Togochi had set up around Mount Burkhan Khaldun, checking in with men and asking for reports. Attacking in this sacred place would be an act against the High Heavens themselves, and he doubted any man would be foolish enough to take such a risk. But after what had happened in Mongke Bulag, he was not about to take any more chances.

The conversation with Mandukhai two nights ago still had Unebolod reeling. She insisted none of those men had raped her, but any time he came near, she trembled in fear. It only happened to him. Boke lived at Mandukhai's shoulder like a perched falcon, and she never once shied away from him. Boke was the one who had failed to guard her. *I still need to have words with him*, Unebolod thought. But he had been unable to get Boke alone.

A great chasm grew between Unebolod and Mandukhai. Unebolod had no inkling on how to breach that gap. He'd meant what he said. Unebolod had given her everything he had to give. Everything but his honor. What more could she ask of him?

Unebolod had initially understood why Mandukhai had wanted to wait before accepting his proposal. Her plan was a reasonable one, and he could not deny her logic. Waiting allowed her time to mourn Manduul's death in the eyes of the people. At the festival, when all the tribes gathered together for games, they would make their engagement official and consolidate their power to install him. It had been a good plan.

But that plan now required change. The Oirat had revealed their intentions. What other lesser khans would step forward to attempt the same? No. He would not allow it to happen. If another man tried to steal her away, he would assert his claim. He could only hope she would understand after the ordeal with the Oirat. It was for her own protection. And once he asserted his claim—given by order of Manduul Khan himself—even she would be powerless to stop it. *Why would she want to stop me? This is what we have wanted for so long.*

He recalled those early days together, when the two of them would lie under the stars and share their dreams. This had always been part of the plan. *Why is she changing the rules now?*

The cloud of dust in the distance shifted abruptly as his army changed tactics in practice, following only the sound of a horn. Unebolod longed to be with the men, but he knew his place now and had to keep it carefully. The men needed to see him as their ruler, their figure of authority. Soke would be *orlok* of the eastern tribes when he became Great Khan, and the men needed to learn how to follow Soke's commands now. When an actual battle came, Unebolod would ride out with them and fight at their side.

Bigirsen would be Unebolod's first target once he became Great Khan. Unebolod knew Bigirsen's men vastly outnumbered his own, but Mongols could easily win such a battle with the right commander at their head. A commander such as himself. By destroying Bigirsen, Unebolod would also destroy the Uyghur hold over the Oirat. Then he would make the Oirat suffer for what they had done to Mandukhai. It would require several layers of trickery to draw out enough of Bigirsen's men to defeat them in smaller numbers until his opponent could not stand against him. Unebolod straightened in the saddle, strengthened by the knowledge that Bigirsen's power would soon end.

Movement in the southeast, far from where his men ran their drills, caught Unebolod's attention. He squinted into the distance. It was hard to see clearly, even with his sharp eyes, so he closed his hands into a scope to narrow his field of vision—an old scout trick.

A handful of riders raced away from camp, and he swept his gaze across the horizon to spot why. In a moment, he could have his men tear down any who threatened his camp. Instead of an army, Unebolod spotted a single rider trotting ahead of a cart. He could not make out much more from such a distance.

Before he could decide whether this was worth investigating, blue banners fluttered around another rider from camp—Mandukhai. She rode

Dust toward this newcomer with her guards around her. Unebolod hesitated only a moment before kicking his mare at an angle to catch her, along with the newcomer. His mount lurched into action. Was Mandukhai determined to be captured again?

Two of Mandukhai's guards broke off to intercept Unebolod as he drew closer, escorting him into her company.

Unebolod turned his attention to the man riding ahead of the cart and noticed the cut of his Uyghur clothing immediately. Unebolod rested his hand on the hilt of his sword. He did not trust *any* man from that tribe.

"Ease yourself, Unebolod," Mandukhai said softly. Though she had not looked at him, somehow, she still knew he was ready to strike. "This man is no danger to me."

Unebolod relaxed his shoulders, but not his grip. She could not just command him to trust a Uyghur.

He turned his attention to the cart, noting the woman and a bundled boy beside her. The boy's head peeked out from the felt and fur blankets wrapped around him despite the warm late-spring air. The hat on the boy's head was too big, and between the hat and blankets, he looked to be peering out at them from beneath a rock. As the cart hit a bump, the boy nearly tumbled out. The woman snatched him and pulled him upright.

Mandukhai's guards fell back as she rode past the Uyghur man, barely giving him a nod, and headed straight for the cart.

What is she doing? Unebolod readied to attack, her warning be damned.

"This is him?" Mandukhai asked the woman in the cart. "How does he fare?"

The woman's eyes cast downward as if suddenly ashamed as she pulled the cart to a halt. "It is him. He rode part of the way here but fell from the saddle and into a stream. Khadag pulled him out. But I fear he suffers from pneumonia now. He nearly drowned in the stream."

Unebolod attempted to make sense of the conversation. But all he could gather was that this boy—who couldn't be much younger than five or six—could not stay in a saddle or stand up in a stream to save himself. What sort of invalid was this?

"What of his other illness?" Mandukhai asked.

"Healed, Queen Regent," the woman said. "Though I wore out three silver bowls doing so."

"You will be repaid," Mandukhai said without a moment of hesitation. "And then some. It is the least I can do." She motioned to her guard, Torgus, who rode forward and untied a sack from his saddle, tossing it into the back of the cart with a loud clink of metal. "You are both honored here at Mount Burkhan Khaldun and have all Guest Rights. No one will harm your family."

Unebolod stared at the boy, who stared back at him with wide, feverish eyes. Golden eyes, he realized. Suddenly, his heart seized as reality slammed down on his chest. Unebolod had only known two men with eyes like those. Molon Khan ... and Bayan.

Mandukhai's ger quickly filled with activity. She kneeled beside her bed, where Batu now lay beneath a mass of blankets and furs as the shaman, Khosoichi, administered salted ginger tea. The boy coughed and sputtered as he attempted to drink the warm liquid. Mandukhai pressed a warm compress to Batu's forehead as he quivered violently enough to make the layers of fur shift. It reminded her of Manduul's illness. *Lord Tengri, please don't take this boy*, she prayed.

Getei, the Ongud soothsayer who had arrived from her own tribe with the Khorchin, shook the bones and cast them several times on the floor. He then crouched down and mumble to himself as he deciphered their meaning.

Esige lit incense at the altar, fanning the jasmine smoke through the air. The girl continually ensured that the water on the stove remained fresh for compresses and drinks, all the while monitoring Nemeku on the far side of the ger. Nemeku clearly sensed the tension in the ger judging by his sober expression.

Unebolod hovered near the doorway. Mandukhai had tried refusing him entry, but he had argued so firmly that she did not want to waste precious time. At least he stayed out of the way.

"How long has he been ill?" Khosoichi asked as he once more propped Batu up and helped him drink the salted ginger tea.

"About four days, according to Saichai," Mandukhai responded, touching the back of her hand to Batu's burning forehead. She had not gone through all this trouble to have the boy die on her here!

Khosoichi frowned and reached into his layered robes, producing a long needle. "Hold him down."

Mandukhai's eyes widened. "What are you doing?"

"His lungs are filled with fluid and his symptoms are not abating," Khosoichi said patiently. "We have to relieve the pressure."

"By stabbing him?" Mandukhai leaned protectively toward Batu, placing her hand over his chest.

"It's either that, or he dies. I leave it to you to decide, Queen Regent."

Mandukhai glanced around the ger for someone else to say something, but no one else moved. Esige was busy with Nemeku. Getei frowned at his bones on the floor. Unebolod's face remained a mask devoid of emotion as he watched with a distant look in his eyes. Mandukhai hung her head, smoothed a hand across Batu's sweaty forehead, and offered him reassurance before she stood to pin his shoulders to the bed. Batu hardly seemed aware of what was happening around him.

Khosoichi pulled down the furs to expose Batu's pale, sunken chest. Mandukhai could see all of his ribs sticking out from the flesh as if attempting to escape the skin. Khosoichi felt along the ribs for the correct placement, then tipped the needle against Batu's chest. He pressed it into the skin, and Mandukhai flinched, unable to watch as, inch by inch, the needle penetrated deeper. Batu released a rattling scream that felt as sharp as if the needle penetrated Mandukhai's heart. Tears welled in her eyes, but she leaned closer to his face, smiling sweetly and offering words of comfort as she pressed down on his bucking shoulders.

Batu's scream transformed into a cough that had Khosoichi cursing as Getei joined them to hold the boy still. Tears rolled down Batu's temples as his golden eyes came into sharp focus on Mandukhai's face.

The needle was drawn out, followed by a rush of air. Blood bubbled up from the puncture and Khosoichi deftly wiped it away and pressed a silver-infused salve around the wound. Batu's coughing eased and his breaths came easier. Khosoichi pulled the furs back up to cover Batu to the neck as Mandukhai leaned close to the boy and pressed her forehead to his, tenderly stroking his cheek.

"It's okay," she whispered to him. "It's over."

Batu whimpered and closed his eyes.

Mandukhai kissed his sweaty forehead and sank back on her heels as Esige produced a fresh, warm compress and applied it to Batu.

"He will need rest, water, and salted ginger tea," Khosoichi said. He dropped a pouch into Mandukhai's palm. "Mix this into his water or tea at least two or three times a day to help fight the infection."

"How long will he remain like this?" Mandukhai asked, tearing her gaze away from the slumbering boy.

"The fever should break in a few days," Khosoichi said, "but the rest of his symptoms will take longer to subside. Pneumonia can take months to fully heal, assuming he survives."

Mandukhai scowled at him.

"I simply want you to be prepared for the worst, my Lady," he said, spreading his hands wide in defense. "Not everyone survives, and his previous illness already weakened his body. You could be fighting a lost cause."

Mandukhai handed the pouch to Esige and rose from the floor, straightening her spine and raising her chin. "I never fight for a lost cause."

"Of course, my Lady," the shaman said, bowing as deeply as he could in the cramped space. Then he slipped past Unebolod out the door with a nod of respect.

Unebolod grimaced, shooting a scowl at Mandukhai briefly before once more studying Batu.

"And you, soothsayer? What did the bones tell you?" Mandukhai asked, rounding on Getei.

He bowed before saying, "His survival depends on you."

Mandukhai nodded stiffly. "Esige, can you please take Nemeku out for some fresh air?"

Everyone cleared out of the ger, leaving Mandukhai alone with Unebolod and the slumbering boy. Without meaning to, Mandukhai maintained at a distance from Unebolod, just out of reach. His entire demeanor had changed after the Oirat attack, and now, with this boy, something else had shifted in him. Unebolod usually wore his emotions plainly for her to see, but now he wore a mask of cold distance.

"You seem to collect strays like rare jewels," Unebolod said once the two of them were alone.

"Because they are, in their own way," Mandukhai said.

Unebolod stood with his arms tightly across his chest, and his jaw twitched as he glanced at Batu, who wheezed as he slumbered on her bed.

"Our immediate plans are unchanged," she reassured Unebolod, but it was clear her words offered no such reassurance.

He scoffed, glaring at the boy with pure hate. "What plans? There was once a time when we had plans, when we believed that once Manduul died, you and I would finally be together, and I could be Great Khan. Now, it seems, all you have are secrets."

Mandukhai flinched and retreated a step. "You make it sound so simple."

"It is."

"No. It never has been. You know that as well as I do."

"Who is he?" Unebolod's gaze slid past Mandukhai to the sleeping boy.

Mandukhai licked her lips and glanced over her shoulder at Batu. "Bayan's son."

Unebolod's armor creaked as his body tensed. "His what?"

"Before he came to Manduul, Bayan and Siker had a son they both believed had died of illness." Mandukhai knew she had to convince Unebolod to spare the boy, and it must be careful work. "My men found him several months ago and brought him to Saichai and Khadag to care for his illness."

Unebolod's jaw slackened. "Months? You have kept this from me for months?" Anger burned in his voice.

"I wanted to be sure he would survive before I worried you with it." Mandukhai hated how that pitch in his tone made her tremble, but she would not back down. "Besides, you would have killed him!"

"I wouldn't have to! Look at him, Mandukhai." He waved at Batu's prone little body. "He would be dead already if you hadn't interfered."

"Interfered?" Mandukhai's blood heated with her own anger as she tensed her shoulders. "Do oaths and duty mean nothing to you now? Have the years so changed you?"

Unebolod took a deep breath and released it slowly. "You speak to *me* of duty? Have I not done my duty and been patient all these years? Have I not upheld my oaths? I have watched these years in *agony* as another man took my title and gave it away again and again, as he held you and kiss you when I could not."

"*Your* title?" Mandukhai blanched, and her hands fell limp at her sides. The words hammered into her heart, knocking the air from her lungs. He presumed the title had been his in the first place? *Who is this man?*

She understood his pain. And she could not imagine what it must have felt like watching her act as a wife with Manduul all those years. But this was the first time in her life Mandukhai had any ability to make her own decisions. Men had dictated her life for too long. Mandukhai was in charge of her own fate, and she was not about to relinquish it so readily.

Unebolod stepped toward her, reaching for her hand. "I'm sorry."

Mandukhai withdrew and shook her head. "You are not. You meant every word. But this has not been easy for either of us. You watched me with him, but I had to give myself to him and every time I wanted to scrub his touch off my skin."

"I know."

"And then, those men ..." Mandukhai's voice trailed off.

Unebolod's stony façade cracked. "I know. I know."

Mandukhai realized she had to share something with him to keep this from cascading out of control, if nothing else, for the sake of Batu. She edged closer, sliding a trembling hand into his. "Unebolod, you have been so patient."

His thumb stroked her fingers tenderly, and he didn't tighten his grip. The small gesture offered Mandukhai some relief, even if she wanted to withdraw from his touch.

Mandukhai swallowed a lump that formed in her throat. "But you must also know that Manduul's death is not a flag for you to seize control. Such a bid when there is no clear, immediate heir will not be so easily stolen. We have to be careful how we handle this."

Unebolod nodded. "So, we agree?"

Mandukhai hesitated. Agree to what? She had not promised him anything in that statement. She only advised caution. Besides, she needed to be certain of Batu's fate, and Unebolod had to understand the boy had rights as an heir of Genghis. She had to tell him about the vision, or at least part of it. Mandukhai opened her mouth, but before she could say a word, Unebolod pulled his hand away.

"It's because of him, isn't it?" Unebolod threw a hateful glare at Batu. "His mere presence is enough to make any man question my right."

"Not if you adopt him as your son and heir," Mandukhai said. "When you and I marry, you will become Great Khan, and Batu will be your heir in another ten years, when he is old enough to claim his birthright."

"Ten years," Unebolod said flatly, and she could see the anger he tried so hard to hide behind a cold, impassive face. "You expect me, in just ten years, to hand over the khanship to this boy? What of *our* sons?"

Mandukhai had known Unebolod would not appreciate this part of her plan, but it was the only way to lend Unebolod legitimacy while Batu lived. "They will be second to Batu and his own heirs."

Unnatural silence fell between them. Neither moved. The only way to tell the world still turned was by the chatter of men and women outside, and the uneven breaths of Batu's slumbering frame. Unebolod edged closer, and Mandukhai shied away as his hands gently grasped her head. His warm breath rolled off her forehead. Then his lips grazed her skin. Mandukhai's stomach twisted in tight, sickening knots.

"My sons will not live in the shadow of another," he said. His lips grazed her forehead as he spoke. "As I have my entire life."

A surge of disappointment raced through her. Unebolod abruptly pulled away. Though he had not outright refused her proposal, the rejection stung all the same. On some level, deep down, Mandukhai had expected this answer. She understood his frustrations under Manduul and Bayan. Perhaps fear of those exact words had her stalled all this time.

He turned to the door, hesitating only a moment at the threshold.

"I will not subject my sons to such torture, nor should you," he said firmly.

Before she could respond, he stepped out and firmly closed the door behind him with a finality that made Mandukhai's knees weak. She sank onto the edge of the bed beside Batu as tears stung her eyes.

Unebolod would understand. He knew that, as long as Batu lived, his own honor would bind him to Manduul's final wishes. Batu was an heir of Genghis, whether or not Unebolod liked it. And she could not just sit back and allow the royal line to die just so the man she loved could become Great Khan. She had a duty as much as he did.

He just needed time. Batu was the last rightful heir, and should he survive long enough, he would follow Unebolod as Great Khan. Those were her terms. Unebolod would come around. He had no other choice.

Chapter Thirteen

Platitudes

As Issama approached the door of Bigirsen's ger, a crash within made him pause. The walls of the ger shook. A moment later, one of Bigirsen's rather harried wives scurried out of the ger, tears streaming down her face. Issama grimaced as he watched her rush off, then turned his attention to the door. No guards. Was that a good thing?

Bigirsen had been extra cruel to his wives lately. It was a wonder one of them had not done Issama's job and drove a dagger through Bigirsen's heart while he slept. *He is in another rage,* Issama thought. But there was no avoiding this. Bigirsen had summoned him, and if Issama didn't show up, Bigirsen would likely hunt him for sport.

Issama called out a greeting, then ducked inside.

Issama's gaze swept the space to pinpoint Bigirsen. The other man stood beside the stove, his shoulders heaving with angry breaths. The moment he turned and laid eyes on Issama, Bigirsen's thick brows narrowed dangerously.

"What have you done, Issama?" Bigirsen hissed.

Issama cocked his head. For once, he felt out of sorts. It was an oddly unpleasant sensation that made his skin tingle. "I'm afraid I don't understand, my Lord."

Did he find out about the proposal Issama had made to Mandukhai? Surely not. Issama had sent one of his own loyal men to deliver it and only used abandoned trails to avoid any potential encounters along the way.

Bigirsen strode toward Issama in two long steps and seized his collar like a viper striking its prey. *Airag* and rotten meat permeated the air, pushing into Issama's face as Bigirsen sneered. "The Oirat. You reassured me you had them under control."

Issama's heart dropped into his stomach. Bigirsen had left control of the Oirat to Issama this past year as he continued his southern campaigns. But now, forced into this demeaning position as Bigirsen's shadow, Issama could not maintain his iron grip on the unpredictable Oirat.

"I'm afraid you have to be more specific," Issama said calmly, easing Bigirsen's arm away as much as he dared.

Thankfully, Bigirsen let go. Issama took a step back, straightening his deel as he glared at Bigirsen. *Old, crazy fool.* It was high time someone younger and more capable took control of the Uyghur.

"They attacked Mongke Bulag and tried to capture that woman." Bigirsen's nose curled in disgust, leaving no doubt who "that woman" was. Mandukhai.

For a moment, Issama hoped the Oirat had succeeded. However, two facts destroyed that hope just as quickly. First, if the Oirat khan got his hands on her, Issama could lose his power and he might have to declare war on the Oirat to redeem himself in Mandukhai's eyes and take back control of the Oirat. Second, Bigirsen said "tried," which implied a lack of success. *This is why I haven't heard from her. She probably thinks I was behind the attack.* That had been his plan months ago, but that plan would no longer work. It was the entire reason he had proposed a marriage alliance to her.

"I cannot control the barbaric Oirat from a thousand miles away," Issama replied smoothly. "And you insist you need me here. They will be like a dog without a rope to hold them back. And with Manduul having no Borjigin heir, they will move in to take control. If you want me to control them, send me back."

Bigirsen's jaw twitched. His hands clenched into fists at his sides. "No. We will conquer the Urainkhai as we have the Ordos and Chakhar, then sweep up the east. The Three Guards commanders say the Urainkhai khan is weakened right now. He sent his son north with half of his men. Now is the time to strike."

Issama balked. "You said we were preparing to invade Ming territory. Half the Urainkhai will not change that, and even if you win, which you likely would, the other half will come back with Tolokan khan's heir to fight back, possibly with new allies from the east. And you know Unebolod has control of the eastern tribes. You will not conquer them. You will make enemies of them … if they don't die first. And then you will have no Nation to rule over."

"I will do as I please!" The vein in Bigirsen's neck pulsed.

"Why do you keep me here if not to advise you?" Issama took a risk pushing Bigirsen when he was in such a state, but Bigirsen likely would be suspicious if Issama did not push back at least a little.

Bigirsen mopped sweat from his forehead with his bare arm, then stalked away toward the butcher's block in the back of the ger. "I have listened to your advice for years, Issama, and look where it has gotten us. I sent you to Mongke Bulag to destroy what remained of the court. Instead, somehow you seemed to have strengthened it."

"Strengthened?" Issama crossed his arms. If Bigirsen believed that, then he truly had lost his mind at last. "Were it not for me, they would have already handed the Nation over to Bayan. I did as you commanded. I entered the court and earned the trust of both Manduul and Bayan. I planted the seeds of doubt in their minds, and when the time was ripe, they sprouted exactly as we wanted. Now both men are dead and you have a chance to take control." Issama edged closer to Bigirsen as the other man poured himself a drink. "Your original plan was a good one. Gather your forces. Attack the Ming."

Bigirsen turned, leaning against the butcher's block. "We cannot possibly outnumber them."

"We don't need to outnumber them, just outmaneuver them." Issama prayed his message would get through the haze of anger roiling around Bigirsen. "We can take Yinchuan. And when we do, the Nation will fall in behind you. Because from there, you will take what Genghis never could, and what Esen failed to hold. They will believe you are blessed by Lord Tengri and the sky father himself."

Bigirsen dipped his chin to his chest. It was a subtle gesture, but enough for Issama to know that he agreed. Bigirsen would abandon his foolish quest to conquer the tribes and would turn his attention on the Ming.

"She has set up camp at Mount Burkhan Khaldun," Bigirsen said at last.

Issama started. "She does not have enough support to name Unebolod." *Please let that be true.*

"Do you honestly believe he needs it?" Bigirsen scoffed. "I have fought him before. He can do far more damage with half a dozen tribes than I can with the full force of my *tumens*. War is coming, Issama. She will name him. The northern and eastern tribes will fall in line, and he will travel south to challenge me and enforce his foothold over the tribes."

"I wouldn't be so sure," Issama said, tapping his lips pensively. He began pacing the ger, thankful that Bigirsen's rage had subsided. "The Oirat may have done us a favor. He may want to exact retribution for their attack before turning south. If you defeat the Ming first, his power will crumble. The tribes would defect to you the moment you win and proclaim yourself the rightful successor of Genghis."

"I am to defeat an empire before he defeats the unruly Oirat?" Bigirsen snorted, then downed his drink and slapped the cup on the block. "Not likely." He paused a moment and Issama could almost hear the wheels in Bigirsen's head turning. "I suppose we stand a better chance in the south. All we need is Yinchuan. Ready the men."

Issama bowed and excused himself to set the task to the men. They would ride toward the Gansu Corridor, and from there, push into Ming territory. If Mandukhai would not accept Issama's offer, he would have to change his plans again, or the Chakhar and Ordos Lords would take his head.

Bigirsen *must* fall.

Unebolod flexed his forearm, eyeing the two-foot-long braided leather whip corded around his arm. The leather handle was firmly in his fist, tucked back up his arm. Days had passed since his argument with Mandukhai, and he still struggled to control his anger. She had known about Batu for months and said nothing. Instead, she served him platitudes every time they spoke of the khanship. The betrayal stung deeply. Now she wanted him to accept that his reign as Great Khan would only be until the boy was old enough to claim his birthright?

He could hope for the child to die. Yet experience taught Unebolod not to take such things for granted. He had assumed he owed the Borjigin line as a descendant of Khasar. He had saved Bayan foolishly when he was only fifteen. He had assumed the boy would not live to become a man.

But he had. Bayan had a child in secret with Siker. Which also meant Batu was not only an heir of Genghis, but legitimate in the eyes of the law because Siker, eventually, had become Bayan's wife. Even if Batu was born a bastard, he was not illegitimate.

Unebolod knew, deep down, the truth. He was not angry with Mandukhai, but with himself. All of this misery came about with his own hands.

Sweat beaded on his forehead and he reached his free hand up to scrub it away. The summer heat reached toward full swing. In just a few short weeks, even the cool breeze from the mountains would relieve no one out here on the steppe.

An *arban* of his Khorchin warriors—ten in total—entered the open wrestling grounds where Unebolod waited on a stack of saddles. In the middle of the group, held by each arm, Odgerel stumbled, attempting to hold her head high as they dragged her along. Her eyes fell on him and she paled, dropping her gaze to the ground in obvious shame. *She should be ashamed.*

The two men holding her pushed her to her knees a few feet in front of Unebolod. A small crowd began forming around the wrestling grounds, curious about this public display.

"I trust my men can let go," Unebolod said. He could not keep the anger from his voice. "You won't get far if you try to run."

Odgerel nodded, still staring at the ground.

Unebolod waved his men back. They released her arms and took a few steps back, but not so far they could not easily capture her again. He waited, allowing the silence to hang like an axe over her head.

"My Lord—"

"Silence! I didn't ask for your excuses."

Odgerel trembled violently, hugging her arms over her chest.

Unebolod leaned forward, and the saddles beneath him groaned. "You knowingly deceived me for months, attempted luring me into bed under false pretenses. No doubt you hoped to end up with my child before you revealed the truth." Anger made Unebolod's neck turn red and throb with intense life. His breaths came in tighter heaves. He tightened his grip on the handle in his fist until it creaked. "By the old laws, do you know the penalty for such intentional lies?"

Odgerel choked on a sob. She dared to glance up at him. Tears formed ribbons down her rosy cheeks. He should have felt bad for her—he did—but he was also upset that she had lied to him for so long. The second their eyes connected, she dipped her chin to her chest and fought down another sob. "Yes, my Lord."

"I am not your Lord," Unebolod said in a low, dangerous tone. "I am the khan of your tribe. I would be well within my right to kill you here and now."

"I b-beg your mercy!" Odgerel cried.

Unebolod scoffed. Mercy had gotten him into this mess. If he had just killed Bayan years ago, he would not have to scrape for the khanship. He would have it already.

The crowd had grown substantial. *Good.* Unebolod needed others to see this, to witness his wrath when someone crossed him.

"The Queen Regent still reserves the right to punish you for your disobedience, and that will probably be the end of you, knowing her," Unebolod continued, making sure he spoke loudly enough for everyone nearby to hear. "You saved my life, and I have not forgotten that." When a plague had ripped through the Khorchin camp, Odgerel had taken care of Unebolod when no one else would. "But I also saved yours. And so we are even. Now, you must suffer for your lies. Take her silk."

The Khorchin warriors closed in around her as she cried out, begging them to stop as they stripped the silk deel from her body, leaving her in a thin cotton tunic she had been wearing beneath, and her trousers. Odgerel covered her chest as one man cut the silk ribbon holding her hair in a braid. She whimpered.

"You are no longer a Lady of the court," Unebolod announced. "You will never again hold the title unless the Queen Regent or a Great Khan restores it upon you."

Odgerel squeezed her eyes closed. Unebolod had little pity. She had lied to him for six months, and more than once attempted seducing him. He had liked her, on some level, and respected her before the truth came to light. Unebolod did not relish punishing her. But it had to be done.

"You will no longer now, nor ever again, serve my house in any manner," he added. Unebolod stood. Odgerel flinched, pressing her trembling body closer to the ground. He stalked toward her, once more flexing his fist around the whip handle.

"I take no pleasure in any of this, Odgerel. If you had been honest with me from the start, I would have been obligated to help you. Your ties to my nephew would have seen it so. You made this choice. Now you must suffer the consequences." He stopped beside her, noting how thin the cotton tunic was—thin enough that he could see through it this close to her. "A lash for each month you deceived me."

Odgerel stiffened.

"You can choose who does it," he said. It was a small mercy. If she knew anyone who would go lighter on her, she could choose him herself.

Odgerel lifted her chin, her face streaked with rivers of intersecting tears. "You do it. Then you can suffer along with me."

His jaw twitched. Odgerel's defiance would get her killed one day. "Hold her steady," he commanded.

Two of the men stepped forward. She struggled to hold her arms over her chest, but their strength proved superior. They stretched her arms out to the sides as she kneeled on the ground, exposing her back through the thin cotton.

Unebolod's jaw twitched. He would take no delight in this. That had been the truth. He had tried giving her some control over the circumstances. But she made her choice. He could not back down now.

A numbness crawled through Unebolod. With a flick of his wrist, the two-foot coil unwrapped from his arm as he turned the handle in his fist. Clenching his jaw, Unebolod raised the whip and released the first crack against her back. Odgerel whimpered, but didn't cry out. Memories of how he had taken care of her during that plague flooded to the surface. He swallowed and shoved everything behind the wall of numbness taking over.

He had tried to pull back the blows as much as possible, but if she did not welt or bleed, it would still make him appear weak.

Silence had settled in the ring, broken only by the whimpers of Odgerel on the ground and the sharp crack of the whip as he snapped it down a second time. This time, she cried out. He flinched.

"What are you doing?" a man roared from somewhere behind Unebolod.

He glanced back in time to see Boke break through the crowd, shoving people out of his way. Another man Unebolod did not recognize hid behind Boke.

"Stay out of this," Unebolod snapped. "It's Khorchin business."

He raised his arm to crack the whip a third time, but Boke seized his arm and grabbed hold of the whip. The end of the whip cracked across Boke's face, leaving a bleeding gash on his cheek he hardly seemed to notice. Unebolod twisted Boke's arm away and slammed his fist down into the hyper-extended joint. It was enough to break contact, but not enough to seriously injure Boke. Mandukhai would never forgive him if he broke her guard's arm.

"You would dare interfere with my business?" Unebolod snapped. He had a different score to settle with Boke. "Shouldn't you be guarding the Queen Regent? Or have you abandoned your post again?"

Boke glowered, clutching his arm as he shuffled a few steps back. "The Queen Regent has reserved the right to pass judgment for Odgerel's crimes."

"She will get her turn," Unebolod replied.

Boke glared death at Unebolod, then shoved his way back through the crowd.

Unebolod turned back to Odgerel, who had dissolved into sobs as blood stained her cotton tunic.

Jaghan refilled the teacups as Mandukhai placed a fresh compress on Batu's forehead. His fever had not broken yet, and she worried whether he would recover at all. Yesterday his cough had taken a turn for the worse, and Mandukhai had buckets of water brought into the ger and placed them on the stove until no more could fit. The roof flap was sealed tightly shut, as was the door, and Mandukhai had turned the inside of the ger into a sweat tent, creating enough steaming water vapor to ease his symptoms. Today, his color appeared better, but his skin remained ashen.

"People are asking questions about this child you have taken in," Jaghan said as she settled down on the other side of the ger. "You cannot keep the truth from them much longer."

Mandukhai stroked Batu's cheek. It was so hot! "I need your help with this, Jaghan. Unebolod is the only other person who knows the truth, and it will be dangerous to contain it. He won't say a word about Batu to the other Lords. It would weaken his claim." Mandukhai sighed as she sank back on her heels beside the bed.

"Has he spoken to you since you made your offer?" Jaghan asked.

Mandukhai frowned and picked at her cuticles. "I think he is hoping Batu will die and he won't have to agree to anything. I suspect Unebolod is waiting this out to see how Batu does with his pneumonia."

Jaghan sipped her tea. "Alright. He won't say anything. I agree. But already I hear the whispers. People want to know who this boy is and why you have taken him in when he is so ill. How do you plan to control the flow of the story?"

"That's why I need you," Mandukhai replied. "Between Borogchin, Esige, and Nemeku, I have a reputation for taking in Borjigin princes and princesses. But I need you to spread rumors. They may not hold for long, but if I am lucky, they will hold for long enough."

"What *is* your story?" Jaghan asked. She leaned forward like a child eager to hear a good tale.

"My mother and step-father died recently," Mandukhai said. "A flu, I heard. If we can get the people to believe this is my half-brother, at least for now, that should allow me some time. But we cannot state this as a fact. It needs to come across as a rumor. That way, when the truth is revealed, no one can accuse us of lying outright."

Jaghan nodded. "And Togochi? Can I at least tell him?"

"Not yet."

Jaghan opened her mouth, but froze when they heard the commotion outside.

Togochi burst through the door with Boke on his heels. Boke's face was crimson with rage and an angry red welt on his face seeped blood. Mandukhai surged to her feet, terrified they were under attack. But Togochi's calmer countenance made her second guess the assessment.

"Unebolod is publicly punishing Odgerel," Togochi said.

"Punishing! He is horsewhipping her!" Boke shouted.

"Did he whip you?" Mandukhai asked as fury burned through her.

Boke touched his face and shrugged. "That was an accident."

"I will watch over him," Jaghan said, nodding toward Batu.

Mandukhai loathed leaving Batu in anyone else's hands, but she could not leave him alone either. Before ducking out, Mandukhai offered Jaghan a grateful smile.

The three of them jogged across the camp toward the wrestling ring, where Boke led them right to the massive crowd. Some men were cheering. The air cracked. A woman shrieked.

"Make space for the Queen Regent!" Togochi snapped as he and Boke forced people out of the way.

Mandukhai broke the edge of the ring to find Odgerel held face-down toward the ground as Khorchin warriors held her arms. Unebolod stood with his back to Mandukhai, but the slope of his shoulders reminded her of his rage during the Oirat attack. Momentary panic seized her.

"Stop this at once!" Mandukhai commanded. The clarity and strength of her voice surprised her, considering how her insides twisted in dread.

Unebolod dropped the bloodied whip on the ground and turned slowly to face Mandukhai. His expression bore a stony resolve, cold and distant. "I'm done, anyway."

"What are you doing?" Mandukhai demanded, marching toward them.

"She committed crimes against me," Unebolod said plainly. "I have punished her."

"By whipping her?"

"Do you have a better idea?"

His retort gave Mandukhai pause. Since the Oirat attack, she had not had a moment to even consider how to deal with Odgerel's defiance. Certainly, it merited some form of action, but publicly whipping her felt like too much.

"Take her to my healer," Mandukhai commanded.

Boke stepped forward, and the way he and Unebolod glared at each other made her blood curdle. The Khorchin warriors appeared uncertain about how to react to this turn of events. They loosened their grip on Odgerel like they were prepared to obey Mandukhai's command, but they also looked to Unebolod for confirmation. It rankled under Mandukhai's skin.

"I told you I reserved the right to punish her," Mandukhai told Unebolod.

"She defied you, and I have not punished her for that, only for deceiving me." He watched as the men stepped back and Boke scooped Odgerel into his arms. "She's all yours."

"She was mine to begin with!" Mandukhai snapped. She took a deep breath to steel her nerves, then let it out slowly. She edged closer and lowered her voice. "I hope you have not taken your anger toward me out on her."

"Why would I be angry with you?" he asked. Was he mocking her? She couldn't tell. Unebolod stepped closer, reaching for her hand.

Mandukhai cocked her head, but panic raced through her entire body, making her skin tingle. She wanted to pull away. Quickly. "Does this mean you have accepted my terms?" she asked.

He dropped her hand, picked up his whip, and stalked away.

CHAPTER FOURTEEN

What is Best

The incident with Unebolod had only expanded the divide between him and Mandukhai. She hated how sudden his withdrawal had been, and how much it hurt her. None of this could be easy for him—she understood that. Yet Mandukhai still hoped he would see reason. What choice did either of them truly have in this?

Days passed. Then a week. By the second, Mandukhai had determined Unebolod simply wanted nothing to do with her anymore. Was he truly so angry?

She waited for the other tribes to arrive, focusing her attention on preparing for the upcoming festival while also healing Batu's illness. She could not allow her heartache to impede her duty. Not when she was so close to *kurultai*.

Mandukhai had remained tethered to her ger as Batu healed. Occasionally, Khosoichi would visit to check on Batu's status, and always under Mandukhai's watchful eye.

Batu had remained too ill to do much more than sit up on the bed during those two weeks. Mandukhai had spent her nights curled up against his side, listening to his breathing until she fell asleep. During the day, she had passed time keeping him from overheating and ensuring he drank enough cooled medicinal tea to keep his body hydrated. Between her herbs, attentive moisturizing of his body and lungs, and feeding him all the broth his little body could handle, Batu's color had turned from ashen gray to pale, then somewhat rosy.

During the third week of care, Mandukhai had taken Batu outside—only a few feet from the ger at a time—to get fresh air. His legs were weak, and she often had to support most of his weight herself during those first days. But slowly, Batu had grown stronger, though not as strong as other boys near his age, like Nemeku.

Batu had said nothing since his arrival. Only whimpers, coughs, or moans gave any sign he could make any noise at all.

Nemeku had attempted entertaining Batu a few times after meals. Nemeku told stories as boys did, with grand flourishes and ridiculous jokes. He clowned around to try pulling smiles from Batu. Nemeku seemed to understand they were family and treated Batu as such.

The first time Batu had smiled it had been such a small, simple thing—faint but welcoming. Relief had flooded through Mandukhai. Perhaps Batu had begun warming up to them. To her surprise, he had smiled at her and not at Nemeku. Still, he would not speak.

Today, Nemeku sat on the floor of the ger with Batu attempting to teach him how to play knucklebones. Mandukhai hovered by the door, chewing her lower lip.

"They will be fine," Esige reassured her. "I won't leave."

Mandukhai had not ventured so far from Batu since he had arrived. She worried about what might happen in her absence. But the other tribes had started arriving, and she needed to meet with the lesser khans individually to discuss the upcoming *kurultai* vote. She needed them to support her decision, which would be a hard sell.

Esige placed her hands on Mandukhai's shoulders and turned her around, nudging her out the door. "Go."

Mandukhai had no choice. She knew that, but she hated going. As she shuffled out the door, she glanced back once more, only to have Esige filling the doorway, waving her onward. Then the girl closed the door firmly in her face.

Squaring her shoulders, Mandukhai marched away toward the Alyghuchid tribe's section of the growing camp. Unige had been a loyal supporter of Manduul, and his wife, Satai, had been a close friend to Mandukhai for years now. This should be the easiest alliance to secure.

The moment she reached their section of camp, Mandukhai recognized the white-domed ger lined with Borjigin blue needlework around the doorframe and the top of the walls. She had spent several afternoons taking tea here with Satai.

Mandukhai called out her greeting and was escorted inside by one of Satai's servants. The inside was even more elaborate than the outside. Silks donned the walls. Persian rugs lined the floor. The posts holding up the roof were a brilliant shade of red, with elaborate carvings of yellow birds in flight spiraling upward. They had poured most of their wealth into this ger.

"Queen Regent, we are pleased to host you," Satai said as she stood and motioned to an empty chair at the table. Only the wealthy had tables and chairs. They were bulky to move, even when broken down.

Unige didn't bother rising for Mandukhai, a sign that did not bode well for this conversation. Did he not recognize her station above him? Unige was in his forties now, and gray streaked his temples and lightened the roots around his scalp. His tired eyes watched Mandukhai inscrutably as she thanked Satai and settled in the offered seat.

Satai poured a tea for Mandukhai, then for Unige. He didn't touch his, so Mandukhai only gave her own a very brief, polite sip—hardly more than a few drops. If he would not drink, she would not either. It made her suspicious about what could be in the tea.

"Lord Unige, you were always loyal to my husband," Mandukhai began. "He often spoke of you with great esteem." She wanted to soften him up before she moved in for the kill.

"Did he?" Unige sounded disbelieving. "I always believed he thought I was a simpleton."

Mandukhai's brows climbed slightly at this. "Why would you believe that? He valued your opinions. Manduul was not in the habit of asking advice from people he didn't respect the opinions of."

Unige sat back in his seat, folding his arms over his chest. "I would love to hear what he said, specifically."

Mandukhai knew she could not hesitate, but Unige had caught her in a trap. She had attempted softening him up but had nothing real to offer him. She had no choice but to lie. Manduul hardly ever talked about Unige. "He told me you were among the first to align with him when he became Great Khan, and he respected you all the more for it. He said that very loyalty was why he allowed you into his private council meetings. He trusted you had his best interests at heart."

The two of them studied each other. Unige remained inscrutable as he weighed the truth of her words. Mandukhai made certain her expression remained gentle and open so that he would swallow every word she fed him. Men often misjudged her because she was a woman, and she needed to use that to her advantage.

"What is it you want from me, Lady Mandukhai?" he asked at last. "You didn't come here to drink my wife's tea."

Mandukhai nodded. "I didn't. I simply came to ask if I have your support as a loyal member of Manduul's council. You know I am capable of handling the selection for candidates at *kurultai*. I sat in on several meetings with you and Manduul over the years and shared my wisdom. When it comes time to put a name forward, can I count on you to support my decision?"

Unige bit the inside of his lip, making his cheek sink in momentarily. Then he cocked his head to the side. "Manduul made his wishes very clear. That is what I support. In the absence of an heir of Genghis, he named Lord Unebolod his successor."

Mandukhai was prepared for this response. She set down her teacup and folded her hands in her lap. "His last will clearly stated, should no heirs remain, the Queen Regent shall rule until a worthy Lord has won her favor and become Great Khan at *kurultai*."

He opened his mouth to retort, but no words spilled out. Instead, he sat in his seat, arms over his chest, slack-jawed as the truth sank in. Mandukhai waited patiently for him to puzzle this out for himself and put the pieces together.

"You do not favor him," Unige said at last.

Satai's eyes widened in alarm as she understood the implication. Everyone had been ready to accept Unebolod.

"I never said that," Mandukhai clarified.

"Then you *do* favor him."

"I never said that either."

Unige huffed and rubbed at his forehead. "This makes my head ache. What is it you intend to do, Lady Mandukhai?"

"I intend to do what is best for the Mongol Nation," she said plainly. "All I ask is whether I have your support to do as Manduul trusted me to do."

Once more, Unige chewed the inside of his cheek as he stewed over her proposal. Not knowing who she intended to name would be the hardest part. But if Unebolod accepted her offer to become Great Khan until Batu came of age, she did not want these Lords believing she would not name him. However, the opposite was true as well. If Unebolod refused, she might have to name the boy. Mandukhai certainly did not want to mislead these men, or they would never support her when the time actually came. She needed their votes to assure her victory should Unebolod not agree.

"I will honor Manduul's final wishes," Unige said at last, but the words sounded like they pained him.

Mandukhai suppressed her grin. She knew going into this meeting that Unige would be easier to convince.

It was the rest of the Lords she had to worry about.

Unebolod stood in Albeq's ger, resisting the urge to pace a hole through the nice, colorful rugs. Albeq's wife would not thank him for that. He and Albeq had a history in combat. Albeq's tribe had nearly been swept into Bigirsen's forces when Unebolod came to his rescue and pushed Bigirsen's men into retreat. In exchange, Albeq had promised Unebolod support just a few months ago, assuming Bayan died. Which he did. What would Albeq do if he knew the truth about Batu? *I cannot tell anyone.*

Mandukhai must have known he could never share the secret of the boy's parentage or it could ruin his chances at *kurultai*. But if he could ensure he had the support, perhaps they would choose him even if she did not. Then he would not be turning against his word to her and forcefully taking what he had worked so hard for. The Mongol Lords would hand it to him, beg him to take it. He needed this plan to work. After that, she could choose for herself what she wanted to do—accept him as her husband or go her own way. He hoped she would see reason and choose him, but he could not hang a lifetime of work on her whims.

He had worked to build his reputation and gather the respect of the other tribal leaders all of his life, hoping he would become Great Khan one day. He loved Mandukhai. There had been a time he thought they had wanted the same thing. Clearly, she had pulled the wool over his eyes. But now he saw everything clearly.

Four of the tribal khans were gathered in Albeq's ger with Unebolod. For nearly an hour, they had been arguing over just how Mandukhai had overstepped her position. Each thought he knew what was best.

"This is pointless," Albeq snapped, drawing a few dirty looks from the other khans. "What is it you want from us, Unebolod? You know you have our support, mine, at least. But you also assured me you had her under control."

"I want nothing from you," Unebolod said. He had to be careful that they did not choose him because he asked them to. They had to come to this conclusion on their own. "And I never once said I controlled her. She made me believe we wanted the same thing. I am just as put out by this as all of you. Perhaps more so. I thought—" He choked off, averting his gaze to the floor. Part of this was an act to make them buy his story. But it was not all an act. He felt betrayed. Unebolod huffed and raised his gaze. "It doesn't matter what I thought. She has not refused me. She simply has not named me. All I ask is that, when the time comes, you each do what you believe is best for the Mongol Nation. No matter what."

Bagatur, the Kharchin khan and his near cousin, adopted an expression of sympathy.

"We have discussed this before," Albeq replied. "You know where I stand."

A few of the others nodded in agreement. Unebolod was uncertain exactly what that meant, but it seemed to bode well for his chances.

Togochi met one of the Tabun horse traders, attempting to strike up a deal to bolster the numbers in his own herd. Tabun horses were not as strong as Oirat horses, but he had little choice in the matter. The Oirat would never trade with him—nor he with them. Not after what had just happened.

As he headed back toward home, something odd caught his attention. He ducked back behind a ger and peered out to watch as Unebolod stood outside of Albeq khan's ger with three other lesser khans. They exchanged words he could not quite hear, then Unebolod shook with each of them. Had Mandukhai chosen Unebolod and now he strengthened his position by meeting these lesser khans?

Unebolod turned his direction and Togochi ducked back out of sight. A moment later, his brother strode past. Togochi noticed the small smirk in the corner of Unebolod's mouth. Something about this didn't seem right. Togochi had learned to trust his gut instincts over the years.

If anyone knew if Mandukhai had confirmed the upcoming vote for Unebolod, it would be Jaghan. Those two women were as close as sisters.

Togochi waited a few minutes to be certain no one would spot him, then slipped through a different set of gers and crossed the massive camp toward his own home. If Unebolod was working against Mandukhai, what would Togochi do? He respected Unebolod far more than other men, and if anyone deserved this title, it was Unebolod. But he had made a promise to Manduul to support Mandukhai's decision. At the moment, he felt like a sheep on a string being tugged in both directions.

Jaghan sat outside in the sunshine with the boys, holding their daughter against her chest as she watched the two boys play. When she saw him approaching, her face lit up with a brilliant smile. Togochi adored Jaghan. *How have I been so lucky when Unebolod has been so unlucky?* Togochi did not understand what he had done to deserve such fortune.

"Torudur, inside," Togochi said.

The older boy sulked and his eyes welled with tears as Togochi scooped up his brother.

"Now!"

Torudur jumped, rushing through the doorway as fast as his short little legs could carry him.

Jaghan frowned as she stood. "What is it?"

Togochi only shook his head and stepped into the ger. Jaghan seemed to understand, following him in and closing the door as he set down Babaquai.

"You are scaring me a little, Togochi," Jaghan said. She sidled toward the bed and laid the baby girl on the mattress.

"Has Mandukhai given Unebolod the agreement?" he asked. It was not the first time he had asked her this question, but something had changed.

Jaghan sighed and strolled toward him, sliding her arms around his waist. "Again? You are too worried about this. She will do the right thing."

"So that's a no." He needed to be certain.

"No. Not to my knowledge. She gave him an offer. He has not yet accepted it."

Togochi's chest clenched. *Then what was Unebolod doing?*

His face must have given away something of his anxiety because Jaghan pulled back and her frown deepened. "What is it?"

"I need you to speak with her."

"Togochi—"

"Before you say anything, this is different," Togochi said. "I ... saw something. Unebolod was striking up some sort of deal with four of the lesser khans. If she hasn't named him ..."

Jaghan's lips parted. She licked them nervously. "I don't understand this thing between the two of them. How can two people who love each other so much be so at odds? Why would they not just accept each other and be done with it?"

Togochi couldn't help but agree with his wife. "There must be some reason she has not named him yet. I just cannot puzzle out what it might be."

Jaghan's gaze darted to the floor. A moment later, she turned and walked across the ger toward the jug of *airag* to pour him a cup.

He scowled. *She is avoiding me.* Togochi stepped toward her. "What do you know, Jaghan?"

"I don't know, Togochi," Jaghan said, but her voice trembled ever so slightly. "She has been through so much since Manduul's death and the attack. It must be a great burden to bear."

He closed his eyes. The attack. That must be it.

Jaghan pressed the cup into his hand. He peeled his eyes open and offered her a thankful smile before taking a drink.

Mandukhai had said those men had not raped her, but would she ever admit the truth? Perhaps it was as simple as that. She was worried about becoming a wife, even if it was with Unebolod. Togochi down the *airag*.

"I still think you need to speak to her," he said, turning the silver cup in his hand. "If he has the support of four lesser khans, she should prepare herself. She needs to meet with Mendu sooner than later."

Togochi could not imagine what would happen if Unebolod and Mandukhai ended up at odds with each other. However, he had given his vow to Manduul to carry out his last wishes. He owed the Borjigin more than he could ever repay in his lifetime for what his tribe had done to Prince Molon years ago. Mandukhai, for now, was the representation of the Borjigin line, chosen for this task by Manduul.

Togochi owed it to Manduul to support Mandukhai. *Hopefully, she truly does know what is best.*

CHAPTER FIFTEEN

The Fool and the Moon

Summer warmth blew on a breeze as Mandukhai rode Dust with Batu seated in front of her. His body could not handle riding on his own like other boys his age, and Mandukhai was not about to risk his health attempting to force the issue. His entire little body was stiff, pressing back against her. His little hands clung to the belt tethering him to her. This was Batu's first ride since the fall that had nearly killed him. She understood his fear.

As she rode toward the base of Mount Burkhan Khaldun, along the rocky path worn smooth by centuries of other Mongols making such a sacred pilgrimage, Mandukhai basked in the sunshine's warmth of her face. Esige and Nemeku rode with them as well, each on their own horses. Nemeku rode like he was born in a saddle, just as Esige had in those early years. While Mandukhai had not had children of her own yet, she adored these children gathered around her as if they were her own flesh and blood.

In a month, enough tribes would be gathered for her to call a vote. The festival would pave the way to *kurultai*. Days of wrestling, archery, and races both on foot and horseback. They would form several groups for each event, beginning as young as seven and breaking off by age all the way up to fifty. Mandukhai could not recall the last time the Mongol Nation had come together for such an event. Had it even been in her lifetime? She hoped enough tribes would come for the festival that she could call for *kurultai* at the end. *I only need the majority*, she thought.

"Can't I enter the horse race?" Nemeku pleaded once more. He put this petition forward nearly every day with the same pitiful expression on his face.

"You are not old enough yet, Nemeku," Mandukhai said firmly. "Two more years."

"I could ride for him," Nemeku said, nodding toward Batu.

The other boy gazed at Nemeku with those always calculating, wolfish eyes, but still said nothing. They all knew Batu was far from ready to ride, let alone race.

"No. And that is my final word."

Nemeku muttered under his breath. Mandukhai could not make out the words, but she understood his sentiment well enough, and had he said that around his father he would have earned a cuffing. *I am allowing him to grow soft,* Mandukhai thought sadly.

How long before Bigirsen came for his son? Nemeku had asked for him a few times. Mandukhai did not have the heart to explain that it was his father who had killed his mother. Someday, he would learn the truth. Would he resent her for keeping it from him?

"The day she lets you ride is the day she lets me wrestle," Esige said. Her tone dripped with resentment.

Mandukhai suppressed a sigh. "Esige, we have been through this. You are a girl and they do not allow girls to compete."

"*You* are making the rules this time," Esige pointed out. She leveled her gaze at Mandukhai. "Lady Altan is competing in the archery contest. How is this any different?"

Mandukhai had to admit, Esige had a point. "She is commander. You are a princess."

"Then make me a commander!" Esige exclaimed. "I've already beaten most of the men here in camp at wrestling, and Chakicha proved a little more challenging, but I still defeated him."

Mandukhai snorted. "Commander! You've never been in—Wait. Who is Chakicha and when did you wrestle him?"

Esige straightened and raised her chin a touch arrogantly. "Last night. Some teenagers were wrestling for fun. I beat one boy and this hulking Tabun guy entered the ring. He insisted on redeeming the dignity of his friend." She didn't even bother trying to hide her grin. "I find big guys like him are easier to beat because they assume their size is their advantage. But it makes them all slow." She shrugged. "He was no different."

Tabun? Anger pulsed through Mandukhai. She took a deep breath to keep her emotions in check. "*Lord* Chakicha?"

Esige's grin broadened. "Yup."

"Do you have any idea what you have done?" Mandukhai hissed. "His is Albeq khan's son. When his father finds out what you have done, I could lose his support. We are grasping at drops of water here, Esige, and you could have cost us." Mandukhai rubbed at her forehead.

Esige sagged a little in the saddle. "Chakicha didn't seem that upset afterward. He offered me a drink of his *airag*, then asked when I considered settling down." She shuddered and grimaced.

Mandukhai's breath caught. "What did you say?"

"That he was climbing the wrong cliff for an eagle he could never catch." She rolled her shoulders, licked her lips, and glanced at Mandukhai. "It was all in good fun."

All in good fun! What sort of damage control would this innocent wrestling match require? Mandukhai needed Albeq, and if Esige insulted Albeq's son, Mandukhai had two choices. She could let it go and pray nothing happened ... or she could offer Esige in marriage. Mandukhai mentally calculated her odds at *kurultai* to have her chosen candidate installed as Great Khan without Albeq's vote. Without Unebolod, it didn't look promising.

"Lady Mandukhai!" Jaghan's familiar voice called out.

Mandukhai heard the hooves galloping to catch up to them and carefully turned in the saddle to see Jaghan racing up to join them. Jaghan reined in to match Mandukhai's pace when she reached them, and her gaze fell on Batu.

"Jaghan, what brings you into our company?" Mandukhai asked, smiling at her long-time friend.

Jaghan glanced at Esige and Nemeku, and Mandukhai understood well enough.

"Esige, why don't you show Nemeku why he is not ready to enter the races this year?" Mandukhai asked.

Esige grinned. With only a few words between them, she and Nemeku shot away along the path. Mandukhai watched them go, smiling with pride.

"Mandukhai, the men are getting restless," Jaghan said the moment the two were out of earshot.

Mandukhai tensed in her saddle. Batu kept his gaze forward, watching the other two children race away.

"Men are often restless," Mandukhai said.

Jaghan snorted in agreement, but she glanced over her shoulder as if anxious, then leaned closer to Mandukhai. "Togochi is asking questions. Keeping a secret from my husband is one thing, but I cannot lie to him. Please. I beg you. Togochi is loyal to you and to his word to Manduul. Tell him the truth."

Mandukhai wanted to trust Togochi. He had certainly earned that trust. Yet Batu was still so fragile. The more people who knew of his parentage, the more danger he would be in. Her gaze drifted down to the boy, only to find him staring back at her with those knowing eyes. Mandukhai stroked his cheek, then raised her chin.

"I need Unebolod to agree to my terms," Mandukhai said. "He has been particularly stubborn. Once he agrees, I will talk with the rest of the men."

"The two of you have hardly spoken since this boy arrived, and that only makes the men more anxious," Jaghan said, then lowered her voice. "Mandukhai, Togochi sent me to speak to you because he is worried. I won't pretend to understand what is going on, but he wanted me to tell you this and hope that we can speak reasonably." She breathed deeply, straightening in her saddle. "Four of the tribal khans have been meeting with Unebolod."

The words pierced Mandukhai in the gut. *Why is he meeting with the khans behind my back? He must be preparing for* kurultai, she told herself. *Does this mean he will accept my offer?*

"Two more tribes are on the way, and should arrive within the week," Jaghan said. "The Ongud and the Urainkhai. You need to speak with Mendu khan before Unebolod has a chance. Togochi is worried that Mendu's allegiance is too volatile. You need to secure the Khorlod. Togochi supports you, but his vote is not as strong as the vote from the Khorlod khan."

"My tribe will support me," Mandukhai said confidently.

Jaghan chewed her lip.

"What?" Mandukhai reined to a halt, suddenly terrified.

"Togochi says he learned Unebolod extracted a deal from Korgiz khan before returning to Mongke Bulag," Jaghan said.

Mandukhai blinked fiercely to rein in her tears. Why would these men not follow her as Manduul had ordered? If he formed some agreement with four of the tribes already, and Korgiz really was on Unebolod's side, that meant the Urainkhai and the Khorlod would be the deciding factor if Unebolod intended sweeping in to steal *kurultai. He wouldn't do that, would he?* He certainly had been distant and angry with her lately.

Silence wrapped around Mandukhai like a protective wall.

A small hand grasped her own, and Mandukhai blinked back tears as her gaze met Batu. Such soulful eyes! How could he have come from two such as Bayan and Siker? Yet his touch, his small squeeze of reassurance, gave Mandukhai strength.

"If you intend to oppose Unebolod, you need at least one more," Jaghan said.

Oppose Unebolod ... Mandukhai had never considered them in opposition. She simply wanted him to respect her. Besides, he gave his word to Manduul. He had made the same vow as every other Lord—that a true heir of Genghis would rise to Great Khan above all others.

"Why do you hesitate to accept Unebolod's offer?" Jaghan asked. "I thought it was what you wanted."

"I did. I do. But Manduul has placed a great duty on my shoulders. It is a great responsibility to be the one who determines the course of our Khans in the future."

"Sounds more like a curse to me," Jaghan said tersely. "As if Manduul wanted to keep you from being truly happy. Isn't Unebolod Manduul's choice as well?"

Mandukhai chewed her lip. "You were there that night. Manduul was clear. In the absence of a male heir to the line of Genghis, Unebolod would be next."

Jaghan fell silent, glancing at Batu as they rode the worn paths together.

Jaghan and Esige were the only friends Mandukhai had left. Satai was not truly a friend, but someone interested in acting like a friend when it benefitted her. Siker—her belly growing with Issama's child—had packed up her belongings and left with the rest of the Uyghur families months ago to join Issama and Bigirsen in the south. Not that Siker had ever truly been her friend. Only the Borjigin and those loyal to Togochi or Unebolod remained.

"I guess I don't understand," Jaghan said at last. "I know he has rights." She glanced again at Batu. "But he is young. And you have been in love with Unebolod for so long. Can you not be with Unebolod and name the boy the heir?"

"I have asked Unebolod the same. But he refuses to answer." Mandukhai stopped, worried that Jaghan would tell Togochi, and rounded on Jaghan. "Not a word to anyone."

"No." Jaghan's eyes were as wide as saucers.

"I need you to swear it, Jaghan."

Jaghan's breathing became shallow as she sweat. But she nodded. "I swear it. I will not tell another soul. But ... does that mean you will not accept Unebolod's proposal?"

Mandukhai's shoulders slumped, and she turned along their path once more. "That depends on him."

They resumed their ride. The weight of this recent development created a hush between the two women. Jaghan knew how Mandukhai felt about Unebolod. She had learned the truth during a drunken confession nearly two years ago now.

"Tell me, Jaghan, are you familiar with the tale of the fool and the moon?" Mandukhai asked, steeling herself. When Jaghan gave no affirmation, Mandukhai glanced at the sky. A sliver of the moon was visible against the blue. "A thirsty man came upon a well for a drink, but when he gazed into the water, he saw the moon. Believing it trapped in the well, he threw down a rope to attempt a rescue. He wanted to bring the moon up to him, to where it belonged. But after giving a mighty yank, the rope whipped up at his face. He fell back only to discover the moon was above him the whole time."

Jaghan's cheeks heated.

From so high up the mountain path, Mandukhai could see the vast spread of the gathered tribes. Thousands of men down there would declare their support for Unebolod.

Tears spilled down her cheeks, and she quickly swiped them away. Mandukhai *did* love Unebolod more than she had ever loved anyone before. More than she could ever imagine loving anyone else. But she had made a sacred vow to the Lords when she was named Queen Regent. To break that vow would destroy her everlasting soul. Choosing a Great Khan was not a matter of love. He had to understand that, or he was no better than the fool trying to rescue the moon.

As long as Batu drew breath, Unebolod would have no choice in the matter. He could either accept her proposal and agree to raise Batu when he was old enough and strong enough, or she would have no other choice but to proclaim the boy in front of everyone—upon threat of her immortal soul.

And then everyone would know an heir of Genghis still lived.

And Siker and Issama would know that Batu had survived.

The Strength of Women

Togochi had insisted on sitting in on this meeting with Mandukhai. He knew that Lord Mendu, the khan of his own tribe, could sometimes be sensitive and Togochi felt it best if he showed the Khorlod khan that he aligned with Mandukhai. It also gave Togochi the ability to wedge himself into the conversation to steer it the right way if Mandukhai seemed to flounder. Not that he had seen her flounder much before, but she had not been the same since the Oirat attack. Togochi would not take chances.

Mendu welcomed Mandukhai into the ger, bowing respectfully as she stepped over the threshold. *So far, so good.*

Bright sunlight streamed through the open smoke hole in the roof. It made the rich red silk walls glow and give the entire ger a reddish hue. Mendu showed his wealth with the silken display, along with the table lined with silver cups and trays—all of which were loaded with food. It was not a garish display, but enough to show off his position in the empire.

Mandukhai seated herself first, and Togochi slid onto the bench beside her. Mendu and two of his advisors settled across the table from them.

"Please, eat," Mendu said, gesturing to the feast.

Mandukhai gave her thanks and added a few pieces of lamb *buuz* to her plate alongside a wedge of melon. The fruit was rare, grown in Hami and exported across the empire. Only men of wealth could afford it.

Togochi also added food to his plate, watching the men across from him as he did. They waited for the guests to make their selection before loading their own plates. No one ate, though. He glanced from the corner of his eyes at Mandukhai, who sat demurely with her hands folded in her lap. She didn't touch the food. She wouldn't until someone else ate first. It was an old habit she had picked up since she was poisoned five years ago. He ate one of the *buuz* on his plate, then washed it down with a drink of *airag* the servant had poured into a silver cup for him. This seemed to satisfy Mandukhai, and she took a sip of her own drink but only picked at the food.

"I was a little surprised you wanted to meet with me, Queen Regent," Mendu said, breaking the silence as everyone ate. "We assumed the matter of succession was well in hand, so your request was curious. What do you want from me if we are already set for the vote at *kurultai*?" He glanced pointedly at Togochi.

Months ago, when he sent the news of Manduul's death, Togochi had assumed, like everyone else, that Mandukhai would choose Unebolod quickly. He blanched a little now as Mandukhai threw a sharp glare at him.

"Is it set?" she asked innocently. Togochi admired her ability to feign ignorance. She played this tune like a horse fiddle with many of the men over the years. He had learned long ago not to underestimate her. "Funny, I have announced no candidates yet. How could the vote be set, then? Unless the Lords are working against me, and against my husband's final command as Great Khan."

Mendu's brows shot up and he failed to cover his alarm as he drank from his own cup. After wiping his mouth, he said, "I understand your husband gave you this gift. A noble thing, really. But let us be open here, my Lady."

"I'm not a Lady. I am your Queen Regent. Since we are speaking openly." She shot a pointed look at Mendu as her fingers toyed with the edge of her cup.

Mendu's jaw twitched.

"I heard Manduul's words myself, my Lord khan," Togochi said, smoothing out the ruffled feathers with his calm tone. "Just moments before he died."

"All the same," Mendu replied sharply. "He gave you this appointment, Queen Regent, as a final gift, a piece of freedom women rarely have. So that you may choose your next husband. Not so you could control how we choose to vote."

Mandukhai took a slow drink and set the cup down on the tabletop primly. Once more, Togochi admired her. Though outwardly she appeared calm and collected, he knew her well enough to understand that a storm gathered beneath the surface. The dragon would soon appear.

"Indeed," she said, nodding once in ascent to Mendu's comment. "I would not dream of controlling the vote. To do so would hinder the fidelity of *kurultai*. What I *do* expect is the respect this title affords me. A title that places me above even you, Mendu khan. I also expect the Lords to honor their oaths to carry out Manduul's commands, even after his death, until a new Great Khan is chosen."

Mendu opened his mouth, but for the moment remained silent. At last, he broke from his stunned spell. "What do you want?"

Mandukhai smiled sweetly. "Respect. And the support of your tribe for whomever I select at *kurultai*."

"In other words, my vote."

"You boil things down too simply. I find this a common problem. Your vote is yours. But if anyone else tries to step in and steal *kurultai*, I expect you to support me. Manduul trusted me with this for a reason. If you don't believe me, you can ask Togochi. He knows how much Manduul trusted my wisdom." She motioned toward Togochi.

He had to admit, Mandukhai had expertly backed Mendu into a corner. If he refused, he risked being outcast once a new Great Khan was selected. Mandukhai would never choose a man who did not support her fully—another reason he still firmly believed she would choose Unebolod. What other choice did she have, really, aside from himself? The idea of becoming Great Khan himself was laughable. And incredibly unappealing. Togochi had no desire to run the Nation. He only wanted to ensure that whatever happened was best for all Mongols.

"Mendu, after everything our people have been through, after everything the Mongols have been through since the fall of Genghis's empire, it is more important than ever to adhere to our traditions," Togochi said, resting his forearms on the table. "The Khorlod have been on the wrong side of history for too long, and I have dedicated my life to setting things right. Do you truly believe I would sit beside her if I did not have faith that this was the right thing to do?"

"I respect what you have accomplished for yourself, Togochi," Mendu said evenly. "And I also appreciate your dedication to absolving the misdeeds of my father—of our people. But if we are to move out of this dark period in our history toward something better, we need strength to do so. You know better than I do that Unebolod is the man we need. Even Manduul knew that."

Togochi sighed softly and nodded in agreement. "You are right. Of course."

Mandukhai shifted, not bothering to hide her alarm as she gaped at Togochi.

He held up a hand to her before she rebutted. "However," he continued, "my understanding of exactly what strength is has changed over the years. The strength of a man comes from the strength of a woman who guides him through life. And I have seen the strength of women. I have underestimated their value and learned to listen when they offered their advice."

Mandukhai's breath hitched beside him. She gave Togochi a look that combined alarm and curiosity neatly together.

He pressed on before either she or Mendu could interrupt. "None I have met have been stronger than Mandukhai, and I value her advice above most others. You would be a fool to not do the same."

For a moment, no one spoke. Then one advisor leaned close to Mendu and whispered into his ear. Mendu grimaced and nodded.

Meanwhile, Mandukhai stared at Togochi with her brows somewhat furrowed, examining him. Her lips parted ever so slightly. Had his words genuinely dazed her so much? She stared at him as if she had never truly seen him before.

"As Togochi said," Mendu said at last, breaking the deep, awkward silence, "we value wisdom and cannot afford to repeat the mistakes of our past. Tradition *is* important." The other advisor whispered something in Mendu's ear, then Mendu continued without missing a beat. "We know such power has been given to women in the past, though it was centuries ago. My fear is that we will end up in a similar situation where it could take years to make a proper selection. With men like Bigirsen clawing at our threshold, we cannot afford to wait years for a Great Khan. We need one now. As long as you intend to give us one before we leave this place, Queen Regent, you have the Khorlod support. But if we leave this place without a Great Khan, all bets are off."

Mandukhai broke from her spell when Mendu called her by her title, shaking her head as if beating away cobwebs. She smiled sweetly at Mendu. "I will be sure we have a Great Khan placed before the *sulde* of Genghis before you leave here. After the festival."

Mendu stood, and Mandukhai followed his lead. The two exchanged a shake in agreement. Togochi rose slowly, watching Mendu for signs of danger. He did not want to believe that Mendu khan would do anything foolish, but Togochi could not afford to underestimate anyone around her. Too many men stood to gain something from her downfall.

Togochi said farewell to Mendu as well, and he followed Mandukhai outside. She walked at a brisk pace away from the Khorlod section of the camp and he rushed to match her stride. Once they were well away from Mendu's ger, she stopped and pivoted to face him, her expression inscrutable.

The sudden stop alarmed Togochi. He jerked to a halt. She stabbed a finger into his chest. He jumped in alarm. What was wrong with her?

"Why did you say those things to him?" she demanded.

Togochi's bushy brows knitted together. "What things?"

"About women!"

He pursed his lips and gave a small shrug. "It felt like the right thing to say at the time. And it's true. Why does it matter?"

Once more, Mandukhai studied him like he was some new thing to dissect. He shifted uncomfortably under that gaze.

At last, she turned on her heel and grumbled, "It doesn't." Then she resumed her march toward her side of camp.

He hustled alongside her, dying to know what that was all about.

Esige had slipped off while Mandukhai was away. She had changed into breaches and a leather haltered top. Her hair hung down her back in intricate braids, swaying as she rushed toward where the wrestlers gathered to practice. Mandukhai would never approve of Esige joining these practices, which was the entire reason Esige had to slip away while Mandukhai was gone. Batu was well-guarded in the ger and in Tuya's care. Nemeku was playing with Jaghan's boys. Esige escaped and found a bit of fun for herself.

A gathering of tribes this large had not been done in her lifetime. As Esige rushed through the camp, she noted the colorful banners and vast number of people. It also meant she had new contenders to challenge her skills. Unebolod had taught her well how to defend herself, and she expanded on his lessons with tricks of her own.

"Here comes the warrior princess," Dawa teased as she joined the ring of young men who had gathered to watch one of the practices.

Dawa meant it as an insult, but Esige took it as a compliment. Better to be a warrior princess them a made-up doll to be paraded around—something she knew she would have to do during this festival.

"I think she's glorious," Chakicha said, grinning at Esige as he joined them.

Dawa eyed Chakicha up, clearly assessing this new male threat to what his misguided mind believed was his. He gulped a little and shrugged. "It would be better if she learned a woman's place."

"The day you defeat me, I will willingly bow to your superiority," Esige replied.

Chakicha chortled. He offered his skin of *airag*, but Esige politely declined as her focus turned to the men wrestling in the ring. She did not want Chakicha to think the two of them were so familiar after the last time. Instead, she studied the way the wrestlers moved, committing each piece to memory and making note of their weaknesses.

The bigger man won, pinning the other facedown in the dirt. Once he was declared the winner, he backed off and raised his arms victoriously in the air.

"Who would dare challenge me next?" he taunted.

Before anyone stepped forward, Esige sauntered into the ring, eyeing him up. She didn't know this young man. He must have been one of the fresh arrivals. His size was impressive, but she knew size didn't matter.

He grinned crookedly at her. "Hello pretty thing. I would be happy to wrestle with you later."

The comment turned Esige's blood hot with anger. Men and their assumptions! She swayed her hips, playing the part he wanted her to play.

"Watch out!" Chakicha called to the young man. "She's a viper."

The young man's gaze swept over her with uninhibited appreciation for what he saw. He reached out to slide his arm around her shoulder. Esige snapped into action. She threw her hip into him to unbalance him. Her hand clamped onto his wrist, pressing her fingertips into the pressure point Unebolod had taught her, then yanked it back at a sharp angle enough to bring him down but not hurt him. He dropped to his knees, startled by her sudden movements. Before he could twist his body around, she wrenched his arm further back and pressed her knee into his back. He fell forward, catching his balance with his free hand.

The men around the ring broke into a roar of laughter.

Esige leaned closer, careful that her braid was away from his grasp. "I think I've seen enough to know you aren't worth my time," she whispered into his ear.

He growled and pulled at his arm.

Esige release him and shuffled back into a defensive position. He surged to his feet and took a few angry steps toward her, violence in his dark eyes.

Before she reacted, a fist flew past her shoulder and connected with the young man's jaw. He stumbled sideways, grasping his jaw as he worked the muscles.

Esige turned to her would-be rescuer with her hands planted firmly on her hips. But her eyes moved up. And up. This man was tall! And older than the others.

"This is Princess Esige," he growled at the young man, "the Queen Regent's ward. Learn a little self-control."

Esige's jaw twitched with anger. She didn't need anyone coming to her rescue! "I had this under control."

"All due respect, princess, but it is one thing to play at wrestling and another to fight off a stronger man," her rescuer replied. He glared over her shoulder.

The sudden shuffle of feet running the other way caught her attention, but she didn't dare look back. She would not flinch.

"I'm Boragan," he said, offering his hand to shake.

Esige raised her brows and crossed her arms over her chest. "So?"

"Heir of the Ongud," he clarified, as if she should have already known.

All Esige knew for certain was that Mandukhai had been Ongud. "And?"

"And I've been looking for you," he said, nodding out of the ring as other wrestlers stepped forward to challenge each other.

Esige marched alongside him, then eyed him impatiently. Somehow, she already knew why he was looking for her and she was firmly against it. "You've found me. Get to the point already."

Boragan scowled, and his jaw twitched. "I had hoped you would be interested in speaking about an alliance."

An alliance... "You mean marriage."

"Is there a difference?"

Chakicha snickered a few feet away, eavesdropping on the conversation.

"Don't you already have wives?" she asked sharply.

"So?"

"How greedy can one man be?"

Boragan's eyes widened in alarm. "It seems you respect one thing." He waved toward the wrestlers. "If you win, you walk away. If I win, we speak with the Queen Regent."

Esige eyed him up and down. Boragan was no bigger than any of the other men she had wrestled, though he was taller. But something in his eyes differed from others. An almost mad determination to prove himself that bordered on dangerous. She shook her head. "I'll pass."

Esige turned away, but took only two steps before he seized her arm. Her heart thumped as his fingers squeezed into her upper arm.

"It would be a mistake to walk away right now," he said.

Her eyes had locked on his hand. A man on the edge of rage was a dangerous thing. Esige could hear her heartbeat as clear as the voices of the surrounding men. "If you don't let go of me, you will regret ever touching me."

The two of them glared at one another, waiting for the other to back down. It only lasted a few seconds before he let go, but it seemed much longer for her. She still felt his grip on her arm even as she marched away, but resisted the urge to rub at it. Esige would not show him any signs of weakness.

Boragan was dangerous.

CHAPTER SEVENTEEN

A Matter of Oaths

Thousands had flocked to Mount Burkhan Khaldun. Mandukhai had never seen so many Mongols gathered in one place in all her life. She took rides on Dust's back up the mountainous slopes with Batu as often as she could, just to see the swelling of gers. Tens of thousands. At the top, they would dismount and gaze across the massive valley floor. A field of domed gers stretched as far as she could see across the valley.

The Shrine of the First Queen had mysteriously appeared one morning, nestled at the base of the mountain path beside a stream. No one could explain the appearance of the shrine. It had disappeared at least a hundred years ago without a trace. The shrine represented the first queen of the Mongols, long before Genghis. Mandukhai had watched people make a pilgrimage to the shrine to make offerings and give prayer since the morning it arrived. One of the tribes at Mount Burkhan Khaldun must have had it tucked away somewhere. Mandukhai saw the arrival of this missing shrine as a good omen. What else could it be?

Mandukhai had avoided confronting Unebolod about meeting with the lesser khans behind her back. The two of them had always confronted things like that together. But now she feared that something between them had broken and she could not fix it. What did it mean that he would do this in the first place? Did he realize it undermined her authority? Some might even see it as treason. Mandukhai could not contemplate branding him a traitor. *How did Manduul find the strength to name Bayan a traitor?* Mandukhai wondered pitifully as she oversaw the construction of the archery ranges. It was no wonder it had killed Manduul. She now understood his predicament. *I don't* know *that Unebolod is committing treason.*

Batu tugged at Mandukhai's hand, pointing at a banner as it fluttered along the edge of the archery range. His banner. Did he know? Mandukhai crouched beside him, pointing at the soaring golden eagle against a blue backdrop as she spoke.

"That is your banner, Batu, the banner of the Borjigin, the banner of Genghis." A memory of her vision with Genghis rushed to the surface. A small boy with a broken body getting picked at by chickens and crying. No one had come to his aid. Tears pricked her eyes. Genghis knew who Batu was back then, but she did not.

Batu stared at her in that curious way he often did. His golden gaze pierced her, as if reaching into her soul and understanding her. But he was just a boy. Such understanding would be beyond his years.

Mandukhai licked her lips and offered a warm smile. "Years ago, the spirits offered me a great gift." She glanced around, but only Boke lingered nearby. Other men and women bustled around on their own urgent tasks further down the mountain pass. Boke watched everyone around the two of them. Mandukhai lowered her voice, just to be certain. Visions were sacred, and the spirits chose whom they spoke with carefully. It was a sacred trust, which was the reason she had not told Unebolod years ago. Soon she would have to, though.

Mandukhai had not told another soul of her vision, but Batu would not speak of it. He never spoke to begin with. "Genghis Khan came to me in a vision. He promised me a great gift when I had lost my only child. I believe he showed me you, Batu. Do you know why?"

Batu's only reaction was a small twitch of his eyebrows.

"Because you, Batu, son of Bayan, are special." Mandukhai stroked his hair affectionately. "You are the last of the Borjigin wolves, heir of the great Genghis Khan. Those banners are yours. And one day, all those men will be as well. But first, we must survive. Our families have abandoned us both. Therefore, the spirits saw fit to bring us together. You are the most precious jewel of all. The jewel of the entire Mongol Nation. I promise you, Batu, that I will do everything in my power to fight for you." *Even if it means opposing Unebolod,* she thought. *If that is the will of Genghis.*

Batu threw himself at Mandukhai, wrapping his arms around her neck and hugging close to her body. The sudden affection took Mandukhai by surprise, but she welcomed it, holding him close to her. Did he understand anything she said to him? For a moment, the two remained locked in the embrace. Batu seemed so different from his father and great-uncle. Perhaps because he was still young. Perhaps because he truly was different. If he was to grow to be a powerful leader of men, Mandukhai would have to be certain she taught him well. He would not be lazy, slow, or cowardly like his predecessors. He would become a true wolf of the plains.

Boke made a small sound in his throat to get her attention, signaling the approach of one of the lesser khans. Mandukhai withdrew from Batu's hug and stood straight, sliding the boy behind her with a gentle nudge of her hand. Batu was used to this already, and he quickly hid behind her flowing deel.

Mandukhai raised her chin as Korgiz khan, of the Ongud, approached on foot. "Lord Korgiz, to what do I owe this pleasure?"

Korgiz glanced past her to attempt glimpsing Batu, but Mandukhai covered the boy well. If anyone could ruin the rumors that Batu was her half-brother and not Bayan's son, it would be Korgiz. "I came to talk to you about Esige."

Mandukhai tensed. "What has she done?"

"Interesting that you would assume such," Korgiz noted. "My son Boragan approached her about a potential marriage alliance and she spurned him."

That Mandukhai was not surprised about at all. In fact, she had to control herself to keep from laughing.

"A marriage would benefit both of us," he continued, oblivious to her amusement. "She does not have to like it for it to happen."

All amusement in Mandukhai burned away in a quick burst. Her body tensed. "I will not force her into a marriage that does not suit her."

"It is how things are done."

"As you did to me?"

"Where would you be now if I hadn't?" Korgiz asked, appearing quite pleased with himself.

Mandukhai had to resist the urge to slap him. Partly because he was so arrogant. Partly because she knew he was right and she hated it. "I agree, but I'm afraid that's as far as I can agree. I mean no disrespect, Korgiz khan. But Manduul and I had several conversations about her future after what happened to her sister. I'm afraid I cannot agree with this."

He grimaced, all the puffed-up pride vanishing in an instant. "She needs a husband. We will circle back to this conversation another time. I also wanted to inquire when you will make your announcement, Mandukhai."

Boke edged closer, but Mandukhai waved him back sharply. Korgiz insulted her by not addressing her as Queen Regent. She allowed it in informal situations with people she trusted, but this was not one of those moments. *Just another in a line of men who do not appreciate my rank above them*, she thought bitterly. Yet this one stung more deeply than the rest. He was the Ongud khan, her own tribe by birth.

"I'm afraid there must be some mistake," she said coldly. "You come to me asking who I will name as Great Khan, yet you do not recognize me in this position. I find this quite at odds."

Korgiz's jaw twitched. "Lady Mandukhai. I have heard you and Lord Unebolod are quite close. You must know by now that most of the men favor him. And I believe your late husband named him."

"In the absence of a descendant of Genghis," Mandukhai interrupted. "I am well aware of my husband's wishes and do not need you to remind me. After all, I believe it was I who remained at his bedside—a bedside you placed me beside. Unless I am mistaken."

Korgiz glanced past her again at Batu, who peeked out curiously at the Ongud khan. Korgiz's frown deepened. "Who is this boy you have been taking such care of? He is too old to be yours and rumors indicate he is your mother's son, but I know that isn't the truth."

"I have taken on a few abandoned children these past few years," Mandukhai commented, nudging Batu back. "Bigirsen's son among them. We can stop skirting what you are after, my Lord. If you seek to trick me into declaring for Lord Unebolod, you are on a fool's errand. *If* I am to declare for him, it will be to him and the sky father, and no other."

"You are too headstrong for your own good, my Lady," Korgiz said smoothly, though an undercurrent of danger lurked in his words. "Just remember that it is a man we need to rule the Mongol Nation."

Mandukhai stalked toward Korgiz. Batu clung to the skirt of her deel, trailing behind her. "It is my father's respect for you that stays my hand right now, Korgiz khan. But understand this clearly. I will not be browbeaten into submission, nor will I tolerate being threatened. If I discover that any of you intend to take what is not yours, I will punish the offender as the law dictates, and I will be well within my rights to do so. What this nation needs is someone of strength to guide it away from the precipice of destruction. I have survived Esen, Manduul, and Bayan. I will survive you, as well."

Korgiz bristled, then spun and stormed away. Once he was gone, Mandukhai's shoulders sagged, and she trembled as she reached for Batu's hand. He slid his fingers around hers.

Unebolod would wear a hole in his rugs at the rate he had been pacing of late. Before Manduul died, Unebolod had been careful to align these lesser khans behind him. Now, with Bayan and Manduul both dead, the Lords were prepared to keep their word. He found it ironic that, of all the people who had given him their support, the one person he had trusted to follow through was the one holding out on him.

Mandukhai coddled that boy and never strayed from his side. Unebolod considered what would happen if the boy were to accidentally die. But just as with every other time he considered this, he dismissed it. He could not bring himself to kill a child, nor would Mandukhai ever forgive him. Still, if he had just Bayan as a boy, none of this would be happening to him. Bayan never would have come to court to cast a shadow of doubt. He never would have sired that boy. That arrogant prince haunted him from the grave.

Without Batu, Mandukhai would have given over to him already.

Togochi stepped into Unebolod's ger. "You needed me?" he said, frowning as he observed Unebolod's apparently agitated state. "What is it, brother?"

Unebolod stopped pacing and straightened as he met Togochi's gaze. "Brother. What does that word mean to you, Togochi?"

Togochi closed the door behind him and edged deeper inside, but a stiffness had taken control of his body. He eyed Unebolod uncertainly. "That we have taken a bond of brotherhood. But you know that already. So why are you really asking?"

Unebolod rolled his shoulders to loosen tense muscles. "You already know."

Togochi said nothing. He was smart enough to know the day would come when he would have to make a choice between supporting Mandukhai or his own sworn brother. He *must* have known. Despite being Unebolod's sworn brother, Togochi supported Mandukhai instead of swaying her.

"I need you to convince her before it's too late," Unebolod said. "The Lords are getting restless. She trusts you."

Togochi scoffed, crossing his arms over his broad chest. "She doesn't trust anyone. You know that. Especially not after what happened to her."

So much time had passed since that Oirat attack. Nearly three months. He had expected Mandukhai to declare him the moment they were reunited, so that this could not happen again. *Then that boy showed up.*

Togochi raised his chin. "Why were you meeting with the lesser khans in the Tabun camp?"

Unebolod's breath hitched. He froze. "Are you spying on me now, brother?"

"No." Togochi held up his hands in supplication. "I just happened to be there talking to a horse trader. It looked highly suspicious, Unebolod."

"I told you!" Unebolod snapped. It carved into his heart deeply that Togochi mistrusted him. "The Lords are getting restless. I am trying to keep them calm."

Togochi narrowed his eyes. "It didn't look like that to me."

Unebolod resumed his pacing, clenching and unclenching his fists at his sides with each stride. "She has lost her mind since that attack, Togochi," Unebolod said. "She has not been herself, shirking those closest to her, closing herself off to everyone, refusing to acknowledge what we all know to be inevitable. I ..." A lump lodged in his throat. Unebolod swallowed it down. He could not voice the words. Saying he loved her only to have her reject him would be the worst sort of betrayal to his heart. "I need her to understand that we are all united in this decision. If we can all gather and convince her, make her see reason, I think I can get through to her. But right now, she wants me to agree to make that boy my heir. Yet if he lives in my home as my son..."

Togochi's brows shot up. "What boy?"

Unebolod tensed, freezing again as he eyed Togochi.

Togochi rubbed his forehead, groaning. "Jaghan." He shook his head. "She knew all along."

Mandukhai had not outright claimed Batu to be a descendant of Genghis to anyone else. But she told Unebolod. Togochi seemed to think his wife knew as well, which meant Esige probably knew, too. "You didn't really think he was her mother's son, did you? By Tengri, Togochi, just look at his *eyes!*"

Togochi released a sigh so heavy it deflated his body and his shoulders sagged. "If it's true, the boy's presence will *always* undermine you. You are afraid the Lords will only see you as Regent and not Great Khan." He shrugged. "Maybe they will. But will that matter? You will still have *her* and the rule over the tribes until he comes of age."

"I don't want to rule the tribes until he becomes a man!" Unebolod snapped.

Togochi scowled. "Then perhaps she can see the truth of your heart, and that is why she hesitates. Regardless of how much you love her, you want this title more. She has given you her conditions, and you have refused them." Togochi glanced at Unebolod's hands, which he had not even realized he clenched in white-knuckled fists. "From where I stand, it appears you are the one coming undone. Not her."

"I will remember who stood with me when I become Great Khan," Unebolod growled.

Togochi's face hardened. "Is that a threat, brother?" He inched closer, arrogant in the way he moved. "You are forgetting one important detail. You are *not* Great Khan, and as long as that boy survives, if he truly is an heir of Genghis, then you may never be. You walk a dark road, and I'm afraid I cannot follow you down that road. You may not need my support to win if you decide to steal *kurultai* from her, but I would hate to draw this line in the sands between us."

The words slammed against Unebolod's chest. He gasped, but Togochi was already striding toward the door. He paused and glared over his shoulder. "If you want my support, accept her terms. She is right. It's the only way for you to go forward with this." He ducked outside stormed away.

Unebolod punched the *uni* pole holding up his ger. The ger quivered. The pole cracked.

Togochi, of all men, was turning against him? Unebolod needed air.

The encounter with Korgiz had left Mandukhai quivering with rage. Had Unebolod sent Korgiz? Was he planning something? She had to talk to him, clear the air, set things straight before they spiraled too far for her to control. In a fury, she marched toward Unebolod's ger with Batu in tow, intent on forcing him to see reason.

Instead, Mandukhai paused outside his closed door as she heard raised voices inside, muffled by the felt of the ger. Togochi and Unebolod were arguing about the khanship and Batu. She glanced at the boy and saw the fear in his eyes. It pierced her heart. As the door opened, she grabbed Batu and ducked around the side of the ger. Until this moment, she had been uncertain if Togochi would choose to align with his sworn brother or keep his oath to her when it came down to the end of this horrible mess. She no longer doubted. Togochi's ultimate threat confirmed his loyalty to her. She would be sure to remember it no matter who ended up taking over.

Unebolod would never accept her terms. Any hope that he loved her enough to accept Batu as his heir disintegrated as Unebolod's words burned into her heart. *I do not want to rule the tribes until he becomes a man!* Every piece of her soul shattered into thousands of fragments the moment he barked out the words.

Such a childish thing, to hope that their love was strong enough to sustain even this. He had always wanted to be Great Khan—more than he had wanted her. All those stolen moments, shared secrets, desires, dreams. *I was a fool.*

A crack resounded from inside, and the ger quivered. A few seconds later, Unebolod strode out. Mandukhai slipped back so he would not notice her. As she made her way to her own ger, each step felt heavier than the last.

Perhaps Manduul had done this to her on purpose. Perhaps he knew Unebolod's desire for the title would tear them apart. There had been a time when she'd thought this was Manduul's final mercy, giving her a blessing—of sorts—to be with the man he must have known she loved. Now, she wondered if Manduul had set this up as a last way to rip out her heart.

"Boke," Mandukhai said as they reached her door. She ushered Batu inside, blocking him off from everyone but the commander of her royal guard. "I need you to promise me something."

"Anything, *Khatun*." Boke bowed.

"You will guard Batu with your life, even above my own."

Boke frowned, glancing at Batu behind her. "I am sworn to protect you. I gave an oath."

Mandukhai swallowed, then stepped closer, placing a hand on Boke's arm. She had no choice but to tell him the truth, but was certain to keep her voice low enough that no one else would hear her. "Boke, Batu is Bayan's son. He is the last Borjigin prince. If anyone comes for him, I will fight to the death to stop them. But I need you to promise me you will as well, even if you must choose him over me."

Boke studied Batu for several painfully long seconds. At last, he nodded and kneeled in front of them. "I give you my vow, Mandukhai *Khatun*. Prince Batu will be safe to my last breath."

Mandukhai nodded sharply, satisfied. "Good. Do not call him prince, though. No one else can know who he is until I say so. Trust no one but Togochi, Boke. Any of these men could be loyal to Lord Unebolod. I do not believe he would harm me, but the same cannot be said for Batu."

Boke rose. "Lord Togochi is his sworn brother."

"You heard what they said in that ger as well as I did," Mandukhai said. "Brother or not, Togochi is loyal first to his oath to Manduul."

"If I might make a suggestion, my Lady?"

Mandukhai nodded.

"Allow me to change your royal guards," Boke said. "We have several Khorchin men whose loyalty I would hate to doubt, but I cannot account for their allegiance."

Her own guards? Had Unebolod's men surrounded her for years? It felt like another twist of the knife in her heart. Had he been planning this all along? Mandukhai swallowed the lump in her throat. "See it done. Borjigin and Khorlod men only."

"Borjigin only," Boke said. "I have heard many of the Khorlod men talking these past months. They follow their Lord and khan, but they admire Lord Unebolod too much for my comfort."

Every muscle in Mandukhai's body felt stretched too thin. Could she truly trust *any* of the men? She nodded in agreement and closed the door.

Batu sat on the bed playing with knucklebones, casting them across the blankets and frowning, then casting them again. Could he read their fortune? Only seven, but he seemed like such an old soul.

Mandukhai leaned against the closed door and squeezed her eyes closed, as if that could block out the agony ripping into her heart.

If she disobeyed the will of the spirits, of Genghis, it could destroy her everlasting soul. But she wanted Unebolod—needed him! How could this be her fate?

CHAPTER EIGHTEEN

The Hunter and the Eagle

The festival approached, and Mandukhai's days and nights were consumed with tasks and meetings. Between attempting to speak with the Mongol Lords—most of whom attempted talking her into naming Unebolod for *kurultai*—and overseeing the organization of events, Mandukhai barely had time to watch over Batu, let alone talk to Unebolod like she knew she needed to do.

Commanders and Lords put forward their best men into archery or wrestling for the big competition. Families entered young men into both the footrace and the horse race.

As the days passed, the inevitable truth approached. Soon, she would have to name the next Great Khan. And Unebolod had yet to agree to her terms.

Mandukhai had hoped to gather support from the Urainkhai khan, but Tolokan khan had sent his son Huoshai in his stead. The message was obvious. The Urainkhai had not come to support a new Great Khan, but to partake in the festival events. Otherwise, Tolokan would have come for himself.

Regardless, Mandukhai needed to garner Urainkhai support. She approached Huoshai as he and his men gathered around racehorses. Dozens of men and women mingled among the horses, talking, exchanging bets, joking with one another. Huoshai proved no exception to this. He grinned as he and his men joked.

Huoshai cut an impressive figure. Mandukhai guessed his age to be around sixteen, but he carried himself like a young khan. Though his posture was relaxed and he spoke lightly with his men, he carried a natural air of command. The sides of his head were shaved clean, and a strip along the top was divided into two braids along the crown, then gathered in a long braid down between his shoulder blades. He only bore the early signs of facial hair. He wore the same simple deel, breeches, and boots as his men, but somehow on him, it looked finer.

As Mandukhai walked toward him, she noticed his gaze repeatedly drifted away from his men. She followed his gaze through the milling crowd and frowned. *Esige.*

"Lord Huoshai," Mandukhai said, raising her voice above the din.

He only cast a glance in her direction. "Queen Regent," he said.

"I hear you have entered the archery and wrestling matches," she said.

"Indeed, I have." He drew himself up proudly, then elbowed the man next to him and nodded ever so slightly.

Mandukhai once more noticed they were watching Esige, and her stomach twisted. She watched as Esige ran her hands along the forelock of a horse, then shook her head and said something to the horse master. *What is she up to?*

That Huoshai practically ignored Mandukhai so he could ogle at her ward sapped away the last of Mandukhai's patience. "Lord Huoshai, I noticed your father has not come with the Urainkhai. Has he authorized you to vote at *kurultai* on his behalf?"

"My father sent me to compete and find a wife," Huoshai said, never pulling his gaze away from Esige.

Mandukhai ground her teeth. "Lady Esige is my charge, and if you touch her, my men will remove your hands. Do I make myself clear?"

Huoshai tore his gaze away from Esige, and it appeared almost painful for him to do. He grinned at Mandukhai until he saw the fury in her eyes, then he paled ever so slightly. Though he clearly understood she meant every word, he persisted. "Is she promised to another?"

Mandukhai had been prepared to deny him any hope, but something else sparked in her mind. She raised her chin and smiled sweetly at Huoshai. "Did your mother ever tell you the story of the Eagle and the Hunter?"

Huoshai shifted feet, apparently fighting to resist staring at Esige again. "The fierce, strong hunter found a powerful, stunning eagle. He climbed a cliff to capture the eagle, but it flew off. The hunter leaped after the eagle, hoping to land on its back, but instead fell to his death, unable to capture the powerful creature."

Mandukhai nodded. "This particular eagle has drawn several ambitious young hunters to the top of that cliff."

Huoshai squared his shoulders, no longer fighting his obvious urge to gawk at Esige. Mandukhai almost felt bad for the young Lord. He would still try. And she would watch him fall off the cliff, just as all the others had done.

The sun burned hot on the first day of the festival. Unebolod opted for a sleeveless deel, but he had nothing to mop up the sweat on his brow. The horse races had begun an hour ago. Bets had been placed on who might win, and which tribes would take the top ten spots in the race. But horse racing was a game for the young. Unebolod knew he could ride hard in a saddle for days, and no forty-mile race would prove anything.

He had put one of his strongest warriors, Ordagaqai, forward in the wrestling tournament. With any luck, the young man would prove himself and rank highly—if not take the top spot. Unebolod had every faith in the massive man and his strength. But as Esige had proven in the past, skill would be just as important.

Unebolod and nine of his best archers waited for the Urainkhai men to finish their shots under the relentless sun. The targets were far away—one hundred yards. A score of thirty-three was required to move on to the next round, and, so far, it had eliminated a handful of competitors. Unebolod had not met the Urainkhai in battle before, so he was uncertain what to expect from their skills. But Lord Huoshai was young, which could sometimes lead to mistakes.

The first volley of arrows flew in tandem from the ten Urainkhai warriors. They released together, arched together, and hit their targets as one. The young Lord Huoshai grinned at the man next to him as the flags from the first shots were raised to signal their score—an impressive ten out of ten on target. The final three volleys followed, each with nearly equally remarkable scores. Their total score of thirty-seven was quite extraordinary. Unebolod had to admit he was impressed.

Huoshai congratulated his men. As they moved off, he patted Unebolod on the shoulder. "Are you sure you are prepared for this, Unebolod khan? I would hate to see a future Great Khan humiliated in the tournament."

Unebolod simply raised his brows and took the comment in jest. "We shall see who is humiliated by the end of the festival," he replied. His own men laughed along, patting Huoshai in commiseration as they passed him to take their positions.

The young Lord stepped out of the way to make room for his Khorchin archers, and Unebolod caught the way Huoshai studied Esige as she stood under the tent on the side of the range with Mandukhai. Esige watched Unebolod like a curious hawk.

Don't let him distract you, he admonished himself as he stepped up to the line and waited for the signal from the other end of the field.

As one, he and his nine men breathed in, drew back with their thumbs, and released their breath as they let the bowstrings snap. Unebolod squinted into the sky as he watched their arrows soar as one. Each struck the target and judges rushed out to see the result. Ten shouts of *"uukhai!"* called back to the line, indicating ten perfect shots. Not that Unebolod had expected any less. His were the best archers in the Nation.

Sweat rolled down into his eyes as he prepared for the next shot, but he ignored it, focused on his target as his men would be. Three more volleys for a total of forty arrows. After the final round, their score ended tied with the Urainkhai. Unebolod patted his men in congratulations and strode toward Huoshai.

"I hope I haven't disappointed you, Lord Huoshai," Unebolod teased.

"You have," Huoshai said, watching as Esige approached them. "By three points."

Unebolod couldn't help but laugh. It felt good to laugh. Huoshai had expected Unebolod to get a perfect score.

Esige threw her arms around Unebolod hard enough to throw him off balance. He hugged the girl back with one arm.

"I knew you would do well," she said, beaming up at him as she stepped back.

Huoshai stood straighter. Unebolod found his preening display intriguing. The look he cast Unebolod behind Esige's back was clear. He wanted an introduction. *On your head it be*, Unebolod thought.

"I couldn't let a young man like this outshine me," Unebolod said, motioning toward Huoshai.

Esige half turned. Her critical gaze swept over Huoshai. Then she shrugged and turned away again as if he were nothing. Unebolod bit the inside of his cheek to smother his smirk.

"No one could outshine you, Une." Esige kissed him on the cheek. "I'm off to the races."

"Not to take part, I hope!" Unebolod called after her as she strode away. Esige simply waved off the comment.

Huoshai frowned as he stepped up beside Unebolod, his gaze tethered to Esige as she disappeared into the crowd. "She has her eye on you."

Unebolod barked out a laugh and slapped Huoshai hard on the shoulder. "Now *that* was funny. I'm not a suiter to her. I'm more like a brother or … or a father." He shot a meaningful glance at the young Urainkhai Lord.

"In that case, we should talk." Huoshai turned squarely to face Unebolod. "Because I do not intend to jump off a cliff to my doom chasing her down. I have something much more favorable in mind."

Unebolod knew instantly he would be in trouble if he gave Huoshai the wrong idea. If Huoshai thought Unebolod controlled Esige's future, he was grossly mistaken. Unebolod clearly recalled the fury in Mandukhai's eyes when Manduul had given Borogchin to Bigirsen. No way would he make that same mistake. All amusement slid off his face.

"Walk with me, Lord Huoshai," Unebolod said. "I have a wrestler I don't want to miss."

Esige convinced Nemeku to play with Togochi's boys and show them around the festival. His excitement bubbled over for days, and the moment she gave him permission, he darted out the door toward Togochi's ger. Mandukhai had taken Batu on a ride around camp to get a grip on the extent of Mongols who would be present for *kurultai*. For the first time all day, Esige was blissfully alone.

She wrapped bands of cotton as tight as she could around her chest to flatten it out. It worked, but only a little. To cover what she could not press flat, Esige swathed herself in a baggy deel and belted it in the fashion of men under the belly. She had pulled her hair back and braided it the same way she saw other men her age doing—tight back from the face and braided thickly down their backs, with two small braided tails over the ears. Sadly, this exposed her feminine features, but she could do nothing about the way her face looked.

Glancing over her shoulder, she opened her trunk and shuffled through her belongings. After a moment, she produced a sword from among her things. She had pilfered this from Manduul's belongings months ago. It was old, but she had cared for it, restoring the chipped and dull blade to a faint luster each night. Esige stood and slid it into her belt, then added her knife. To finish things off, she slipped on a pair of boots she had bartered off an old man two days ago, along with a lightweight *toortsog* hat. They were worn, but simple. Perfect for her needs. The ornately decorated boots Mandukhai gave her would never help her pass off as a man.

Once satisfied, Esige cracked her door open and peered out, looking for her guards. While the men were well-meaning, Esige did not want to be accompanied on this mission. Over the years, she had perfected her ability to slip in and out of guarded spaces without notice. Today, she would use that skill to her advantage.

The coast was clear enough. One guard stood with his back to her, several feet away. She could tell by his posture that he watched the crowd milling along the thoroughfare in front of her ger. Esige tiptoed out and eased the door closed silently. Keeping a careful eye on him, she followed the edges of the ger around to freedom.

It was not until she blended into a crowd over twenty yards from her ger that Esige relaxed. Even if her guards had not spotted her, any of Mandukhai's guards or loyal nobles could have. She had planned her path carefully to avoid going anywhere near any of the noble gers.

An energy buzzed around Mount Burkhan Khaldun. Between the excitement of the festival events and the upcoming *kurultai*, everyone had come out of their gers to participate. Some people—men, women, and children alike—offered trades or sales for goods. Some wares were foods, others were homemade items. Anything Esige could have wanted could be found somewhere in the massive camp.

Everyone walked around with a drink in their hand. The endless flow of *airag* permeated everywhere. Esige had taken a few drinks herself occasionally, but she was always careful who she accepted from.

Overall, the atmosphere reminded Esige of one massive party that would last for days. She heard swells of the horse fiddle and throat singing as she crossed the camp. Children played games with each other, ducking and weaving around adult legs. Everyone had light spirits.

When she reached the line to sign up for wrestling, Esige craned her neck to get the full scope of how long the wait would be. At least a dozen men stood in front of her. She avoided the conversations—mostly about women or boasting their manliness—and kept her head down as she inched forward.

At last, she stood before the table and dropped her silver .

"Name and tribe?" the scribe asked without looking up at her.

Esige's heart lifted with hope. If he didn't look at her, she would be registered and no one could stop her. Except for Mandukhai.

"Altan, Borjigin," she said, attempting to lower her voice and sound more manly. She had chosen one of the most common names on purpose, and figured she should at least be forthright about her tribal affiliation. There was no reason to lie about that.

"Sponsor?" he asked, sounding bored with the entire proceeding.

"Goji," she said. Goji was a drunk. If anyone asked him and he couldn't remember sponsoring anyone named Altan, no one would care, assuming he had just been too drunk.

The scribe jotted down the name, and he reached for the silver coin he paused, looking up at her.

Esige's heart stopped beating entirely. She attempted wearing the cool warrior's face that Unebolod often wore, hoping this scribe would not see through her mask.

He narrowed his eyes as he swept his gaze over her. "Lightweight class."

"I can handle heavyweight."

He snorted and shook his head. "Lightweight class."

Esige wanted to slap him. She could perfectly handle bigger men!

He touched the ink-tipped quill to the paper, then hesitated, cocking his head as he studied her again.

Please don't realize I'm not a man. Please! She held her breath and tried to remain calm, but something about the way he studied her made her stomach twist in horrific knots. "Is there a problem?"

She glanced past him and saw a young Lord studying her in amusement. *What was his name again? Huoshai!* Unebolod had introduced them earlier in the day. Judging by the look on his face, he recognized her. *Please don't say anything!*

A scratch of the quill tip against the paper drew Esige's gaze down at the scribe. He was scowling as he crossed her name off the list.

"What—?"

"The Queen Regent warned us you might try something like this," the scribe said. He waved her off. "Take your silver and go, princess."

"I am stronger than most of these men!" she protested, waving flippantly at the queue behind her.

The protest drew several chuckles from the men all around. Her face heated, and she opened her mouth to give him a good tongue lashing, but hesitated. It would do no good. Not if Mandukhai had told them not to allow Esige in.

"This is unfair," she grumbled.

Huoshai appeared beside her as if by some sort of magic, leaning closer to her as he whispered. "I agree." He cleared his throat and stood straighter, raising his voice for the entire crowd. "We should start a women's division. High Heavens knows there are plenty of tough women in our camps."

Esige pushed Huoshai away. She didn't appreciate his showmanship. Nor his familiarity with her. "I don't want to fight women." She stepped toward the table. "These matches are meant to find the strongest among the tribes. Who says that has to be a man?"

The scribe sighed and set down his quill, leveling his gaze. "Listen, the rules are the rules. I don't make them. I only enforce them. If you have a problem, take it up with the Queen Regent. She is the one who banned you."

Esige quivered indignantly as she snatched her silver off the table and stormed away.

Huoshai dogged her steps, whistling as if impressed. "You must have really done something to get personally banned by the Queen Regent."

"I'm not interested," Esige snapped.

Huoshai waved his hands in surrender but didn't stop walking alongside her. "I get it. You're a strong, independent woman. I can respect that."

Esige glanced at him and noticed the way his gaze swept over her. It made his words sound stale. "I don't think you *do* get it."

Huoshai sighed. The act of a suave young Lord melted away. His arms dropped to his sides. His back slouched slightly. He gave a small shrug. "I do. You value your own worth and don't think that any guy could ever truly appreciate it. To them, you're a princess and a womb. Good for one thing."

Esige jerked to a stop and rounded on him, her eyes wide. How dare he speak to her like this!

Huoshai stopped as well and chuckled. She did not know what he thought was so funny, but she didn't appreciate it. "You should see your face. Before you punch me, let me finish. Please?"

Esige crossed her arms and raised her brows impatiently.

"I won't bother challenging you like all those other idiots," he continued. "And I won't jump off a cliff chasing down a girl who is clearly not interested. There are plenty of other prospects in this mega camp. Besides, the Queen Regent and Lord Unebolod both warned me about you. I just wanted you to know that I don't see the same thing as the other men."

Mandukhai and Unebolod warned Huoshai about her? What did that mean? What had they told him? Esige's pulse quickened.

"I'm not interested in playing games," she said sharply.

"Me either." He turned and walked away.

Esige's heart hammered in her chest. If he didn't see a princess only good for having children ... "What do you see, then?"

Huoshai glanced back, grinning. "A caged rabbit eager to break free. Have a good evening, Lady Esige."

A caged rabbit. Esige stared after Huoshai as he strolled away. She couldn't stop swallowing. Her nails bit into her palms and she realized she had clenched them into fists. Esige eased them loose. A mild pain spread across her chest, making her lightheaded.

The observation struck so close to true that it left Esige stunned. She had often felt like a caged rabbit, wanting to race across the steppe but forced to remain in her ger and act as a princess should.

In a matter of minutes, Huoshai had stripped her bare.

And she didn't like it.

CHAPTER NINETEEN

A Vision of Unity

The heat of summer seemed to burn down from everywhere. Issama was not a big fan of the heat, but gusts of cool air sometimes blew through camp from the Huang Ho River, offering some relief. Overall, Issama found the climate within the great loop of the river preferable to that of northern Mongolia. Hot days were not unbearable—as a Uyghur he was used to desert heat—but he certainly had grown to appreciate more temperate climates.

Issama stood within the walls of Bigirsen's command tent as Bigirsen poured over maps he had looted from Ming officers and captured cities. Issama had placed markers across the maps, noting where the Ming had marked out the heaviest concentration of soldiers. They could not outnumber the Ming. Even if they defeated all the forces along the border, hundreds of thousands more hid behind the Great Wall. A head-on attack would not work.

Bigirsen's determined campaign against the southern tribes would have failed even if he had attempted sweeping across the map. All he would have seized would be land. Many of the Mongols had gone north for a festival. Issama suspected *kurultai* would follow the end of the festivities. Then Mandukhai would name Unebolod, and he would turn his attention south. They had perhaps weeks until that happened—and it would take the Mongol forces nearly a year to reach this far south.

One year. That was all the time they had to finish this mission against the Ming.

One year to take Yinchuan and kill Bigirsen.

It is enough time, Issama thought.

Since turning away from the east, Bigirsen had led the southern Mongols with a fevered determination. The Ming emperor was weak, and the empire distracted by its own internal strife. It presented Bigirsen with numerous opportunities to chip away at the borders and force the Ming deeper into their territory

Issama had to admit there was a level of brilliance to Bigirsen's strategy. The Mongols could capture the Gansu Corridor with swift, decisive action, but they could never hold it with the city of Yinchuan so close, or with the city of Yulin providing the Ming forces with supplies. Instead, Bigirsen turned toward the harsh land within the great loop of the Huang Ho River, launching raids against Ming commander Wang Yue. The Mongol forces had become serpent-like shadows, striking out swiftly at Ming supply trains, then disappearing into the darkness once more as if they had never been.

Wang Yue had attempted to lure the Mongol army out of the shadows with supply caravans, hiding his own forces in the surrounding landscape to attack the moment the Mongols arrived. Unfortunately, Wang Yue neglected to recognize the savvy of Mongol organization.

"We have another force hiding in the hills here," Issama said at last, growing impatient as he waited for Bigirsen to speak first.

Bigirsen looked at the hills Issama pointed out and nodded. "Same size as before?"

"According to the scouts, there are about five thousand," Issama said. "It's a significant force. They are growing more determined to bolster their numbers." Usually, they encountered legions of roughly two thousand. "The caravan is coming from here." Issama drew a line from Yulin, through a gap in the wall, and right toward where the scouts found the awaiting force.

Bigirsen shook his head. "Idiots," he muttered. "They never learn."

"They have learned," Issama corrected. "They have more than doubled their numbers."

"So you think we cannot handle them?" Bigirsen leveled a hard glare at Issama, making it clear enough he believed Issama insulted him.

He has grown so touchy.

"We will handle this as we have all the rest," Bigirsen said. "Send in a raiding party to capture the supplies. Follow the Ming forces and close in around them when they attack."

Issama had been skeptical of this strategy the first time Bigirsen had commanded it, but as Bigirsen drove the Mongol army deeper into the great loop, it was clear his strategy worked. They would send in a raiding party to steal the supplies, then send in a secondary force to distract and chase away the Ming forces. The Mongol army had captured hundreds of miles of land within the Ordos basin.

The land itself mostly had no potential for irrigation and farming, so the Ming who lived here eagerly gave up their land to the might of Bigirsen's men. The shifting sands, salt lakes, and dry gravel proved ample for hardy Mongol herds to find grass to graze. The animals were just as tough as the people.

Thousands of southern Mongol families had set up gers within the Ordos basin, guarded by enough men to see that women and children were safe. People from all the Ordos subtribes, the Chakhar, the Three Guards tribes occupied the recently conquered landscape. Meanwhile, Bigirsen continued to push forward.

Once he controlled the Ordos basin—which would be soon now—Bigirsen would launch his campaign against the Ming cities along the border.

Ending at Yinchuan. Then, Issama would solidify his own vision of unity.

"Send in a second wave *tumen* to follow the first," Bigirsen said, breaking the studious silence. "That should teach the Ming they no longer have control of these lands."

Mandukhai had taken an interest in all the events for differing reasons. Good, fast riders would make great scouts and messengers. Accurate archers would become elite warriors. The strongest wrestlers would make the best guards—assuming she could count on their loyalty. What began with over two thousand fierce warriors ended the second day with fewer than fifty.

The *bökh* wrestlers had warmed up for days before the festival. Men and women had passed the wrestling rings to watch the contenders. Kids pushed their way between legs to get a better view. Fortunes could be made or lost betting on wrestling.

The first day of competition had weeded out the old and weak. A few men had sustained injuries that prevented them from competing further in the tournament.

One of Unebolod's men, Ordagaqai, won his last bout of the day. Mandukhai watched as Unebolod strolled up to his chosen warrior and congratulated him. She had not seen such joy on his face since he had heard of their child. *So long ago. What has it been now, five years?* Their child would have been close to Nemeku's age. Mandukhai knew, deep down, that was why she protected Nemeku so fiercely. On some level, she saw Nemeku as the son she had lost.

Mandukhai glided toward the Khorchin men. "Congratulations on another successful day, Ordagaqai. You have done your tribe proud."

Unebolod stiffened the moment he heard her voice. Mandukhai watched his gaze flit around her as if seeking Batu. But Mandukhai had left him with Boke and Tuya back in the ger when the boy had been worn down by the events of the day. A few of Boke's chosen guards remained with her.

"Queen Regent," the wrestler said, bowing deeply to her.

Mandukhai raised her chin, beaming at the show of respect.

The tension in the air grew thick between her and Unebolod as they stood beside each other. The handful of men around them seemed to sense it, finding their excuses to slip away. Some cited the late hour, though the sun had just begun to set. Others complained of hunger and went to seek one of the many fest tables around the camp. Soon, Mandukhai and Unebolod were alone, with only her guards around them and a few people milling at least twenty or more feet away.

"May we?" Mandukhai asked Unebolod, motioning toward a path leading away from the festivities.

"I would not refuse our Queen Regent," Unebolod said evenly.

His response caught under her skin like a burr. She brushed her hands over her bare arms to smooth out the hair rising there.

The two of them walked in complete silence with only her shadow of guards trailing several feet away. When had they last engaged in natural conversation? *Not since the Oirat,* she thought. The night before that attack, they had spent a glorious night of passion. Mandukhai was uncertain if she would ever feel passion like that again in her life. As much as she denied it to everyone else, what those Oirat men had done to her, the way they had touched her, had seared into her flesh so thoroughly that every touch reminded her of them. Even Unebolod's own hands.

They rounded a corner, away from the last line of gers. She glanced back and saw her guards following, but no one else was around in this space. They were too far from all the music, feasts, and events for anyone to venture here.

"Have you considered my proposal?" Mandukhai asked.

Unebolod stiffened his back. His face set in a grim line. "I hoped you had considered mine."

Mandukhai's heart sank. "It isn't so easy for me."

"Why?" His sharp tone startled her.

Mandukhai swallowed the lump that had jumped into her throat. She summoned the courage to tell him the truth, or at least enough of the truth for him to hopefully understand. The idea of being with any man—even him—terrified her. "What those men did to me has ... broken something, Unebolod." Admitting this to him had taken all the courage she could gather. "I cannot stand to be touched anymore. I'm afraid I would make a poor wife. I am uncertain I could perform as a wife should."

"Is that what this has all been about?" Unebolod asked. "Why have you not said so sooner?"

"I can barely say so now," Mandukhai murmured. Her throat tightened. Anxiety pressed against her chest. She had to confront him about his meetings with the other khans and Lords. "I know what you have been doing these past weeks. That you have been gathering support."

"What choice did I have?" Unebolod asked. He clasped his hands behind his back as he walked alongside her. "We are coming down to the end of the rope, Mandukhai. If I didn't prepare for *kurultai*, we would both be in serious trouble."

"So you admit you have been forming alliances with them?"

He scoffed. "I started doing that before Manduul even died. I told you I would travel east to gather support, and I did. Now I just wanted to reaffirm what these men have already promised me. If we wait until the morning of the vote, someone else could step in and declare both of us inept."

Mandukhai stepped in front of Unebolod. Her hands trembled, so she clasped them behind her back so he could not see her fear.

"Manduul killed Bayan for such acts," she said, ashamed of the quiver in her voice.

Unebolod's expression darkened. Despite the anger on his face, the pain in his eyes pierced her soul. "Are you … are you threatening me? Mandukhai! See reason! We both *know* this is inevitable. No one will support the boy, which means you and I will go forward with our plan, as we agreed. I have given you the space you requested. I have given you everything. I told you before I will light your fire for you. We can grow stronger *together* and create the family we have wanted for so long."

Mandukhai turned her gaze toward the sacred mountain. His promise was carved into her heart. How she longed to be his wife, to have his children, but she could not give herself to another man. Not after everything. Not so willingly. Somehow, she had to make Unebolod understand. The last thing she wanted was to make an enemy of the man she loved. *I need to tell him everything*, she thought, attempting to convince herself this was the only way forward.

"I had a vision that day, when I …" Mandukhai glanced past him at her guards, then lowered her voice and prayed they could not hear. "When we lost our child. I did not fully understand it at the time."

Unebolod relaxed somewhat, crossing his arms over his broad chest. He did not interrupt.

"In it, I walked a dark path to the sacred Mother Tree," she said, "where a spirit guided me. He showed me Bayan's death in the desert … and he showed me the boy. He promised I would become the mother of wolves."

"But Bayan did not die for years after that," Unebolod said, furrowing his brow. "What spirit was this?"

Mandukhai smoothed her hands over her deel and took a breath to steady herself. "Genghis."

Unebolod chuckled and shook his head. "The spirits are toying with you, just as they have been toying with me for years. They don't want to see us together. You did not see Genghis. You saw what they wanted you to see to make you believe what they wanted you to believe. If you think this is the true path, I beg to differ. To me, it sounds like lunacy."

Mandukhai bristled. How could he mock her like this? She knew he had lost his faith long ago, but he knew she firmly believed in her own. "It was him! Unebolod, it didn't just look like him. It was not just some spirit dressing the part. He carried the lost wolf-head sword. He *gave* it to me! And the world around him bent to his will. There was something about him I can't even explain! Like … like an air of power. I watched him cut

Esen down from the Mother Tree and punish him for over-reaching. And if it was not true, then how did I see Bayan's death long before he died? How did I see Batu before I knew he even existed?" Mandukhai shook her head. "It was Genghis. If you have ever had faith in me, have faith in this."

For a moment, he didn't even move. Unebolod froze in place, rooted to the earth like stone. Then his face crumpled. His arms fell at his sides. Mandukhai watched his chest heave. "Wha—I ... I don't understand."

"I don't think I did either," Mandukhai said. "Not fully. Over the years, I have turned his words in my head repeatedly, trying to find a logical solution ... trying to find any excuse that might mean he intended the next Great Khan to be you. And I wanted to tell you sooner, but the spirits are deliberate with—"

Unebolod waved her comment off. "Yeah. I've heard it before." But he didn't sound angry with her. In fact, all the anger in his body extinguished. Unebolod appeared on the brink of collapse. He shook his head, shuffling half a step toward her. "What—why do you think any of it was true? Perhaps it was a fevered dream from the strain you underwent. It was not an easy loss for you. It could have been nothing more than fevered dreams."

Mandukhai stepped toward Unebolod, yearning to console him but unable to find the strength to touch him. In his desperation, she could feel him grasping for any excuse to discredit the vision. "It could have been ... but again, how could I have known where or how Bayan would die in the desert alone? How could I have seen Batu as a small boy, broken and abandoned?" Mandukhai shook her head. "Had those visions been wrong, I might have agreed with you. But ... I know what I saw. I just need you to believe me."

Unebolod's chin dipped to his chest. "I do," he muttered. All the fight fled from him. "What did Genghis say about me?"

"Nothing ... exactly." Mandukhai closed her eyes. Unebolod would not appreciate this part of her vision. "But before Genghis appeared, you came to me."

Unebolod's head shot up at this, hope renewed in his dark gaze.

Mandukhai averted her own. "You attacked me, Unebolod."

He shook his head firmly, horrified. "No."

Mandukhai's heart hammered as she recalled that part of the vision. Her voice shook as she told him the horrible truth. "I lay on a bed of furs, and you came over me with such fury. You raised a wolf-head sword over my heart. I thought you would kill me."

The last of Unebolod's strength left him. He sank to his knees in front of her, gazing up with such profound sadness Mandukhai could no longer resist reaching out to him. She placed her hand on his head, sliding her palm over his looped braids. The guards shifted in the distance, but she gave a subtle motion for them to stay back and give the two of them space.

"I would never hurt you," he insisted. His voice shook. He took her hand and pressed it to his lips. "Mandukhai, I swear it. Should I ever hurt you, let the spirits tear my limbs from my body."

The vow swept away Mandukhai's breath. Her knees gave out, and she sank down in front of him. To sever the limbs from the body was to sever the soul. She had loved no one so fiercely before, so certainly. Every part of her being gravitated toward him. For the first time since the Oirat attack, his touch did not repulse her. Unebolod clung to her hand as if she were the only thing allowing him to cling to life.

"Please," he pleaded softly, as tears rolled down his cheeks. "Let me hold you."

It surprised Mandukhai to discover herself crying as well. She took a great breath to stifle her sobs before they could begin. Once more, he asked for her permission, just as he had the first time they had given in to their passion. She tried to speak, but no words came out. Instead, Mandukhai nodded stiffly.

Unebolod swept her into his arms, holding her close with so much longing it made her soul ache. His grip was firm but not harsh, full of warmth, but not passion. This embrace was unlike any other she had experienced before. A desperate love. A shelter from the storm. Mandukhai clung to him.

"Only the one who carries the spirit can reunite the One Nation," Mandukhai whispered into his ear. "Only he of my bone will have the might to hold it."

Unebolod's muscles tensed as she uttered the words of Genghis. His fingers pressed into her back for a moment before he pulled back and rested his forehead on hers. "What does it mean?"

Mandukhai swallowed, still clinging to that lingering hope. "Genghis told me we have forgotten the call of the wolf, abandoned his vision of unity. He told me that the people need a strong leader to follow if they are to save his fractured empire. He also said I would give my heart twice." Mandukhai ran her fingertips along his scarred face. "Once to passion. Once to compassion."

Unebolod closed his eyes at her touch, pressing his cheek into her palm without pulling away from her forehead.

"I believe he means for us to work together," Mandukhai said. "That the two of us have the spirit to reunite the broken Nation, but Batu is the one who will have the power to hold it together."

"I have no choice in this, do I?" Unebolod whispered pitifully.

Mandukhai shook her head. "Nor do I. Please. I beg you. Accept my proposal. I cannot do this without you."

"He is so weak and small, Mandukhai."

"Then we will make him strong." Mandukhai kissed his cheekbone. "Unebolod, this is why you and I were brought together. This is why the spirits took our son from us. This destiny is not ours. Unless you accept my proposal, I ..." Mandukhai squeezed her eyes shut as if it could close out the pain. "I cannot be yours. Would you consume the vessel of our Khan, of Genghis himself?"

The silence between them stretched long and thin, much like the air Mandukhai struggled to pull into her lungs. She understood what she asked of him. Unebolod would be her husband as long as he accepted Batu would become Great Khan when he came of age in ten years. Meanwhile, the two of them would bring the nation together for Batu to rule.

"You are a Queen and a widow, Mandukhai, and the people are without a Lord to rule them."

Mandukhai dared to open her eyes. Unebolod stared intensely at her. She wanted to draw away. She wanted to press her lips to his. The fear and passion inside her soul waged war with each other. "Give me your word, and this is done."

Unebolod pressed a tender, loving kiss to her lips, then wiped away the tears on her face, and sank back on his heels. "You have had years to think through this, and months to determine your course. At least give me a night to think it over. I can't promise I will agree. I have spent the last twenty years of my life dreaming of this. I never expected you. I would gain one of my heart's deepest desires, but sacrifice the other. No matter what I decide. And when I come to you with this decision, it needs to be public, so that everyone knows how the two of us intend to go forward."

Mandukhai nodded. What else could she do? What she asked of him was an impossible choice. Such a thing could not be determined in a moment. "Have faith in the High Heavens, Unebolod, and they will guide you to the right path."

His lips thinned, but he nodded. Once more, he pulled her close and kissed her ... and she feared it would be their last.

Unebolod helped Mandukhai to her feet, and the two clung to each other as they meandered back toward the camp in silence. When they reached the gers, he broke away, casting a look of deep sorrow at her.

Mandukhai watched him disappear. No matter what he decided, in just two more days she would be placing a new Great Khan before the sacred *sulde* of Genghis. It was time she had someone prepare it for the ceremony.

CHAPTER TWENTY

Two Ribbons, One Fate

U nebolod stalked back to his ger, taking the longest, most indirect route he could just to distance himself from everyone else for as long as possible. Mandukhai's confession had driven a spike through his soul. She feared him, and she loved him. But her fear stemmed from something he could not control. Not the Oirat—*I will make them pay for this as soon as we finish here!*—or what he had done to the men who assaulted her. He should have done far worse to the man he killed, tortured him to the edge of death. Unebolod had dreamed up a hundred ways to punish that man, each more disturbing than the last. Though shoving his dismembered cock down his own throat before killing him had offered some pleasure.

Mandukhai feared Unebolod because of what she had seen in that vision. Nothing more than a nightmare as far as he was concerned, but it had clearly stuck with her all these years. He stroked the hilt of his sword as he turned away from his home and marched between gers. His was not a wolf-head sword. Just a well-cut piece of iron and steel, forged by a master craftsman. No man had a wolf-head sword anymore. The sword of Genghis had disappeared centuries ago, after the death of Kublai Khan.

Perhaps it was the symbolism of the sword that worried her. The wolf-head represented the title of Great Khan. Perhaps she feared he would kill her in the future if she gave him control of the Mongols.

Yet that logic did not make complete sense. Mandukhai had offered the position to him until Batu grew old enough to rule. She had offered herself as well. Would she remain his, though, when he gave the khanship to the boy? Or would she transfer with power as well? *No, that's not possible. A man does not just give up his wife like that.*

The moment he had laid eyes on Mandukhai six years ago, Unebolod knew she was different. The day she had married Manduul, Unebolod had seen the shadow of a great eagle pass over her ger—an omen of strength. At the time, he'd did not know what that had truly meant. But he had quickly learned just how strong she was. Mandukhai had been beaten, assaulted by her own husband, poisoned by the mysterious Altan, and faced down the full force of Manduul's court after he'd died so that she could carry out his final wishes.

Unebolod's stomach clenched and twisted. Manduul's final wishes. Unebolod would be Great Khan, only if no other Borjigin heir remained. Everyone heard the proclamation in Mongke Bulag that night, so long ago now. Yet also only two years ago. So much had changed since then.

Unebolod slowed his stride, then stopped altogether, turning to take in his surroundings. Deep in thought, he had unknowingly wandered up the sacred path on Mount Burkhan Khaldun. From this high up, he could see the expanse of fires all across the rolling valley. Birch and fir trees dotted the mountain and riverbanks. Herds of animals grazed free, little more than specks of moving shadows at this distance. The darkness of night masked the colorful banners, giving them the illusion of one color—black. The color of war.

Far below, Lords and lesser khans from a dozen tribes, large and small, waited for *kurultai*. Most of them had given him their support. He had not meant for his alliances to seem like treason to Mandukhai. He had simply been preparing for the inevitable vote at *kurultai*. They needed someone strong, wise, and fair to follow. Mandukhai had once told him as much, clearly hinting that the man was him and not Manduul. But he had a duty to uphold. An oath to keep. *I still do*, he realized.

Those men would follow his lead. If he took the title—and her—they would not challenge his judgment. *But she will. Every step of the way.* Unebolod knew how fierce and dangerous Mandukhai could be when she dug in her heels. He also respected her far too much to force her into anything. Unebolod had vowed to never harm her, and that included such an obvious violation of her emotional wellbeing. If he ceded his claim to her judgment, they would also follow him—though certainly not without a need for explanation. If he accepted her offer, Unebolod would never truly be Great Khan. He would be a Regent until Batu came of age. Even if Mandukhai gave him the title, the Lords and lesser khans would not. Unebolod would be little more than a placeholder.

I would not be Great Khan, but I would have her. He huffed in irritation. It was a terrible choice.

The scuff of approaching feet from up the path attracted Unebolod's attention. He rested his hand on the hilt of his sword, just in case. One could never be too careful. Two men strolled around a bend in the path together, pausing when they noticed him.

"You are late," Getei said. The Ongud soothsayer had joined Unebolod months ago, after he had visited the Ongud khan the previous fall. Mandukhai needed Getei, he had told Unebolod. How and why, he had never explained.

The other man was Khosoichi, the Borjigin shaman. Manduul's shaman. Both of them stared at Unebolod as if they had truly expected him some time ago.

"Were we to meet earlier?" Unebolod asked, frowning.

The two shared a secret smile that set Unebolod's teeth on edge. *Shaman and their secrets*, he thought bitterly. *They probably had some sort of fore-knowledge of this encounter because some dumb spirit had told them as much.*

He grimaced. "Never mind that," Unebolod said. "Since you are here, I am hoping you can answer some questions for me."

Both men straightened and eyed him with knowing suspicion.

"How common are visions of Genghis?" Unebolod asked.

"Men claim such all the time," Khosoichi said.

"And women?" Unebolod released his sword and crossed his arms over his chest.

Both men shifted. "You are referring to our Queen Regent," Getei said.

"Did she tell you of her vision?" Unebolod asked.

"She didn't need to," Khosoichi said. "We confer with the spirits daily, in our own way."

Unebolod's heart tumbled to his stomach. Somewhere deep down, he had hoped maybe she had been mistaken, and it had been a fevered dream, regardless of how accurate her vision had been. That these two men seemed to know about her vision without her telling them made the truth undeniable. Genghis had not been a phantasm of her fevered, grieving imagination.

"You know, then, of her offer?" he asked them.

Both men nodded slightly.

"Tell me," Unebolod said, taking a desperate step toward them. "What answer should I give?"

They stepped away from him in unison and dipped their heads as if ashamed. *No, they are not ashamed. They are skirting my request.*

"Throw your bones, man, and tell me what to do!" Unebolod demanded, waving madly at the ground.

Getei shook his head. "I cannot."

"What?"

Getei raised his chin, a hardness in his gaze. "I have cast the bones to find the answers you seek. It would be ill-advised to tempt fate a second time. Uncertainty leads to madness."

You're telling me! Unebolod had to breathe deeply and let his breath out deliberately to control his rising temper. "If you already know," he said slowly through his teeth, "then tell me what you know."

Getei drew himself up and his jaw set stubbornly. Unebolod knew what the soothsayer would say before the words tumbled from his lips. "I cannot."

Unebolod seized Getei's collar and yanked him close until his breath rolled off the soothsayer and back into his own face. "This is my life you are toying with, man."

Khosoichi rested a firm, yet reassuring hand on Unebolod's arm, encouraging him to let go. "Duty is a mountain, my Lord," he said. "And we have ours to maintain, just as you do. He is not refusing you because he chooses to. He refuses because our interference in this changes the entire course of the Mongol Nation."

How long have they been discussing this? It seemed everyone had secrets to keep from him. Unebolod's shoulders heaved with angry breaths, but he released Getei and stepped back. They already knew his fate, yet would not share it with him. It was infuriating, and he wanted to yank the hair out of their scalps for answers. He wanted to do it to himself as well. He turned accusing eyes on Getei.

"You knew her fate all this time, didn't you?" he asked harshly.

Getei nodded. "Since her birth. But some things I am not at liberty to say, for it could change her fate. It could change all our fates. Including yours. I cannot give you the answers you seek, but I can tell you this. Your destinies are tethered. No matter what you choose, she will need you."

Khosoichi nodded. "It is time you find your faith, Lord Unebolod, and make amends with the High Heavens." He motioned up the path as the two of them stepped aside, leaving space for him to continue onward.

Unebolod turned and continued up the path as he heard Khosoichi and Getei carry onward down the mountain path, away from him.

Genghis had come to this mountain for protection. He had come here to plead with the gods. Tonight, Unebolod would do the same.

Over the centuries, men and women had climbed this very path, wearing down the stone into a nice, level surface. Only a few tree roots rose from the earth. Unebolod climbed with caution, aware that slipping too far to either side could end in him plummeting to his death at this late hour. It was fully dark, and only the moon and stars high above offered any light. The path was wide enough for two horses to ride abreast, but the sheer cliffs of the mountain on either side still made this a treacherous place to be at night.

At the head of the path, at the top of the mountain, a tall, twisted tree stood alone against the night sky. Blue ribbons fluttered from branches, and rocks of all shapes and sizes circled the base of the trunk. These ribbons and rocks were sacred offerings from others who had come before him. Unebolod had nothing to offer as he stood before the Mother Tree.

As a young man, he had heard the stories about Esen's death. How the men who killed him dragged his body up this hill and hung him from the tree like one of the blue ribbons—an offering to the gods to show they did not support a non-Borjigin Khan. This realization did not bode well for Unebolod's chances, either.

Unebolod drew his sword and laid it on the ground in front of him, then kneeled before the rock base of the tree and bowed his head. Would he be strung up the same way if he tried to claim the title, now that a Borjigin heir lived? While he had close ties to the Borjigin, as long as Batu lived, he would be just another non-Borjigin who attempted seizing control unjustifiably.

"Lord Tengri," Unebolod said, his shoulders hunched, "I come to you for guidance, a humble descendant of Khasar. I have tried to live my life as my father taught me, and as his father taught him. To be a man of honor and strength. To uphold my oaths and protect the Mongol Nation. To have the strength of will to do what is right, no matter the personal cost."

Unebolod sank back on his heels, gazing up at the branches of the tree as a breeze ruffled the blue ribbons like a glowing blue *sulde*. "I fear my strength is waning, my soul torn in two, with no way to mend this breach. I have spent my life in envy and find now this shameful demon taunting me. I can no longer have all I desire.

"For almost twenty years, I have wanted to become Great Khan, to restore the strength of Genghis and bring the fractured empire together once more. I believed my success in battle and at court affirmed my abilities to complete this mission. Yet I understand that the only way I could ever truly be Great Khan would be at the end of the line of Genghis." He bowed his head and closed his eyes momentarily, centering himself. Then Unebolod lifted his gaze to the tree. "I thought that unfortunate fate had come at last. But there is another. A weak, sickly boy who cannot even ride a horse. Am I truly to believe that this is the boy Genghis has chosen as his heir? Once the Mongol Lords realize this boy exists, they will turn against me as they turned against Esen fifteen years ago."

He ripped a strip of cloth from his belt, then tore it in two, holding them up in the breeze and watching the yellow ribbons flutter. "One piece of my soul is consumed with a desire to honor what my ancestors built, even if that is not my right by birth, and take the khanship. The other piece of my soul desires something far more fleeting, yet just as fulfilling ... the woman who has stolen my heart. It will never belong to another, no matter what guidance I am given this day." He observed the way the breeze made each ribbon whip and spin in his fists, as if just as uncertain which direction he should go.

"She asserts Genghis guides her," Unebolod continued, raising his voice over the rising winds. "That he vowed she would have a pack of wolves. That he believes we are destined to unite the Nation once more so that Genghis' heir can hold it together."

Everything inside of him coiled in a nauseating mass. Unebolod struggled to force the next words from his mouth. "My heart has shattered. I face a terrible choice. One I cannot face alone. Do I accept her offer, take her as a wife, and help her raise the boy—knowing the Lords will not accept me as their Great Khan? Or does this destiny to restore the fractured empire belong to her and the boy? In which case, I stand to lose everything. Mandukhai. The khanship. All of my deepest desires. My selfish heart cannot accept it. I leave my choice, my fate, to you."

Unebolod reached for his sword, careful not to let the ribbons catch in the breeze and fly away. His fingers fumbled as he tied each of the yellow strips of cloth to the hilt of his sword, keeping the ties loose and clasping them in place under his fist. Then he thrust the tip of his sword into the hard dirt, driving it deep enough to make the metal vibrate and bounce back and forth, but not fall. Unebolod kept his hand over the ribbons, then turned his gaze to the Heavens.

"I resented you for years, for taking my wife and son, for allowing a man to poison Mandukhai and kill my second child. For wiping out half of my tribe with terrible tragedies. Your will seemed unjust. I lost faith in the High Heavens and the guidance of Lord Tengri, for what had I done to deserve such torture?" Unebolod bowed his head in shame. "I understand now. My sins of envy and greed have destroyed my foundations as surely as the gunpowder destroyed my family home. Now, I kneel before you, submitting to your will."

One ribbon he had tied shorter than the other so he could easily distinguish the difference between them.

"The long ribbon represents my endless love," he explained, and his chest ached to hear the words whipped back at him on the breeze. "If I am to be with her, leave the longer ribbon on my sword, and I will keep it there eternally, just as my love for her is eternal. I will accept her offer, help her unite the Nation, and become her husband. Whether or not I am accepted as Great Khan.

"The shorter ribbon represents my honor and the oath I gave Manduul, even if it means I live my life as I always have—in the shadow of another. If I am to maintain my vow to Manduul, support the heir of Genghis, and serve a higher purpose, leave the short ribbon on my sword. I will never lay it down as long as I live. I will give up my claim, fight for her Nation, and release her to serve as Genghis desires. Let the ribbon of my eternal love fly away on wings so I may focus on this task."

Unebolod's hand ached from clenching the ribbons against the sword. He eyed the yellow tails as they rippled on the breeze. "Togochi was right. I cannot have her and maintain my honor. To have one, I have to sacrifice the other. But I cannot choose. I do not possess the strength. Lord Tengri, High Heavens above, show me the way. I submit my fate to your will, as I should have long ago."

Unebolod's chest tightened as he released his clammy hand and rose, moving back from the sword. Each breath became a struggle as he watched the yellow ribbons flap in all directions on the breeze. The knot on the longer ribbon loosened but did not slide away. Unebolod could not blink as he watched. His eyes stung as the wind hammered at him. His heart pounded against his ribs. He would accept the will of the High Heavens.

The knot on the shorter ribbon slipped loose as it flapped in the wind. Unebolod held his breath, willing it to fly away. Every part of his being wished for this short ribbon to fly away.

With both knots loose, either could sail away at any moment. Unebolod stood back stiffly, hands clenched in fists at his sides. How would he survive if her ribbon flew away? How could he live if he could not hold her? *At least I will still be near her*, he reasoned, trying to console himself.

Yet if he was destined to be Great Khan, to be with her as he believed would one day happen, his own sons would not carry on the flame. Unebolod would dedicate his best years to building an empire for another man to take over. Not his own sons. *At least I will be with her*, Unebolod thought. He could accept the sacrifice if it meant being with her. Hopefully, their children would not destroy what they built as Genghis' heirs had done.

Unebolod's mouth ran dry as he waited. The breeze fell away. The ribbons ceased fluttering just as he was certain hers would break free and fly away. It was as if the High Heavens themselves held their breath, waiting for judgment. Every second that passed created further agony in his soul. Could he get an answer from nowhere? First, the soothsayer had refused, then the shaman, now the gods themselves. Unebolod had never felt so alone, so abandoned.

"Please," Unebolod whispered, squeezing his eyes closed. Every part of his body was wound so tight it could snap at any moment. "I must know your will. Tengri, Genghis, whoever is listening to me, just give me an answer. Tell me your will."

A soft breeze curled up around Unebolod like a caress and his eyes snapped open, locked on the sword, on the ribbons as they twitched. Despite the cool air in the mountain, sweat trickled along Unebolod's temples. His fingers jerked, and he ground his teeth so hard his jaw ached. The muscles in his arms twitched, eager for something to do, for him to move. But he was rooted in place, staring at his two fates. Unebolod's throat hurt. His skin heated unnaturally without the aid of the summer sun.

After several long moments of twitching along with the two ribbons, Unebolod could no longer contain his anguish. He howled into the wind. "Answer me!"

The breeze swirled around him, then away, creating a whirlwind of leaves that spun around the sword. He held his breath. This was it.

The breeze kicked upward, tearing a ribbon off his sword and carrying it north, away. Unebolod stared at the remaining ribbon, too stunned at first to grasp what had happened. The breeze died, leaving him alone with his sword, the tree ...

And the short ribbon.

Unebolod's knees gave out. He grasped the hilt of his sword to catch his balance. Hot tears burned in his eyes. His chin dropped to his chest as the grief ripped through him. The hammering of his heart dropped to a dull thudding as if to confirm that a piece of his heart had died. His dry mouth was sour, and an impossibly painful lump swelled in his throat until he was certain it would cause his throat to rip open. Unebolod could not sob. No sound would escape through the lump in his throat, but his shoulders shook with grief all the same. The truth was too much, and he wanted the earth mother to swallow him up forever.

Mandukhai was not his, no matter what her heart may want.

She never had been.

Unebolod did not know how long he crouched in a heap, silently shaking as the grief ripped through him. Moments? Hours? He remained there until only a shell of his former self emerged. Inside, all had gone hollow.

Trembling and weak, he pushed himself to his feet and tightened the knot of ribbon on his sword. Unebolod's muscles twitched in protest as he yanked it from the earth. He sliced his hand and approached the tree, pressing his palm to the rough bark—a blood oath to uphold his end of this terrible bargain. After cleaning off the blood, Unebolod slid the sword into his belt.

Hollow, Unebolod turned from the Mother Tree and marched down the sloping path of Mount Burkhan Khaldun. He had come up the mountain a candidate as Great Khan. He would return to camp as what he had always been.

The Steel Soldier—inside and out.

CHAPTER TWENTY-ONE

The Black Road

The night was still young, and the encounter with Unebolod had left Mandukhai broken. Batu was still safely tucked away in her ger sleeping, with Boke and his men guarding the home like an impenetrable wall. Mandukhai's heart split in two. Why should she be forced to suffer this ill fate? Is this truly what Genghis wanted for her?

Too restless to return home just yet, Mandukhai shifted course and headed toward Jaghan's ger, her guards still trailing in her shadow. Perhaps her friend could help her find a way to mend her heart—or reassure her that Unebolod would do the right thing.

Along the way, she crossed paths with Togochi. *It's time for him to know the truth*, she thought.

"Togochi, a moment?" Mandukhai said, drawing his attention away from the men he had been drinking with.

The rest of the men eyed her as if she were some great puzzle. Togochi nodded and moved away from the group. Mandukhai shifted to be sure his back would be to the other men. They remained far enough away that the men would not hear her. She signaled for her guards to remain further away as well.

Togochi frowned slightly. "This is wearing you thin, Mandukhai."

She nodded. "It's time you understood exactly why. I have presented Unebolod with a choice. Tonight, he considers his answer. Right now, our future depends on him."

"I know. I'm aware of what you proposed to him. And who the boy is."

Mandukhai flinched. "Did Jaghan tell you?"

"She didn't have to. I've gathered enough hints." Togochi hung his arms at his side, clinging to a small jug of *airag* in his fist. "Korgiz is denying that the boy was your mother's son. People are asking questions, and if anyone looks closely enough, they will see his eyes. Which also means you have presented Unebolod with an impossible decision. This isn't just a matter of being with you or being Great Khan. It's a matter of his honor. To have what he wants, he will be breaking his oaths. You must understand that."

Mandukhai blanched. She had not considered that. Togochi was right. If Unebolod wanted to be with her and accepted her offer, he would be breaking one of his vows, discrediting his own word. Who would ever trust him? She closed her eyes, feeling the sting of tears attempting to form. She would have to take this decision away from him then, and she did not know if she had the strength within herself to do that.

Togochi placed a sympathetic hand on her shoulder and squeezed gently. "For what it's worth, I'm sorry this has fallen on you. I won't tell another soul until the two of you have decided how to handle this. But the truth has to come out."

Mandukhai smiled weakly. "Thank you. Enjoy your evening, Togochi. Tomorrow will be a big day."

Togochi bid her good night and returned to his friends. She watched for a moment as the men questioned Togochi, and he casually brushed everything off.

As she approached Jaghan's ger, Mandukhai slowed her steps. Voices rose from within. Women. Inviting women in for an evening of entertainment would not be unheard of, particularly as the festival approached the last day. But they had not invited Mandukhai to this celebration. That *was* unusual. Especially for Jaghan.

After a quick glance around, Mandukhai waved her guards back and edged toward the side of the ger, then tiptoed around toward the door. It was firmly closed. Still, the layers of felt did not hinder the voices within.

"... make her see reason," a woman said. Not Jaghan, but a familiar voice all the same. Mandukhai struggled to pull back the name to match that sharp tone. "I thought you said she wanted to choose him. Why has she not made that decision?"

"She does *want* to choose him," Jaghan said. "I am certain of it. Mandukhai's feelings for him have always been ... complicated. But this isn't a simple matter."

"We need a Khan or we are all doomed to walk the Black Road," another woman said.

The Black Road. A road to war, destruction, death. Did they truly have so little faith in Mandukhai's abilities?

"Yes. A woman cannot rule. We need a strong man to lead. Unige is worried that she intends to take over."

Mandukhai's jaw clenched. *Satai.*

These women spoke about Mandukhai behind her back. How many would be inside? How often had they done this? How could Jaghan allow this under her roof? Not only did the women doubt her, but Jaghan hosted this swarm of cackling hens. The betrayal seeped into Mandukhai's bones and made her weary. Could she trust no one? Her shoulders drooped, and she pressed her fingers to her lips as her stomach twisted painfully. Jaghan wouldn't have told them the truth about Batu, would she?

"The Queen Regent is young and beautiful," another woman said. "She has years of producing strong children ahead of her. Children who could one day be Great Khan. I do not understand why she would refuse a man like Lord Unebolod."

Mandukhai's back stiffened. Her stomach hardened. She had *not* refused him! Not yet. Pressing her hands to her stomach, Mandukhai raised her chin and approached the door. Enough was enough. These women would learn who she was. Mandukhai was not a prize, not a simple woman. She was a queen.

As Mandukhai reached out to open the door, a roiling heat grew in her belly. She pushed the door inward without bothering to knock and strode in as if it were her own home.

All the women fell silent, except for a few gasps of alarm. Mandukhai turned cold eyes on each, but held the longest on Jaghan, whose face flushed red with shame. It occurred to Mandukhai that these women did not know she had heard anything they said. Their shame stemmed from their guilt. Mandukhai lifted her chin and plastered on her most innocent smile.

"So many of you gathered in one place," she commented sweetly. "I must have missed my invitation to tea."

Jaghan flicked her wrist toward the back of the ger. Odgerel moved swiftly into action, pouring a cup for Mandukhai as one of the other Ladies vacated a seat and offered it to Mandukhai. Who was the woman? Mandukhai examined her clothing but could not determine who her husband might be by the style of her apparel.

Odgerel dipped her head and looked away the moment Mandukhai made eye contact with her. Ten women had gathered. And Jaghan had welcomed Odgerel—employing her as a servant, it seemed—knowing how Mandukhai loathed that woman.

"I apologize if I interrupted your conversation," Mandukhai said as she accepted the tea from Odgerel, eyeing it suspiciously. Of all the women in the ger, Odgerel had the most reason to poison her. "Please, carry on."

No one spoke. No one made eye contact with her. The silence grew thicker with each passing moment. Mandukhai reveled in their discomfort, forcing them to stew in the pot of their own design. Giving Odgerel a pointed look, Mandukhai innocently sipped at her tea. She would not show Odgerel that she feared her.

"This silence is unnerving and makes me think perhaps you were all gossiping about me behind my back," Mandukhai said with a light laugh. "But surely such noble women as yourselves would not stoop so low."

Odgerel raised her chin, glanced at the other women, then broke their silence. "The Ladies were just wondering why you haven't yet accepted Lord Unebolod's offer."

Mandukhai shot a fierce glare at the girl. "I do not give *you* permission to speak here."

Odgerel flinched and shrank away.

Mandukhai smothered a smile of satisfaction. "Are your wounds properly healed?"

"They are better, Queen Regent," Odgerel said softly, staring at the rugs.

"Good. I have been so busy holding this Nation together, I do not believe I have punished you for your defiance, Odgerel," Mandukhai said, all pretenses of innocence shattered.

"Lord Unebolod has punished me," she said timidly. "As you know."

The other women watched the exchange with intense curiosity burning in their eyes. Mandukhai would show these women who she was.

"He punished you for deceiving him," Mandukhai said. "A lesson I hope you have learned. But I reserve the right to punish you for your defiance toward myself, as well as the devious nature of your crimes. You created division and doubt, acts which I could consider treason."

For a moment, Odgerel simply waited. Mandukhai allowed the discomfort to stretch, for Odgerel's mind to travel to all manner of terrible places. At last, Odgerel trembled and sank to her knees. "Please, my Lady—"

"I am your *queen*!" Mandukhai shouted.

All the women shrank away.

Mandukhai surged to her feet and stalked toward Odgerel, who remained on her knees, bowing to Mandukhai. "But I am not without compassion," Mandukhai said. She reached down and cupped Odgerel's face, pleased at the way the girl flinched at her touch. Mandukhai tipped Odgerel's face up to meet her eyes. "You are a young woman without parents to guide her or arrange a marriage. It is only natural you would gravitate toward such a powerful man. Unfortunately, he is not meant for you. As Queen Regent, I will find you a suitable husband in the absence of your parents."

Odgerel's eyes widened in fear. Her lip trembled.

The other nine women watched with the sharp eyes of those prepared to share juicy gossip. Word of what Mandukhai did here would spread like fire through all the gathered tribes. *All the better to make these people respect my authority*, Mandukhai thought.

"There is no point in wasting time," Mandukhai said. "You are young and healthy and would make any man happy. Your noble birth allows you some rights."

"Queen Regent, Lord Unebolod has stripped me of my title," Odgerel said meekly. Her voice trembled.

"As was his right," Mandukhai replied evenly. "But as Queen Regent, I may decide where you belong. I will honor you, Lady Odgerel—something you certainly don't deserve. Your marriage will keep you forever in a position of honor, close to my side, where I can keep my eyes on you. I will choose a husband I trust, whose loyalty to me is so absolute you could never seduce him away. A man who would be thrilled to have a beauty like you in his bed every night, where you *will* perform your duties as his wife. By giving you to him, I will further solidify his loyalty to me. And if I catch a *whiff* of you plotting against me or refusing your husband, I will consider it another open act of defiance. Then my judgment will not be so merciful."

Odgerel shook her head, still cupped in Mandukhai's hand. Abject terror filled her eyes. "I beg you—"

"Do not beg!" Mandukhai snapped. "It is beneath a Mongol woman. Lady Esige has informed me of someone with great interest in you, and I trust him more than most men in this camp. Tomorrow, after the festival concludes and I have named the next Great Khan, you will marry Boke Temur."

Murmurs of approval rippled through the women collected. Mandukhai released Odgerel and turned away as the girl sank back and buried her face in her hands. Boke had expressed interest in the girl before, and he needed a wife. Mandukhai knew she could trust him to observe Odgerel, and he had been loyal to the Borjigin line all of his life. Odgerel's swaying hips would not steer away him.

As Odgerel shrank away from the rest of the women to reconcile herself to her fate, the other women appeared more interested in what would happen next. *They shouldn't be*, she thought.

"Does this mean you will accept Lord Unebolod's proposal?" a gray-haired woman asked. She held herself like a khan's wife. Mandukhai could not be certain which of the lesser khans she was married to.

Mandukhai settled back in her seat and picked up her tea after Jaghan refreshed it. "Perhaps, since you all seem determined to share your expertise on the fate of the Nation as if you know all the facts, you can advise me on how to proceed when I have a powerful Lord, favored by the tribes, eager to become my husband, take the khanship, and ignite the flame of my soul." Her tone oozed with sharp sarcasm. "You can tell me how I, a queen, should carry out the final wishes of my dead husband and the will of the High Heavens when it may oppose his wishes to accept this Lord. Perhaps, you all know better than me which road is the black road—leading to war that none of you want—and which is white, which leads us to a brighter future."

Each woman froze—except for Jaghan, who already understood Mandukhai's struggle. Mandukhai observed each as they picked apart her words, and the implication that another in the line of Genghis survived. Brows furrowed. Some chewed their lip in thought. Others turned their teacups in their hands, staring into the depths as if it contained answers. All remained silent.

"Clearly, you all understand my dilemma now," Mandukhai said. "While I would love nothing more than to give in to the whims of my heart, would your husbands accept him if they knew the truth, that this was not, in fact, what Manduul Khan had wanted? Would it take this Nation down the Black Road to war and division if I chose what my heart desires? Or would Lord Unebolod have the strength to hold the Nation together, even amidst doubt? This decision is not only mine to make. It is his, and he understands the impossible choice. I do not hesitate because I want to hold this power, as your husbands likely led you to believe. I hesitate because my very decision will determine the future of everyone ... forever. It is a heavy burden."

The women exchanged ashamed glances. Even Odgerel, her eyes red with tears, had the good sense to recognize the problem facing Mandukhai.

Satai licked her lips and shifted in her seat. "Queen Regent, I consider you a friend and hope you consider me the same. We have shared many cups of tea over the years. I understand you know Lord Unebolod well. I have watched the way he looks at you. You know his words are good. He will do as he promises."

Several of the women nodded and murmured in agreement. This actually gave Mandukhai hope for a moment. These women had the ears of their husbands, all highly ranked. If the women agreed, it meant their husbands would as well. However, it did not resolve Mandukhai's dilemma. The Lords might follow her and Unebolod, but what if they learned the truth of Batu?

Mandukhai's gaze stopped on Jaghan, who chewed her lip as a dog would a bone. Their gazes locked, and Jaghan raked her teeth over her lower lip, then licked nervously at them. Why was Jaghan so distressed? What did she know? Togochi must have said something to her.

"Speak, old friend," Mandukhai said. "You know my heart better than any other here. What am I to do when faced with this impossible choice?" Jaghan would understand the implication of her questions, being one of the few who knew the truth about Batu's parentage. Jaghan also knew what Mandukhai had offered to Unebolod. "Do I trust his word if he agrees to my terms? Should I believe he would step down once he is Great Khan, should an heir of Genghis be uncovered? And would the Lords and lesser khans accept his will?"

The questions made each of the women more uncomfortable. Several shifted, tapping toes on the rug. Mention of an heir of Genghis drew several alarmed glances. Mandukhai had been careful not to state that she knew of another, but that there could be one out there ... somewhere. It was as honest yet evasive as she could be under the circumstances.

"What would your husbands do?" Mandukhai asked pointedly, challenging each woman present. Most of them quickly looked away. She understood the reaction well enough. It meant they knew their husbands would hold the power just as surely as Unebolod would. Any man who could become Great Khan would not give it up. Not for anything.

Jaghan took a deep breath. "I know your heart, as my husband knows the heart of Lord Unebolod. He loves you as you love him. He will honor you as you deserve. But he has wanted this title as long as my husband has known him. He would not give it up willingly once he has it."

Mandukhai's heart clenched as if Jaghan had wrapped her long fingers around it and squeezed. Yet she knew, deep down, Jaghan spoke the truth, even if it was not the truth she wanted to hear.

"Should an heir of Genghis come forward, contention for the title of Great Khan will direct the Mongol men into war," Jaghan continued, and her tone shifted to a more formal register.

Mandukhai wondered why Jaghan made this change. Perhaps to show the weight of this moment?

Jaghan stiffened. Mandukhai heard the sorrow in Jaghan's voice as she continued. "Under those circumstances, if you go to a descendant of Khasar—and not that of Genghis—you will travel the Black Road to war and further division. You will no longer be a part of your whole people, and you will lose your title of *Khatun*. For others will no longer recognize it."

Mandukhai blinked to stop the burning in her eyes, sipping her tea slowly to cover the clear pain of those words. It was not the title of queen Mandukhai desired, but she refused to be the woman who ripped apart the Nation once and for all. Genghis had been clear. This decision would alter the course of their entire future. Not that Mandukhai could tell any of these women about her vision.

"Should an heir of Genghis be unearthed," Jaghan said, "if you choose to support descendant Genghis, you will be treated well by the High Heavens, govern the whole people as you have so wisely done in the shadows and in the light these past years, and make famous your name. You will follow the White Road and rule the Nation as you make famous an unrivaled name. If you want to know what my husband would do, or if the other men will follow, you already know the answer in your mind. It is your heart that is steering you astray."

Mandukhai remained silent, allowing these words to sink in. Jaghan spoke the truth as honestly as she always had. Unebolod likely knew the answer as certainly as she did. The Lords and lesser khans would end up divided if she gave him the title. Those loyal to the Borjigin line would never truly accept him, and Unebolod would not so easily give up the title once he had it. To reignite the flame of the line of Genghis, Unebolod could never be Great Khan.

Tears pricked the corners of Mandukhai's eyes as this reality pressed down against her shoulders, threatening to crush her under the weight of a mountain. The moment the Lords and lesser khans realized who Batu was, Unebolod's reign would be over. But he would still fight to hold on to it. *I have presented him with an unreasonable option*, Mandukhai realized. *Togochi was right. I have asked the unthinkable of Unebolod. The moment he loses his honor, all bets are off. Break one vow and you can break them all.*

Mandukhai took a careful breath to regulate her increasing heartbeat. "Unebolod insists the men need a strong Lord, and that I am a widow queen without a Khan," she said softly. "While I do not believe he sees me as weak and he respects me, he still sees what all men see. A woman."

"He is right," Satai said firmly. "We *do* need a strong man to lead."

This comment from Satai inflamed Mandukhai's anger. She had expected as much from the men, but the women Mandukhai had hoped would understand. As her face heated in anger, she glanced around the ger. Many of the women nodded in agreement with Satai. They all saw this so simply. Mandukhai was a woman. Her job was to produce children and be a good wife. To them, it ended there. But Mandukhai knew her talents were wasted, and if she gave in to the demands of the men now, then she was condemning women forever. Who could ever respect a woman's decision if she proved, again and again, to be worth one thing only?

All the anger bubbled to the surface. Mandukhai surged to her feet and threw her cup at Satai. The other woman yelped as the hot liquid poured out on her clothes. Most of the other women scrambled away. The gray-haired Lady rushed forward to help Satai.

"And because I am a woman, I am unequal to the task?" Mandukhai snapped. "Have I not guided this Nation when the men were too weak to do so themselves? For years, I steered my husband's hand. I advised him to bridge gaps instead of causing further divides." Mandukhai's anger rose into a heat that burned in her face and eyes. Her chest heaved with mounting fury. "You see me as the men do—weak simply because I am a woman. Yet I was the one who governed when Manduul Khan rode to battle. I was the one who prevented him from starting a war against Bigirsen; a war that would have destroyed us all! And who did he entrust this important task to? Not Unebolod or Togochi or Unige. He understood what no one else seems to understand—that I have been guiding this Nation from the moment we married! And I will continue to guide the Mongol Nation toward better days so that *your* husbands don't have to fight each other and die for nothing!"

Mandukhai clenched her hands into fists at her sides. "Perhaps, Satai, you have given yourself to whatever man had the courage to claim you as his," she spat.

Satai blanched. Unige had done exactly that after her first husband had been killed in the very charge Unige had been leading. Instead of fighting back to honor her dead husband, Satai climbed into his killer's bed.

The anger made Mandukhai's hands tremble with rage. "But such a fate is not my path! I am not a prize to be claimed by the victor. I am a queen."

Enraged, Mandukhai strode toward the door, afraid of what else she might do if she remained a moment longer. "Lord Unebolod will accept my terms and give me his vow, or he will get nothing."

Lord Tengri, give him more sense than these women! Mandukhai thought as she stormed out of the ger and into the darkness of night, allowing it to swallow her whole.

Upon returning to her ger, Boke bowed to Mandukhai. He obviously noted the storm cloud surrounding her, but he said nothing. Mandukhai paused at the door, taking a breath to steady herself and calm down.

"Tell me, Boke, have you considered taking a wife?" she asked. "While I appreciate your dedication to serving me, I understand that men have needs and a right to have sons. I would not want you to assume that your service restricts you from having a family. As long as you maintain your oaths to me."

Boke's brows climbed his forehead. "I have considered it but have not yet found a woman who would have me."

That admission startled Mandukhai. What woman would not want Boke? He was strong, respected, well-positioned ...

"I have someone."

He shifted feet and glanced at the other guards forming a ring around her ger. "*Khatun?*"

"Tomorrow night, after I have named the new Great Khan, you will have a wife, if you want her." She had not given Odgerel a choice because the woman had lost her right to choose. But Boke earned the respect to make this decision on his own.

"May I ask who you have in mind?"

"Odgerel," Mandukhai said.

Boke gaped. He placed a fist over his heart and bowed. "If that is your will, I would not refuse the command of the *Khatun.*"

"Command?" Mandukhai shook her head, placing a hand on his shoulder. "No, Boke. I will not command you to marry her, but I was led to believe you had an interest in her."

Boke righted himself, raising his chin. "I did. I do. I just assumed she had ... other interests."

Boke did not have to say whom he meant. The implication was clear enough. He had noticed her interest in Unebolod.

"She also understands that is not an option for her, and you are a good man. I will not force this on you. If you so choose, she is yours."

"Thank you, *Khatun*," Boke said, nodding with far more respect than other men showed her. "I am more than happy with this arrangement."

The thrill of this minor victory lifted Mandukhai's heavy heart. "Just remember who you are loyal to."

"Until my last breath, *Khatun*," he said.

While the win was small and could not abate her own woes, Mandukhai still managed a smile as she ducked inside.

The air inside was warm and thick. Esige sat on the floor with Nemeku, telling him a story as Batu slumbered in the bed. Both gazed up at Mandukhai with heavy lids. The excitement of the day, coupled with the exorbitant amount of food everyone consumed, would make all the people at Mount Burkhan Khaldun tired. Some sooner than others. But Mandukhai feared she would not sleep this night as she awaited Unebolod's answer.

"How is he?" Mandukhai asked, sidling to the edge of the bed.

"He gets tired real easy," Nemeku pointed out, peering over his shoulder at Batu. "Why don't he talk?"

Mandukhai poured water from a bucket into a kettle and set it on the stove. "He has had a very hard life for one so young. It's hard to trust anyone when everyone has abandoned or hurt you."

Nemeku puffed his chest out. "But I will protect him. We are family ... aren't we?"

Esige ruffled Nemeku's hair. "Yes. We are. But sometimes even family has to leave." Her gaze shifted meaningfully to Mandukhai, but Mandukhai could not for the life of her figure out why. What did that look mean?

The door opened as Mandukhai placed the tea in the kettle. Boke ducked in.

"Yes?" Mandukhai asked. Her gut twisted. Was it Unebolod with his answer already? "Who has come to see me?"

"Not you, Khatun," Boke corrected. "There is a Lord Huoshai here to see Lady Esige."

Mandukhai snorted. "Let him in."

Boke's gaze flicked to Batu.

"It's all right, Boke," she reassured him.

He bowed back out the door.

A moment later, Huoshai ducked through the door, standing respectfully beside the threshold as he slid his hat off his head.

"Queen Regent, I apologize for the intrusion at this hour, but I was hoping to speak with Lady Esige," Huoshai said, twisting his hat in his hands.

Mandukhai expected Esige to refuse him outright, but as she watched the girl, prepared to say it was Esige's choice to speak with him, she noticed the way Esige's eyes lit up. Mandukhai's breath hitched. She knew that look. She had observed it many times before on other women. Jaghan. Borogchin. Odgerel. Countless others she could not name. *I'm not ready for this,* Mandukhai thought. For the first time, Esige seemed to have an interest in a boy.

No, he is not a boy. He is a man looking for a wife. Mandukhai was prepared to tell him to leave, but she had promised to let Esige make her choices. *I don't want to let go yet.*

Esige turned her hopeful gaze to Mandukhai, clearly struggling to tear it away from this handsome young Lord.

"I want your guard with you, Esige," Mandukhai said firmly. "Do not even attempt evading them, or I will know."

Esige climbed to her feet with such care that Mandukhai knew the girl was toying with Huoshai. She moved slowly and deliberately as if in no hurry to speak to him. Mandukhai knew better. Esige contained her emotions well—she always had—because if she did not, she would already be skipping out the door and dragging Huoshai along.

Nemeku made a face of disgust as he gagged the moment Esige and Huoshai disappeared into the deepening darkness outside. Mandukhai thumped him in the back of the head. "It is time for bed, Nemeku."

He rolled to his feet with all the grace of a young wolf ready to play, then moved to the small stack of felts Mandukhai kept in her ger for him. Despite his young, lithe energy, it was obvious the excitement of the day had exhausted him. He curled up on the felts, not bothering to pull one over his small body. He watched Mandukhai for a moment until his heavy-lidded eyes drifted closed.

Mandukhai turned to Batu. He had rolled to his side with his back to the rest of the ger, clutching the blankets in his little hands as if afraid the blankets might vanish. How different these two boys were. One wild, free, and unashamed. The other timid, restrained, and cautious. She settled on the bed beside Batu, wrapping an arm around his thin body. Even in his sleep, he trembled.

Unebolod was right. Batu was small and weak, but he was also only a boy, and boys could grow stronger. Batu could be properly raised to be strong. To do that, she would need Unebolod's help. No matter what he decided, she would need him.

Mandukhai lay beside Batu, holding the terrified boy, worried about what the future would hold.

CHAPTER TWENTY-TWO

Whispers in the Dark

Esige trailed alongside Huoshai across the expanse of the camps, un-certain where he was taking her. Here and there, they would step out of shadows into the light of another campfire before passing into shadows once more, like two wraiths on a mission. Esige glanced over her shoulder as her stomach coiled in a mass. Her two guards trailed a few feet behind them. She had not heard their footsteps over the jovial noises of the camps or the rise and fall of music. It reassured her to know the two guards remained with her. While she was not afraid of Huoshai—Esige didn't fear any man—she was unsure of his intentions.

"Usually when people walk together, they talk to one another," she said, shattering the comfortable silence between them.

Huoshai shrugged. "You didn't seem terribly interested in talking to me before."

"Then why are we doing this?"

He grinned at her. "Are you interested now?"

Esige rolled her eyes dramatically and grunted. "Don't flatter yourself." But the way he grinned at her made her stomach flip. "I just don't see the point of us walking if we aren't talking. Unless you are playing a game with the other Lords interested in me, trying to show your dominance."

A laugh rolled out of him. "What sort of world have you been living in?"

Esige sulked, turning her attention away from him. She didn't bother answering. Was her suspicion a result of the world she had grown up in? Esige had just assumed it was the same everywhere. Why wouldn't it be?

Everyone wants something, Unebolod had told her, *be careful what you give in exchange.*

But now Esige wondered if Huoshai was toying with her, or if he truly meant he thought her suspicion odd. What was life like among the Urainkhai?

Huoshai nudged open a path through a group of teens their age, sliding his hand into hers to pull her along with him. Esige had half a mind to yank her hand away, but she worried she might lose him in the crowd. Once again, she glanced back to see her guards pushing their way along to keep up as the gap closed behind her. *Is he trying to lose them? Mandukhai will string me up by my toes if I slip my guards with him!*

Cheers erupted all around them. The crowd jostled Esige. She tightened her grip on Huoshai's hand. He pulled her closer and put his arm around her so they couldn't be separated. Her guards fell further back into the mass of bodies.

"I thought you might want to break free from your cage," Huoshai said, leaning close so she could hear him over the crowd. Even then, it was hard to hear him clearly.

His arm remained around her waist, keeping her tight against his side. His warmth radiated through her clothes and ignited some unknown sensation in her core. This close, she could smell leather and sweat mingled with the powerful scent of campfire smoke. Did he always smell like that?

Huoshai wedged an elbow between two teens in front of them, then brought his arm between the bodies to pry them away from each other.

Through the gap, Esige spotted the wrestling ring. Another cheer erupted loudly over the regular commotion of the crowd. She grinned, pushing between the bodies to the front, easing away from Huoshai as she jockeyed for a better position.

The wrestlers had their arms locked together, and their feet danced around each other as they both attempted sweeping the leg of their opponent. If any part of the body besides the feet touched the ground, that wrestler would lose. The two continued in their odd dance of feet, torsos swinging back and forth as they fought to overpower the other. It looked like a dance to Esige.

Huoshai stood at Esige's shoulder, grinning and cheering with the crowd. He remained close enough for her to smell him, but paid her no attention otherwise. Esige allowed herself to get swept up in the moment. The roar of the crowd. The struggle of each set of wrestlers. A skin of *airag* passed by and she took a generous drink, then swiped her arm across her mouth and passed it on. Huoshai's fingers brushed hers as he took the *airag*, and the touch sent a jolt throughout her body. Was that normal? Esige certainly had never felt it before.

Eventually, the crowd broke apart as wrestlers cleared out and a group of teens entered the ring, striking up music. Her guards had somehow remained nearby, and they drew a few curious glances from other teen boys and girls around them. Esige hoped no one knew the guards were there because of her.

She waited for Huoshai to offer a dance, but the two of them remained on the side, watching the other teens dance and laugh. Her stomach twisted, and she realized she was disappointed that he hadn't asked her to dance. *I won't jump off a cliff chasing down a girl who is clearly not interested*, he had told her last time they talked. So what were they doing tonight, then?

Another guy she didn't recognize offered to dance, and Esige hesitated a moment, glancing at Huoshai. He offered a nonchalant shrug. Her stomach tumbled in disappointment. Esige smiled at the guy and joined him in the line of dancers, entering the *Biyelgee* dance. The lines rolled back and forth through each other like waves as everyone moved together. Esige managed her perfect balance, something she had perfected in her own training with Unebolod over the years.

Despite the cool summer night air and the breeze that swept over the crowd, sweat beaded on Esige's temples. It rolled down her back as she continued dancing. Her partner shifted to the side, joining the next girl in line, and Esige was startled to see Huoshai in his place. Had he been dancing with another girl instead? Esige didn't like the jealousy brewing in her gut.

The two of them moved fluidly around each other as the lines shifted forward and back. She twirled around and dipped her shoulder, offering out her hand. His fingertips grazed her own and their gazes tethered to one another. Esige was transfixed and knew she could not look away if she had tried with all her might. He had trapped her as surely as a mouse in the sights of an eagle.

He was not like the other boys who had approached her. His flippant attitude about courting her only intrigued her even more. The fact that he had clearly told her he wouldn't chase her down made her wonder why. And as they danced, gazes tethered to each other, the torchlight created a dance of their own in his dark eyes. That excitement in his eyes belied all of his exterior nonchalance.

The swell of the music dipped down, indicating the end of the song approached. Esige lifted her arms, continued the dancing twitch of her shoulders, and swung her body down from the waist, delicately swooping her arms forward, palms to the sky. Even bent over, her gaze remained locked on Huoshai. Her insides writhed with crazed excitement.

Why was it the one boy she wanted to have chase her was the one who clearly stated he wouldn't?

As the song ended, the two of them walked away from the lines of dancers. A new song began, but they moved as if of the same mind toward a small barrel of *airag*. They waited their turn, standing so close their arms almost touched. The heat from his skin was hotter than it had been before. He dipped the ladle first but offered it to her. Esige smiled shyly and took the drink.

After Huoshai had his own drink, they began walking further from the music, much closer than they had been on the walk toward the celebration. Once more, bubbles of excitement rolled up from Esige's toes.

"Thank you," she said once they were far enough away they no longer had to shout over the noise of the crowd.

"For what?" He glanced at her, then past her at the guards.

"For helping me escape the cage, even if only for the night."

He said nothing. As they strolled alongside each other, she wanted to reach for his hand, but would that be proper for her to do? It might give him the wrong idea. Or was it the wrong idea at all? Esige did not like the uncertainty. But she loved the way just being with him made her entire body come alive. She loved wrestling, riding, archery, but this ... this felt different.

"Is that the end of our evening and conversations, then?" she asked. "You walked me there in silence. We stand together for a while. Dance a little. Now you walk me home in silence?"

"It's what you wanted." Huoshai said it so matter of fact that Esige worried he meant what he said before. This was nothing more than a means of helping her escape for a little while. It meant nothing else.

"You are only returning me to the cage," she said, pouting a little. If only she could have a little more time outside before she had to return to her duties.

Huoshai slipped his hand into hers and Esige's knees trembled. He stopped, turned her to face him, and slid his free hand along her cheek, cupping her face. He edged so close she couldn't breathe without inhaling his breath.

Her stomach bottomed out. *He's going to kiss me!* she realized. What would her guards do? She did not know if they would tear the two apart, report it to Mandukhai, or do nothing at all. Their job was to ensure no one harmed her. Did it end at that?

"I don't want to keep you in your cage," he whispered. Huoshai's eyes tore into her with burning intensity. "I want to set you free."

She swallowed and licked her lips. "Then set me free."

Huoshai's lips brushed hers, and the heat of the sun itself burned her from the inside out. Her pulse quickened. Her heart raced. She leaned against him, absorbing every second of this touch, committing it to her memory to sustain her in the years to come. Esige had kissed other boys before, but nothing had ever been like this. Not even close. His lips brushed hers, taunting. His tongue teased her mouth. Esige took the hand she still clasped in her own and pressed it to the small of her back. Then her arms snaked around him, fingertips feeling the muscles in his back through his thin summer deel. She parted her lips, brushing her tongue against his, and a small sound of delight escaped her throat.

Suddenly, Huoshai broke his mouth away. She moaned in disappointment, arching her neck to reconnect. He stepped back.

"I think we should get you home," he murmured. His own voice was breathless.

Esige's head spun, stuffed full of cotton and pure delight. Home was the last place she wanted to be. "I thought you wanted to set me free."

His palm stroked her cheek, and that consuming intensity in his eyes once more made her stomach drop. "I do. But your guards are watching. No matter how interested I am, I'm not sure I could stop myself if we carried on too long. You burn like an unquenchable fire, and I long to be consumed by the flames."

Disappointment made the butterflies of excitement transform into a churning mass of sludge. "I see."

Huoshai flinched. "Your tone suggests otherwise."

"Congratulations, Lord Huoshai. You have played your game and received your reward," she said sharply. "Now you can go brag to all your friends that you chipped away at the warrior princess."

Esige spun on her heel, whipping her hair out at him.

"Wait, what?" Huoshai rushed forward, cutting her off. "Esige, don't you get it? I came here with no idea what I would find, if anything. But the second I heard about you, laid eyes on you, that was it. You burn brilliant and bright like a flame, drawing me in. I did not know what I wanted when I came. Now ..." He swallowed.

Esige crossed her arms over her chest and raised her eyebrows. But she already knew what he was about to say. Had all of this been a trick to break down her wall? "Now what?"

Huoshai took both of her hands, pulling her arms down, and eased himself to his knees. "Now I'm at your mercy. Name your price. I will pay the world."

Suddenly her heart hammered so hard she could feel it in her throat. "What?" she asked, too stunning to put the pieces together.

"I will never trap you in a cage," he said. "I will always open the door and let you roam to your heart's content. All I ask is that, when you are satisfied, you return to me. Tell me, what can I do to earn your heart … forever?"

"Mandukhai would want—"

"I'm not asking her what she wants," he said. "Esige. What do *you* want?"

What did she want? No one had asked her that before. Mandukhai told Esige she could choose, but some part of her always knew Mandukhai would still have to approve. Would she approve of Huoshai? Excitement and terror made terrible stomach mates. Esige was not sure if she would throw up or bubble over with happiness.

Huoshai had not treated her like the others. He listened. He *saw* her.

"I'm getting a little worried down here," he said.

Her hands were clammy. He had to have noticed. But was he trembling? What did he have to be afraid of?

Esige could not deny that she had been drawn to him all night. "I want you to beat me in a race," she said.

He chuckled. "You won't make it easy for me, will you?"

"Never."

He climbed to his feet and brushed his lips over hers. "Then I will do my best to be worthy."

"I sure hope so."

The two of them resumed their walk back to Mandukhai's ger, fingers laced together. Neither said another word. Esige wondered if Huoshai's insides were as much of a mess as her own. What if he couldn't beat her? She wanted him. There was no doubt in her mind about that. But if he lost, she would lose as well.

They approached the ger, pausing a few feet away from the guards.

"She still had to agree to this," Esige said, worried that this could still fall apart. "And after what happened to my sister, I'm not sure she will."

"What happened to your sister?"

Esige swallowed the grief that leaped into her throat.

"I didn't mean to upset you," he blurted.

What must she look like if he could read her grief so easily? "No, it's not ... My uncle married my sister to Bigirsen, but he killed her the moment she showed him defiance. Nemeku is all I have left of her." Esige could hear how thick her voice had become. She sniffled and angrily swiped her tears away. "Mandukhai is overprotective of me now. She may not agree to any marriage."

"I leave that to your skilled hands," he said. "You seem to have a way with her." He kissed her hand and started away, glancing back and grinning at her.

"Hey," she called.

Huoshai turned and walked backward. "My Lady?"

"I won't be toyed with."

He paused, bowing. "I would never dream of toying with a woman like you." Then he spun around again and disappeared around Togochi's ger.

Esige bit her lip and steeled herself, then tiptoed into Mandukhai's ger with hope, excitement—and a bit of fear—blooming in her chest.

Mandukhai lay on the bed beside Batu, and she rolled over as Esige entered, watching her cross the ger. Esige made her way toward Nemeku to check on him, then tucked the blanket around him and brushed her hand over his forehead. Would this mean she had to leave Nemeku behind? She loved him almost as much as she would love her own son.

Mandukhai sat up and rubbed her tired eyes. "What bothers you? Did he hurt you?"

"No." Esige glided silently across the ger, then bit her lip as she stopped beside Mandukhai's bed. "Mother, I would like to race in the morning."

Mandukhai stiffened. "You cannot enter the races, Esige. We have talked about this. Besides, it is too late."

"Not that race, Mother." Esige held her breath as she watched Mandukhai's reaction. It was a mixture of shock and fear.

"I hear he is a good man, and a future khan of his tribe." Mandukhai eyed Esige curiously. What was that look about? "Will you let him win?"

Esige laughed. "You know me better. No. I would let no man win." Though if he was close, it would sorely tempt her.

Mandukhai appeared to calculate something as she considered this. She probably assumed the odds were not in Lord Huoshai's favor. Perhaps they weren't. *There will be only one way to know*, Esige thought.

"I will make the arrangements tomorrow morning," Mandukhai said. "If you are certain."

Esige bit her lip to smother her smile, but it failed miserably. Everything inside of her twisted in a maelstrom of chaos. "I am."

"I am happy for you, then." Mandukhai spoke the words, but Esige could hear the sadness bleeding through.

How would she even sleep tonight?

CHAPTER TWENTY-THREE

Duty is a Mountain

Mandukhai's heart weighed heavily as she worried over Unebolod's decision. To assuage her soul, she sought guidance from the High Heavens. Mandukhai moved to the altar at the back wall of the ger and lit incense. The sage quickly filled her senses. She kneeled before the altar. Her prayers were no simple matter. The fate of the Mongol Nation rested on her shoulders, and the burden of that decision weighed on her pleas to Lord Tengri. She prayed for answers, for guidance, and for strength, pouring every ounce of her will and desire into each precious thought.

Should the High Heavens approve, surely they would send her a sign. Soon. For tomorrow, Mandukhai's and Unebolod's decisions would forever shape the future of the Nation.

The incense continued to burn as Mandukhai climbed into bed beside Batu, resting a hand on the boy's chest. Death was behind him, but his heart still felt too weak.

As Mandukhai drifted into the world of dreams, Unebolod consumed her thoughts. His decision could bring them together at last or tear them apart forever. To place such a burden on him was unfair, but Mandukhai could not make this decision alone. Nor would it be fair to do so without him understanding the implications of what would happen.

Jaghan's warning also pressed on Mandukhai's mind as she struggled to fall asleep. Would it truly take her down the Black Road—a path of war and destruction—if Mandukhai chose Unebolod? Ruling the Mongols these past months, since Manduul's death, had been exhausting. Someone always opposed her simply because she was a woman. Could she truly handle ruling the Nation until Batu came of age, should Unebolod not accept her offer? Surely Genghis could not have meant for her to walk the White Road of wisdom and enlightenment alone. Her last thought before drifting off was a prayer to the High Heavens to guide her soul.

The world of dreams had a different feel than the real world, like a half-truth that carried only the weight of what *might* be instead of what *would* be. Mandukhai could not put the sensation into words. Yet even within the world of her dreams, she perceived a shift, a certainty that carried her very soul and made her body come alive in a way she could not produce by any other means. Most dreams were forgettable or excusable, while a rare few were so grounded in a heavenly reality that they pulled her inexorably forward. She could not control the way such heavenly dreams moved her body alone a predetermined path. It often felt like a combination of the surreal and real.

This dream was no different. With Dust beneath her and the wind in her hair, Mandukhai raced across the steppe with a sense of freedom. Yet another sensation pressed in around her, as if she was trapped in a prison she could not escape.

It is time, a voice in her mind said as Mandukhai crested a hill along the plains on Dust's back. The voice was not her own. Mandukhai could not say what it was time for.

A breeze caressed her skin, carrying with it that surreal sensation despite the very real foundations of the world around her.

At the top of the hill, Dust snorted and stopped, stamping his hoof into the dusty ground. Mandukhai gazed at the plains ahead. The space felt both familiar and foreign like she had returned home after years away living another life. What did this dream portend? *I prayed to the High Heavens for a sign. Is this it?*

Another rider drew up beside her. She expected to find Unebolod there, but instead, a burly man in rich, thick furs sat in his saddle on a fine armored horse. He gazed across the plains as well. His looped braids hung long and low over his shoulders, covered only by his fur hat. The way he sat in the saddle exuded a comfort that came from years of experience, along with a deadly grace. Mandukhai's breath quickened. She had seen this man before.

"Lord Genghis," she said formally, bowing in her saddle.

Genghis turned his wolf-like golden eyes on her, his hand resting casually on the handle of his wolf-head sword. The black horsehairs that hung from the hilt swayed in the breeze. Mandukhai knew he could kill her in an instant. She found herself both terrified and mesmerized by him, just as she had been the first time he had come to her. *I prayed for a sign, and this is it.*

For a moment, the two of them sat in their saddles, side-by-side, staring across the dusty plain. In the distance, the horizon burned red and orange as if a great fire consumed the world. The scent of campfires carried on the wind, accentuating the sense that everything was ablaze. The sun no longer shone in the sky, and gray clouds covered the normal hues of blue high above as if smoke filled the sky and choked out the world. An ominous sensation rolled down Mandukhai's spine as she observed what she could only relate to as the end of the world.

"I gave them an empire, and they have forgotten their unity and purpose," Genghis said, his voice drowning in sorrow. His face wrinkled in disgust as he stared at the burning horizon. "I left the greatest empire in the world, but my line is ending. The men know only one solution. They will tear each other apart before uniting. They have forgotten the One Nation."

The disgust shifted as his face sagged. Mandukhai could *feel* his sorrow profoundly in her own heart.

"My vision is burning," he murmured.

Tears welled in Mandukhai's eyes as she sensed the great depth of his words. The Mongol Lords would ignite the flame of war once she named a Great Khan. This would be the fate of her world. "I have failed you."

"No, Daughter," Genghis said.

Mandukhai tore her gaze away from the horizon to meet his penetrating stare. A firmness set in his jaw. He straightened in the saddle. How could he not see this as a failure? The world would burn, the Nation would crumble, and she was the one in charge of it all.

"I told you before," Genghis said. "I have seen the strength of women. I have underestimated their value and learned to listen when they offered their advice." Thunder rumbled across the sky, matching his dangerous and stormy expression. "*You* must be the voice of reason."

"I fear some may not want to listen," Mandukhai said, slumping in her saddle. "Unebolod has wanted to be Great Khan all his life. How can I deny him?"

Genghis cocked his head as his mount danced beneath him. "You misunderstand me. Perhaps time has dulled your memory. You have given your heart to passion. Now, it is time to give your heart to compassion. Only one can hold true power over you."

Mandukhai flinched. Her love for Unebolod had consumed her like an eternal flame, never relinquishing. Passion was a simple, yet poor word for how she truly felt about Unebolod. But the weight of a nation was great, and duty was as heavy as a mountain. Such a thing could not simply be handed over without due consideration.

Jaghan's words echoed in Mandukhai's mind. Unebolod had wanted this too long to hand over his power when Batu came of age.

"Remember, only the one who carries the spirit can reunite the One Nation," Genghis said, pulling her from her inner turmoil. "And only He of my bone will have the might to hold it."

Mandukhai nodded solemnly. "Unebolod and I are prepared to be that spirit, I believe." Was she certain, though? Only his response would reveal the answer. Years ago, she had assumed Genghis meant her compassion to be for Manduul, as she had certainly been compassionate toward him in those final years. Now she knew better.

It was Batu.

It had always been Batu.

She and Unebolod were the spirit. Batu was the bone. Somehow, the three of them were tethered in this fate together.

That was why Genghis had shown her the boy years ago. To prepare her. "Batu is too young, and still so weak," she said. "I fear the worst is not over for him yet."

"I have told you already that the strength of a man comes from the strength of the woman who guides him through life." He shifted in his saddle to face her more directly. His words burned with a passion that Mandukhai felt press into her own soul. "Be that strength. One arrow alone can be easily broken, but many arrows are indestructible."

Mandukhai nodded. Alone and divided, this future before her would be certain. The world would burn. But together, perhaps she could raise Batu to be the Khan the Mongols needed. Perhaps that weak boy simply needed more arrows to help make the Mongols indestructible once more.

"How does one set aside her heart?" she muttered to herself.

Genghis snorted. "Spoken like a true woman. Remember who your heart truly belongs to, daughter of the dragon, queen of the wolves. You drank from my cup of destruction when we last met. Now, with the blood of the wolf in your veins, you will birth a pack of wolves to complete what I could not."

Mandukhai bowed her head. While his words made sense, what did that mean for her and Unebolod? Could they unite the Nation together?

Mandukhai knew she could not walk away from him. She had waited years for this chance to be with him and did not have the strength to refuse him. The more she considered this, the more certain Mandukhai became. She could no more refuse Unebolod as a husband than the moon could refuse to let the sun rise. Was he telling her that she had to let him go, or that her plan to marry Unebolod and make Batu Great Khan when he came of age would be sufficient?

Genghis seemed to sense her hesitation and said, "My brother Khasar was a great warrior, but he did not truly understand the breadth of what I was trying to accomplish. He failed to see my true struggle. Conquering the world on horseback is easy; it is dismounting and governing that is hard. This will be your destiny, Mandukhai. You may desire one thing, but remember that a leader can never be happy until his people are happy. It was my greatest mistake. The merit in action lies in finishing it to the end."

Genghis turned his horse away from the burning horizon and faced Mandukhai head-on. "You know in your heart what must be done. Now, it is up to you to find the strength to do it."

"I cannot do this." Mandukhai's heart seized as if in the grasp of some giant. "You have made a mistake."

"I leave you a heavy burden to bear, but duty is a mountain, and I have waited these centuries for a firm hand with the strength and spirit to do what needs to be done." He drew his wolf-head sword and offered it to her. "Mandukhai the Wise, I leave you the monumental duty of restoring the greatest empire in the world. Only you can rebuild what my kin has broken. Only the boy can hold it together."

Mandukhai eyed the wolf-head sword—the sword of Khans. Genghis offered it to her, a woman, freely. Such a gift represented a sacred trust. All her young life, Mandukhai had dreamed of being strong, of carrying the spirit of Lady Khutulun. Now Genghis offered her something far more valuable.

His own spirit.

Solemnly, Mandukhai wrapped her hand around the hilt of the sword and accepted the duty placed upon her shoulders.

As she grasped the sword, the truth moved like magic from the handle, through her hand, up her arm, and into her mind. Genghis' warning about his own brother sparked in her mind with clarity and absolute certainty, like he passed his knowledge on to her through the sword.

Unebolod wanted to be Great Khan, but like his ancestor, Khasar, he was a great warrior who did not truly realize what it meant to rule. She saw as much through the years. Unebolod had no patience for the daily tasks of a Great Khan. He wanted the title because of the prestige—because he felt he deserved it. But now, with the sword of Genghis in her hand, she realized the terrible truth.

Unebolod's path as Great Khan would lead to destruction as surely as the horizon ahead of her. He would not focus on uniting the tribes but on conquering them. The distinction was fine, but clear. He would lead as all men did—through destruction and bloodshed. Once she gave him the title, she would be powerless to stop him.

Mandukhai *had* to take another path.

Genghis wanted her to choose his own heir. Yet she could not fathom a life without Unebolod. Just imagining it created a fracture in her heart.

Genghis did not explain further. He did not need to. The sword passed his knowledge on to her. Instead, he simply galloped into the darkness behind her. His voice carried on the breeze as he disappeared. "Remember, be of one mind and one faith, that you may conquer your enemies and lead long and happy lives."

Mandukhai turned her attention to the horizon. Love was a burden that clouded her judgment. Duty was a mountain. To choose the right course, she had but to ride with the One Nation in her heart. Mandukhai kicked Dust into a gallop toward the burning horizon.

Someone had to extinguish the flames.

CHAPTER TWENTY-FOUR

Thresholds

Mandukhai's eyes fluttered open to discover the wolf-like golden eyes of Genghis staring back at her. She jumped, startled by his presence here in her bed, before realizing it was only Batu. In his eyes, Mandukhai saw the future, but she also saw the loss of her own personal desires.

The certainty of her own decision in the dream carried over into the waking world. How could she refuse Unebolod the title while also allowing him this decision? Surely he had spent his night in just as much grief as she had, worried over what was best. If Mandukhai took that choice from him, he would have every right to resent her.

Genghis had chosen her for this task. The spirits of the Khans had faith in her ability. *I have waited centuries*, Genghis had said. She could not fail him. She could not fail Unebolod, either.

"Has my life ever been my own?" she mumbled, stroking dark hair away from Batu's forehead.

The corners of Batu's mouth curved further downward. The boy seemed to wear a perpetual frown, with a rare exception when Nemeku's humor drew out a smile.

"A lot is riding on the two of us, Batu," Mandukhai said softly. "But I fear for our future if you cannot speak. Please tell me something. Make some sound to show me you have a voice of your own. You will need it in the years to come."

Batu simply stared at her with those penetrating, soulful eyes. He had made some noises before, she knew. When Khosoichi had pierced Batu's lungs to allow in air, the boy had shrieked loudly enough to rattle Mandukhai's eardrums. He must have a voice with which to speak, and somehow Mandukhai would need to draw words from his lips. Even if only for her.

"It's okay," Mandukhai murmured, then kissed his forehead.

Duties of the day waited, but the wolf dawn gave Mandukhai a little more time before she needed to be up and ready. Tuya would enter soon to stoke the fire and get breakfast prepared. Then they would dress Mandukhai for the day—the most important day of her life.

How could Mandukhai tell a boy of seven just how important he was to her future? "Do you like stories, Batu?"

He nodded ever so slightly.

"Once, there was a young girl, the same age as you are now, who dreamed of being a fierce warrior like Lady Khutulun. She dreamed of flying with eagles, riding fast horses, and fighting for the Mongol Nation to preserve what Genghis Khan built. As she grew older, the girl was instead married to the Great Khan. He was a man of good intentions but weak ambitions, and she could not give her heart to him, no matter how hard she tried.

"Then, one day, she met a fierce and handsome warrior. This girl, now a queen, saw something special in this warrior." Mandukhai's throat tightened as grief seized her heart. "And he loved her with a passion fierce enough to consume the world. When the Great Khan's body failed him and he passed away, he left the Mongol Nation in his young queen's hands, and she thought she knew for certain that this warrior she loved with all her heart would be her husband's successor." Tears burned in Mandukhai's eyes, slid along the bridge of her nose, then dripped into the pillow.

As she continued, her voice thickened with pain. "But this warrior's passion was all-consuming. She realized that, to save the world from his black road, she would have to release the hold he had over her heart. An impossible task. For how does one move mountains?"

Mandukhai's chin quivered. She took a moment to attempt collecting herself. It failed miserably. Instead, her sorrow deflated her entire body. Her muscles and bones ached. She stroked Batu's cheek as he continued staring at her as if deciphering a puzzle. His eyes burned with curiosity.

"The queen knew she could not do this alone," Mandukhai continued, barely holding herself together. "She needed someone to guide her, to hold her heart in his hands and protect it from the crushing weight of the mountain. She needed someone she could trust with her heart and soul. She needed him to be her shield so that she could restore the fractured empire." Mandukhai's throat seized as a lump the size of a boulder grew in it. She tried to speak further, but no words would come out. Only choked sobs.

Batu studied her. Mandukhai was uncertain if it was her own tears masking her vision, or if he cried as well. And then he spoke, his voice small and timid, but still laced with conviction. "I will."

Suddenly, Batu threw his arms around her and buried his face in her neck. His tears soaked into her skin. Mandukhai could no longer control her grief. She pressed her cheek to the top of his head and allowed herself to let go of all the agony she had fought to hold at bay. Somehow, without saying a word, Batu had unlocked her pain and her fear, then lifted the burden from her soul.

Even if those were the only two words he ever spoke, they contained more power than anything anyone else could say with a hundred words. She hugged the boy tight, afraid of losing him as she had lost everyone else she cared for. His words bonded to her heart stronger than any other oath ever could have.

The door opened and Tuya slipped inside quietly. Mandukhai pulled back from Batu, scrubbing the tears from her eyes.

He had taken on her burden.

Now she had one to take on for him.

Unebolod should have felt dread or sorrow as he stepped out his door. Instead, he felt nothing at all, as if some great fist had reached into his chest, ripped out his insides, and left a husk. As he passed other gers, men nodded respectfully to him. Unebolod wore a warrior's stony face, not slowing his stride. It was better to do this now and be done with it.

Mount Burkhan Khaldun buzzed with excitement all around him, and he loathed every moment with intense resentment. How could others be so happy when he was not?

Today, the festival would end, and the victors would be forever marked. Everyone wanted to know who would win the wrestling tournament. Great fortunes had already changed hands over the past two days as horsemen won or lost races, archery teams had been eliminated from rounds, and wrestlers either advanced to the final rounds today or were eliminated from the competition. Runners had raced for miles yesterday in a brutal footrace that was not only a test of stamina but strength. A young Khorlod boy had taken first place.

Unebolod's archers had made the final round, as had Huoshai's. He knew he should focus on the competition, but he could not do so with this sword hanging over his head. His wrestler also had made the final round of the tournament with resounding success. The last of Unebolod's pride hinged on his wrestler and archers.

For most of the Mongols, today would be a day of victory and celebration. For Unebolod, it would be a day of mourning as the last of his hope died.

He rounded Togochi's ger as Nemeku darted out the door, followed closely by a stumbling Torudur. The boys nearly ran into his legs, unapologetically rushing away. Togochi barked a command from inside for the boys to come back, but there was no helping it. They wouldn't listen.

Unebolod passed by, his gaze focused on just one door.

Boke stood guard outside, as he always did. Upon seeing Unebolod approach, Boke tensed, and his face creased in scowl lines. The two of them had unresolved issues but now was not the time. Unebolod didn't care about Boke.

Unebolod and Mandukhai had agreed he would declare his decision publicly, but he wanted to go inside and avoid prying eyes. He didn't want others to witness his misery. The public display had been his idea, though, and he knew logically that it was necessary so that everyone understood how the two of them would proceed with *kurultai.*

"I came to speak with the Queen Regent," Unebolod said evenly, raising his voice so anyone nearby could hear. "I believe she is expecting me."

With a subtle twitch of his head, Boke commanded one of his men to inform Mandukhai.

Unebolod waited patiently, aware that the surrounding space slowly filled with warriors, Lords, and Ladies who were curious what was happening. At the edge of his vision, Unebolod spotted Togochi. He wore his sword on his hip, his body visibly tense. The two of them had hardly spoken since the fight in his ger two days ago. What was Togochi expecting would happen here today?

Unebolod clasped his hands behind his back and stood stiff and straight as he waited. He was as cold and solid as the steel at his own hip.

As Mandukhai stepped over her threshold, Unebolod saw his grief mirrored in her own eyes. Somehow, she knew his answer before he even spoke it. This was not a conversation he wanted to have so publicly, but they had agreed.

Staring into her eyes, Unebolod felt cracks in the wall he had raised around his emotions last night. If anyone could break through, it was her. *I cannot allow the walls to come down*, he thought. If that happened, it would consume him whole. Unebolod stood tall and proud, raising his chin.

The slight change in his posture had been signal enough for her. Mandukhai's lips thinned, and she nodded stiffly. For several agonizingly long minutes, the two stood silently staring at each other. No words could truly breach this chasm.

Getei and Khosoichi rounded Mandukhai's ger and joined the growing crowd where Mandukhai and Unebolod faced one another. The shaman observed the scene with knowing eyes.

Unebolod glanced around to take stock of who was present, aside from the three he already knew. Lord Unige and his wife Satai. Jaghan and her children, with Nemeku. Korgiz, Albeq, Esige, Soke, Altan ... It was quite a crowd that continued to grow. Unebolod was certain if he turned to examine the circle, he would see other Lords he had made deals with. How would they take this? Probably not well.

Everyone watched curiously.

"What is happening?" someone whispered.

"I think she is making her declaration," someone else responded softly, as if afraid to shatter the fragile silence.

Unebolod drew himself up and attempted to summon the words he had rehearsed all morning.

Bayan's son hid in the shadows inside the ger, watching with his golden eyes. The boy should have died years ago. He never would have been born had Unebolod not saved Bayan from certain death. *This is a monster of my own making. I cannot blame a child for my sins.*

"The will of the High Heavens has spoken," he said, praying his voice did not shake as much as he thought it did. He lifted his voice high enough for everyone to hear him. "My heart is full and empty. To have what I desire, to light your fire and guide our people with you at my side, I would lose all honor."

A murmur rippled through the crowd as everyone speculated on this confession. How would he lose all honor? Why could he not become Great Khan? Korgiz grumbled something under his breath. Togochi offered Unebolod a sad, knowing look of sympathy.

Unebolod cleared his throat and lifted his voice, afraid that if he spoke at a normal level his voice would break. "To keep my oath to Manduul

Khan, and keep my honor, I must yield my claim to any surviving heirs of Genghis. Even if it means giving up all that my heart desires."

Whispers rippled through the crowd. "An heir of Genghis lives?" "Who is it?" "Is it the boy Nemeku? We cannot have a Uyghur Khan." "Who is the other boy?"

Mandukhai had guarded her secret well, but the truth had to come out. Nothing else would explain why Unebolod revoked his claim on the title. No one would understand.

Mandukhai strode toward him in just three long steps, pressing her fingers to his lips. The walls around his emotions quaked. The mortar shook loose. *Let me finish!*

"Lord Unebolod," Mandukhai said, her own voice tight with emotion, "flame of my heart, my eternal soul is bound to the last wishes of my husband. To fulfill those wishes, I must reject all that my heart desires." She took a breath and let it out slowly. "You have a tent flap I must not raise."

What are you doing? he thought desperately. That last sentence was the arrow through the last of their hope. It formally declared that she could never live in the same ger with him so long as she was bound to her duty. He wanted to stop her, but was powerless against her will.

Her eyes shined with unshed tears. "You have a threshold I must not step over." The words seemed to be dragged out of her.

Don't do this. Don't close the door forever. Yet no matter how much Unebolod wanted to speak up, to stop her, he knew the will of the gods. This was always inevitable.

Mandukhai's eyes bore into his soul, pleading with him not to interrupt, baring her own inner struggle. The two of them remained locked in this dance of their souls, and bricks began falling from his wall. Time stood still. No one around them dared to move or breathe, as if they were aware of the delicate balance of fate prepared to tumble over the edge with the slightest breeze. Then Mandukhai stepped back, folding her hands in front of her and raising her chin proudly.

Don't say it.

But he knew she had to, just as he knew he had to refuse her.

"As long as there is a descendant to my Khan, I cannot go to you," Mandukhai said, her voice strong. It carried on the air, amplified in his ears.

With those words, Unebolod's wall reformed taller, thicker, laced with molten steel so nothing else would ever get through again.

With those words, Mandukhai had closed the door to him for as long as Batu—or any of his descendants—lived. She had given her life to the Mongol Nation.

Unebolod would need to do the same. For her.

Mandukhai did not know how she had not collapsed under the strain of the confrontation with Unebolod. Perhaps the eyes of the Lords and Ladies around the clearing gave her some unknown strength. He bowed formally before spinning on his heel and striding away. The crowd parted for him, watching as he marched away. They whispered, eyeing Mandukhai as if waiting for some further confession from her lips. Only a handful gave knowing nods as if they had guessed the truth long ago.

That look Unebolod had given her told Mandukhai all she needed to know. He would not accept her offer. Not that she had expected he would after what Togochi said. This decision was a matter of Unebolod's honor, the last piece of himself he had to cling to. She had given him a choice that had not been a choice.

Yet the fact that he had turned her down was a relief as well. If he had accepted, after her dream with Genghis, they would have to have another private conversation about how to proceed according to the will of the spirits. And if that conversation ended with him revoking his claim, it could have been just as discrediting.

"Who is the heir of the Khan?" someone asked from the edge of the ring of onlookers.

Questions were hushed as all eyes remained on her, waiting. She heard every question, but refused to acknowledge any of them.

"Is it the boy?"

"I told you he wasn't her mother's son."

"How can the boy be an heir of Genghis? Who is his father?"

"Who will be Great Khan, Lady Mandukhai?"

"I still think she intends to make that Uyghur boy Great Khan. I won't follow him."

Mandukhai remained fixed in place, unable to look away as Unebolod disappeared through the crowd. With these witnesses, Mandukhai knew she could never go back now. She had closed the door to him, just as Genghis had wanted. She just hoped she had the strength to finish what she had started—what Genghis had demanded of her.

A small hand slipped around Mandukhai's arm, and she turned her gaze down to Batu. He stared at her as if he understood the depth of her pain. Relieved to have him beside her, Mandukhai dropped her arms and slid her hand into his.

"Come, Batu," she whispered. "We have a big day ahead of us."

Together, they crossed the threshold of her ger to prepare.

And the crowd eyed the two of them, knowing without a doubt who he was.

Batu was in more danger now than he had been when he came into her care on the threshold of death.

Esige had stepped outside when she heard the growing whispers from the crowd. She stopped beside Togochi when she saw Unebolod and Mandukhai face to face. A tension filled the air between them. *What is going on?*

Yet Esige knew the answer. Unebolod had grown restless these past weeks waiting for Mandukhai to name him as her candidate for *kurultai*. Esige had caught him a few times speaking with lesser khans to secure their support for him. She hadn't told Mandukhai, afraid that it would only end in a fight. Even if Mandukhai named him, he would need to support of the Mongol Lords by majority.

But what would happen if the two of them had a different idea on how the vote should go? Mandukhai had not been terribly forthcoming with Esige either.

Unebolod spoke first, formally withdrawing himself from contention for the khanship. Esige gasped, pressing her hand to her mouth. Tears welled in her eyes. With one breath, he confessed his love for Mandukhai so profoundly it made Esige's heart ache—how could Mandukhai stand there?—and with the next breath, he renounced his claim.

A murmur of alarm ripped through the crowd as Unebolod mentioned an heir of Genghis, and her gaze darted to the shadowy form of Batu hiding inside the ger. She had resented no one as much since Bigirsen. Such a small boy to cause so much heartache. Esige had wanted Mandukhai and Unebolod together for so long ... perhaps since only a few months after her sister had left Mongke Bulag. It had seemed like such a perfect pairing—a powerful warrior and even more powerful queen together conquering the world.

But Batu spoiled all of it.

Worse still, Mandukhai spoke up, and her vow essentially closed the door to Unebolod forever. Fury burned in Esige's veins. Fury, resentment, grief, loathing, sorrow. As Mandukhai headed inside—ignoring all the questions circulating around her ger—Esige remained frozen in place, glaring at the boy's back until the door closed. Even then, she remained, glaring in anger as if she could burn a hole through the door and straight into Batu's soul.

A hand fell on her shoulder.

Esige swiped the tears from her cheeks and spun around.

Togochi offered a sympathetic frown. *I don't want his sympathy!*

"How could she do this?" Esige snapped. She shook her head, chest heaving in angry breaths.

"Duty is a mountain, Esige," Togochi said. "I will see to him. She will need you."

"You're right about that." Esige set her jaw in determination. "I will set this straight."

As she turned to march into Mandukhai's ger and call her out for rejecting Unebolod, someone grabbed her hand and pulled her back. Esige swung around with her free fist.

Huoshai snatched it and pulled her against him in a tight hug. "Let's walk."

"No!" She pushed against his chest, but he held her fast.

More tears escaped, and she hated her eyes for giving her away. Huoshai tightened his hold, rubbing at her back. She buried her face in his neck, ashamed of how openly she cried. As she did, Huoshai guided her away from the clearing so no one else could see her grief.

By the time they reached a small cluster of trees, her tears died up. Huoshai released his hold on her and leaned against one of the birch trees, hooking his thumbs on his belt. He didn't watch her with sympathy as Togochi had. Instead, Huoshai simply waited patiently for her to speak, a brow raised.

Esige did not know where to start. Or what she should even say. Mandukhai had not openly said who Batu was. People could only make their assumptions. She flicked her gaze toward the camp and spotted her guards lingering nearby. *Of course they are.*

"It was a really powerful reaction, Esige," Huoshai said. "I expect you have *something* to say. You have something to say about everything."

Esige briskly wiped the tears from her cheeks as she attempted collecting herself. Huoshai produced a square of silk from his belt and offered it to her. She murmured her thanks as she accepted, then used it to dry her face.

"I don't have something to say about everything," she said at last. Her throat hurt.

He chuckled, but remained expectant.

"Fine. Alright. So some childish part of me wanted them to be together. Mandukhai is the closest thing I have known to a mother. Unebolod was more of a father than Manduul ever was." Not that Manduul was Esige's father. She hoped Huoshai understood that much. "She has been crying so much lately, and I know it isn't about Manduul because ... well, I just know." Esige folded the silk square in her long fingers. The brilliant shade of red had darkened in a few spots where it became wet with her tears. "I know they love each other. It's so obvious."

"I'm pretty sure they said as much in front of the world today," Huoshai replied. He glanced at the guards. "But you know there's no going back now. He withdrew his claim. She rejected him. In front of everyone. And it was pretty formal." He kicked the toe of his boot casually against the tree's root. "So, do you know who the heir is, then?"

Esige tensed, narrowing her eyes at him. "Don't mistake my anger or grief for carelessness."

"I'll take that as a yes," he replied. He shrugged his shoulders. "I was just asking. My father tells me all the time that, when you are in charge, it's important to remember that the good of the people has to come before my own desires."

Esige placed her hands on her hips. "So you would do the same?"

He pursed his lips, and his gaze swept over her. Then he shook his head. "Not if it meant giving you up."

Her heart skipped. Did he really feel so strongly about her, or was his interest rooted in something baser? "There is no way you care about me more than they care for each other."

"You underestimate me."

"I hardly know you."

"You will." He pushed away from the tree and strode toward her.

Esige's pulse quickened as she noted the intensity in his eyes she had seen the night before. Huoshai skimmed his fingers along her cheek, then leaned closer and brushed his lips over hers. Her breath hitched, and a hunger for more overwhelmed her senses. Before she could push forward and have her fill, Huoshai stepped back.

"Upon my eternal soul," he said, and his breath rolled down her neck, "when I win that race and win your hand, I will do anything to keep it. Even if I have to give up the world."

Esige's knees weakened. Her chest heaved. Heat rose in her cheeks. Huoshai hadn't just made a passing promise. He swore it on his eternal soul. Suddenly, Esige's mouth went dry. She swallowed. *Don't let him know he flustered you*, she thought, though it was likely too late.

"*When* you win? I think you mean if."

"Again, you underestimate me." Huoshai kissed her cheek. "Losing is not an option." He kissed her other cheek. "Because it means losing you."

Their lips melted together, full of hunger, longing, and whispered promises. But unlike Mandukhai and Unebolod, Esige would keep hers. She would eagerly cross the threshold into her new life. If Huoshai won, she would give herself to him completely, heart and soul.

CHAPTER TWENTY-FIVE

Jumping off the Cliff

Unebolod stood in the center of his ger, beside the cold stove, and stared at nothing. All thoughts drifted from his mind. All emotion drained from his body. He stood in a void of nothing like some bizarre, lifelike statue. It was done. Now he had to focus on the events of the day ahead. Esige's race against Huoshai. The archery and wrestling finals.

Kurultai.

By the end of this day, Mandukhai would plant that weak boy in front of the sacred *sulde* of Genghis Khan and reveal him as the only true and rightful heir to the title. The Lords would have no choice but to select Batu at *kurultai* as he would stand in front of that sacred banner, a place that belonged to Unebolod, as all the Great Khans before him had done. Unebolod was not sure if he could stomach watching. He was not sure if he could avoid it, either.

He closed his eyes, wishing Kilgor was still with him. In moments like these, he missed his dog. She kept him from feeling so lonely.

A gentle rap on the door pulled Unebolod back to reality. A moment later, he heard Togochi calling to him through the door.

Unebolod marched over and pulled the door open.

Togochi's dark eyes swept over him and he frowned. "I came to check on your wellbeing, brother."

Unebolod stepped back to allow Togochi to enter. Without a word, he poured two cups of *airag* and held one out to Togochi after the door had been closed. The two drank in silence until, after they finished their cups, Togochi sighed.

"Don't close yourself off completely," he said. "She still needs you."

"I know." His voice sounded hollow, even to himself. He truly understood, though. Mandukhai had not chosen the easy path. Nor had he. She would need his battle skills going forward. Without him, her chances were slim. It was just another knife in his already bleeding corpse.

"If there is anything I can do to make this easier for you ..."

"I appreciate the effort, Togochi, but I will be fine." The lie slid so easily past his lips. Unebolod would not be fine. He would never be fine. Certainly not if he had to remain close to her, help her, and never hold her. *I must become the Steel Soldier inside and out.*

Togochi narrowed his eyes. Clearly, he didn't believe the lie. "The offer stands if anything changes." He set down the cup. "Esige's race starts soon."

"I will be there." Unebolod would never miss watching some poor Lord getting crushed by Esige's skills in a race like this.

Togochi nodded and opened the door.

"Togochi," Unebolod called after him.

His brother paused.

"Please make sure Jaghan is watching Mandukhai." His voice cracked over her name and he swallowed the lump that leaped into his throat.

"She will."

As soon as everyone heard Esige and Lord Huoshai would compete in a Capture the Bride race, wagers had been placed. Unebolod watched small fortunes placed on the line. Some people knew how strong of a rider Esige was and they had placed their bets in her favor. Most assumed she could not out-ride a khan's son and bet on Huoshai. Besides, some reasoned, why would she agree to the race if she was not interested in capture?

Unebolod waited near the back of a knot of Lords and Ladies gathered in long rows of canopies beside the start and finish line. While many still preferred to watch the wrestling tournament, which began shortly after breakfast, hundreds gathered along the course Esige and Huoshai would ride. In the distance, perhaps a quarter-mile off, a mountain of shale broke the horizon. The race would travel around that mountain and back to this point. If Huoshai could capture Esige off her horse before she crossed that line, he won the race. Unebolod knew she would not make it easy. Whether or not she was deeply interested in this arrangement, Esige was a proud girl.

Huoshai would have a tough ride ahead of him. Unebolod didn't envy that at all.

Near the starting line, Mandukhai and Esige spoke quietly to one another. Unebolod stood back and waited behind the crowd. He had no desire to be near Mandukhai yet. The longer he could keep distance between them, the better. At some point, he would have to talk to her about all of this, find out what exactly she needed him for—because she *would* need him. The longer he could avoid that conversation, the happier he would be.

At last, Mandukhai glided away from Esige toward a small cluster of Urainkhai men who surrounded Huoshai and his mount, near to where Esige stood. Batu clung to Mandukhai's side like an extension of her. Unebolod averted his gaze and strode to Esige.

"I will admit, I did not expect this day to ever come," Unebolod said as he stopped in front of Esige's mount—a stallion with wide shoulders that promised strength.

Esige adjusted the saddle strap, then smoothed her hands over her riding deel. "Is it wrong to be nervous?"

"I suppose that depends on why you are nervous in the first place," he said. "Is this what you want, Esige?"

She chewed her bottom lip and glanced toward the Urainkhai men around Huoshai. They parted for Mandukhai and Batu, leaving a line of sight to Huoshai. Her cheeks turned red. "He is different," she said at last, then her dark eyes pierced Unebolod's. "Like you."

"I expect you won't make this easy for him," Unebolod said, somewhat amused by her comparison. He supposed, if he considered what he had learned of the young Lord these past few days, he could see where she would reach that conclusion.

Esige grinned, mischief dancing in her eyes. "Never."

"Even if he wins, he still will need Mandukhai's final approval," Unebolod said, almost choking on her name.

Esige noticed. The grin slid off her face, and she edged closer to him. "I don't understand what happened between you, Unebolod," she said, lowering her voice. "Why did you cede your claim? I thought you wanted her."

"There was more at stake than my desires," he said.

"It's that boy, isn't it?" Esige's face heated in anger, and her forehead wrinkled. The way she said *that boy* left no doubt she resented Batu. "Why can't you still be together? I just don't understand." Her hand fell on his arm.

Unebolod wanted to pull away, but he didn't have the strength to move. Every part of him suddenly felt like it had been cast from iron.

"This was difficult for her," Esige said. Her voice as it flooded with compassion. "I heard her crying this morning. She puts a good face on the surface to cover her broken soul inside."

This broke him from his spell, and Unebolod stepped back. "Good luck in your race, Esige. Ride hard. May fortune turn out in your favor."

Unable to hear another word, not wanting Esige's pity or reassurance, Unebolod turned abruptly and strode away. He had never wanted to be the source of Mandukhai's pain. The longer he remained around here, the more it would hurt her.

Batu clung to Mandukhai's hand as she approached the Urainkhai men gathered around Huoshai. Roughly ten men clumped together, offering Huoshai advice or making jokes about marriage. When they laughed, their happiness cut into Mandukhai's heart. She had lost Unebolod, and if this race ended as Esige hoped, she would lose the girl as well. Nothing about this day offered Mandukhai any form of happiness.

As she drew near the Urainkhai, their jokes died away and they parted, revealing Huoshai in the center of their ring with his horse. While the others grinned in amusement, his face was set with determination while he ensured his mount was ready for the race.

"Lady Mandukhai," Huoshai said, bowing to her.

"Lord Huoshai, I hope you are prepared to jump off that cliff," Mandukhai said in a sweet voice. "Lady Esige will not pull any punches. She fully intends to test you."

"I would jump a thousand times." The corner of his mouth twitched in amusement. "I would expect no less. She is quite spirited."

"And I trust you will not try to break her spirit, should you win. Women like her are rare."

"I know." Huoshai shifted, grasping his reins as the horse grazed.

The men around Huoshai ribbed each other but said nothing and glanced toward Esige. Mandukhai followed their gazes, and her stomach twisted in uneasy knots as she spotted Unebolod speaking to Esige. *Of course he would*, she thought, *she was like a daughter to him as well*. A knot tightened in her throat and she struggled to force it down. Her eyes burned, but she had no more tears to shed today.

Mandukhai stepped forward, running her hand along the horse's shoulders to get a feel for the animal. She would be fast, but Mandukhai was not sure if it was strong enough for what Esige had in store. "Do you need your father's blessing for this marriage?" Mandukhai asked.

"He sent me to find a wife," Huoshai said, puffing up slightly at being given this choice for himself.

Most boys in his position would not have much say in the matter. A khan's son should have a suitable match, and he could draw powerful allies. What would his father think of Mandukhai as an ally?

Huoshai shifted. "He will be pleased with the results."

Mandukhai nodded. How could his father be less than pleased? If Huoshai won, he would return to his father with a Borjigin princess. What better match could there be outside of herself? "She has a sizable dowry," Mandukhai said. "He will be pleased with that, if nothing else. He has arranged no other wives for you?"

Huoshai eyed her curiously, then shook his head. "He has left this to me."

Mandukhai had done some inquiring since he had first showed Esige interest a few days ago. Huoshai was just sixteen, and she already knew he had no other wives, that his father had put this on Huoshai, expecting he would choose a wife before he turned eighteen. At that point, his father would take over. "Most boys in your position have something arranged by the age of twelve. Why has it taken you so long to choose a wife?"

Huoshai hesitated, his brows knitting together as he considered his response. "I have no suitable answer to that question. Except, maybe, I knew something was waiting for me. Or someone."

Though his face remained a mask of determination, Mandukhai saw the light in his eyes. While she could not pretend to know what he was thinking, she recognized that look. He was besotted with Esige. Mandukhai was pleased enough with that reaction. It meant his heart was in this just as much as his ambition.

Huoshai raised his chin proudly, confident in his abilities today. "We will need to discuss bride-service."

Mandukhai smiled. "First, you must win. Do that, and we will discuss the terms."

Esige had made herself quite clear only moments ago. Should he best her traps, outrace her, and capture her from her horse, Esige had no intention of letting him slip away. Mandukhai had given Esige the right to make this choice. Now she would have to respect the outcome, even if it emptied another piece of her heart to do so.

Huoshai bowed, followed a moment later by his men doing the same.

Mandukhai gave the horse one more pat. "Good luck to you then, Lord Huoshai. You will need it."

With that, she strode away, holding Batu's hand for dear life. Something told her that, by the end of this day, she would have only his hand to hold.

A tent had been set up near the starting line where Mandukhai, Batu, Nemeku, and several of the highly ranked men and women close to Mandukhai would watch. Jaghan and Togochi were among them, along with their three children.

Nemeku, Torudur, and Babaqai played off to the side of the tent, but Batu sat in his seat at Mandukhai's side, watching the race with a gleam of curiosity in his eyes. He had spoken only those two words—his timid promise to protect her. Mandukhai wondered when he would be comfortable enough to share the thoughts clearly racing through that young mind of his.

Her gaze had drifted several times to the far end of the tent. Unebolod leaned back in his seat, crossing his arms as he gazed out at the start line. Her heart ached every time she looked at him, yet she could not stop herself. Would her draw to him diminish over time? *I don't want my feelings to diminish*, she thought pitifully. What she wanted was to kneel in front of him, beg his forgiveness, offer herself and everything she had to him. Did he feel the same?

As if he sensed her gaze, Unebolod turned his head to stare at her. His expression bore no emotion. That void thrust another blade into her bleeding heart. How could he feel nothing? *Have I broken him?*

Mandukhai dipped her head and stared at her hands. They had not yet spoken since he ceded his claim and she closed the door to him. In fact, this was the closest he had been to her since walking away—so close, yet still so far apart. They would need to talk at some point. She knew that, but was not ready. Would she even be able to speak if she tried? Mandukhai still needed him. Would he understand or reject her? How could she even ask him to train Batu and help him grow strong? It seemed like a deep betrayal of everything they had dreamed of for years. But she needed him still. In every way.

Esige and Huoshai waited on their mounts at the starting line. The horses snorted and stomped impatiently. Esige would be given a brief head-start, as tradition dictated. She and Huoshai exchanged playful glances as they gripped their reins, awaiting Mandukhai's signal to start.

Mandukhai patted Batu on the arm, then rose and approached the edge of the tent, close enough to be seen and heard, but far enough that she wouldn't taste dust when they kicked off the race.

Mandukhai gave the signal for Esige to begin, releasing the blue strip of ribbon into the wind. Esige's stallion launched into action, displaying its powerful strength. Mandukhai turned her attention to Huoshai.

"If you win, you have Esige's blessing," she said. "But you will still need mine."

Huoshai nodded stiffly, all business as he stood in the stirrups and leaned closer to his mount's neck, prepared for his own start. Mandukhai raised the second blue ribbon, watching for Esige's stallion to cross the line that indicated she had completed her head start. Huoshai's muscles tensed, exposing a strength that belied his young age as his bare arms showed the swelling of his arms and shoulders. Esige's stallion crossed the head start line far sooner than expected, and Mandukhai released the second ribbon.

Huoshai kicked his mount into action. It sprang forward at an alarming rate. But speed would not be his problem in this race. Esige knew the strengths of her stallion. She would make him climb.

Mandukhai strode back to her seat and settled beside Batu, who leaned forward as he watched the race. Her attention turned to the horizon as Huoshai slowly closed the gap. She heard about the bets some of the men had placed on Huoshai capturing Esige within the first mile. Those men didn't know Esige as she did.

Huoshai's confidence was apparent in the way he relaxed slightly in the saddle. Mandukhai smirked. Esige was toying with him. Some men and women watching murmured to one another, certain that he would win the race swiftly. But Mandukhai saw exactly where Esige was headed.

A quarter-mile ahead of them, to their right, the mountains offered a rocky slope to climb. Esige would force him to follow her up the slopes, and if his mount was meant for speed rather than strength, he would lose ground swiftly.

Much to the alarm of everyone watching, Esige rose from the saddle like a practiced warrior, twisting around with her bow and guiding the stallion with her knees. She drew back. Huoshai ducked as the arrow flew past. She would not mean to harm him, only distract him or slow his pace. Huoshai hardly had time to recover before Esige released another arrow, forcing him to veer to the left and lose ground. Some men watching grumbled, but one laughed.

Mandukhai glanced down the line of nobles to see the amusement on Unebolod's face as he openly laughed at Huoshai's struggle. His delight cut deeply, making her breakfast turn to bile in her throat. How could he be happy when she was so miserable?

As Mandukhai had predicted, Esige pivoted her stallion right toward the rocky slopes. To Huoshai's credit, he had predicted this as well and turned his own mount in almost perfect rhythm to Esige.

Climbing the slopes slowed Esige down for a moment as her stallion fought for footing. Loose shale shifted beneath the stallion's hooves. Esige glanced back over her shoulder to discover Huoshai only a step behind, leaning forward and reaching a hand toward her. For a moment, Mandukhai thought he would get a hand on Esige, but Esige leaned slightly away, urging the stallion on. The mount surged his great muscles and pulled away from Huoshai. The gap continued to expand as his own black horse fell behind, unable to navigate the shale as deftly as Esige's stallion.

Then Huoshai turned back. Mandukhai sank back in her seat, inwardly smiling to herself. Perhaps she would not lose the girl after all.

Huoshai guided his black horse back down the slippery slope. He had not gone far up yet. Though she didn't want to lose Esige, Mandukhai was a little disappointed that he had given in so quickly. She had expected better.

The black mare turned north, around the crest of the shale slopes, away from the tent and those gathered. Mandukhai's heart thumped in her chest, and she leaned forward, gripping the arms of her seat as she stared at the horizon.

Esige vanished over the top of the slippery slope.

Huoshai disappeared around the edges. *Perhaps he is not a fool, after all,* Mandukhai thought.

Huoshai's black mare could not outpace Esige's stallion up the shale, but he knew the mare's merits. At the pace Esige could move over the mountain, he could race around and cut her off—or at the very least, meet her on the other side and resume the race. Mandukhai loathed being unable to see what was happening.

Esige reached the crest of the shale mountain and loosened her grip for a moment to let her tense hands relax. She glanced back over her shoulder to see how much of a lead she had on Huoshai.

No one was behind her. She reined in, sweeping her gaze down the slopes as disappointment and terror clenched her belly. Had she been too hard on him? Did he change his mind and decide she wasn't worth the climb?

A wave of cheers rose from the spectators lining the path around the mountain. Hundreds, perhaps thousands, had shown up for the race. A Capture the Bride race was a rare event, and surely it only enhanced the excitement of the festival to everyone else. Esige examined the cause of the cheers and spotted Huoshai, small and distant, racing around the mountain. A grin curled the corner of her mouth. He knew he would lose ground on the mountain and thought he could beat her around the edge? *I will show him!*

Esige whipped the reins and kicked her stallion onward. The stallion raced down as quickly as he dared. His hooves slipped on the loose shale, but he kept his legs under him. Esige held her breath and prayed that she would make it down without hurting the mount. A few times, she dared a glance to her left, attempting to spot Huoshai's progress around the mountain until her glances no longer revealed his black mare. With any luck, she would reach the bottom before he rounded the base. But he had disappeared from sight.

It wasn't so much that Esige wanted him to lose to her as much as it was a matter of her pride. Esige was known to be fierce and strong. If she let him win just because she wanted him, it would make her look like every other weak girl who let a boy win the Capture the Bride race. Esige would not be weak.

The stallion reached the base of the mountain, and she breathed a sigh of relief that he had not been injured. The second he had steady legs under him on the valley floor, Esige whipped him to a faster pace.

The wave of cheers erupted, echoing off the walls of the valley. She dared a glance over her shoulder as a black streak darted out of the trees, straight for her. Huoshai was close enough for her to see his excitement clearly, but far enough back that she had a decent head start. To reach the finish line, she would have to circle back across his path. *I need to slow him down and throw him off course.*

Esige unhooked her bow once more, drawing back and firing arrows in rapid succession at the ground in front of his mare. Huoshai deftly guided his mare away from the arrows exactly as she wanted. Esige's pulse pounded with excitement. In a straight race, his mare would likely beat her stallion. She had counted on the mountain slowing him down. She needed a new plan.

Swinging wide and away from him, Esige circled back toward the mountain pass he had emerged from a few minutes ago. The shouts and cheers rose to a crescendo, drawing her gaze back over her shoulder.

Huoshai had cut across the path, as she had predicted he would do, and now leaned tight to his black mare's neck. The excitement had transformed into fierce determination. Her stomach danced in delight. Adrenaline already pumped through her veins, but it reached a roar as she heard the beating of her own heart over the noise of the crowd and thump of horse hooves. Esige hooked the bow again, knowing he was too close to fire now, and reached into the bag she had attached to the saddle.

The caltrops pricked her skin, but she ignored the pain as she spread them in her wake, careful to space them out enough that his horse could not easily leap over them.

A hush fell over the crowd.

The black mare leaped into the air and soared forward.

Esige dropped more caltrops as Huoshai landed on the other side of her first batch.

Once more, he guided the mare into a jump instead of going around and increasing the distance.

The crowd roared in delight, clapping, cheering.

Esige turned her gaze forward, closing the bag. She had not expected him to jump over the caltrops. One misstep and his mare would be lame for weeks—if not longer. It had been a bold move.

As they darted back and forth between trees, flashing in and out of sight of the lines of spectators egging them on, Esige yanked her knife from her belt. Huoshai was close now. In another mile, he would be upon her. Perhaps less. She could slice at his arm if it came to that.

Shouts and cheers from the other side of the shale mountain echoed off the valley walls, carrying back to Mandukhai and enhancing her pounding heart. What did that mean?

Without realizing it, Mandukhai had edged to the end of her chair. Her knuckles turned white. Her nails dug into the wooden arms. *Lord Tengri, unless this union serves a higher purpose, do not take her from me!*

Huoshai couldn't win. Could he? Esige was skilled. She had beaten countless boys and men in races and wrestling. If any held the spirit of Lady Khutulun, it was Esige. Was she meant to be the wife of a lesser khan?

The cheers from the other side of the mountain grew to a crescendo. Several pulsing heartbeats later, Esige shot out from around the mountain with Huoshai neck-and-neck with her horse. Mandukhai surged to her feet as Esige reached out to him. Something flashed in the sunlight, and Mandukhai realized Esige used a knife to slice at his arm and prevent him from grabbing her.

The finish line approached. If he did not capture Esige soon, he would lose. Mandukhai pressed her hands against her pounding heart. Down the line of nobles, Unebolod was also on his feet, cheering Esige on. His face lit up with excitement, swept up in the moment. Mandukhai could not look at him for long, afraid she would miss something. Mandukhai could not find the breath to cheer.

Huoshai wrapped a leather strap around his arm without losing momentum. When Esige swung her knife out again, her eyes widened in alarm as the blade glanced off the leather.

Huoshai grinned and drew his sword from his hip.

The finish line drew near.

He cut the reins from Esige's hands with a careful swing of his sword. Before she could reach out for the mane to keep her grip, Huoshai tossed the sword carelessly away and seized her arm, pulling Esige closer. The knife fell from her hand. The horses raced so tight together now that their sides bumped against each other. Esige brought her other arm around to punch his ear, as Unebolod had taught her. Mandukhai held her breath.

Huoshai sank back in the saddle, causing Esige to miss. He maintained an iron grip on her arm. His free arm wrapped around her waist.

No. Please. I'm not ready for this. Mandukhai's eyes burned.

Esige struggled, but Huoshai firmed his grip and yanked her out of the saddle.

Mandukhai's heart sank as she watched Huoshai pull Esige into his saddle with him, less than ten yards from the finish line. And once she was there, Esige didn't struggle anymore. Huoshai yanked the reins, holding Esige close to him. The black mare reared before the finish line.

Esige's eyes shined as she smiled at Huoshai. Blood dripped from a cut on his cheek and seeped around the leather he had wrapped around his arm, but his face was alight with delight.

Mandukhai trembled, hoping no one else could see just how devastating this loss was to her. Unebolod appeared just as stunned as she felt.

Huoshai whispered something in Esige's ear, making her flush a brilliant shade of red. She murmured a response. A moment later, Esige slipped out of the saddle, bouncing on her toes as she had done so often as a little girl.

An Urainkhai warrior had rushed forward to stop Esige's riderless horse.

Mandukhai stiffened her spine and strode toward the two of them while Huoshai hopped out of the saddle.

"It appears congratulations are in order, Lord Huoshai," Mandukhai said loud enough for everyone around to hear.

He bowed to her, clutching the leather-wrapped arm with a wince. "Not without injury. You were correct. She certainly didn't make it easy." He beamed at Esige, who stepped up beside him, watching Mandukhai expectantly. "The caltrops, in particular, were a surprise."

"His mare had a longer jump than I expected," Esige said, as if she needed to explain why he had bested her in this particular challenge.

"I have done as requested and won the favor of the Lady," Huoshai said.

"Have you?" Mandukhai asked, seeking confirmation from Esige.

"He has." Esige had never sounded so sure of herself.

Mandukhai was uncertain how much more of this day her heart could take.

"Do I have your blessing, though, Queen Regent?" Huoshai asked as the nobles edged close to them.

"That will depend on whether you agree to the bride-service," Mandukhai replied.

Esige deflated, watching the two of them with worry clouding her face.

"Walk with me, Huoshai," Mandukhai said. "This is a matter of family and does not need to be so public." Mandukhai began strolling away from the crowd, shooting the gathered throng a meaningful glance. "Yet."

Huoshai frowned at Esige as if he had expected this to be simple. Had Esige given him the impression that Mandukhai would simply give them her blessing? Surely the girl knew her better than that.

As if sensing she needed comfort, Batu appeared at Mandukhai's side, sliding his small hand into her own.

Huoshai hesitated, falling behind. Esige flicked her hand to encourage him along, forcing him to jog a few steps to catch up to Mandukhai, clutching his wounded arm close to his chest.

"Esige is not like other women," Mandukhai said, lowering her voice so that only he could hear. "She is a princess, and I expect whatever man she marries to treat her as such."

Huoshai glanced back over his shoulder. Mandukhai followed his gaze to see Esige standing with Unebolod, who slid his arm around her as she wrung her hands. Agony clutched at her chest, but Mandukhai forced it down. She didn't have time for it now.

"Have I given you the wrong impression?" Huoshai asked. "I have met a lot of girls, but none of them have ever stirred something in me as Esige has. She is a jewel on the crown of this Nation. I would never treat her as less."

"She is like a daughter to me, Huoshai. Just as your father has given you some freedom to choose your own path, I have done the same with Esige." Mandukhai slowed her strides, wishing these words did not hurt so much. "Perhaps you two were meant to come together like this. I can see that she did not give in easily." A smile tipped the corner of her mouth. "She nearly beat you," she teased.

He chuckled, sliding his finger almost affectionately across the cut on his face. "She did."

"Her sister's life was cut short too soon by her own husband, a man of ambition who did not cherish or respect what he had." Mandukhai stopped, squaring off in front of Huoshai. "I will not send Esige into the same fate."

Huoshai's grin slipped. "She told me what Bigirsen did to her sister."

"I would put her within his reach if I allowed her to marry you and join the Urainkhai in the south," Mandukhai said. "Which makes me uncomfortable. I need to be certain he cannot touch her, and that you will never harm her."

"I swear it on my very soul," Huoshai replied with conviction. "I loathe him as much as she does."

"I doubt that. No one hates him as much as Esige." Mandukhai raised her chin, knowing what she was about to ask of him could be the very thing that broke this exchange. "Lord Huoshai, we will have a new Great Khan by nightfall. Your father has revealed his disrespect by not coming to show his support at *kurultai*. I cannot give the hand of the princess to someone who does not respect the house of the Great Khan, of Genghis."

Huoshai's face fell. A flurry of emotions crossed his face. Doubt. Disbelief. Outrage. Grief. Confusion. "You know all of this before you agreed to this race. What was all of this about if you never intended to give your blessing?" He glanced at Esige, who watched them from a distance, clinging to Unebolod as if clinging to the edge of a cliff. Her face shined with hope. And fear. "Why would you do this to *her*?"

"Do you think you are the first to try winning her hand? I warned you about the cliff."

Huoshai's jaw dropped. His glare mingled with anger and disbelief.

"I am not here today to tear away hope or happiness," Mandukhai reassured him. "But the bride-service I request of you is no small thing."

He shook his head, working his jaw as if attempting to snap out of his shock. "Anything."

"I demand you give yourself to serve myself and the Great Khan, above all others," Mandukhai replied smoothly. "Above your tribe. Above your father. For there is no station more divine than the blood of Genghis."

Huoshai's brows knitted together. His gaze fell on Batu, who stared back as if watching a curious bird. She could see the wheels in Huoshai's head turning. It only took a moment for him to put the pieces together. Silence fell between them so deep Mandukhai could hear the chattering of the nobles watching them from a distance, speculating.

Huoshai crossed his arms. His gaze bounced back and forth between Mandukhai and Batu, calculating something. "If I agree, then I have your word that we have your blessing?" he asked after several painfully long minutes.

"On my very soul."

Huoshai's jaw twitched. He straightened his shoulders. "Then you have my service."

"I'm afraid I need you to make the oath to us, Lord Huoshai, under the Eternal Blue Sky where the gods can hear you."

Huoshai flinched.

Mandukhai was no fool. Without giving the official oath, he could take Esige home, then back out on his word without breaking any sacred oaths. She understood what she asked of him. Should Huoshai's father not agree to follow the will of his new Great Khan, Huoshai's oath would bind him to her over his father. He weighed this predicament, as she knew he should. If he gave the oath without hesitation, she would be concerned about his trustworthiness.

Huoshai sank to a knee and bowed his head as if a terrible, great weight suddenly pressed down on him. Was this grief over losing Esige, or resignation? Mandukhai held her breath.

"I give my oath freely," Huoshai said, his voice thick with grief, "that I will serve the Queen Regent and the house of the Great Khan with salt, gers, horses, and blood, until such a time that either sees fit to free me from their service."

Mandukhai stepped toward Huoshai, placing her hand on his shoulder. Wind picked up, kicking her deel around her legs. She held tight to Batu's hand.

"I give you my blessing to marry Lady Esige," she said.

The words drove another spike into her heart.

CHAPTER TWENTY-SIX

A Dangerous Proposal

Heat pressed down on Unebolod, making sweat roll down his temples and stick under his arms. Short sleeves offered no relief from the brutal sun shining directly on his back. The final round of the archery tournament had already begun, with only three teams of ten remaining. He blinked sweat away from his eyes as he watched the first team line up—a group of warriors from the Jalair tribe, led by Lady Altan. He should not have been surprised that her tribe had made it this far under her guidance. Unebolod had not met a woman so adept at leading battle strategy as Altan.

As her men stepped up to the line with her, she glanced at Unebolod and Huoshai, who watched from the side, their men at their backs. The corner of her mouth curled up in a smirk and she winked at them. Unebolod grimaced at her arrogance. Huoshai chuckled.

Four rounds of arrows flew toward targets. The final round put the target at one hundred yards away. At such a distance, only an expert archer could hit the target with perfect accuracy. Unebolod watched each volley fly, shielding his eyes from the sun as he squinted into the distance. Only the judges at the other end would give any clear indication of the team's success with their flags. The Jalair final score was respectable.

Huoshai and his men went next. Just as the Jalair had done, the Urainkhai men fired in unison all four rounds and awaited their score. The Jalair beat them by one point.

Altan approached Huoshai, elbowing him in the ribs. "Maybe you should have saved your race for after the tournament," she teased.

Huoshai shook his head, glancing at the canopy nearby where Mandukhai and Esige watched the event. "I would prefer that result to this one any day."

"She must be some woman then," Altan said.

Unebolod noticed Mandukhai there as well ... beside Batu. He turned his back to all of them and marched to the line. This was not the time to let his heart distract his mind from focusing on victory.

Yesterday, he had fired expecting to show the people the sort of warrior their Great Khan would be. Today, he felt no purpose. For the first time in his life, Unebolod felt old, like a thing of the past, while warriors like Altan and Huoshai would be the future. Suddenly, his back ached. His bones felt heavy with exhaustion. Unebolod was not old, he knew. Barely in his thirties, he still had years of good fighting ahead of him. But what was he fighting for?

Unebolod gazed down at his hand, now packed with silver and bandaged tight around the cut he had made across his palm, sealing his promise to the High Heavens. *My word is iron,* he thought, remembering the oath he had given last night. But even iron melted or bent under the right heat or pressure.

No, he would not let his men down by losing this final round. Perhaps he would not become Great Khan, but Unebolod knew he was still a force to be reckoned with. The sooner everyone understood that, the better. He would not live forever.

Unebolod drew in his breath as he pulled back on the string in tandem with his men, then released the arrow as he breathed out. One. Two. Three. Four. With each, he heard the thump in the distance but could not see the result until the judges raised their flags.

A tie with Altan's warriors.

The crowd collectively gasped, then a roar of applause lifted into the air. Ties rarely happened. Now, each team's commander would face off until a winner could be declared. Unebolod scrubbed his arm over his forehead and wiped the sweat off his temples, flicking it aside as the judge explained how the final round would go.

Unebolod and Altan would each get four shots. If it remained a tie, the targets would move back another twenty yards, and they would try again. This process would repeat until one of them won.

Unebolod no longer wanted to do this. He was hot and sticky with sweat, and too tired to care about winning. Were it not for his Khorchin warriors watching their khan, or Mandukhai's hawk-like gaze locked on him from the tent, he might have given up the fight.

Instead, he stepped up to the line.

"Don't worry, I'll go easy on you," Altan teased.

Unebolod pulled back an arrow as he glared at her, releasing the first shot without bothering to break his gaze from her. The crowd collectively held its breath. Altan's eyes widened as she watched the arrow fly. Unebolod just stared at her as he heard the thump of the arrow in the distance. Then the crowd erupted in cheers.

"I'm not worried," he said.

Altan set her jaw and turned away from him, releasing her first shot. Judges would reserve marking points until they had fired all four arrows.

The sun baked Unebolod's skin as they continued their contest, and he was certain the sky father was determined to burn him alive. It was so blisteringly hot out today!

Unebolod's stunt had thrown Altan off, and he beat her by two points. He shifted his bow to the wrapped hand and offered his other hand to shake. Altan grinned at him as she clasped his arm.

"I will count this as one of the highlights of my life," she said. "To face off against the Steel Soldier and survive."

Unebolod grunted in amusement and let go of her arm. "Let's hope this is the only time we face off."

"Let us hope we all remember we are on the same side," Mandukhai said as she joined them.

Unebolod stiffened, giving a tight nod. For a moment, their gazes locked on each other. Her eyes watered, but she blinked the tears back. They would need to talk at some point, but now hardly seemed like the place. Besides, the two had never been very good at sharing their feelings honestly when it would hurt the other. Unebolod would rather hide from Mandukhai than face the inevitable conversation.

"Lady Altan, I would love to speak with you privately later," Mandukhai said, averting her gaze from him. "You have shown yourself impressively in this tournament."

Altan bowed respectfully, but Unebolod noted something in her body language. Altan was not interested in any private meetings with Mandukhai. "At your leisure, Queen Regent. Just send me word."

Before Mandukhai could say more, Altan spun on her heel and marched away. Her warriors closed in around her. Unebolod's frown deepened as he watched her go. A curious exchange.

"Unebolod," Mandukhai said.

His heart seized, and he flicked his gaze to her.

Mandukhai watched him with a mask of formality that would make any warrior proud. But he knew her better than anyone and could see the truth. It offered him some comfort to see her struggle with this separation as much as he did.

"I can think of no one more deserving of this victory than you," she said. "I would like to offer you and your men a position of honor as a reward."

Unebolod sensed his nine warriors lingering behind him. They hung on her every word, just as he had done for so long. Before she could speak, he wanted to decline, to turn as Altan had done and just walk away. Yet duty, honor, and passion bound him in place.

"I would like to offer you the sacred *sulde* of Genghis," she said. "No one is more deserving of its stewardship."

Unebolod blinked. The *sulde* of the first Great Khan was a sacred object. Manduul had entrusted it to Unebolod until Bayan had come along. It gave the bearer power as an heir should there be no clear line of succession. Stewardship of the black *sulde* was one of the highest honors a Khan could give. *But she is not a Khan.*

At his back, Unebolod's men muttered under their breath. He could not hear them, but judging by the fierce glare in Mandukhai's eyes as she stared them each down, she understood the sentiment well enough. Only a Khan could give the sacred banner. But a Great Khan would not bear it himself. Mandukhai had just drawn a wider line in the sand between him and the title.

This was also something he could not refuse outright. To do so would shame not only him, but his entire tribe.

"It would honor me to accept this responsibility again," Unebolod said as evenly as he could. "Once a Khan is present to hand it to me."

Mandukhai frowned, pain shining in her eyes even if she did not show it on her face. Unebolod did not want to hurt her, but tradition was tradition, and he would not risk the anger of the tribes. Not even for her. Not anymore.

"Then I assign you the duty of retrieving the *sulde* from where I have stored it and bring it to me tonight," she said. Frost crept over her tone. "Then, once I have named the new Khan before the sacred *sulde*, as custom requires, I will have all authority to give it in his name. Would that be satisfactory?"

Unebolod gritted his teeth. Was she putting on a show for these men, or did she truly mean to be so cold to him? Surely she couldn't be bitter about what had happened this morning. It had been her choice long before it had been his. With his disbelief gripping his veins, he could only nod, afraid of the words that might come out if he tried to speak.

Mandukhai strode away from them, with her young shadow trailing alongside. Batu turned around. His wolf-like eyes watched Unebolod as he walked away, giving Unebolod a sense that the boy had placed Unebolod on a scale to weigh and assess.

He is already more of a warrior than his father ever was, Unebolod thought.

Evening approached far too quickly for Mandukhai's taste. Sunset would come in just two hours' time, and she could not delay the inevitable much longer. A few more alliances would go a long way. When Unebolod arrived with the *sulde* of Genghis, Mandukhai would have to speak with him to ensure he would still support her and Batu, even without the title. She would need him in the years to come. While she did not think he would oppose her decision, that did not mean he would show up at *kurultai* and vote in her favor either. Unebolod could just as easily walk away.

She had a lot of work to do to prepare Batu, but the meeting with Lady Altan needed to happen before *kurultai*. Perhaps Mandukhai could solidify an alliance with another woman who might sympathize with her cause. If there was some way to ensure Unebolod's happiness, Mandukhai would do everything she could to see it happen. Even if it killed her a little more inside.

Tuya finished cooling the tea and set a small jar of *airag* on the table as well. Altan was more likely to enjoy *airag* than tea, but Mandukhai wanted to be sure all options were available.

Batu sat on the bed, playing with a set of wooden puzzle blocks. He picked each piece up, studying the angles and connections. It was meant to be taken apart and reconnected properly. Nemeku could take them apart easily enough, but rarely remembered exactly how they fit back together. She wondered how Batu would do with the toys.

Lady Altan ducked in after a brief announcement from Boke. Her gaze swept the inside of Mandukhai's ger briefly, no doubt assessing her situation. Her dark eyes settled on the tray of snacks and drinks on the table.

"Please tell me you didn't invite me over for tea," Altan said.

"You don't strike me as a tea woman," Mandukhai replied with a warm smile. She gestured to the table. "Please. Sit. I would like to talk about your performance in the festival ... and your future."

Altan grimaced but crossed the ger and settled at the table. Tuya poured her a cup of *airag* before melting into the background again. Altan took a generous drink and held it out for a refill. Tuya quickly moved to comply.

"What do you know of my future?" Altan asked tersely.

"I don't presume to know anything, but I know what the men expect," Mandukhai replied, cradling her cup of tea in her hand. "How long before one of them tries to take what belongs to you?"

Altan snorted and shook her head. "That won't happen."

She sounded so confident that Mandukhai could not help but envy her a little. What was it like to be so certain?

"You assume the two of us are alike, but we aren't," Altan said, then drained her cup and set it on the table. "I have been fighting and hunting for as long as I can remember. My father never had sons. He had me, and so I was raised like his son. The men respect my position because I have earned it. How have you earned yours?"

Mandukhai's jaw twitched. She took a sip of tea to calm her anger. "I'm disappointed in you, Lady Altan."

Altan made a fist on the tabletop but didn't move. Her own anger colored her face.

"I thought you would see what the men clearly cannot, being a woman who has worked for everything she has," Mandukhai continued. "But, like the men, you see what is on the surface. A woman dressed in silk. Don't understand what lurks beneath the surface. Even a crane can be deadly when provoked."

The corner of Altan's mouth twitched up in a grin. "Are you threatening me?"

Mandukhai smirked right back. "I wouldn't need to. I'm simply stating a fact."

Altan leaned back in her seat, cocking her head as she examined Mandukhai. The woman seemed to have a good grip on weighing the merit of a person upon examination. "Well, you have somehow garnered the support of some of the more powerful men, so you can't be as delicate as a lily." She rapped her fingers against the tabletop. "What is it you want, Queen Regent?"

Mandukhai nodded. She appreciated Altan's no-nonsense attitude. It was a breath of fresh air compared to the other women she spoke with. "You are right about one thing. I have some support, but I cannot seem to align the Lords behind me." She glanced at Batu. "I will need to do that soon."

Silence fell. Altan studied Batu, chewing the inside of her cheek as she contemplated something. Mandukhai wished she could read this woman, but Altan was so different from everyone else. Not soft and predictable like the women. Not hard and expectant, like the men. Mandukhai could not help feeling a kinship with Altan.

"It's him, isn't it?" Altan said at last, pointing at Batu. "He looks like Bolkhu. Did he have an illegitimate son no one knew about? If so, I am not surprised that you are the one to find him."

The truth would be dangerous to Batu, but Mandukhai knew she could not hide it much longer. If people did not already know who he was, they would by the end of this day. "Yes. But he was not illegitimate. His mother is Lady Siker."

Altan let out a low whistle. "That explains so much. So I assume you are naming him as the last heir of Genghis?"

Mandukhai didn't bother nodding. She simply met Altan's gaze without flinching.

Altan huffed, then leaned forward, resting her forearms on the table. "I don't mean to discredit your strength. The mere fact that you could do all of this—" Altan waved around grandly, though Mandukhai understood she was not talking about the inside of the ger, but everything that had happened these past weeks, "—says something about your strength. But *kurultai* is a whole other matter. Those men will gather, and they will select whomever they choose, no matter whose name you put forward. And if you put that boy in front of the *sulde* and try making him Great Khan, he will either end up dead, or the Lords might turn and walk away. No one wants to follow a boy and a woman."

"But your men follow you."

Altan nodded. "They do. Because I have proven myself. I fought at their sides. I saved their lives. I've been soaked in the same blood as them. Men only respect two things, Mandukhai. Tradition and battle strength. If you want their respect, earn it."

In battle. How could Mandukhai ever earn their respect in battle if she could not get a chance to *show* them her strength? They had to follow her first.

"What does this have to do with my future?" Altan asked bluntly.

"I need to know I can count on your support." There. She had said it.

Altan's lips parted. Her eyes narrowed.

Sensing that she might lose the other woman, Mandukhai leaned forward, setting down her tea, and met Altan's gaze without flinching. "The men respect two things. I am supporting tradition and will continue to do so for as long as I am able. But if I want to prove myself in battle, first I need a reason to go to battle. If I have to fight for every single one of those votes at *kurultai*, I will. But I would rather keep our men off the battlefield as much as possible. For every vote I have to fight for, we potentially lose good men. If I cannot even get your support, none of those men will follow me either. Why should they when even you would not?"

Altan scoffed. "A woman's power is always meant to dangle by a thread. If I follow you, I risk my own credibility. If you get enough support, I will back you. But I will not be alone at your side. I hope you can understand my position, Mandukhai. I mean no offense. It's simple politics."

Mandukhai glanced at Batu. He had disassembled the toy and now attempted to piece it back together again. As he worked, his eyebrows scrunched together, and he bit his lower lip. All of this was for him. Did he even want any of it? He was just a child.

"Can I ask why you rejected Unebolod?" Altan asked.

Mandukhai flinched, jerking her eyes to the tabletop. The grains flowed like a river along and around each other. She could not tell Altan the truth. Unebolod knew of her vision, but no one else did. Mandukhai would not speak of it to another soul—except Batu.

"Just like everyone else, I gave my word to support an heir of Genghis above all others," Mandukhai replied. "Unfortunately, as Manduul's only living wife, that puts me in an awkward position. I am destined to forever be chained to the line of Genghis. Unebolod is not. He deserves better. He deserves a wife who can give him what he wants, and sons who would inherit his legacy. If I chose him, he would get neither." Which brought Mandukhai to her next point. She took a breath to center herself, then straightened and met Altan's gaze. "Unebolod respects strong, powerful women. He is drawn to them. Which is why I think you would make a great match for him."

Altan choked on her *airag*. She coughed, thumping a fist against her chest. When she looked at Mandukhai again, her eyes were watered. "Are you trying to arrange a marriage for him?"

"Yes. And no." She sagged a little. "I have cherished him dearly for years. And even if I cannot be with him, I want him to be happy. I want him to have sons. He is one of the few men I know who would not try to force you to give up your position in exchange. If anything, he might expect you to maintain your leadership role." Mandukhai smiled sadly. Her heart broke speaking these words, but she truly wanted him to be happy, and Altan seemed like a perfect match. "As I said, he is drawn to strong women."

Altan stood, stared down at Mandukhai, then strode toward the door. As she opened it, she paused. "I have no interest in marriage, and I'm insulted that you would see me as the men do."

Mandukhai surged to her feet, worried that she had lost Altan. "No. That's not what I mean. You would still keep your position."

"Right." A dangerous glint entered her eyes as she swept her gaze over Mandukhai. "If you want him to be so happy, spread your own legs. Not mine."

"Altan!" Mandukhai moved around the table, but the other woman stormed out and slammed the door.

Mandukhai held her hands to her mouth, taking careful breaths. That had not gone well at all. And she was fairly certain she would lose Altan's support for good now. If Altan told Unebolod ...

Would he change his mind about supporting her as well?

Tears shimmered in her eyes as she turned away from the door. Batu stood beside the bed, hands in little fists at his sides, watching the door. When he saw her tears, he shuffled toward her and wrapped his arms around her waist.

Mandukhai hugged him back, worried that she had just sealed his fate and the Lords would kill him before nightfall.

Chapter Twenty-Seven

The Sacred Sulde of Genghis

Issama reclined across the wide table from Tolokan, the Urainkhai khan. They sat in an open field surrounded by rolling hills of green Populus trees in all directions. Issama brought along Nahai and one of the Ordos Lords—Ulum—to help smooth out ruffled feathers among the Urainkhai khan. Tolokan had launched several small-scale raids against Bigirsen's camps when they set up too close to Urainkhai borders. The stance was clear. Tolokan did not welcome Bigirsen's army.

The sun heated Issama's skin, and he was thankful for the sleeveless deel today.

"If it weren't for the nice weather, I might be less inclined to sit here with you," Tolokan announced. He grasped a goblet of *airag* as if Issama intended to take it away from him. Tolokan was not old, by any means, but gray flecked his hair here and there. He had shaved most of his head and only wore the looping braids along the sides and the forelock in the front. As he narrowed his eyes over the edge of his goblet at Issama, crow's feet spread out from the corners. He wasn't old, but he showed signs of age.

The Urainkhai were a powerful force in the south and were content to raid the Ming borders instead of involving themselves in Mongol politics. The lack of interest in political matters made it harder for Issama to predict what Tolokan would do next. But they guarded their borders like a rabid pack of wolves. Since their territory stretched the length of the eastern border with the Ming, Issama needed to find some common ground. If he needed that access, he needed an ally.

"You need to stop raiding our camps," Issama stated in a casual, yet plain tone.

Tolokan wiped *airag* from his upper lip and snorted. "Move away from my land and we have a deal."

Issama suppressed a sigh. "I would like to form an alliance with you, Tolokan khan. That is why we have moved closer."

Again, Tolokan narrowed his eyes. "You open your mouth like a man yet speak like a yak. I would sooner trust a mountain lion than trust you. I know what your master has been up to. Bigirsen thinks he can take whatever he wants and leave the scraps for the rest of us." Tolokan spit at the ground, then glared at Issama. "You don't come here to make friendly with me. You come here to do his bidding."

Issama picked through the bowl of plums, finding one with supple skin. He brushed his thumb over it, making the skin wrinkle beneath his finger. "He's not happy that you sent your son north for *kurultai* with Lady Mandukhai."

"I didn't send him for her," Tolokan snapped. "I sent him to find a wife. He seemed unable to find a suitable one here. Tengri knows he tested a few of them out."

"You sent your heir north, where she controls the hearts and minds of the people with her witchy ways," Issama replied as if explaining why water was wet or the sky was blue. "Do you truly believe any wife he finds there will not manipulate him with the power between her legs?"

Tolokan's face reddened. "My son is not weak, but my patience is getting there. Tell your master to get his slaves away from my borders and we won't have a problem."

Issama winced, pressing his thumb into the skin of the plumb. "Did you know that if you apply just the right amount of pressure to the skin of a plum, you can create a minor break?"

Tolokan eyed him warily as he took another drink. Issama continued pressing his thumb into the plum until a bit of juice slipped past his finger.

"But all it takes is that one tiny, minor break to create a rupture that will destroy the plum from the inside out." With a touch more pressure, the plum exploded outward in his palm. "And all you are left with is the pit."

Tolokan's jaw twitched. Issama saw the khan calculating his warning. "Huoshai is strong. I would not have trusted him on this journey if he were not."

"And when was the last time your wife bent you to her will?" Issama wiped his hand on one of the cloth squares on the table.

The question thrust Tolokan into silence. Issama fought off his smile. He had the Urainkhai khan. Tolokan would consider the merits of supporting Mandukhai vs. supporting Bigirsen. Either way, he would be pinched off between the two of them and would have to choose a side.

"Save yourself the trouble, Tolokan," Issama said. "Ulum has a daughter near enough to Huoshai's age. Keep your title. Join us against the Ming, and you will have a suitable, agreeable, delicate wife for your son to produce his own heirs."

A servant shuffled over and refilled Tolokan's goblet. He took a deliberate drink before responding. "Fine. But if Bigirsen attempts taking my title or my tribe, I will cut his throat myself."

Issama raised his hands in supplication. "I won't stop you."

MOUNT BURKHAN KHALDUN – SUMMER 1470

Unebolod knew he should work on retrieving the black horsehair banner of Genghis from Mandukhai's storage space in the gathering tent, but the events of the day had worn him thin. Instead, he sent his warriors to do the task for him and headed for a path through the alpine trees along the edges of Mount Burkhan Khaldun. How much longer could a day be? Unebolod felt as if he had not slept for a week. A bit of isolation would help soothe his weary mind.

He passed the Shrine of the First Queen as a young couple kneeled at the doorway with their offering of milk. The sight made his heart ache. He turned away, deeper into the trees. Where that shrine had appeared from, he could not say. It had been missing for so long, and he heard the whispers. People gave the shrine almost supernatural reverence, as if the appearance were herald for the strength of the next Great Khan—and the strength of Mandukhai.

In less than a day, everything had changed. Genghis had chosen Mandukhai for this task, and not him. All his life, Unebolod had never felt so worthless, so utterly lost. She didn't need him. The people didn't need him. The Nation didn't need him. What had the purpose of his life been?

Togochi had reminded Unebolod he was still khan to his tribe, but this was something Unebolod had never aspired to be. He had been content not so long ago to allow his brother to rule the Khorchin while he ruled the Nation. They would have been a powerful duo, just as Genghis and Khasar had been.

He moved through the woods, making no sound. It was an unconscious thing to him, moving with stealth. It came as naturally to him as breath.

Voices drifted to him through the trees, distant but still somewhat distinct. Unebolod paused, straining to hear more. Several voices exchanged words, but he could not make out anything they said. He crept closer.

"... an insult like this," Korgiz said.

Unebolod stiffened as he recognized the Ongud khan's voice.

"She has no idea what she is doing," Albeq khan said.

"She never has," Korgiz snapped. "We cannot allow her to do this."

Unebolod edged closer, watchful to not step on sticks so the men would not hear his approach. What they spoke of could be considered treason. Mandukhai would be within her right to kill them both. He peered through a gap between trees, careful to remain in the shade.

Half a dozen of the highest-ranked Lords gathered in this secret place, voicing their animosity toward their Queen Regent.

"I still think we should have spoken to Huoshai," Unige said. Since Manduul's reign began, Unige had been loyal to the Borjigin. Now he met with other tribal leaders in secret. "The Urainkhai are a powerful force in the south, and he will be married to the princess. We need him on our side."

"He kneeled in front of that woman," Korgiz said, then spit on the ground. His nose curled in a sneer. "He would be of no help. We all know he gave his oath. To a woman!"

Unebolod ducked back out of sight as his heart clenched in his chest. These men would not follow Mandukhai, even if she raised Batu to Great Khan. They wanted someone stronger, a warrior fierce enough to lead them into battle and help them conquer the world as they had done under Genghis and his sons. *They want me*, he realized.

If he wanted it, Unebolod could step out of the shadows, rally these men, and take the title. Mandukhai would never forgive him, but when the Mongol Nation was at stake, would that matter? *She once had faith in my abilities.*

Unebolod had to take a stand right now. He could lead these men as they wanted, as their Great Khan. Or he could declare to support her choice—of the will of Genghis and the High Heavens—and be the shield around her.

The cut in Unebolod's hand suddenly burned, as if the High Heavens reminded him of his oath the night before. His jaw twitched. He was still unsure of his faith, but an oath was an oath. He flexed his fist, pressing the tips of his fingers into a fist over the bandage on his palm.

"She won't survive," Bagatur, the Kharchin khan, said with absolute certainty.

Unebolod released a slow breath and closed off his emotions once more. *I have given my word, and my word is iron.*

"Who won't survive?" Unebolod asked as he stepped around a tree to join the ring of startled Lords. He did not want them knowing he had overheard the first part of their conversation.

All the men stiffened and averted their gazes the moment they realized he had found them. Each one either appeared ashamed or uneasy. Had Unebolod overestimated their support for him? No one dared to speak.

Unebolod maintained a cold warrior's face. "I'm not sure what is more condemning," he said, standing straight with his hands laced behind his back. "Is it the fact that you are now silent, or that you saw a need to meet in secret in the woods?"

Albeq cleared his throat and lifted his gaze from the stump he sat upon. "Mandukhai has gone too far, Unebolod. We came here to support you. You led us to believe you had her under control, but she has closed the door to you and attempted to give your men charge of the sacred banner. As if she were a man with any right to do so."

"Control?" Unebolod laughed, but the sound was hollow. "Can a mortal control the sun? Can a man control a dragon?" He paced in a circle, staring each of them down. "I never said I controlled her."

"We will not follow her," Korgiz said. His beard quivered indignantly. "A man will lead Mongols, as always. Any authority she believes she has is little more than a veil full of holes. Water runs straight through."

Unebolod halted his steps in front of Korgiz, glaring down at the man. Silence settled over the gathering. Korgiz shifted, but Unebolod did not relent. Even the wind seemed to cease blowing through the small clearing.

"Allow me to tell you a story," Unebolod said coldly. "Of a mouse, bullied and abused by an elephant." Several men squirmed, but no one interrupted. "The mouse was small and weak, and the elephant thought it better, bigger, stronger." Unebolod moved again slowly, each step a threat.

"But one day, the mouse warned the elephant that if it did not stop, the mouse would have no choice but to declare war. Of course, the elephant still thought itself superior, so it laughed at the mouse."

Unige crossed his arms tight over his chest, as if attempting to shield himself. The man had been a loyal member of Manduul's court. He had seen how Mandukhai rose to power. How she showed all the men her strength. How could *he* doubt her? *Because he is weak willed and happy to follow the pack.*

"When the elephant did not desist in its bullying, the mouse was ready," Unebolod continued. He adopted a dangerous edge in his voice. "The mouse destroyed the elephant from the inside."

Each of the men nodded as if they understood his meaning.

"That is what she will do to us all," Korgiz proclaimed. "She will destroy us from the inside out!"

Others raised their voices in agreement.

Unebolod moved to the center of the small circle, resting his hand on the hilt of his sword. His fingers brushed the yellow ribbon. *Fools. All of them.* He now knew with absolute certainty what he would do by the end of this day.

"No, Korgiz," Unebolod said evenly, confidently. "This war between the mouse and the elephant laid waste to all. I will not make the mistakes of the elephant. Above my position, above my personal ambition, I will fight to preserve this land and this Nation. As I vowed to do. Gentlemen, I will make peace with the mouse."

Stunned silence followed Unebolod's proclamation. Unebolod had taken his stand. He had chosen his side. Now, he just had to hope these men would follow his lead. If not, he would face them down on the battlefield to ensure Mandukhai carried out the mission Genghis had laid at her feet. *This is my purpose*, he thought with certainty. *This is why I am here.*

"And if we don't?" Bagatur asked.

"Then one day, the *sulde* of Genghis will cast a long shadow over your tribe," Unebolod said.

Each of them eyed Unebolod, weighing the implication. If Mandukhai put that banner in his hands, that meant they would face him. None of them wanted that. They all knew of his skills.

"She needs a Khan," Unige said.

"She has one. Mandukhai fights for the Borjigin line, gentlemen. For tradition. And she fights with the spirit of Genghis Khan at her back. Huoshai was wise enough to recognize this." Unebolod marched toward the edge of the clearing. "When she declares our Lord, I will give my oath to her, just as promised. For the future of the Mongol Nation."

Unebolod left the Lords to contemplate his words as he strode back toward the sprawling camp at Mount Burkhan Khaldun's base. They now knew exactly where he stood. And he knew what they had considered. It hung over their heads like an executioner's blade. They could accept her, or they could face the drop of the blade.

Mandukhai shaved Batu's head clean, as was the custom for young boys, but left two long tails at either ear. He did not move as she ran the blade over his scalp. He didn't even flinch. Such was his trust in her steady hand. Tonight was the night, and she would be certain Batu was as much a Borjigin heir as she could make him appear.

Once she finished shaving his head—leaving the forelock on his forehead—she set to work on the looping braids around his ears, as warrior men wore.

Boke announced Jaghan's arrival and Mandukhai welcomed her friend inside as she continued her work.

Jaghan watched as Mandukhai prepared Batu. "How are you feeling, Mandukhai? I'm concerned about your emotional state. This has been a hard day for you."

Mandukhai's throat tightened, but she managed a reply. "I will be fine. This will be an auspicious day."

Jaghan sighed, folding her hands in the sleeves of her deel. "There is no way you are fine. You had to let go of the two people closest to your heart today."

Mandukhai smiled, but it did not reach her eyes. "My heart is safe." She leaned forward to gaze at Batu. "Isn't that right, Batu?"

He straightened and nodded once, but with so much certainty that it truly bolstered Mandukhai's heart. She continued braiding his hair.

"And tonight, we will have a new Great Khan," Mandukhai said with certainty.

Togochi ducked inside. "The boys are under Nemeku's watchful eye for now. That won't last long."

Jaghan sighed, then cast one last glance at Mandukhai, imploring her with eyes alone to just let go of her sorrow. "I am here if you need to talk."

"We are fine," Mandukhai insisted. But no matter how many times she said it, the words did not feel any truer.

Togochi waited for Jaghan to bow out and chase down the boys. The moment the door closed behind her, Togochi turned toward Mandukhai. The set of his shoulders and the way he crossed his arms made it apparent he was ready for a confrontation.

Mandukhai tied a strip of leather to Batu's braid to complete the second loop. As he ran his hands over his new hair, Mandukhai stepped back to give him more space.

"So, you intend to follow through with this plan," Togochi said, eyeing Batu curiously.

"I do."

Batu rose slowly from his seat. Mandukhai shook out the new silk deel she had made for him. Batu ran his hands along the blue cloth, accepting it from her.

"You truly are closing the door on Unebolod," Togochi said as he watched them prepare. "I thought this was what you wanted. Why would you choose the boy over him?"

Mandukhai grimaced as she smoothed out the shoulders of the deel and helped Batu with the ties. "I told you already. The fate of the nation cannot be guided by the whims of my heart. I have a duty to uphold, just as much as you. Perhaps more so."

Togochi lowered his voice, leaning closer. "If you do this, if you raise this boy to Great Khan, he will be dead in a year."

Mandukhai had considered this. Young Khans rarely lived long. Some were assassinated, others died in battle prematurely. It was the whole reason she had Boke swear his life to the boy.

But she could not do this alone. She needed allies. Strong ones. A few guards alone would not be enough. "Which is precisely why I need you, Togochi."

"No. That's why you need him!" Togochi stabbed a finger outside, as if Unebolod stood right outside her door. "I know how stubborn you can get once you choose a course, Mandukhai, but I would like to think you respect my advice. So listen to me now. Where Unebolod goes, those Lords will follow. You can either tame the beast or set him loose so he can come back to bite you."

Mandukhai rounded on Togochi, stabbing her finger into his chest. "You listen to me, Togochi! I am guided by divine right. This boy is the last of Genghis Khan's heirs. Would you like to be the one who fails Genghis?"

Her chest heaved with angry breath. Her hands trembled. "You gave me an oath, Lord Togochi. To follow my lead."

Togochi ground his teeth. "Until a new Khan is chosen."

"And he will be!" Mandukhai waved a hand at Batu. "Tonight. Then, you will give that oath to him."

Togochi swatted Mandukhai's hand away. "My loyalty is now and always to the Mongol Nation. Wherever that may lead me."

The two glared at each other. Mandukhai did not want to be angry with him. She needed Togochi on her side. If she lost his support, she might have no choice but to crawl back to Unebolod on her knees and beg his forgiveness. Just the thought made her eyes sting with tears. Especially since she knew he would accept her back. It only punctuated how deeply she had hurt them both.

"This is hard on us all," Togochi said, his tone softening.

"It will be hardest on him." Mandukhai turned to Batu, who brushed his fingers over the silver embroidery on his deel.

Boke opened the door, glaring at Togochi before turning his attention to Mandukhai. "Lord Unebolod is here for you."

"At last." Mandukhai huffed and marched out the door.

Unebolod stood stiffly with his men, his face a stony mask. Mandukhai's gaze swept over the men, and for a moment she feared he had changed his mind. Could these men overpower her own? They had no banners to give her.

"It's gone," Unebolod said.

Mandukhai's heart clenched in her chest. "What is gone?"

"The *sulde* of Genghis Khan," he replied. "It's not in your storage space."

Mandukhai's world splintered. Without that banner, she could not install Batu as Great Khan.

If she could not place Batu in front of the *sulde* of Genghis, there could be no *kurultai*.

Chapter Twenty-Eight

Jewel of the Soul

Mandukhai paced the rugs of her ger, unable to stand still. The *sulde* was gone. She had left it secured in her storage space in the gathering tent, and only a handful of people had access, which narrowed her list of suspects. She could not consider its absence a coincidence. Just a week ago, it fluttered in the breeze outside the gathering tent. It had been removed for safekeeping before the festival, precisely because she feared something like this would happen.

One week. Someone could take it far from Mount Burkhan Khaldun in a week. But who had left? Had they left at all?

Confidants crowded her ger. Togochi and Jaghan sat beside each other on a long bench, along with Esige and Huoshai. Nemeku kept the other three boys corralled along the north wall, out of the way. Boke stood guard just inside the door to one side, with Unebolod on the other. The rest of Mandukhai's guards surrounded the ger outside.

The smoke flap above remained open to the blue sky. Mandukhai paused below the opening, hands on her hips, staring up. Sunset was not far off. The Lords would be waiting for *kurultai*. Anger bubbled in her chest. These men, the so-called Lords of the Mongol Nation, undermined her at every opportunity. But this ... to steal the sacred banner of Genghis! *I cannot trust anyone!*

No one else dared to speak. They all watched her with curious eyes, well aware of the anger rolling off of her in suffocating waves. Mandukhai closed her eyes and prayed, *Lord Tengri, Genghis, guide me now so I may carry out your will.*

A hand fell on Mandukhai's forearm. She tilted her head away from the smoke hole. Batu stood beside her. Once again, his touch soothed her soul and smothered the flames of her anger. How could one so young have such power? *Perhaps he truly is divine*, Mandukhai thought.

Mandukhai placed her other hand over Batu's, and something passed between their gazes. Understanding. Gratitude. Trust. She breathed in, then turned her attention to Unebolod. The pain in his eyes as he watched her with Batu wrenched at her heart. The last thing she wanted was to watch him suffer, but she needed Unebolod close.

"You are certain it is not here, somewhere around Mount Burkhan Khaldun?" she asked Unebolod.

He and Batu seemed locked in some silent calculation. "No," Unebolod said at last, tearing his gaze away from Batu. "It is a large encampment. In a week, someone could have stashed anywhere it. Or it could be hundreds of miles away by now."

Everyone shifted uncomfortably. If the banner was not in camp, there would be no *kurultai*.

Togochi rubbed his hands together anxiously. "You cannot name the next Great Khan without that banner," he said. "The Lords will not allow it. Tradition—"

"I am aware of that, Togochi. Thank you!" Mandukhai hadn't meant to snap at him, but she did not need him to state the obvious either. They had named every Great Khan all the way back to Genghis in front of that banner. While the Lords all preferred performing *kurultai* in Karakorum, they would do it anywhere, as long as the banner was present. Without that banner, anyone could question a Great Khan's right to rule. "Search the camps. I need it found by tonight."

Unebolod balked, crossing his arms over his wide chest. "That's impossible. Even with the full force of all of our men, we cannot possibly search the entire encampment in one night. Thousands—hundreds of thousands—of gers cannot be searched with even a full *tumen* in such a time. Mandukhai, you have a bigger problem here than the missing banner."

"I know of my challenges," Mandukhai said, heat rising in her voice. "I don't need you to remind me."

"I don't think you *do* know," Unebolod said, not backing down. "Several of these Lords have openly stated that they will not follow you. Not even with him." He glared at Batu as if his gaze could burn the boy alive. "They won't follow a woman and a child. This could be a ploy to keep you from naming him, a stalling tactic to buy them more time to find their own candidate."

"How do you know?" Mandukhai snapped. Yet she knew the answer already. Unebolod had his finger on the pulse of the Mongol Lords for some time. Was he one of those men who would not follow Batu? Was he their candidate? She swatted her question away. They would discuss that soon. "I don't care about why. I only care about where. And if you know who they are, you know where to begin the search. That should make it more expedient."

Huoshai shifted. His discomfort in this ger was clear, no matter how casual he tried to appear. "If I may?"

Mandukhai turned toward him slowly. Huoshai shrank back and said nothing, waiting for her to allow him to speak. *At least one of these men understands how to show proper respect.* Mandukhai nodded.

"Perhaps I can help," Huoshai said, pulling away from Esige. Their proximity to each other grated on Mandukhai's nerves. It was like salt in an open wound. "I am more of a neutral party here. I could ask around with some of the other Lords, see if anyone knows anything. If you go hunting for that banner, it will vanish forever. Whoever took it will not want to be caught, and they will find a more secure place to hold it."

Unebolod grunted and shook his head. "You are not a neutral party. Not anymore."

Huoshai glared at Unebolod. "What does that mean?"

"We all saw you kneeling to her," Unebolod nodded toward Mandukhai. "It doesn't take a smart man to put together why. They won't trust you. Not anymore."

Huoshai bristled, then sagged slightly.

"Thank you for the offer, Huoshai, but I'm afraid he may be right," Mandukhai said, trying to smooth over irritated tempers. "You raise a good point as well, though. If the thief knows we are looking for the banner, they will hide it far from my grasp." She hated this. How could they search for the *sulde* if no one could know they were searching for it?

"Mandukhai," Togochi said slowly, as if something terribly important just occurred to him. He straightened his back and as his gaze met hers, the worry in his eyes confirmed her suspicion. He must have realized something awful, and she did not want to hear it. "If what Unebolod says is true, and these Lords are working against you, then you are facing an exodus ..."

His words hung in the air, thick and suffocating like smoke. Mandukhai's head spun as she considered this. She could lose not just her power and title, but the support of these people around her now. And Batu. They would either capture him and keep him until he grew older, as had happened to Batu's father, or they would kill him, which would open the door for Unebolod. *I will not allow that to be Batu's fate. There must be another way.*

Huoshai stood, then bowed to her respectfully before straightening. "Queen Regent, let me leave tonight. I will take my men, make the Lords think the exodus from this sacred ground has started. Then I will circle back and trap those trying to follow. We will find out who is against you. Lords Togochi and Unebolod can bring their men in behind these traitors, and we can seal them off and force them to kneel."

War. He wants war. Mandukhai turned, watching for reactions from the others.

Unebolod and Togochi exchanged impressed glances. Unebolod stroked his narrow beard. Mandukhai knew that look. He considered the value of this plan.

Batu sank to the rug at her feet, picking at the sleeves of his deel. Did he understand what they were discussing?

"No." Mandukhai said the word so firmly everyone in the ger froze. "I will not sanction attacking my own people unless absolutely necessary. If they want to leave, let them go. Let them think I am nothing more than a weak woman. Their votes and minds are their own. Before I am through, they will see the error of their ways."

Togochi smirked at this, but Mandukhai could not understand why.

Genghis would not have chosen her if he had not believed she could succeed. Bolstered by her own confidence, she continued, "I have been given this divine task. When I ride, it will be with the blood of Genghis at my side. According to Mongol law, His is the holy power above all others. The Lords can leave if they wish, but the blood of Genghis will come for them—it will *always* come for them—and they will bend to His will, eventually. Without bloodshed, if possible. For if we break the rules of the great Genghis, all doors of destruction will be opened."

She resumed her pacing, but this time it was with fevered passion burning in her soul and not seething anger. "I have seen this fate. The fires burning on the horizon to the east, threatening to consume the world. Only by uniting behind the blood of Genghis can we avoid this fate. They will all see this before I am done."

Huoshai paled at her declaration. Togochi's eyes widened. He glanced at Unebolod, who remained as stone-faced as ever. He already knew Genghis chose her.

Esige rose and stepped up beside Huoshai, raising her chin with all the pride and confidence of a true daughter of Genghis.

"Mother, this is why the High Heavens have brought Huoshai to me," Esige said confidently. "You know what I am capable of. I will go south with him, back to the Urainkhai and amid the other southern tribes. I will keep my ear to the ground and my eyes on the horizon. I will feed their appetites with pride and fill their ears with the divine power of the blood of Genghis so that when you arrive, they will fall at your feet. Though it pains me to leave you, it fuels my spirit to know I can serve you still."

Mandukhai's heart filled with pride as she gazed upon this young woman Esige had become. She was so much smarter and stronger than her sister had ever been. Perhaps they could not have a new Great Khan tonight, but there was still much to celebrate. She glided across the rugs and held Esige's face in her hands.

"Remember always who you are, Esige." Mandukhai placed a kiss on her forehead. "You are a daughter of Genghis. And tonight, I fear I must set you free." She released Esige to face Huoshai. "Do you need to wait for your father before you are married?"

"No, Queen Regent." Huoshai stood taller. "He would much rather I return with a wife than a promise."

Mandukhai nodded. "Then you shall have a wife. Tonight."

Esige bounced up on her toes, beaming.

"I am trusting you to protect one of my most precious jewels, Lord Huoshai," Mandukhai said. "There is no greater gift of trust I can offer."

Huoshai bowed. "I am honored, Queen Regent. And I will shelter her from danger."

Mandukhai smirked. "Just don't smother her."

Esige snorted to show what she thought of this statement. Mandukhai doubted any man could ever smother her.

Mandukhai turned toward the door. "Boke."

He squared his shoulders.

"You will also have a wife tonight."

"I wish to wait a few more days," Boke said. "If what these Lords have said is true, you will need me here tonight."

Mandukhai admired his determination, but she knew the truth. "There will never be a good time, Boke. One night will not change that."

Boke frowned. "With all due respect, Queen Regent, one night *did* change everything. And I lost good men that night."

Unebolod grimaced.

Mandukhai flinched.

Boke need not say more for her to understand what he meant. The night of the Oirat attack. And it had changed everything. But she could not focus on the tasks ahead if she worried about Odgerel's potential orchestrations. Boke would be loyal to Mandukhai first, and she needed him to watch over Odgerel. Besides, Mandukhai didn't trust that Odgerel would not still test her luck and pursue Unebolod again. He would need a wife to carry on his legacy, but not Odgerel. *Never* her.

"It will be tonight, Boke," she said, plainly ending the conversation.

There would be no Great Khan, but there would be a cause for celebration.

Esige's stomach became an incessant maelstrom of butterflies as Tuya finished fixing her hair and placing the bridal headdress on. How could things have changed so swiftly? Just a week ago, Esige never would have imagined getting married. Now, she couldn't wait to become Huoshai's wife. She still did not understand how he burrowed his way into her heart so quickly when no other guys ever could. Perhaps it was because he saw her plainly—the real her and not the made-up princess everyone else saw.

Other men, such as Boragan or Chakicha, would have expected her to settle down and produce sons instead of wrestling or bow fighting. Huoshai, however, made her feel as if she would not be sacrificing that piece of her very soul just to be with him.

What will his father think of me, though? Princess or not, his father was a khan and his expectations might vary from Huoshai's. Without knowing his father at all, she did not know how he would receive her. Huoshai seemed strong and capable, but even strong men could crumble under the expectations of their own fathers.

Esige held her arms out as Mandukhai and Tuya worked together to fasten the red deel in place. She tried to meet Mandukhai's eyes, but her mother avoided her.

Mother. Mandukhai had not given birth to Esige, but she was the only mother Esige had ever known. Despite her newfound purpose in the south, Esige could not help the terror that clenched her limbs at the very idea of riding away from Mandukhai. *It isn't forever, Esige*, she reminded herself. *We will still see each other.*

But Mandukhai never saw her own mother again after riding off to marry. Her mother had died of a fever. Would something happen to Mandukhai while Esige was a thousand miles away?

Mandukhai stepped back to let Tuya finish. As Tuya adjusted the shoulders of the deel, Mandukhai approached with a belt. Her hands trembled slightly as she held it up for Esige to examine.

The belt was simple, made of gold with a few gemstones imbedded in the links.

"My mother gave this to me before I rode north to marry Manduul," Mandukhai explained. A sadness bled into her voice as she spoke. "I never had a chance to wear it on my wedding day, but I would be honored to give it to you for yours."

"The honor is mine, Mother," Esige said. Tears welled in her eyes as Mandukhai fastened the belt around her waist and adjusted it with tender, caring hands.

Overwhelmed with emotion—love, sorrow, honor, grief—Esige wrapped her arms around Mandukhai and pulled her into a tight hug. *Don't cry. Don't cry.* She fought to hold back the tears as the lump in her throat swelled to ridiculous size.

For a moment, they embraced, both unwilling to let go first. But they could not hug all day. As they both drew back, Mandukhai brushed a loving hand along Esige's cheek. Unlike Esige, Mandukhai did not bother holding back her tears. They flowed freely down her face.

"You are strong, bold, and far too intelligent for your own good," Mandukhai said, her voice thick with sorrow, or perhaps pride. Esige could not tell. "Be careful whom you trust. And if something should go wrong, you are always welcome back in my ger. You are the pride of my heart, the jewel of my soul. There will always be a place for you at my side."

"I'm terrified, Mother," Esige said, hearing the tremble in her voice which affirmed her statement. "Why does he scare me so?"

Mandukhai smiled in that way that always helped soothe Esige's nerves. "It's a scary thing to give yourself to another, body and soul. And it requires a great deal of trust to place your life and your future in the hands of another. But love—" Her words choked off, and she stepped back, brushing her hands against her cheeks to wipe away the tears. When Mandukhai continued, her voice no longer sounded like her own, but as if something had lodged in her throat to speak through her. "Love makes all the pain less. I'm sorry."

Mandukhai spun away and crossed her arms, then pressed her hand to her mouth.

Esige's heart sank. Amidst her euphoria, she had not even considered how hard this must be on Mandukhai, how watching Esige marry Huoshai could cause her so much pain. As Mandukhai quietly cried, Esige stepped around her. Even with her eyes squeezed closed, Mandukhai's tears rolled in waves down her cheeks. Surely Mandukhai had assumed that today she would marry Unebolod.

Esige pulled her mother into her arms and stroked Mandukhai's back, murmuring reassurances. The gates opened and Mandukhai's sorrow poured out. She leaned against Esige and sobbed for several heartbreakingly long minutes.

Suddenly, some stubborn pride must have struck Mandukhai because she stopped weeping and jerked back from Esige's arms. Briskly, she swiped away her tears with her hands, but it did nothing for the redness in her cheeks or eyes.

"I'm so please that you will find happiness," Mandukhai said. The way she struggled to fight through the pain and lock it away was obvious to Esige. "One of us deserves bliss."

Esige reached out to comfort her again, but Mandukhai drew away and marched toward the door. "I should see to Boke's wedding. I look forward to watching you become a woman, Esige."

Mandukhai strode out and closed the door behind her, drawing Batu along with her.

Esige smoothed her hand over the belt. Did she deserve this happiness any more than Mandukhai deserved her own?

Two Weddings, One Surprise

Unebolod had spent as much of the early evening as he could attempting to seek the missing *sulde* of Genghis. It had become a matter of pride. While he had not actually possessed the *sulde* yet since Mandukhai had given it to his care, he still felt responsible for it. Without that banner, there could be no Great Khan and he would be forever shamed for failing in his sacred duty.

Perhaps that had been the intention. Whoever stole it would have known Unebolod had taken a stand today, and they might have wanted to shame him and strip away what little respect he had left. Or it could have been someone who had not supported him from the start. But that only left the Oirat and Bigirsen's men, along with the few tribes who had not come to Mount Burkhan Khaldun. None of them would have been within grasp of it even a week ago.

The list of suspects included almost every Lord with something to gain from Mandukhai not naming Batu as the next Great Khan. Korgiz certainly had been firmly against her, and if he took the banner and headed south with it, he might decide someone like Bigirsen was better qualified for the title. The very idea of a Uyghur Great Khan filled Unebolod with fury. He would rather burn everything to the ground than see Bigirsen become Great Khan. *I will burn everything to the ground to find that banner, if I have to*, he decided.

As Esige's wedding approached, Unebolod had a few personal matters to attend. First, Mandukhai had asked him to retrieve the shaman for the ceremonies. *It's like she is trying to get under my skin any way she can,* he thought as he stomped toward the Ongud section of the massive encampment.

Khosoichi had been consulting Getei about something neither would talk to him about. Unebolod did not press the issue, distracted by Korgiz passing by not far away.

"Just get ready for the ceremony," Unebolod said sharply, watching Korgiz with intense curiosity. What was he up to? "On the Queen Regent's orders."

"So, you have come to your decision," Khosoichi said.

Unebolod clenched his jaw and said nothing. Did they have to rub his face in it? His hand twitched as he fought off the urge to strangle each man with a bare hand ... simultaneously.

"No need to tell us," Getei said, striding alongside Unebolod. It felt a lot like he was being corralled by them instead of escorting them to the site for the wedding. "We already know your decision."

Unebolod's nostrils flared in anger. These men were toying with him, poking at him. Did they want him to snap? Because he was very close to it.

"We know this is hard to accept," Khosoichi said. "But it is necessary. The vision was clear." Khosoichi's eyes glazed over as he stared at the eastern horizon.

The fires burning on the horizon to the east, threatening to consume the world, Mandukhai had said. Did shaman know of this part of her vision? It shamed Unebolod more than he would care to admit that this could be the fate of the Nation if he took over. How could he cause such destruction?

"I must check on Huoshai," Unebolod said sharply. "I trust you can find your way from here."

He veered away from the two of them before they could say any more. Before he lost his temper. They were close enough to the tent Mandukhai had constructed for the ceremony that they could not get lost if they tried.

Korgiz had passed nearby, drawing Unebolod in his wake. He watched as the Ongud khan approached Albeq and the two participated in a hushed but no less passionate exchange of words. Unebolod could not hear what they said from where he hid, but by the look of it, they conspired in some fashion. His jaw twitched.

Then Albeq broke out in a booming laugh that drew a few glances from passersby. It grated on Unebolod's nerves. Korgiz patted Albeq on the shoulder and strolled away. Albeq approached Unebolod's hiding place.

He stepped out, cutting Albeq off. "What have you two done?" he asked.

Albeq drew up short, alarmed by the sudden appearance of the other man. "What are you on about?"

"If it was you, I will know," Unebolod said, lowering his voice and leaning closer to Albeq.

"What? Have you lost your wits today, Unebolod?"

"Korgiz seemed to have a secret to share with you," Unebolod snapped.

"Secret?" Albeq's expression darkened. He crossed his arms and puffed out his chest. "So, after admitting you will bend the knee to her, you are accusing us of conspiring against her? Is that it?" He shook his head. "If you must know, Korgiz found out that Esige and Huoshai are getting married tonight instead of holding *kurultai*. He isn't happy for more than one reason. Frankly, neither am I. We came all this way, and now Mandukhai postpones the vote after spurning you. And her little protégé takes after her, spurning both of our sons and throwing herself at the Urainkhai Lord's feet eagerly. It's insulting."

"Is that why he took it? Because Esige refused his son and Mandukhai made him angry?" Unebolod's anger was not entirely directed at Albeq, but fueled by the shaman. He knew that, but still could not contain it.

"Took what?" Albeq's brows knitted together. "He said he came all this way for *kurultai*, to support *you*, and if there will not be a vote tonight, he has no reason to stay."

Unebolod's stomach sank. The Ongud would leave at dawn. How many others had Korgiz encouraged to leave as well?

"Good luck, Unebolod," Albeq said as he stepped around him. "If you really intend to follow her, you will probably need it."

What does that mean? Unebolod turned, staring after Albeq. Too much had happened in one day and he couldn't handle much more. This day needed to end. He needed to find the banner.

Unebolod stalked to Huoshai's ger, pounding his fist against the door. Another young Urainkhai man opened it, his eyes widening when he saw Unebolod.

The open smoke hole offered the only light in the large space. Huoshai stood on the far side of the ger, anxiously checking the buttons on his ceremonial deel and the embroidered, corded vest layered over the top.

In the dim light, the blue silk reminded Unebolod of ripples in water. Huoshai swatted one of his men away so he could check the golden buttons and adjust them himself.

"Lord Unebolod, what—is everything alright?" Huoshai asked, his face falling as he looked up at the newcomer. Unebolod wondered what his face must look like to cause such a reaction.

"All is in order. We will be ready soon."

A few of the men in the ger grinned at Huoshai, but he did not return the sentiment. Huoshai's shoulders were tight, his face screwed up in anxiety. He looked ready to snap apart at any moment.

"Good. Great." Huoshai chuckled nervously.

In short order, this bundle of nerves would be married to Esige. Unebolod wondered if Huoshai knew the enemies he made by marrying her. She had always been like a daughter to Unebolod, so he wanted to make sure his message today was received clearly.

Unebolod raised his brows. "It is normal to be anxious," he said. "But you have nothing to worry about." He stepped closer, resting his hand on the hilt of his sword. "Unless you allow harm to come to her."

Huoshai flinched. "I would never. She is more likely to harm me." Over the past week, he had exuded an air of confidence that would one day make him a good khan. All of that confidence disappeared this night, revealing the boy beneath. Unebolod enjoyed seeing this side of Huoshai. It uncovered his true feelings. This was no marriage of convenience for him.

The sleeves of Huoshai's deel draped wide from his arms as he dropped them at his sides. One man swathed a fine layer of fur over his shoulders and fastened it in place with a golden chain. Another stepped forward and placed a matching *toortsog* hat with long golden tails on his head. Huoshai raised his arms again so a belt matching the patterns of his deel could be wrapped around his waist and fastened in place.

"Ready?" Unebolod asked.

Huoshai's face transformed into a serious mask. He gave a small nod.

"Good. We should be on time to catch Boke's wedding," Unebolod said, turning to duck back out the door.

Huoshai and his Urainkhai men followed.

Mandukhai had not mentioned whom Boke would be marrying. Not that it mattered to Unebolod.

They reached the tent and slipped in along the edges to avoid interrupting Boke's ceremony, which was already underway. Boke stood at the head of the tent with a young woman at his side. Unebolod could not see either of their faces. They kneeled and offered their prayers to the High Heavens, then Boke pulled back the heavy red layers of the veil as they turned to face each other.

Unebolod gasped, and his gaze darted around the tent seeking Mandukhai. She stood near the front of the crowd, watching with her chin held high, appearing quite satisfied with this marriage.

Boke had married Odgerel. This made Unebolod's chest ache. He had no deep feelings for Odgerel, save an attraction that any man would have felt. Yet this felt like a ploy on Mandukhai's part to keep the girl away from him.

She does not want me, but she doesn't want me to have anyone else. Unebolod should have been angry, but it didn't matter. Odgerel no longer had a title to give her a place at his side. Besides, he had already determined up on the mountain that he would never marry. He had given his oath to Mandukhai, and that meant something to him. His honor was all he had left.

The ceremony concluded and Boke and Odgerel led the processional to his ger, where they entered together. Unebolod followed, swiping the milk across the doorframe with everyone else as an offering of fertility. It was just as well that this had happened. He could not afford distractions.

When he returned to the ceremony tent, Mandukhai had disappeared. Huoshai waited at the back, forcing smiles at those who came along to pat him on the shoulder and offer him luck. Unebolod slipped to the front of the tent, where he would have a better view of Esige's ceremony.

Mandukhai appeared beside him with Batu clutching her hand as if it was all that held him upright. The boots he wore were too tall for his short legs, coming up well past his knees.

"Did you arrange Boke's wife?" Unebolod whispered, aware of the others around them.

"She was pleased with the match," Mandukhai said sweetly. "As was he."

Unebolod doubted that very much, but he did not bother questioning Mandukhai.

Both were silent for a moment, and he could tell she was working up the courage to say something. But the words that came from her mouth stunned him.

"You should find a wife," she said. He could hear the agony in her voice. "For the sake of your tribe."

"No." He would not take this command from her. Unebolod did not even glance at her, keeping his gaze fixed up the narrow aisle past the fires near the entryway. This should have been his wedding day.

"Une—"

"Now is not the time," he hissed as Esige approached Huoshai outside the tent.

Mandukhai shrank back.

The red of Esige's wedding deel nearly complimented Huoshai's blue clothes. The long sleeves covered her hands. Layers of gems, coral, and pearls hung from her neck and from the headdress draped over her head. The women's *toortsog* hat on her head matched the patterns on her dress perfectly, and a long blue ribbon streamed from the tall peak. Thick layers of plaits fell over each of her shoulders, adorned with wide silver clasps at regular intervals.

But it was not the way she was dressed that made Unebolod's heart seize up. It was the brilliant smile on her face, bright enough to light up the night sky on her own. Esige glowed with joy. Unebolod had not felt that kind of happiness since he married his first—and only—wife. Would he ever be happy again?

Unebolod had not intended to get choked up, but as he watched the young couple pass the cleansing fires burning in massive copper pots on either side of the aisle, his throat tightened and his eyes burned. Esige had been the closest thing he would ever have to a daughter. Between Mandukhai's lessons and his own, Esige had transformed into a formidable young woman. How many of those could he lose in a day?

Khosoichi blessed their path with sprinkled mare's milk for fertility, leading them to the head of the tent. Unlike Odgerel, Esige wore no veil.

As the two kneeled at the front of the tent, Khosoichi offered blessings from the High Heavens, then bound them together in spirit.

Even though the current of the River is powerful,

It flows to the slope of the mountain.

Even though steel is strong enough,

It can be made supple in the hot fire.

The white silk was wrapped around Esige's hands, then Huoshai's. The two continuously exchanged excited glances back and forth. Khosoichi took that white silk and bound their hands together, and Unebolod noticed how their fingers brushed on another.

Unebolod struggled to swallow the lump swelling in his throat. Stolen glances. Small, tender touches. He would never experience that again. His love for Mandukhai was deep; his duty to her Nation binding and lonely.

When the couple rose again as man and wife, Unebolod realized his fingers were woven through Mandukhai's. A knot tightened in his stomach. He did not know who had reached out to whom, but the warmth of her hand created an icy shell around his heart. As he glanced down, he noticed Batu staring at their hands as well. *Does that boy ever talk? What does he think about?*

Unebolod slid his hand away from Mandukhai's and marched after the couple to Huoshai's ger, eager to put space between himself and Mandukhai. He dipped his fingers in the bowl of milk and roughly swiped the door frame, then stomped away. Before he had gone ten steps, Mandukhai appeared at his side with Batu—*always with that boy. Why does she keep appearing as if by some evil magic?*

"Can we talk now?" Mandukhai asked.

Did she not notice how they held hands only minutes ago? Unebolod could not stomach this conversation. Not tonight.

"Is that a request or command?" he asked sharply.

Mandukhai flinched. "A request," she said breathlessly.

"Then no."

"We must, at some point, Unebolod," she said.

"We have both made our decisions," Unebolod said. "What more is there to talk about?"

"I need you to understand."

"I do." He increased his steps to put distance between them. Mandukhai could match the pace, but Batu could not. "Enjoy your celebration tonight, Mandukhai," Unebolod said roughly. "I have a banner to find."

Mandukhai froze, and he was more than happy to leave her behind.

Mandukhai had returned to her ger after Unebolod stormed off. She needed to be alone. Or as alone as she could be with Batu always nearby. The moment the door closed, the agony in her heart poured over. Her knees grew weak, and she sank down on the edge of the bed, weeping.

Unebolod had reached out to her tonight. He had taken her hand and stroked it with such affection as they watched Esige marry Huoshai. Then he had withdrawn as if she had bitten him.

Batu climbed into Mandukhai's lap, snaking his arms around her waist and pressing his head against her chest. Mandukhai held him tight. This boy was the rope that kept her from falling off the cliff.

The door to the ger closed behind Esige, and she couldn't help trembling as she stood frozen in his ger. Their ger. While she understood what was expected of them, Esige had not considered this part of the evening when she had agreed to it. She glanced at Huoshai from the corner of her eyes as he strode across the ger. His broad shoulders were drawn up high. Did that mean he was nervous as well?

He poured two cups of *airag* and turned to her, holding one cup out.

Esige edged closer, eyeing him like a hawk.

"I expect nothing from you, Esige, no matter what anyone outside expects," he said.

She took the cup, brushing her fingers over his hand. Her stomach churned as terror clenched her entire body. *How can I even drink this? I'm just as likely to puke it up on him. Wouldn't that be a charming story?*

"To reforging steel," he said, holding his cup toward her in a toast before taking a drink.

A weak smile crept across her face as he recalled the benediction at their ceremony. Esige studied his face as she took her sip. Her husband. How had this happened? Huoshai was only a couple years older than her, and his eyes still shined with the thrill of youth. The lines of his face were smooth—sturdy, but not hard.

Then he winced. A second later, he began removing the vest over his deel. The drink of *airag* rose in her throat and she took an impulsive step back, unprepared for where this would head. Huoshai raised a brow at her as he shrugged out of the vest and tossed it aside. Her cheeks heated and she had never felt so foolish. He was simply uncomfortable. She had to admit, the silver hanging from her head was not exactly cozy either.

She swallowed as she gathered the strength to speak. "Have you been with other girls?" She reached up to remove the headdress and hat.

His body stiffened. "Yes."

Esige froze. Of course he had been. Why wouldn't he? What boy wouldn't?

"You?" he asked.

Esige smiled coyly as she finished removing the headdress and hat. "No. No other girls."

"Very funny."

"I have my moments." She turned to set the headdress on the table beside the door, careful not to knot up the hanging threads of silver.

When she turned again, Huoshai stood directly behind her. Esige's breath caught in her throat and her heart hammered against her ribs. His proximity made her head spin. The way his eyes burned into her very soul didn't help matters.

"When was the last one?" she asked breathlessly.

"Months ago," he replied. His fingers grazed the skin on her neck. Heat pushed up through her body. "Before I left home."

"Should I be expecting some girl waiting to shove a knife in my heart when we arrive?" Esige asked playfully.

"Probably," he said, then brushed his lips over hers like a whisper of silk over skin. "But something tells me you can handle it."

Esige wanted to come back with a witty retort, but terror and anticipation made her adrenaline spike and she could no longer think straight. All of her curiosity about sex, and about boys, could be answered at her whim. Yet she did not feel ready for this.

Stop looking at me like that! Huoshai's dark eyes burrowed into her with such longing she didn't know how long she could resist.

"We don't have to do this now," he whispered. His warm breath rolled over her face.

For the first time, Esige couldn't take charge of the situation. She felt helpless, immobilized by her warring excitement and fear.

Huoshai stroked her cheek with his thumb. "If you wa—"

"Shut up and kiss me already," she said firmly, before she could lose the courage.

This time, he didn't bother grazing her lips with his own. He pressed a firm, passionate kiss to her lips, and all her fear dissolved.

Mandukhai woke in the morning, unaware that she had fallen asleep curled up with Batu. Esige and Huoshai had not emerged from the ger to join the feast, so Mandukhai had hidden within her own.

Now, as the wolf dawn broke through the smoke hole, Mandukhai sat up straighter and rubbed her eyes. Commotion outside drew her to her feet. She shuffled toward the door. As she pulled it open, Togochi drew up short, clearly ready to wake her.

"It has begun," he said gravely.

Mandukhai slammed her door closed behind her, ordering the guards to remain around Batu as she rushed off on Togochi's heels.

They climbed the crest of a hill, allowing her a better view of the expanse of the valley floor...

... and the lines of carts and horsemen riding away.

Mandukhai watched, powerless to stop the exodus.

CHAPTER THIRTY

The White Road

H ordes of Mongols rode away from Mount Burkhan Khaldun in a mass exodus, just as Mandukhai had feared. The carts bobbed away in wide, long lines. Masses of yaks, horses, and sheep trotted along, kicking up clouds of dust as horsemen kept them herded together. Everyone headed east, and colorful banners fluttered in the breeze. Mandukhai could not stop them without using force. Somehow, the tribal leaders had learned that the *sulde* was missing, or assumed that her inability to carry through with her promise to name a Great Khan last night indicated she planned to hold on to her power.

Unebolod stepped up beside Mandukhai and Togochi, gazing in the distance as the other tribes departed. He said nothing, but the implication of this departure was clear to all of them.

Mandukhai had failed.

Genghis had given Mandukhai this task, to install the new Great Khan and unite the Mongols. She had done none of it. She gazed at the Eternal Blue Sky as if it held answers. Without a Great Khan, she would still be Queen Regent. The Lords could still come together another time for *kurultai*. The Mongols had gone without a Great Khan for as much as ten years before making their selection before. Yet Mandukhai sensed this was different. Her power was not absolute or divine. The departure of these noble Lords clarified that none of them recognized her as an authority figure in the government.

The dream with Genghis of the burning horizon slammed back with full force.

It had burned in the east. The same direction in which these Lords rode. Mandukhai's heart thumped against her ribs. Did this failure mean that fate would come? That the empire, the world, would burn?

The breeze curled around her like an embrace. Mandukhai closed her eyes. She knew who had gone. Jalair. Tabun. Half a dozen lesser tribes. But most painful of all had been her own tribe, the Ongud.

"We need that *sulde*," Togochi said, his voice taking on a hard, anxious edge.

In her experience, Togochi had always been an endless spring of hope and optimism. That hope was now replaced with anxiety. *A true testament to my utter failure*, she thought.

"What we need is a Great Khan," Unebolod said.

I will not let this failure defeat me! She could not accept it. If Togochi had no optimism to offer her, she would hold it for herself. She would hold it for everyone.

Mandukhai turned to face the two men, surprised to find Huoshai, Esige, and a small collection of remaining nobles gathered at their backs. Fewer than a dozen men and women had arrived on the hilltop to watch the tribes leave. Khorchin, Urainkhai, Borjigin. These people were waiting for her to fix this, to rescue the Mongol Nation before it fell apart—or worse, devolved into bitter warfare over the title.

The *sulde* of Genghis may have gone missing, but Mandukhai still had a divine shrine to use. It would not make Batu the official Great Khan yet, but it would give him enough divine right to hold the title until *kurultai* could be held in front of the *sulde*. One way or another, she had to name him. And her oaths would need to be unbreakable in the eyes of all Mongols.

"We will have a Khan," Mandukhai said confidently.

"How?" Unebolod asked. She hated that spark of hope in his eyes, knowing she would once more kill it—for good this time.

Mandukhai wished she had more time to explain all of this to him, but time was not her ally. They had to act quickly before anyone else could leave. "Remember what you told me? There are four kinds of queen. Which of them do you see me as?" she asked him.

The corner of Unebolod's mouth tipped up ever so slightly. No one else would understand the question ... but Unebolod would know what she meant. He had asked her the same question during one of their first conversations—cowardly and cowed, careless and complacent, ruthless and greedy, or strong and wise. On the hilltop, with all the other nobles watching, he only gave a small nod.

"Esige, walk with me," she said.

Esige withdrew from Huoshai's arm and proudly strode up alongside Mandukhai.

Only one option remained. If she didn't get this right, she would lose the support of the few who remained.

Togochi shook his head as he watched the tribes ride away without a new Khan. It was not unheard of for Mongols to hold together for as much as ten years before naming a new Great Khan. But this hurt him deeply. Everything he had dedicated his entire life to trickled through his fingers. All of his hard work would be for nothing if she did not bring these people together and install the rightful heir.

Jaghan rubbed at his back, and the touch made him jump. He was too tense. Everything was coiled tight, ready to snap.

"I should go follow up on a few leads before people venture too far," Unebolod muttered.

"Come," Jaghan murmured in Togochi's ear. "Let's go check on the boys."

The two walked down the hilltop together, but every movement, every step, felt as if Togochi's body slowly turned to stone.

The Khorlod had betrayed Molon Khan when he was just a boy, imprisoning and abusing him. It brought so much bad luck to the tribe that they eventually released Molon with offerings and apologies. But those had not been enough to mend what they had broken. A sacred trust had been fractured. Togochi vowed himself to the service of the Borjigin line. He swore himself to a lifetime of making up for the mistakes of his people. What had that all been for if the line of Genghis fell and the Lords broke what remained of the empire?

This thought drew Togochi up short. His gaze drifted toward the Khorlod section of camp. Unlike many of the others, the Khorlod had not left. It lifted his spirits. Perhaps he had made some difference.

"Go. I will meet you later," he told Jaghan.

She kissed his cheek, offered a sad smile, then glided away.

He turned and marched toward the Khorlod gers. Mendu khan had not run like the others. Perhaps Togochi could find out where Mendu's loyalties now lay.

As he drew closer to the Khorlod camp, Togochi's heart tumbled all the way to his toes. His feet moved slower, as if cast in iron.

The tribe buzzed with activity as families tore down gers and packed them into carts. They prepared to leave as well.

Emboldened, angry, Togochi stormed toward Mendu khan's ger. The guards outside stopped him from entering. One pressed a hand firmly against Togochi's chest and eased him back from the door. The guard's gaze darted to the weapons in Togochi's belt. With a huff, Togochi yanked out his sword and knife, pressing them forcefully into the guard's chest. As the other man wrapped his hands around the weapons, Togochi pushed past him.

"Mendu, where are you going?" Togochi snapped as he burst through the open door.

"Back where we belong," Mendu replied tersely. He busied himself packing belongings into one of the traveling chests.

Togochi edged deeper into the ger. "You gave your word. You can't just leave!"

Mendu handed a stack of cups to his wife, who eyed Togochi with apparent disapproval but said nothing. Mendu squared his shoulders. "I told her I would remain as long as she placed a Great Khan in front of the banner."

"This isn't over." Togochi's anger bubbled to the surface. He struggled to hold it in check. His own tribe could not leave. What would Mandukhai think? "She plans to finish this today, even if she doesn't have the banner."

Mendu shook his head and crossed his arms. "No, Togochi. She is grabbing for power that does not belong to her. Without that banner, she has nothing."

"She has me!" Togochi snapped. He roared, unable to hold back his rage any longer, and threw his fist into the *uni* pole holding up the roof. It quivered. His fist left a dent in the wood. He opened and closed his hand, rubbing the aching knuckles. "I will not allow you to leave. We owe a debt to the blood of Genghis!"

Heat rose in Mendu's face, and his mouth curved downward in anger. "You are getting arrogant, Togochi. I have always respected you, but you go too far. Regardless of what titles you may have held in the Khan's court, I am still your tribal khan. You will show me more respect!"

Togochi closed his eyes and took a deep breath. The shuffle of boots scuffed the ground behind him. "Keep your dogs off me," he growled. "I don't need my weapons to teach them a lesson." He opened his eyes slowly, but had failed to collect himself.

Mendu waved back the guards looming behind Togochi with their weapons. "It's time for you to leave. Stay at her side, if you wish. And if something changes, I am open to conversation. Until then, and as always, I do what is best for my tribe. And that means leaving. Today."

Togochi growled deep in his throat. He clenched his fists so tight his nails bit into his palms. "Tuck tail and run like an honorless dog while I stay behind and do the dirty work for you. *Again.*"

He spun around, glaring at the two men blocking the doorway. His blood burned hot. He could feel the vein in his neck pulsing with rage. Togochi had never been so angry in his life.

The guards stepped to the side and Togochi brushed past them as he stormed back outside, retrieving his weapons.

Mendu had left him to clean up after his father. Now, it seemed, Togochi would have to clean up after him as well. *Like father, like son.*

Unebolod did not understand what Mandukhai was planning, but he appreciated the sort of queen she would be. Fiercely strong and wise. Despite everything that had happened between them, she had asked him for trust with that question.

The morning had been full of questions Unebolod could not answer. Men who respected him asked what the Queen Regent would do, if she would change her mind and name him Great Khan. Unebolod could not say he wasn't curious as well, but he knew Mandukhai well enough to be certain that, if she intended to name him, she would have told him and helped him prepare. No. This was still about that boy.

Unebolod had also spent his morning reassuring men that she knew what she was doing, while simultaneously prodding for information about the *sulde*. The guards on duty around the gathering tent had not understood how anyone could have stolen the banner. No one unauthorized had entered the space.

By late morning, Unebolod inspected the storage space hidden in the gathering tent. Some clue had to be left behind. Failing to uncover the *sulde* would be more shaming than never discovering who had killed his and Mandukhai's child years ago. One shame was private. The other would be public. His inspection of the storage space brought him to thick layers of silk along the outer wall. He ran his fingers over the colorful cloth. They shifted and fluttered under his touch. The banner had been here, hidden away in a chest. Someone broke the lock on the chest, which meant they knew exactly what they were looking for.

He straightened and stood upright, knuckling at the small of his back as his gaze swept every inch of the space. If no one had come in, how had they gotten the *sulde* out? *Silk.* Unebolod yanked back several layers of silk hanging over the outer wall, then brushed his fingers over the felt beneath. The cut had been so careful and precisely done. Straight across the lattice frame where two sections met. He pulled the cut in the felt opening and stuck his fingers through. They brushed against the horsehair rope wrapped around the gathering tent.

Unebolod rushed outside and around the gathering tent, seeking the cut, and could not find it. He wrapped his hand around the rope and pulled it carefully away from the wall.

There, beneath the rope, a slice in the felt ran horizontal wide enough to get a full man in and out. This theft had not been impulsive. It had been planned, deliberate. *How long has it been missing and no one knew?* he wondered. This could have been done yesterday, or a week ago. There was no way to tell.

The thunder of hooves drew Unebolod's attention. Tension sprang into his shoulders as he grasped his sword.

But it was not an attack. Men, women, and children had mounted and were riding north. Unebolod hopped on his mare and rode to catch up to Soke amidst the whirlwind of excitement.

"Where is everyone off to, Soke?" he asked.

"They are following Mandukhai to the mountain," Soke said, not slowing his mount as he joined the pilgrimage toward Mount Burkhan Khaldun. "Something is happening."

Unebolod's chest tightened. He nudged his mare into a canter through the throng of people. Thousands of Mongols rode across the rocky valley floor toward the sacred mountain. A dozen scattered *ovoo*—rocks piled like a miniature mountain to worship the bones of the Father—remained untouched by passing horses. Nobody—human or horse—would tread over the sacred mounds.

Unebolod nudged his way through the growing multitude of people toward the front, where he might have a better view. Women leaned close to each other and whispered about the Shrine of the First Queen. Men murmured about divine right and sacred oaths. The reverence of the people only increased Unebolod's curiosity.

The procession had come to a halt at the base of a small stream. Someone had set up the sacred Shrine of the First Queen weeks ago for men and women to worship beside this stream. No one would ride within several yards of it, afraid of disturbing the spirits. The shrine was a wide felt ger with a doorway broad enough to fit several men shoulder-to-shoulder. The shrine dwelled beside the stream as a direct homage to the earth mother, whose life-giving parts were of the water and caves. Worshippers could come to honor the sacred female spirit in this divine location.

Unebolod had not visited this shrine. He saw little point. The gods had never favored him. Inside the tall ceiling and wide walls, relics of female ancestry were available for worship. A totem of Alan Goa, the woman from whom all Mongols descended. Sacred mementos of Hoelun, the mother of Genghis Khan, as well as a few relics from the wives and daughters of Genghis.

The Shrine of the First Queen had been hidden years ago from Esen's vengeful reign to protect it from potential destruction. Until the tribes gathered at Mount Burkhan Khaldun this summer, no one had seen this shrine. No one even knew where it had disappeared to or who took care of it. While it was not as revered as the *sulde* of Genghis, it came in a close second and could afford potentially powerful declarations.

She said we would have a Great Khan, Unebolod thought. His heart beat a little faster as he watched from atop his mare. *Is this her plan to make the declaration before the sacred shrine?*

High above, clouds covered the expanse of the blue sky like a white and gray fluffy blanket. Unebolod did not need to shield his eye to see who approached the doorway to the Shrine of the First Queen.

Mandukhai dismounted from Dust's back with a horde of spectators at her back on their own mounts. She wore all white—a color for purity and new beginnings—with her hair down in two simple pigtail braids, as was the style for young girls. She wore no jewels, and only a brilliant yellow belt added any color to her outfit.

Unebolod froze along the western edge of the crowd, watching Mandukhai move through the gathering toward the shrine. They parted for her as if ordained to part by Lord Tengri himself. The very sight of her on this spiritual journey stirred awe in him that he could not reasonably explain. It reminded him of the night she had entered Manduul's council and disrobed before all the Lords. She exuded such an air of majestic confidence that anyone watching would be hard-pressed not to feel the hands of the High Heavens guiding the moment. Unebolod unconsciously rubbed at his bandaged palm.

Boke held Dust's reins. Esige was mounted beside Dust, with Batu in the saddle in front of her. Esige had her arms protectively wrapped around the boy. Much like Mandukhai, Batu wore a fine deel of blue the color of the sky with a matching hat, and boots so high they passed his knees and made his legs stick out in front of him. The boy had eyes for only one thing.

Mandukhai.

She is taking a tremendous risk here today, Unebolod thought as he watched Mandukhai call out at the doorway of the shrine. Not that anyone could hide within such a wide opening. Yet such a call had become customary after the last time a national leader had come before a sacred shrine of Genghis. An arrow fired by the spirits had killed the supplicant. Since then, people were more apprehensive about attempting to approach these shrines to install a Great Khan. *Please let the spirit of Tengri and Genghis protect her.*

Mandukhai poured an offering of *airag* on the ground outside the threshold of the Shrine of the First Queen. Her voice rose clearly to be heard by the gathered Mongols. It carried past them on the wind, strong and formal. "I act as a daughter-in-law in a place where the color of a black horse cannot be distinguished. Because I have declared the descendant of your Great Khan, the Mongol Lords will not follow me."

Unebolod gasped at the audacity of her words. Mandukhai came before this sacred shrine and called out clearly her distaste and distrust for the Mongol Lords, lumping all of them together. He glanced around, seeking a wayward arrow.

"I act as a daughter-in-law in a place where the color of a multicolored horse cannot be distinguished," she continued formally, despite the murmurs at her back. "Because your descendant is small, these Lords claim they will take me."

The words twisted like a knife in Unebolod's heart. Was she referring to what he had said? That felt so long ago now. Weeks, for certain, and only to protect her. If it had come down to himself or another make attempting to take her as a wife and steal the title, Unebolod would not have hesitated to secure her and his place at her side.

"Fearful for my life, and the life of your descendant, I come before you," Mandukhai said. She bowed her head as if ashamed, putting on a show for everyone watching. "The Borjigin line is under threat of extinction. Only one of your descendants remains. The Mongol Lords have turned to discord and violence in favor of righteous reason, as Genghis and Tengri have taught us. We can no longer see the difference between good and evil. The state of the world is not stable. My will is not stable." Mandukhai's breath shuddered. "My blushing face is broken. And so, I seek your guidance, sacred Mother, *Khatun* of all Mongols."

The crowd seemed to hold its collective breath. A few wayward glances strayed toward Unebolod. Rumors had circulated around the two of them and their affair months ago, before the Oirat attack. Mandukhai confessed it to all now by proclaiming her blushing face had broken. It would no longer be secret.

Somehow, he kept his eyes fixed forward on Mandukhai without giving himself away. Surely they knew she spoke of him even if she didn't use his name, but to say such things so bluntly and in the open might induce questions about their relationship—as well as the validity of any oath she made here. Mandukhai risked everything in favor of begging the First Queen for forgiveness. How many of these people would accept that forgiveness? How many would insist even more firmly that she grant him the title?

"Your descendant, Genghis, has come to me in my dreams," Mandukhai continued, smashing all the insinuating conclusions of her previous statement with utter shock.

Men whispered to one another but were hushed by those fearful of missing anything. They all hung on Mandukhai's every word.

"Genghis has set forward a path, but I fear I have not the strength of will to carry out his wishes," Mandukhai said, ignoring the murmurs behind her. "He has shared with me his cup and sword. However, without your guidance, I am but a weak woman." Mandukhai stood, raising her eyes toward the entrance to the Shrine of the First Queen. "Lord Unebolod is fierce, strong, and powerful. He possesses the spirit of the nation and the roots of my heart. But, for your descendent and the path of Genghis, I cannot go to him. If I do, I beg you, First Queen, punish me harshly."

While the formal words made sense, the reality turned Unebolod cold inside. He already knew she would declare Batu as Great Khan and rightful heir. To make Batu's reign begin without question, Mandukhai would have to close the door to Unebolod as firmly as she ever could in front of everyone. In front of the sacred shrine. Otherwise, the Lords could still petition to Unebolod to seize control. Mandukhai had not just closed the door on him with these words. She had slammed it shut and sealed it with steel, locking Unebolod on the other side to wither away and die alone.

The only way he could be with her now that she had proclaimed this in front of the sacred shrine with thousands of witnesses would be to kill Batu—something he knew he could never do. *Hope is a tool for fools*, he told himself.

"Take and snare me," she continued, squaring her shoulders as if proud of her words. "And should he despise your descendant so much that he take me, then snare and take Lord Unebolod khan."

Everything spun. The ground tilted. Unebolod gripped his reins tightly, pressing his thighs into his mount's sides to keep from sliding out of the saddle as everything shifted. Mandukhai had not only commanded the spirits to snare her should she give in to him, but that should he try to take her—as if he would!—then the spirits should take him instead. No. The world was not spinning. It had completely dropped out from beneath him. Mandukhai had ripped away all hope once and for all.

"Should I bring harm to your people or fail to protect them, then you may rip apart my body," Mandukhai said, her voice rising to a fevered pitch. "If I fail to uphold my oath to your people and your descendant, I submit my life to you so that you may separate my shoulders from my thighs."

The crowd buzzed now. No one had ever heard such a powerful oath in their lives. Such an oath, to mutilate the body and tear apart the oath-breaker would sever all connections between Mandukhai and everyone she had ever known. It symbolized breaking the bones of the father and the flesh of the mother. This was an oath of men. An oath stronger than any Unebolod had ever taken. It was an oath to the sky and earth, and nothing would bind her more highly. No marriage. No promises to anyone else—not even to Genghis himself. Mandukhai submitted herself to the will of the Gods and to her intent to serve the descendants of the First Queen.

"My purpose is first to your descendants, then to your people, and I submit my life to that purpose," Mandukhai said. "I come before you as a daughter-in-law. If, with the flame of the Nation in my heart, you grant me seven sons, I will give them all the name of Bolod, for they will be the steel that binds and holds the Mongols together as Genghis envisioned."

Many people chattered openly now. Several dozen—perhaps hundreds—stared at Unebolod as if expecting him to speak. What could he say? Mandukhai's words bound her to Batu until he was old enough to take a wife. She belonged to him now. It would be Batu's decision to marry her when he came of age.

Unebolod's only hope of ever being with the woman who possessed his heart would be with the death of Genghis Khan's descendants, or Batu's own sympathy when he grew older. Unebolod did not favor his odds. If he killed the boy himself, he would be cursed.

No. The High Heavens made their will known days ago. Unebolod was a servant to the Khan and nothing more. Still, Mandukhai had given Unebolod one final honor. She would name her sons after him, even if they would not be his.

The great gathering stirred, openly exchanging opinions about this unprecedented turn of events. Unebolod simply sat statue-still on his mare's back as Boke helped Batu down from Esige's saddle.

"From our Lord Bayan, a son has been born," Mandukhai announced loud and clear. It brought the gathering to silence once more.

The small boy marched awkwardly, nearly stumbling in his step as he approached Mandukhai and the shrine. He was certainly not a man, but a weak boy in triple-soled boots that went past his knees. *How can a child hardly capable of walking on his own two feet guide the Mongols? He cannot even command a horse!* Unebolod heard his own thoughts echoed in whispers among the gathering. Surely Mandukhai must have heard something, but she waited patiently at the threshold for Batu to join her.

Unebolod had to admit, the boy certainly showed some courage marching in his oversized boots in front of the sacred shrine. Batu didn't even take Mandukhai's hand when he joined her side, as he always had before. He stood somewhat tall for a boy of seven, and Unebolod could see the pure, unfiltered admiration shining in Batu's eyes as he gazed up at Mandukhai.

"By coming to your tent," Mandukhai continued once Batu stood beside her, "I wish to make your descendant Great Khan, though he is only a young boy. I will guide him, protect him, and build the Mongol Nation for his rule, as decreed by Genghis. My life now belongs first to the will of the High Heavens, next to the will of my Great Khan, and finally, to the protection of my people."

Batu's little legs trembled visibly in his boots as they threatened to give out beneath the weight of his body, but somehow he remained upright without her holding him. Mandukhai simply placed a hand on his back, raised her chin proudly, and completed the ceremony.

"From this day forward, he will be Dayan Khan, the Khan of khans, twenty-seventh successor to Genghis Khan and ruler of all the lands and peoples within," Mandukhai proclaimed loud enough for all to hear. "He will be the Whole Khan."

Everyone watched Unebolod to see how he would react. She had proclaimed their next Great Khan. Dayan Khan, or the Whole Khan, was an auspicious name that made clear her intentions to overcome the division of the tribes, unite them as a whole, and rule as *Khatun* until Dayan Khan was old enough to do so himself.

Now that Dayan Khan had been named and installed here at this sacred shrine with such a solemn and serious oath, the remaining Lords would either give their oath to the new Khan, or they would reject him and further the division Mandukhai clearly sought to mend. Unebolod knew he had to act first. The men respected him. If he took the oath and kneeled to this boy, those who remained would follow his lead.

Unebolod froze in the saddle, unable to force himself into action one way or another as everyone stared at him. *Tengri, if this is your will, give me a sign and I will keep my oath.*

Mandukhai's sharp eyes burrowed into him like the tip of an arrow.

The blanket of rolling clouds parted, allowing streams of sunlight through the break in the clouds. Unebolod's breath caught. He swallowed a sudden lump in his throat.

The sun shined directly on Mandukhai and Dayan Khan.

What more could he want as a sign? The clouds had literally parted and let the sun shine only on those two.

Unebolod swung out of the saddle and strode toward the couple. Mandukhai's gaze never once shifted from his own. His hand rested on his sword, fingers brushing the yellow ribbon. This was the will of the gods, and he was powerless against it. Unebolod drew his sword so swiftly Mandukhai's guards pulled their own. He sensed a dozen blades at his back.

I would follow you to the ends of the world, he thought. *My strong, wise Khatun.*

Unebolod kneeled and placed his sword at Dayan's feet. He cleared his throat, still staring at Mandukhai, unable to look away. This was what she wanted, and she would watch agony.

"Dayan Khan, Mandukhai Khatun," he said, lacing his heart with steel. "As the rightful heir of Genghis, I give my oath to you. I will follow where you lead with horses, salt, gers, and blood for as long as I draw breath, from this moment until my last. Should I break my oath, I beg the spirits to punish me harshly, as my Khatun commands."

As his oath forced past his lips, Unebolod knew all of his own dreams had died.

Mandukhai held her breath as Unebolod approached. Hopefully, he would forgive her for this, but she had no choice. While she had refused him before, her oath before the Shrine of the First Queen meant they could never be together unless Dayan allowed it when he came of age. But as long as the temptation of Unebolod's arms remained, she would be enticed to succumb. It was better this way. Duty was a mountain, and she had just bound herself to Dayan more wholly than she could ever bind to another. Only Dayan could release her now. To break her oath was to break her spirit in this life and all others.

Unebolod's face was like stone, his eyes empty. It broke her heart to see what this had done to him, knowing it was her fault. But he understood. This was the will of Genghis, of the High Heavens. For the two of them, duty had always come first.

Mandukhai's guards inched closer as Unebolod stopped only two feet away from them, hand on his sword.

It happened so fast. Unebolod drew the sword, offered it in front of Dayan, and kneeled to take his oath, even with her guards armed at his back. And his oath to follow the two of them was almost as binding as her own had been. He did not have to give such a binding oath to them, and Mandukhai fought off her own shock.

Once it was done, Unebolod stood, slipped his sword back into the belt, and gave them a tight bow before mounting and riding away. The Khorchin men rode away behind him.

As the other Lords gave their oaths to Dayan, Mandukhai continued staring southwest after the Khorchin dust cloud.

That part of her life had died. Now, she had to raise a Khan and unite the Mongols for him. She would walk the White Road of enlightenment.

CHAPTER THIRTY-ONE

Farewells

T he hills around Mount Burkhan Khaldun hummed with energy as the people celebrated the return of the line of Genghis Khan, and their new Khan, Dayan. Togochi, along with other tribe leaders and Lords, had given their oaths to Dayan Khan and Mandukhai both. While he was not the youngest Great Khan the Mongols ever had, he would need protection and a firm hand to guide him. Knowing she already had such men around her came as a relief.

Mandukhai swelled with pride watching the boy accept each vow without wavering. Batu maintained a steady, knowing look in his wolf-like eyes. He had mimicked Mandukhai's own gesture earlier, dismissing each man after they had spoken their oaths.

One day, he will speak to me, and I look forward to hearing the wisdom hiding behind those eyes, she mused as she waited in the new gathering tent.

Without the *sulde* of Genghis Khan, installing Batu as Dayan Khan had taken creative thinking. Mandukhai had known that her oath at the Shrine of the First Queen had to be powerful enough to remove any doubt from those watching. Esige had done her part, spreading rumors of the Queen Regent's pilgrimage up the mountain on horseback, then preparing Batu for the ceremony. Mandukhai had been pleased with the result when she climbed onto Dust's back and began the journey up. Dozens followed her, then hundreds, then thousands. The crowd had swelled in size quickly as she rode.

By installing the boy as she had, Mandukhai had also bound her fate to his—and removed any opportunity for Siker to come forward and reclaim the son she had abandoned. Issama would have to start a war to claim the boy, and he would have to kill Mandukhai.

Mandukhai had also been careful how she worded her oath to the First Queen. Should Unebolod attempt to harm the boy, he would be cursed to never lead. However, should the boy die by other means, it left the door open for him, as the closest descendant of the First Queen and Genghis after Batu. In a way, it bound Mandukhai to Unebolod as well. She belonged with Batu, but if he died and no other heir of Genghis lived, she belonged to Unebolod. *Dayan Khan. He is no longer Batu*, she thought as her gaze slid to the young boy perched beside her on a throne far too large for his tiny body.

The oath Mandukhai gave also effectively married her to the boy, though they would not act as man and wife until he came of age. Then it would be his choice to decide if she had fulfilled her purpose. He could release her if he so chose. Until then, she belonged to him and no other, and Mandukhai would risk no one else coming between them. Dayan was in her care, and she would raise him to be better than his father and uncle had been. He would be a Khan worthy of his lineage.

Genghis had been correct. While Mandukhai's passion for Unebolod had not waned, her compassion for Dayan was stronger. It must have been, or she would never have had the strength to speak that oath. Above wanting to be with Unebolod, she felt an overwhelming need to protect Dayan from others.

The remaining Lords entered Mandukhai's gathering tent, showing deference to Dayan before taking their seats along the edges. She had summoned them to this meeting to announce their first acts of service to Dayan Khan. Boke had insisted on being positioned beside the two of them, armed with swords, bows, and three of his best men. She entrusted the security of Dayan to Boke's expertise. He stood on one side of the dais with Torgus on the other side. The four guards created a protective box around the Khan.

Unebolod arrived last, marching in with his Khorchin Lords and commanders. They assumed a position to the left of the aisle, standing with their backs straight. He did not glance in her direction. *I'm sorry, Unebolod.*

Mandukhai steeled herself. In time, the two of them would get past this. She raised her chin and articulated so that there could be no doubt every man heard her.

"Noble Lords and commanders of Dayan Khan," she began, "You have shown great wisdom and courage today. Your loyalty to the Borjigin line is commendable and will not be forgotten in the years, the centuries, to come. Where others turned from the path the great Genghis Khan has set at our feet, you bravely turned toward it. You, my Lords, walk the white road beside Dayan Khan. You will be the forebears of our reunified Mongol Nation. Men will tell stories of this day, when you of superior birth and great intelligence chose the path to salvation."

Mandukhai rose from her throne and glided with slow, deliberate steps down the dais steps and along the aisle, meeting each man in the eye as she spoke. "But this road will not be easy. Since the death of Taisun Khan sixteen years ago, we have grown weak, complacent, satisfied to allow outsiders to control our lands and our peoples. We have allowed our tribes to forget the dream of Genghis, and his One Nation. We have permitted the Oirat and the Ordos to grow in power and oppose the will of Genghis himself. Those days are over!"

Stunned faces met Mandukhai's hard gaze as she continued slowly gliding along the aisle, pacing like a stalking lioness. "Are we weak Mongols?" she asked, raising her voice to a fevered pitch.

"No," several men responded.

"Are you, noble Lords and commanders of Dayan Khan's empire, prepared to lay everything at his feet so that he can restore this fractured empire?"

A few nodded, some appeared uncertain.

Mandukhai turned slowly in the center of the tent, challenging each of the men who hesitated. "These outside rulers will oppose your Khan of khans. They will challenge his right, call him weak, raise the black banner against him. It is up to me, and each of you, to show these barbarians the *strength* of a united Mongol Nation—that one arrow alone can be easily broken, but several together are unbreakable. So said Genghis!"

"So said Genghis," the men echoed, their voices rising in reverence.

The heat in their voices, the determination she could feel mounting in the gathering tent, stoked Mandukhai's fire. She allowed them this moment to absorb the implication—that she intended to create a strong, united Mongol empire once again—as she marched back to her seat and settled beside Dayan. The fire burning in her reflected in his golden eyes.

"A Great Khan is only as weak as the men following him," Mandukhai said at last. "And as Genghis bound his horsehair banner to bring together all colors into none, so shall we bind ourselves, from this day forward, to Dayan Khan and his empire."

Dayan didn't flinch. Mandukhai was certain the boy could see far more than any of them, as if he had the gift of the Sight.

"Our first order of business is to secure the flow of goods we have grown accustomed to since the time of Genghis," Mandukhai said. "Men like Bigirsen have controlled our wealth for too long. The Oirat have controlled the Silk Road for too long. At dawn, the Khan and I will make an offering to the High Heavens to bless us on this white road. The Khan's men will break camp and head southwest to the Ongi River, where we will set up camp for the winter. Then, we will take back control from the Oirat!"

Murmurs of approval rippled through the gathered men.

"Go with the blessing of your Khan," Mandukhai said. "Prepare your men and inform your people. Tonight, we celebrate Dayan Khan. Tomorrow, we ride."

One by one, the Lords and commanders stepped forward to bow to Dayan Khan before leaving. Each murmured the same phrase to Mandukhai. "Your will, Dayan Khan and Mandukhai Khatun."

Those words struck a chord in Mandukhai and she struggled to keep her face even. For the first time since she had married Manduul, the men saw her not just as a queen, but as their ruler. She had lost several tribes during the exodus, but she still had enough of a foundation to build her empire.

Huoshai stepped forward to bid goodnight, but Mandukhai leaned forward, placing a hand on his arm. "Wait, Lord Huoshai. I have need of you still."

She also held back Togochi and Unebolod, ordering them to dismiss the rest of their men.

Soon, only Mandukhai, Dayan, Togochi, Huoshai, and Unebolod remained, with Dayan's guards still lingering nearby. Mandukhai allowed herself to relax a little. These men, she must trust. If she could not trust these three around her and Dayan, she would surely fail.

"Huoshai, you will take your Urainkhai warriors back to the rest of your tribe," Mandukhai announced. "But your task will not be a simple one. My spies report Bigirsen has been absorbing the southern tribes under his rule, but he is not a Mongol Lord no matter how many titles he steals. If your father has submitted to him as the others have done, he will have *one* opportunity to swear himself and his people to Dayan Khan. Your mission is to convert him to our white road, where he will be welcomed alongside his Khan. But he will only be allowed one opportunity."

Huoshai paled. Mandukhai knew he understood where she was headed with this.

"You have given yourself to your Khan above all else," Mandukhai continued. "Should your father not comply, the Khan and I trust you to see justice done."

Togochi's thick brows climbed his wide forehead, but he did not interrupt. Though Unebolod seemed to understand what she meant, he did not show the same shock Togochi had shown.

Huoshai fumbled a moment, glancing at Dayan. "You want me to kill my father?" he finally asked Mandukhai.

"Refusing to accept his Great Khan is treason," Mandukhai said, hardening her voice as she stiffened her spine. "I understand this is no small thing I ask of you, but I trust you can make your father see reason and accept my terms. If he refuses, I expect you to carry out the Khan's justice. He must become an example to be sure that any others who might oppose their Khan see clearly what the Great Khan's justice will be. Is that clearer, Huoshai? Are you capable of delivering the Khan's justice?"

Huoshai shifted from one foot to the other, fiddling with the sleeves of his deel as he weighed her commands. Mandukhai felt bad for him. He was far too young to bear such a burden, but he had given her his oath, and she needed to be certain he would carry through with it.

Unebolod's stony expression slipped. He eyed Mandukhai with a hint of alarm leaking through the cracks of his hard face. She pretended not to notice.

Huoshai glanced at the other two men as if seeking help. Mandukhai frowned. Would he refuse and back out on his oath? She would be within her right to have him killed, but Esige would never forgive her, and his father would declare war. *Please just accept!*

"Huoshai!" she snapped. "Can you do this, or shall I ask your wife instead?"

Huoshai's back went as straight as a staff, and he lifted his chin, then bowed stiffly. "Your will, Mandukhai Khatun."

"Good. Go celebrate this night. In the morning, you will return home." Mandukhai dismissed him.

Huoshai pivoted and marched out of the tent, every movement stiff and stilted as he left. Togochi shook his head as he watched the young Lord leave, then eyed Mandukhai in amusement.

"You truly are a dragon in women's clothing," Togochi mused.

Mandukhai smirked at him. "And let's hope those weak Lords and lesser khans learn that sooner rather than later." She glanced once more at the opening to the tent, and her expression shifted to worry. "Do you think he will carry out the Khan's justice?"

"He is a man of his word," Unebolod said. "Though you have certainly not asked a small thing of him."

Mandukhai arched a brow at him. While his words were true, his answer was evasive.

He shook his head. "I believe he will carry out the Khan's justice, but it will change him, Mandukhai. I hope you are prepared for the consequences."

"Esige can handle him." Mandukhai brimmed with pride for the woman Esige had become. Strong and wise beyond what Mandukhai had been at her age.

Mandukhai turned her attention to Togochi. "You have shown your loyalty these past months, Togochi, and I have noticed. It cannot have been easy for you either. But the coming years will not be easy for any of us, and I will need you close to my side. I cannot trust many men as I have learned to trust you and Unebolod."

Togochi had the grace to blush at the compliment. "My people have a lot to make up for. I dedicate my life to seeing it through. Our treatment of Molon was a terrible thing, and I am beyond ashamed of what my predecessors have done."

"You were a child, Togochi," Mandukhai said softly. "Do not be so hard on yourself." Mandukhai rose and strode toward Togochi, standing close to both of the men. Batu remained on his oversized throne, watching the exchange like an eagle. "You are a leader of your people in heart and soul, and a wonderful example for your sons, *Orlok* Togochi of the northern *tumens.*"

Togochi's jaw slackened as his eyes widened. He glanced momentarily toward Unebolod, who previously held this title and control. She did not fail to see the wounded look in Unebolod's eyes, though he said nothing. *I will not take everything from you*, she thought. *I swear it.*

Mandukhai had other needs for Unebolod, and it would take him away from her small army.

"You honor me, Mandukhai Khatun," Togochi said, bowing.

Mandukhai placed her hand on his shoulder. "I fear you have that the wrong way around. I know you will serve your Khan with wisdom and courage."

Togochi placed his fist over his heart as he straightened. "Your will. If I may be blunt, you are far stronger and wiser than Manduul, Bayan, and

Molon together. Teach Dayan to be as strong as you, just as you did with Esige, and the Mongols will be in capable hands."

Mandukhai glanced at Dayan, who shifted to the edge of his throne, but he did not rise. "You will help me with that as well, Togochi. Dayan Khan's future is in our hands."

Togochi nodded. Mandukhai dismissed him and he marched out proudly.

She watched Togochi leave, then turned to Unebolod, glancing past him at Dayan, still surrounded by the guards on the other side of the gathering tent.

Unebolod's eyes wrinkled in the corners, giving away the pain he tried to keep from his face. His shoulders rose with tension. He lifted his chin proudly. Or perhaps as a form of defense. She could not be sure.

Mandukhai wanted to reach out and touch him, smooth those lines and feel his warm skin. But she could not touch him like that again. Her chest heaved as she stared at him, drawn into the dark pools of his eyes. *You will always consume my heart*, she thought sadly.

"I know this is not the future we dreamed of together," she said softly, folding her hands together in the sleeves of her deel to keep from touching him. "I need you to know this was difficult for me. It hurts still, and I'm uncertain that pain will ever go away."

"I understand better than you might think." Unebolod clasped his hands behind his back. He obviously struggled not to touch her as well.

"You deserve better, Unebolod." Mandukhai released a shaky breath. These words would be hardest of all. "Should anything happen to Dayan, your line is still the named successor. The Khorchin will need an heir, and it's unfair of me to ask you to wait and hope that Dayan might one day free me from my oath." Her voice cracked. "You should find a wife. You need sons to carry on your line."

Unebolod's jaw twitched. The sharp lines of his face grew even more distinct. "I will not marry."

Those three words pierced her already aching heart. He sounded so certain. Mandukhai wanted to argue this point, but all she could manage was a single question. "Why not?"

"My word is iron. I swore myself to you and only you. Even if I have to wait until my bones are old." Unebolod's eyes burned with intensity, with suppressed longing as he inched closer. His shoulders relaxed. "That was the oath I gave you, and as I see it, that has not changed."

Mandukhai shook her head. It was a fool's oath to leave nothing behind, have no wives or sons to carry on a legacy when the entire tribe depended on him. "I release you from that oath, Unebolod."

"You do not hold that power, Mandukhai." He smiled sadly. He brushed a hand tenderly along her jaw.

Mandukhai tilted her face ever so slightly into his touch, then tensed as she remembered Dayan and the guards watched. What would they make of this exchange?

Unebolod lowered his voice, only for her. "Only the High Heavens can release me from that oath. My life, my purpose, is tethered to you. They have determined it to be so. I am but a mortal instrument to their will."

Tears burned in Mandukhai's eyes. Why did he have to make this so much harder?

"Your tribe will need an heir."

"It is your tribe, not mine." Unebolod's declaration was soft-spoken, simple, but powerful. By her own words tonight, he was right. But the idea of the line of Khasar dying with Unebolod did not settle well with Mandukhai.

"How am I to serve my Khan and Khatun?" he asked.

Mandukhai struggled against the lump in her throat. It took a moment to manage any words. His hand lingered on her cheek, making all of this even harder to stomach.

"Track down the sacred *sulde* with your Khorchin warriors," she croaked. "The Lords have accepted him for now, but without that banner, it won't last for long."

He nodded in agreement, but desire burned in his eyes. Were it not for the binding oath she had given today, or that Dayan and the guards watched the two of them, Mandukhai's will would have crumbled. While an innocent touch would break nothing, Mandukhai could never give herself to Unebolod again. How would she live without his arms around her? *This isn't the time for wallowing*, she admonished.

"Bring the eastern tribes into the Great Khan's fold, just as Huoshai will bring the Urainkhai," she said, distracted by how close he stood to her. "They respect you. Rally them in the name of Dayan Khan alone, and you will be *orlok* of the eastern *tumens*. Then return to me, Unebolod." Mandukhai feared that reunion already. What would it be like when he returned? Would the distance help them mend their wounded souls, or would it make the longing even stronger? "Dayan will need a talented soldier to train him in battle and military strategy."

"Your will, my Khatun," he murmured.

Their breaths mingled. Unebolod inched closer. Mandukhai's pulse hummed in her ears. Sending him away was the most painful thing she could do, but it would be for the best. The distance may give them both time to accept their fate. *I'm not sure I can ever accept this fate.*

"I have one last request," he whispered. "One last kiss to abate a warrior's bleeding soul."

Would this be breaking her sacred oath? Surely one kiss couldn't hurt. One last, bittersweet kiss. Then he would leave and she would pour all of her attention into Dayan and their future. Boke wouldn't speak of it, nor would he allow his guards. Dayan wouldn't know better. If anyone asked, Mandukhai could excuse it for what it was. A farewell offering. A final goodbye.

Mandukhai acquiesced with a small nod of her head.

Unebolod cupped her face in his hand as he brushed warm, soft lips over hers. Everything spun. Mandukhai became light-headed. The kiss was gentle and chaste but contained no less heat or passion than any other time he had kissed her. Aware that she would never feel his lips again, Mandukhai pressed more firmly against him, but Unebolod pulled back. The lump in his throat bobbed. His hand slipped away. As he took the first step backward, her heart twisted. The second step made her soul scream out for him. By the third, she struggled to catch her breath.

Unebolod turned and marched toward the door. She watched him leave, utterly helpless.

"I *do* need you, Unebolod," Mandukhai called after him. "I always have. I always will."

Unebolod spun toward her from the door and bowed, fist over his heart—the same gesture Togochi had given a few minutes before. "I am yours, my Khatun. As I have always been."

He stepped out of the tent and out of sight. Everything inside of Mandukhai fractured, and her knees weakened.

Dayan slipped his hand into hers, and the world once more became solid beneath her feet.

Mandukhai felt no joy in her heart as she sat at the low table in the open gathering space. Dayan sat beside her, picking through his food silently as he listened to the storytellers weave heroic tales of Great Khans of the past.

An *arban* of guards remained vigilant, and every piece of food and sip of drink given to Dayan had to pass inspection first. Mandukhai would take no chances that anyone would poison him now.

Horse fiddles sounded in the distance. Men and women raised their voices in song all around what remained of her camp.

Over the course of the evening, Mandukhai's gaze scanned the open space several times, seeking out signs of Unebolod, but he never appeared.

Nearby, Boke sat with his new wife, his arm around Odgerel and his eyes on everyone else. Though Mandukhai had given him this night to spend with his wife, he would remain vigilant and watchful of Dayan. Whenever he kissed Odgerel's cheek, she would force a smile and glare at Mandukhai. *She could have done much worse*, Mandukhai thought. After losing her title and rank, Odgerel was lucky to have been married to a man like Boke. Still, it was apparent that Odgerel did not appreciate Boke's advances. Subtle nudges against his hand or pulling away from his body gave it away clearly enough.

Mandukhai also noticed that Huoshai had left after eating very little. He never even glanced at Mandukhai and kept his head down. At some point, he excused himself with a whisper to Esige. She had frowned but didn't protest, though she remained in the gathering space.

As the feast wore down, Esige stretched and marched over to Mandukhai. *Does she know what I asked of her husband? What does she think?*

"I would like to take Nemeku with me when I leave tomorrow," Esige announced.

Mandukhai scanned the open space and spotted the five-year-old boy playing with Togochi's sons.

"I'm not sure that's a good idea," Mandukhai said slowly. "He has friends here, and if you take him south, he will be within his father's grasp. Bigirsen has been sweeping up the tribes under his rule."

Esige crouched and laid her palms flat on the low table. "Mother, he is my sister's son, and all I have left of my family. I cannot leave him. He belongs with me. I can protect him. I would rather die than see him in his father's hands again."

"That's hardly reassuring, Esige."

"Please. You will have your hands full, anyway." Esige's gaze flitted to Dayan for just a moment, and the corners of her mouth twitched downward. It happened in the blink of an eye, then Esige was smiling at Mandukhai again. "If you launch a campaign against the Oirat, Nemeku will be no safer with you than with me. And you will have far more to distract you than I will."

Mandukhai smirked. "A new husband is not distraction enough? What does Huoshai think of this?"

Esige's cheeks flushed. "We discussed it at length this morning. He understands and is more than happy to help me protect Nemeku."

"I'm not ready for this."

Dayan leaned against Mandukhai's arm, drawing her gaze down at the boy as his eyelids fluttered closed, then snapped open again. She sighed. Esige was right. And maybe it would be better if Bigirsen thought Nemeku was with Mandukhai when he was actually far away.

"Alright."

Esige leaned forward and kissed Mandukhai on the forehead. "I love you to the ends of the world, Mother."

The words touched Mandukhai's heart. Tears pricked the corners of her eyes. Before she could find a suitable response, Esige left the gathering space, headed toward the Urainkhai section of camp.

Something had happened in the gathering tent earlier in the evening. Huoshai had not come straight back to the ger, as Esige had expected. It was not until the feast that she finally saw him, and he seemed withdrawn. All the excitement she remembered from their night at the wrestling match and dancing had disappeared from his eyes. She had tried asking him at the feast, but he dismissed her abrasively. It had cut her deeply. Did he regret his decision to marry her? *It's too late now.*

Leaving Mandukhai would be hard enough, but if Esige had to travel with someone who no longer wanted her around, it would be like the final knife in her heart. *At least I will have Nemeku*, she thought as she opened the door to their ger.

Huoshai slumped on the edge of the bed with his head in his hands. The tail of his braid hung low over one shoulder. Esige closed the door softly and shuffled toward him, uncertain what to do. *It would help if I knew what was wrong.*

He sniffled and released a shaky breath.

He's crying, she realized. Was this situation really so bad to him now, that he would be so distraught?

"What's wrong?" she asked.

His clothing stretched over his muscles as he tensed. A few shuddering breaths later, he scrubbed the heels of his palms into his eyes and rubbed his sleeve across his face with another sniffle. Bloodshot eyes met hers with ferocity and grief.

"I didn't hear you enter," he said, but his voice was unnaturally deep, as if he had dropped his pitch to cover the tension in his throat.

"Sorry. Old habits." She edged toward him. "What's wrong?"

Huoshai regarded her with intense skepticism. She didn't like the way he calculated her, as if deciding if she could be trusted. Finally, he shook his head. "Don't worry about it."

Esige bit her lip and could no longer meet his gaze. She remembered the way Manduul had treated Mandukhai when they had first married. The doubt and mistrust. The dismissive way he disregarded Mandukhai's value for so long. The way he had abused her, and she had tried to hide it. *Have I made a terrible choice? Will that now be my fate? Was it the fate of all women?*

"Hey." The softness of Huoshai's voice drew Esige's gaze back to him. "This has nothing to do with you. Thus, nothing for you to worry about."

Esige bit her lip.

He dipped his head again, rubbing his hands slowly together as he studied them.

She shook her head, not that he saw it, and glided over to perch beside him on the bed. "Wrong. We are married, Huoshai. Whatever has you this worked up does concern me. What happens to you happens to me as well. I won't be left out."

He released a brief chuckle. "No, I imagine you won't."

Esige brushed a hand across his back and the muscles were so tense they hardly twitched. She remembered how they had contracted under her hands just that morning and hated how she felt heat flush her cheeks at the memory.

"Mandukhai gave me a mission," Huoshai said, and the way he said Mandukhai's name made all the excitement in Esige's body flush away.

So much distaste!

"She wants me to convert my father to one of her followers," he said, then laughed at something Esige didn't understand.

"Of course she does. She made herself perfectly clear. Her mission is to unite the Mongols." Esige didn't understand why this bothered Huoshai so much. Surely he understood this before he had raced Esige.

Huoshai shook his head and straightened his spine. Her hand fell down his back. The serious lines on his face seemed to belie his young age. He sneered. "No, no Esige. It's not a choice. He either converts, or ..." The lump in his throat bobbed, and he clenched his jaw.

The implication came across perfectly clear. "Oh." Mandukhai could not afford to have resistance to her cause once she started sweeping across the empire. If Huoshai's father resisted, Huoshai was his heir and had given his oath already. The cold calculation made sense to Esige. "What are the chances he will refuse?"

Huoshai rolled his eyes. "My father is the most stubborn man I have ever met. And traditional to a fault. The Urainkhai are proud of their ties to Kublai Khan, and that pride often impedes reason. So the odds are not good."

Esige considered this. Kublai Khan had been a grandson of Genghis and had been one of the vital pieces leading to the civil war and division of the nation. If his father was proud of those ties, he likely was just as stubborn as Kublai had been centuries ago. A smile crept across Esige's face as something else he said struck her.

He scoffed. "What are you smiling about? She basically told me to kill my father. Could you kill her?"

"No." Esige reached over and took Huoshai's hand between both of hers, then leaned her head against his shoulder. "But you said he is traditional to a fault."

Tradition meant Tolokan khan would have to respect the rights of the last heir of Genghis. If they played this carefully, he would fall into place. As Esige explained this to Huoshai, he nodded slightly, but didn't seem to believe her idea would work.

It had to work. Because if Huoshai had to kill his father, it would break him. She could see that plainly.

I will do everything in my power to stop that.

Early the next morning, Mandukhai and Dayan returned to the Shrine of the First Queen to make an offering of milk and salt. By the time they returned to camp, gers had been broken down and packed up. Dayan rode in the saddle with Mandukhai as they made their way southwest.

But at the crest of a hill, Mandukhai paused to watch the line of Urainkhai snaking away with Esige and Nemeku beside Huoshai. And far ahead, the Khorchin became dots on the eastern horizon.

CHAPTER THIRTY-TWO

Crumbling Defenses

Bigirsen arched his back, pressing his fists into his lower back and rolling his neck. Issama had waited patiently as Bigirsen studied the maps and chose their next point of attack. Villages fell first. They proved a vital source of supply for the Ming forces and cities. Once Bigirsen cut off supply to those cities, the Ming would send out more caravans to lure him out.

Bigirsen turned to face Issama. "Have the Urainkhai arrived?"

"They will be here tomorrow," Issama said. "Tolokan khan agreed to the terms and is sending a thousand of his best fighters, but he will not give up his title as the other khans did."

"He will learn soon enough that there can be only one leader," Bigirsen said, waving it off. He needed the Urainkhai reinforcements and their superior strength. It left Bigirsen with no choice but to accept the khan's decision. "Once I have captured Yinchuan, he will see." A fire burned in Bigirsen's eyes. "They will all see."

Issama understood who Bigirsen really meant. Mandukhai and Unebolod were a thorn in his side. *They are a thorn in mine as well.* Mandukhai's lack of response to Issama's offer clarified she had no intention of accepting. He would have to change his own strategy. How, he did not yet know. Those pieces would come together soon enough. They always did.

Commotion outside the command tent drew their gazes toward the flap. A moment later, Bigirsen's guards held the flaps open, and a messenger entered. He kneeled before Bigirsen, holding up his message.

Bigirsen scowled, glaring down at the messenger. "What is this?"

"From the Khan and Khatun, my Lord," the messenger said. His voice trembled as he spoke.

The Khan ... Sweat prickled on Issama's forehead despite the fall chill in the air. This was it. Mandukhai had named Unebolod. *How could he have won* kurultai *with so many of the Lords still in the south with us?* Issama's gaze flicked to Bigirsen, attempting to gauge his reaction.

Bigirsen turned away from the messenger, returning to his maps. An air of arrogance rolled off of him. "I have given no oath to any Khan."

The messenger's eyes widened in panic, darting to Issama as if seeking help. To Bigirsen, no Great Khan could be named because he controlled most of the Mongol Lords. *It is folly to dismiss Unebolod so blithely*, he thought.

Issama's own curiosity got the better of him and he swiped the message from the rider. Bigirsen might act like he didn't care, but Issama did. Before he opened it, Issama gave a jerk of his head toward the exit. If this rider did not leave immediately, he was likely to lose his head to one of Bigirsen's sudden fits of rage. Thankfully, the rider had the sense to obey.

The Khan *and* Khatun. Those words finally sank in. Mandukhai had not given up her position. Somehow, she had given it strength instead. Had Unebolod given her this title? He broke the seal and opened the message.

They had named a new Great Khan. Dayan Khan. Issama frowned, unfamiliar with this name. Had Unebolod taken a new name? Certainly an auspicious one, claiming to be the Whole Khan. To the Ming, this name would clarify that the Khan believed he still held rights to rule the Ming. To them, it would mean Great Yuan, asserting his position over the old Yuan Dynasty.

As he read on, Issama's stomach dropped out. *No. This cannot be true.* His gaze shifted to Bigirsen, who remained at the table studying his maps. *If he reads this, he will kill Siker. Or me.* Issama scanned the message once more, but the truth was unmistakable.

Dayan Khan, Borjigin heir and son of Bayan Mongke, bone of Genghis Khan, blood of Siker, Mongol Great Khan and ruler of all under the Eternal Blue Sky.

How could she not tell me she had a son with Bayan? And when had it happened? The boy couldn't be much older than a few years. She and Bayan had not been together that long. How had she kept this boy hidden?

Feeling deeply betrayed and in need of answers, Issama folded the message into his deel and straightened. First, he had to divert Bigirsen's wrath.

"Well?" Bigirsen snapped, pressing his fists into the tabletop. His back hunched again. "Is it that arrogant Khorchin Lord?"

"No, my Lord," Issama said smoothly. He had to keep his fear contained until he could gain control of this situation. "She has named a Borjigin boy."

Bigirsen stiffened, rising slowly as he turned to face Issama. "There *are* none. Except ..." His long eyebrows knitted together, and the corners of his mouth pinched tight, creating long lines in his face. "Did she name my son?" The words were low, drawn out.

Issama had not even considered this possibility. Nemeku would be a boy, only five or six now, and though his father was not Mongol, his mother was a Borjigin princess. Nemeku was Uyghur, not Borjigin, despite his link to the line of Genghis. For the moment, Issama would have to cling to this until he could sort out the truth from Siker.

"It doesn't seem so," Issama said honestly. "Apparently, Bayan fathered a son before my men finished him. The boy can't be more than a few years old."

Bigirsen's shoulders heaved. Rage burned in his eyes. "She does not know the mistake she has made. I will finish what I have started here, take Yinchuan, and march against her to kill this boy and reclaim my son. She has no right!"

Issama nodded briefly in agreement. "I will send your message to her, but what shall I say?"

The vein in Bigirsen's neck pulsed thick and angry red. "The truth, Issama. That I have taken no oath to a Khan. That I will come for her to take my son back, with the full might of the Mongols and the blessing of Genghis at my back."

Issama bowed, thankful Bigirsen had not questioned him further. It had been dangerous to skirt the truth and avoid mentioning Siker. He excused himself to compose the message, but he would not send Bigirsen's message to Mandukhai. He had his own reply.

Nothing mattered more than speaking to Siker. Before Bigirsen learned the truth. Surely the same message would be sent to Lord Legusi and Lord Guden—or perhaps had already arrived. Bigirsen would hear of Siker's involvement soon enough. Issama had to figure out how to deflect Bigirsen's inevitable wrath. To do that, he had to hear the truth from his wife.

How could Siker keep such a secret from him? He was of half a mind to gut her himself. Yet he could not. Not now. Siker was the mother of the Great Khan. That would be worth far more than anything else. It might even help assuage the chaffed moods of the Lords he had promised to help take down Bigirsen. But why would Siker give her son to Mandukhai? And why would she not tell him, her own husband?

Issama had never ridden so fast in his life. The trip to the family encampment was three miles. He had to get there and back before Bigirsen noticed he had left instead of sending his message to Mandukhai. Cold wind bit into his face as he raced north toward the camp. It stung his eyes, but he did not slow until he reached the edge of camp. From there, he rode casually toward Siker's ger.

Siker sat on a stool outside, nursing Issama's son, Burani. When she spotted him, Siker frowned. Issama rarely returned from the army encampment so his appearance would likely raise her concern.

"What is it?" she asked, rising and clutching Burani close to her chest.

Issama twitched, wanting to tear the baby away from her arms. He could not kill her. She was the mother of his only son, and mother of the Great Khan.

"Get inside," he snapped, turning her and nudging her toward the door.

Siker yelped but stumbled inside. As he closed the door behind him, Siker set Burani down on the bed. The infant immediately began crying, so she gave him a leather strap to suck on.

"This is not your first child, is it?" Issama pointed at their newborn son and hissed, keeping his voice low so no one outside would hear them.

Shock ripped across Siker's face. "W—what?"

Issama stalked toward her, and Siker stumbled back away from him, rounding the ger.

"Did you have a son with Bayan?" Issama snapped.

Siker's face crumpled. Her entire body trembled. "I—we …"

"Answer me, Siker!" Issama roared. Spittle flew from his mouth as he leaned over her.

Siker pressed her back to the doorframe, her hand fumbling for the handle. Issama seized her wrist and yanked her hand away from the door.

"Don't. Tell me the truth. Now!"

"Y—yes. But he was crippled, Issama! And so sickly. Bayan abandoned us. I thought the boy died!" She seized his deel in a trembling fist. "Please. I had no idea—"

"Why didn't you tell me?" Issama pressed her other fist into her own chest.

"I thought he died!"

Issama swung his free hand, backhanding her face hard enough that, were they not clinging to each other, she would have fallen to the floor. An angry red mark sprang to life on her cheek.

"Forgive me," she whimpered. "I only wanted to move on with you. Issama, I love you!"

"Not enough to tell me the truth," Issama spit. "The boy did *not* die, Siker. And when Bigirsen learns of this, he may very well kill me and force you to become his wife so he can claim your son. You have undone *everything* I have worked so hard for." Issama pushed her back into the wall, releasing his grip as he began pacing the rug.

Siker tumbled back, then slid to the floor. Her tremulous gaze turned up to him. "Batu lives?" Her voice was so timid he almost wanted to kick her for being spineless.

Burani wailed on the bed as if sensing the tension in the ger. Siker didn't dare move from the floor as she cowered at Issama's feet.

"Batu?" Issama paused in his stalking, glaring down at his wife. "No. You see, Siker, Mandukhai has the boy now. And do you know what she has done with him?"

Tears rolled down Siker's cheeks. She swallowed hard and could only shake her head in response.

"She has made him Great Khan, wife! *Your* son has taken everything we have been working toward."

Siker sniffled and swiped the back of her hand over her tears in a feeble attempt to collect herself. "But ... he is only seven."

Seven! Issama did a quick calculation in his head, but the results only fueled his anger all the more. He straightened his back, clasping his hands behind him as he stared down his nose at her. "You have known about this boy from the first time we met, when we first came to our agreement."

Siker glanced at Burani but wouldn't dare rise from the floor to go to him. "I told you about the arrangement between Bayan and me long ago. I was young and naïve and he took advantage of that."

Issama snorted, clenching his hands tightly behind him to keep from slapping her again. Women did not know how any of this worked! "Bayan was naïve until the day my men killed him. How stupid must you be to be dumber than him?"

Siker sniffed and straightened on the floor, glaring at him. "I never loved him. I told you as much, and I did not lie. I love you!"

"Love is abstract, Siker," Issama snarled. "But do you know what isn't? Power. Who else knows of the boy that could support Mandukhai's claim that he is Bayan's son?"

Siker sniffled again, scrubbing her sleeve across her face. "Togochi's wife, Lady Jaghan. And my mother. But she would never speak of it. That child was our great shame."

Issama snorted in disgust. She did not know how true that was. "Lord Guden did not know?" Jaghan he could have killed easily enough, but Guden would pose a problem.

Siker shook her head. "My parents hid my pregnancy from everyone because ... because Bayan refused to marry me. The baby was misshapen from birth and always so sick. Then Bayan abandoned us to join Manduul. I could not care for the baby, so I left it in the Gobi. How could I have known he survived? He was less than a year old!"

Issama crouched in front of Siker and she flinched back. "You could not have, Siker." There was no genuine compassion in his words. For more than a year, she had seemed so smart, so much more adept at this game than either of his other wives. Issama had been so wrong. He brushed the tips of his fingers along her cheek tenderly. "You will stick firmly to your story when Bigirsen questions you. And he will. But when you tell him the truth, you will make the boy seem on death's doorstep to solidify your certainty that he died. Bigirsen will question me as well, and I will be honest. I will tell him I knew nothing about this until today. Tengri help me, I will be forced to grovel at his feet so he does not remove my head!" Issama spit on the floor to show what he thought of such an act. "Do you understand what I ask of you? Make that baby's death a certainty in your eyes so that Bigirsen will have no reason to doubt you."

Siker nodded, but fear still shined in her eyes.

Issama brushed a kiss over her cheek. Siker's warm, shaking breath washed over his face. Both of their fates now depended on her ability to convince Bigirsen and beg his mercy. Issama did not like his chances.

Siker threw her arms around Issama and he hugged her close.

If they could not garner mercy, he would have no choice but to fight Bigirsen, then take the Mongols north to seize control of the Great Khan—in the name of Dayan Khan's mother.

Before returning to Bigirsen's camp, Issama raced north to the Chakhar encampment. He needed to find out how widespread this knowledge of Siker's son would be, and Guden seemed the best place to start.

When he reached the edge of the Chakhar gers, a group of warriors stopped his horse.

"I need to see Guden khan immediately," Issama snapped, breathless from the hard riding.

"He's not here."

"Where did he go?"

"A messenger arrived, and he left immediately thereafter to speak with you."

The world listed slightly to the side. If Guden sought him, he would have gone to Bigirsen. Would Guden hold his tongue or spill the truth?

Issama yanked the reins to spin his mare around and whipped her into action. They bolted across the hard, dry grass and his heart beat hard and fast, in perfect rhythm with his horse.

The moment Issama drew near Bigirsen's command tent, a handful of Bigirsen's guards grabbed Issama's horse by the bridle as others yanked him out of the saddle. Somehow, he would have to slither his way out of certain doom. Curse his wife for dropping him into this pile of sheep dung!

"I can walk on my own!" Issama snapped, but the argument was pointless. Bigirsen sent these men to capture him, not escort him. They closed around him like a wall, forcing him into the command tent by the arms.

Lords Legusi and Guden stood along the edges of the open space inside, surrounded by their own guards—but not as prisoners like Issama. Bigirsen prowled the head of the tent like an agitated predator. His guards shoved Issama to his knees in front of Bigirsen, holding him in place. Despite the rug, Issama felt a rock digging into his shin.

Issama considered acting like a fool unknowing of the truth, but Bigirsen would not buy it. Not when news already buzzed through the camp and Issama had already read the message from Mandukhai. He would have to lean into his story, just as he told Siker.

"Bigirsen, you must know I had no idea," Issama said smoothly. The last thing he wanted was to show weakness at this moment. He needed to remain calm and confident.

Bigirsen halted, spinning slowly to face Issama. He bared his teeth in a feral snarl. One moment Bigirsen glared at him; the next, he held the edge of his sword to Issama's throat. "You are like a snake coiling around my ambitions and strangling them slowly. I never should have trusted you."

Issama lifted his chin to lessen the push of the blade against his neck. "When have I done this? I have followed your orders to the letter, my Lord, from the start."

"Tighten the coil, Issama," Bigirsen growled. "And learn how I cut the head off snakes. You did not mention that this boy Khan was your wife's son!"

"I wanted to get the truth from her myself, my Lord," Issama replied calmly. "The news was a shock to me as much as you. But given their relationship, we should have expected this." The blade pressed against his neck. "*I* should have expected this!"

"So?" Bigirsen paused, leaning closer as he clenched the sword in place. Issama could see the whites of Bigirsen's knuckles.

It took Issama a moment to understand what Bigirsen asked. "She thought the baby died. It was deformed and sickly, and when Bayan abandoned her, she abandoned the baby to death in the Gobi."

Bigirsen's nose flared. The stench of *airag* rolled off his breath. "If her story does not match yours exactly, I will kill you." Bigirsen stood and drew the sword away, twisting it around and sliding it into his belt. "I might kill you and take her either way. If I cannot be Great Khan, I will become his father."

Issama's heart lurched. Not for the child, but for his wife ... and his own neck. As angry as he was with Siker for keeping this truth from him, the idea of losing her pressed against his heart. *Curse you twice, woman!* Lord help him, he loved her.

Siker's cries drew near. Issama could not stand with the guards holding him on his knees, but he twisted his head around to see her slung over the shoulder of one of Bigirsen's men with her arms and legs bound like a sheep. When the warrior dropped her on the ground beside Issama, a fresh wave of anger rose in him. Blood trickled from the corner of her mouth. She had struggled and lost. Siker shifted to her backside, her eyes widening when she spotted him on his knees beside her.

Bigirsen pointed at Issama. "Not a word from you until I'm done with your wife. Interrupt and I make you watch me kill her slowly. Then I will kill you."

Issama swallowed. More than anything, he wanted to drive a knife through Bigirsen's ear right into his brain.

Bigirsen stalked toward Siker and crouched in front of her. His calloused fingers brushed her jaw. "Dear, sweet Lady Siker. You have fooled us all."

Siker whimpered and flinched from his touch.

"Why have we never heard of this boy you had with Bayan before?" Bigirsen asked. The sickly sweet tone in his voice was layered with contempt.

"He—he—" Siker squeezed her eyes closed to fight off her tears. They spilled freely from her eyes, regardless. Issama wanted to reach out to her, comfort her, protect her from Bigirsen, but he was powerless. Legusi and Guden wanted Bigirsen dead, but with Bigirsen's loyal guards around him, the two khans wouldn't dare make a move. "He died."

"He did *not* die," Bigirsen said firmly. "Try again, Siker."

She opened her watery eyes and stared at the floor. "He was dying. I—I left him. In the desert. I couldn't—" A sob wracked her body.

"Shh." Bigirsen lowered a knee and pulled her close. Issama tugged at the men holding him down, only to have one of them press a sword to his throat. "It's okay. You can tell me." Bigirsen whispered into her ear, then kissed her temple.

Siker sucked in a shuddering breath that skipped past her lips. Issama ached to rescue her from Bigirsen's clutches.

"Bayan abandoned us," Siker whispered, her voice hoarse. "I couldn't care for a sick baby. So I ... I ... left him in the Gobi." Siker's body shuddered with sobs. "He was less than a year. And I ... I ..."

Bigirsen pulled back, hooking his finger under her chin and tilting her face up to meet his hard gaze. "I am not without mercy, Siker. You have already grieved this loss, haven't you?"

Siker swallowed, nodding as tears rolled freely down her face. Issama wanted to reach out to her, but the men braced him in place.

Bigirsen stroked her cheek, brushing away the tears. Issama had never experienced so much hate in his life. "He is dead to you, Siker. He is dead to all of us. That baby died in the desert." He kissed Siker with such compassion. Right on the lips.

All Issama could see was red. He lurched forward against the men holding him, nearly breaking their grasp. The blade bit into his neck, drawing blood and forcing him back. Issama growled.

Bigirsen stood and glared down at Issama. The guards released him, but he didn't dare move with Bigirsen towering over him.

"You will no longer whisper in my ear, snake. But you will serve." Bigirsen scraped his nails over the top of Issama's head. "I cannot afford to waste this mind." He grabbed a fistful of hair and yanked Issama's head back. "The *only* council you will offer is where to move the *tumens*. Lady Siker will remain close to my wives for safekeeping. If you betray me in even the smallest measure, I will kill your infant son, you will die, and she will replace Borogchin."

He released his death grip on Issama's hair and kicked him in the gut for good measure. Issama collapsed onto his side, gripping his stomach as hot pain shot out from his ribs.

"Issama, if the Ming do not fall, you will. And when that is done, she will either become my wife, or she will die."

Issama glared at Bigirsen with open contempt. Just out of his reach, Siker trembled, hugging herself tight.

Bigirsen ignored the derision and rolled his shoulders. Issama spared a glance for Siker and noted how the color had drained from her face. If Issama did not defeat the Ming, Bigirsen would kill his entire family. But when they defeated the Ming, Bigirsen would have to kill him to take Siker as his wife. And if she fought back at all, Bigirsen would then kill her.

Issama had no claim on the boy Khan, but Siker did. Which meant *she* was the source of power against Mandukhai.

"Noble Lords, you will see," Bigirsen said. "The Ming will fall. I will complete what Genghis could not. And you will *all* agree that the boy died in the desert. Just as his father did." Bigirsen made his final statements a matter of fact. Accept that the boy Mandukhai claimed was Bayan's son was not, and that the baby had died in the desert years ago, or suffer the consequences.

With the ultimate declaration, Bigirsen strode out of the command tent with a trail of his guards. Issama straightened, casting imploring gazes at Legusi and Guden. The first offered a frown of sympathy. The second curled his nose at Siker before ducking outside.

Alone in the command tent with only Issama, Siker collapsed on the floor, trembling violently. Issama crawled to her and pulled her into his arms, stroking her hair. Bigirsen believed he had won, but this was far from over. He believed he had cowed Issama, but by threatening his son and wife, instead Bigirsen had made his worst enemy yet.

Bigirsen's confidence would be his downfall.

CHAPTER THIRTY-THREE

Bones of Winter

Unebolod had sent a few warriors back to the grasslands of the Khorchin homeland with the families who did not wish to travel with him. The months or years to come would be hard riding for everyone, and he could not afford to have families slow his pace. Warriors would move back and forth, visiting their families when time permitted, but the bulk of his *tumen* needed to continue moving through the eastern territories.

His first stop on the quest for the *sulde* brought him to the edge of the Jalair camp, where Lady Altan commanded thousands of warriors—a command she earned after Bayan killed her father, the khan. Before Bayan, the Jalair had close ties with the Oirat. If anyone had stolen the *sulde*, his first suspect was their leader.

Unebolod had met Altan before, at the festival where he had bested her at archery. Meeting her on the battlefield felt much different. The tension in the brisk winter wind was palpable as warriors waited on their mounts. Unebolod had only brought a thousand with him, as was his right as a lesser khan and commander. Altan commanded at least five times his number. Should this encounter go sour, his men would need to act quickly.

Unebolod casually rode toward Altan. He did not want to instigate a fight here. The warriors with him waited a short distance back—close enough to land an arrow in her eye should she try anything, but far enough not to hear the conversation.

Altan grinned as she reined in before him. "It looks like the tournament was not the only time we were meant to face off, Steel Soldier," she said.

"I have not come to fight," Unebolod said evenly. "I come in the name of our Khan."

Altan's brows climbed up her forehead. "*Our* Khan?" Her mount danced, eager to move. She controlled it with expert ease. "Or *your* Khatun? I heard all about her display."

"Too bad you ran away before it happened," Unebolod teased.

Altan scowled. Implying that she had run from anything was clearly not appreciated. "Without the sacred banner, she could not name him. Yet she did it anyway. I should think you, of all people, would have opposed this."

Unebolod chaffed. This woman purposely goaded him. She was infuriating. "Perhaps you should not have taken it, then."

Altan threw her head back as she laughed, then wiped tears of amusement from her eyes. "I didn't mark you for a man with a sense of humor." Her horse edged closer until she sat in her saddle directly beside him. "Clearly I was wrong. About a few things."

Unebolod's jaw twitched. He rested his hand on his sword hilt. He would have to face the scrutiny of the Lords and khans for allowing Mandukhai to seize control. Yet he understood the path Mandukhai walked, even if it made him hollow inside. The High Heavens had spoken. None of these tribal leaders would understand that. Not as he did.

Altan eyed his movements, mirroring them as she rested her hand on her own sword. "Everyone said you were a sure thing."

"I gave my word." It seemed he repeated this line a lot of late. But if he did not uphold his word, he was little more than an honorless dog. "The *sulde* was placed in my care, Lady Altan. I need it back."

She snorted. "I don't have it."

Unebolod wanted to believe her, but with the ties the Jalair had to the Oirat, he could not take her word for it.

Altan seemed to understand this. Her lips thinned, and she turned her horse away from him. "Come to my camp and see for yourself, Unebolod khan. Let your men search for it. I have nothing to hide." She flashed a coy smirk over her shoulder. "I give you and your men Guest Rights. You will be safe in our camp."

Guest Rights would protect him and his men, but it would also protect Altan from retribution if they found the banner here.

Unebolod called Soke to his side as he nudged his mare into a trot to join Altan. "Organize the men. Spread out and search everywhere. Every ger. Every cart. Every hiding place. Leave no stone unturned."

Soke nodded. Since Dayan Khan had been named instead of Unebolod, Soke had become more sullen.

Hooves crunched the snow-covered ground as thousands trampled it into mush. The conditions would make this a treacherous battleground should Altan break her word. It still amazed him that these men willingly followed her. As Mandukhai's stunt had shown, men could be prickly about following where a woman led in politics and war. *She must be fearsome to keep these men in check*, he thought as he rode through the gers alongside her.

The Jalair camp was not massive, but Unebolod suspected that many of the families were scattered across the northern territory. One tribe did not congregate in one area together for long or they risked overgrazing and depleting resources. His own people would scatter across the mountains and Kherlen River, now that the festival was long over.

Smoke pumped across the sky from the smoke holes in the gers all around the camp. The air was pungent with the stench of the burning lumps of dried-out dung. This far to the north, men herded and rode reindeer nearly as frequently as horses. They would not ride the reindeer into battle unless they had no other choice, but the care of the creatures was apparent. Their thick hides provided great fur for the cold winters, and they would turn the meat into food if the animal had to be killed. The antlers made excellent knives or horn handles for the construction of bows. The Jalair had a firm grip on a valuable part of the Mongol economy.

Altan stopped beside her ger and dismounted, then dramatically waved around the camp. "You are welcome to inspect the camp, if that makes you feel better."

Unebolod dismounted and hobbled his mare so she couldn't wander far.

"Or, you are welcome to come in for tea while your men search," Altan offered as she opened her door. She paused on the threshold and grinned at him. "Or *airag*."

With that, she disappeared inside, leaving the door open behind her. The rest of her men dispersed, leaving him alone outside her ger. They might construe refusing her invitation as disrespectful, especially after Altan had offered him Guest Rights. He ducked inside and removed his helmet, placing it beside the door.

The inside roiled with heat from the blazing stove. Unebolod closed the door to ward off the chill of the winter air outside. Altan's ger was much as any other. Chests for her belongings, a bed along one side, a butcher's block for trimming meats, and an altar for worship. Instead of benches or a table, Altan's ger offered a layer of furs and pillows on the ground that could accommodate several visitors. She motioned toward the pillows as she poured him a drink. He removed his sword and settled on the furs.

"We are away from prying ears, and far from her now," Altan said as she joined him on the furs. She handed him a skin of *airag*. "You can speak freely with me. What do you really make of Mandukhai's choice?"

Unebolod took a long drink to cover the grimace. What he truly thought was of no consequence. "It was not a choice. Her duties bound her as much as my own."

Altan took the skin and drank more of the *airag*, then swiped her sleeve across her lips. Thin, pale pink lips. Unebolod averted his gaze to examine the contents of the ger.

"Your reputation for being stubborn is almost as well known as your reputation in battle," Altan mused. "You will not tell me, will you?"

Unebolod reached for the skin, and Altan placed her hand over his. "Do you know what she told me about you, Unebolod?"

His chest tightened. He did not want to know, but could not say as much.

"When she spoke to me, she offered me a position of power, to elevate my rank, because you would need a strong woman beneath you." Altan pulled her hand off of his. The tips of her fingers grazed his skin and sent a jolt of heat through him.

Unebolod recoiled, yanking the *airag* away. Had Mandukhai attempted arranging a marriage alliance with Altan on his behalf? A bold move. And he found the notion deeply offensive.

"I would advise you to travel south and join her," Unebolod said, glaring at the flames dancing in the stove. "She needs strong support. Give your oath to the Khan. He will need your warriors."

"Of course he will. He is a boy, not a man."

Unebolod's gaze was drawn back to Altan. She differed from most women. Strong, fierce, assertive—like Mandukhai. Except that, in a lot of ways, she was more like a man than a woman. But Unebolod noted the curve of her back as she sat upright beside him. She had shed layers of fur when she entered the ger, leaving her only in her deel. It made her appear womanlier.

Altan's eyes shined as she licked her lips like a hungry viper flicking out its tongue. "I could ride with you, instead, Unebolod."

Every part of Unebolod pressed inward, as if some invisible force created a fist around his body, crushing it into a ball. "It would still be in service to your Khan."

Altan leaned closer, sliding her hand along his knee. "Would it?"

Unebolod had not been with any other woman since Mandukhai. Only Odgerel had made him even consider another. But Altan was nothing like Odgerel. One woman was delicate, servile, eager to please. The other was rough around the edges, assertive, and he did not doubt for a moment that Altan would be as wild as an unbroken mare. The temptation burned in him.

"I cannot, Altan," Unebolod said, but even he heard the strain in his voice.

Altan shifted her body so she could face him, and her hand slid further up his thigh. "She rejected you."

He recoiled as if she had slapped him, his jaw going slack. It took a moment to recover. "I gave her my word, and my word is iron. Only the gods can release me from my oaths. I will not take a wife."

Altan smirked, and her lips brushed along his jawline. "Who said anything about a wife?" she whispered in his ear. "I have no interest in a husband. You have needs. I have needs. That's all this has to be. No reason to make it complicated. It will take your men most of the day to search the camp. That leaves us plenty of time."

The heat of her breath against his skin amplified the growing fire inside of him. Unebolod felt as if he were being pulled apart at the seams. His desire warred with his heart and his mind. Each had their own idea of how he should proceed. Before he could choose a course of action, Altan straddled his lap.

She grinned as she pressed her body down against him. "I don't think that's your knife."

Unebolod grabbed Altan's hair and pulled her back to create distance, but it only amplified her heaving chest. A grin spread across her smooth face.

"Don't overthink this," she said breathlessly. "It's just a bit of fun. That doesn't break your oath, does it?"

Unebolod's heart hammered against his chest as he realized she was right. He had sworn not to take another woman as his wife, but that did not prevent him from bedding any woman he wanted. And right now, he knew exactly what he wanted.

Altan must have noticed this revelation in his expression because her hands immediately went to work removing his belt and opening his deel. And he gave in quickly, grazing hungry lips across her neck and ripping open her own deel to expose soft, battle-scarred flesh. Altan's lips crashed into Unebolod's.

Women would be the death of him. He was certain of it now.

SOUTHERN KHANGAI MOUNTAINS – MID-WINTER 1471

Togochi dipped his chin to his chest as Jaghan massaged a salve into his bare shoulders. Her hands were warm, and the pressure pushed deep into his muscles. The stove burned hot, warming the inside of the ger enough that he sweat despite the cold winter beside the mountains. The chatter of his sons on the other side of the ger offered some relief to his soul—a salve in its own way.

"You are too tense," Jaghan said softly as she scooped more of the salve into her hands and rubbed it between her palms.

"Just imagine what she must feel like," Togochi commented, attempting to inject some humor into the moment. "And she doesn't have anyone to rub her shoulders."

"She has Tuya."

"That's not even close to the same," Togochi replied. He sighed as her warm hands resumed their work. The aroma of eucalyptus invaded his senses. "I should be there protecting them. Instead, she has me hiding in the mountains while she sits out in the open. Unebolod would skin me alive if he found out."

Jaghan snorted. "Well, she has Boke and Torgus, as well as Alayitung. Mandukhai is in good hands. You cannot do everything, Togochi."

He wanted to argue her point but couldn't summon the motivation. She would probably win anyway.

"At least we have the winter to fill this ger to the brim with sons," he teased, lifting his head and grinning over his shoulder at her.

"How many babies do you think women can have in just a few months?" Jaghan asked, incredulous, but teasing as well.

Togochi moved too fast for Jaghan to react. He grabbed her around the waist and swung her body around and down on the bed, then climbed over her. "At least one. Maybe three."

Jaghan laughed as he kissed her neck. "You expect me to have a litter? Maybe it's time you find a second wife, then. Because I cannot handle that many tiny versions of you on my own."

He pulled back, grinning down at her. "I'm a gem of obedience," he said in mock indignation.

Her giggle filled his soul. The way she wrapped her arms around him and pulled him against her sent a wave of excitement through his body. How could he ever consider a second wife when the one he had was so utterly perfect already?

Togochi grabbed a thick fur and tossed it over the two of them to block them off from the rest of the ger. Waves of passion rose and fell as their bodies moved together. A desire to keep their voices low stifled the moans of joy. But the rhythm, the way they shifted in perfect unison, brought something deep within to the surface. Perfect bliss.

As the passion abated, Jaghan pulled the fur blanket off their heads and took a deep breath. The air under the blanket had become so hot that even the warm air of the ger felt cool and crisp in Togochi's lungs. He stroked her arm, holding her against him.

"Togochi," Jaghan said softly. "I was not really joking about a second wife."

"Jaghan—"

"Please listen before you say no." She propped her chin on his chest. "I'm not sure how many more children my body can handle. Our daughter was so hard on me. What if ..." Jaghan released a shaky breath that rolled over his chest. "What if the next one is too hard and I don't make it? You cannot raise them alone *and* serve the Khan. I'm not saying you have to find one tomorrow. But I think it's a good idea. I don't want to share you with anyone, but necessity makes some of these choices for us."

The reasoning was strong. If something happened to Jaghan, Togochi was not sure how he would pick up the pieces and hold everything together. He was already under so much stress. Another wife would help Jaghan and him both.

Togochi hugged Jaghan tight against him. "I will keep an open mind. But I'm in no rush."

"Me either." She smiled, and for a moment his heart stopped.

A knock on the door drew a groan from his lips. "What is it?" he barked.

"A message from the Khatun," a muffled male voice said from the other side of the door.

Togochi grumbled as he pulled away from Jaghan and wrapped his deel tight around him. He shuffled toward the door, tucking his arms tight to his body as the blast of cold air hit him the moment he opened the door. The man gave him a message and bowed, then marched away.

After closing the door and rubbing his arms, Togochi broke the seal and read.

All remaining warmth drained from his body.

"What is it?" Jaghan asked.

"She is preparing to attack the Oirat in the spring." Togochi muttered a curse that his oldest son repeated with a bright smile.

Mandukhai did not want him to worry, but it seemed to be Togochi's only state of being these days. He had hoped for more time. And the return of Unebolod.

Mandukhai stood on the narrow deck of the massive cart, watching the approaching Khorlod banner ripple in the breeze. Behind her, Dayan sat on his oversized throne within the walls of his gathering tent. Mandukhai had constructed it using pieces of Manduul's old gathering tent, but she had engineers secure it to a massive cart, just as Genghis had once done. It showed the people that their Khan would not sit in his ger and allow the empire to fall apart, as Manduul had done. Dayan Khan would move across the Mongol lands and enforce his will.

The rough, rocky terrain around the Ongi riverbed was unstable, but the ground beneath the gathering tent was solid and the harsh winter would not freeze the earth as it did in the north. She had chosen this location after weeks of travel past the rings of former Mongke Bulag, around the gleaming white walls of Karakorum, to the unforgiving lands on the edge of the Gobi. While the riverbed was dry at this time of year, springs could bubble up from beneath the surface to provide water. Mandukhai had ordered a few wells dug up once they had set up camp.

The open land along the dry Ongi River suited Mandukhai much better than the hilly, forested space she had lived in with Manduul. Her warriors could see for miles. Enemies would have nowhere to hide to sneak up on her camp. It also served as a gateway for her first campaign as the Khatun. Roughly thirty miles to the west, the land spilled into open expanses along Oirat borders. There, she would make her first stand come spring.

The winter wind was bitter and ripped through her fur-lined deel. Mandukhai's eyes stung, but she did not flinch away from the cold even as the breeze made her tall *boqta*—the royal crown—sway and pull at the strap, securing it in place.

Togochi had insisted they meet in person to plan for the spring when she had sent him a message asserting her intentions against the Oirat.

To the north of camp, the mountains offered a backdrop that blocked the harsh winter winds. The Khorlod made camp near the mountains under Togochi's direction. He had argued against leaving the Borjigin without more warriors to protect the Great Khan, but Mandukhai had refused to bend. The smaller her camp, the less of a threat it would seem to the Oirat. And without the support of other tribes around her, those who had not sworn fealty to Dayan Khan might believe her to be weak and alone. It provided Mandukhai with the element of surprise.

The ruse seemed to work. So far, the Oirat were content to ignore her—or hadn't noticed her small camp at all.

Togochi dismounted near the cart and left his mount to dig up food for grazing. A contingent of four men accompanied him—men from his tribe whom Togochi insisted he trusted. Mandukhai had little choice but to trust his judgment, not knowing the men as he did. The Khorlod leaders climbed the cart steps and bowed to their Khatun.

"Any news from your brother?" Mandukhai asked Togochi.

He frowned, which was answer enough. Unebolod's journey eastward to find the *sulde* of Genghis Khan would take him months, if not longer.

Mandukhai waved her question off and entered the gathering tent ahead of the men.

They had covered the rough wooden planks of the cart inside the tent with the finest rugs Mandukhai owned. Along the center of the tent, leading to the raised dais where her throne sat beside Dayan's, rugs clearly marked out the main aisle with bright colors. At the sides of the aisle, darker rugs covered the planks. The smoke hole allowed light and air into the space and could be easily closed by servants with ropes and levers attached to the outer walls. The same silks and jewels Manduul had put on display in his gathering tent decorated this one, but they created a rainbow of colors that swirled out from the smoke hole, along the ceiling, and down the walls.

Thick red poles supported the structure, attached directly to the cart for more stability. The entire construction required a team of oxen to pull it. Mandukhai was quite proud of this structure and imagined the courtly space of Genghis had been much the same.

She settled on the ornate throne beside Dayan. Benches along the walls of the gathering tent offered visitors spaces. A few of the Borjigin leaders were already waiting. Togochi and his men took their seats and waited for Mandukhai to begin.

"I am not sure your visit was necessary, Togochi," Mandukhai said evenly. "Though I appreciate seeing you."

"You mentioned preparing to take the Khan on campaign in the spring," Togochi said evenly. "If you and the Khan are riding into battle, we need to strategize. I am your northern *orlok*, and currently the only one you can command directly. We are riding south to remove Bigirsen, I assume."

Mandukhai rested her hands on the grooved arms of her seat and glanced at Dayan. As always, he sat silently, staring at the gathered men with those soulful, wolf-like golden eyes. *I wish I knew what he was thinking*, she thought. Even after months of teaching him to read and write, Dayan had said only those two words at Mount Burkhan Khaldun.

"No," Mandukhai replied. "We are not."

The men murmured in disapproval. Like her, they wanted to see the Uyghur usurper removed from power. Mandukhai certainly had considered it, but to do so would leave a dangerous enemy at her back.

"Gentlemen," Mandukhai said, raising her voice to quiet their meager protests, "we cannot ride south and leave an enemy at our backs to close in and pinch us off. Issama has sent word to the Great Khan that Bigirsen is engaging with the Ming along the Gansu Corridor and into Yinchuan on what he considers a divine crusade. I am not worried about him at this point."

Again, the men murmured. Dayan tipped his head slightly to the side as he eyed one of Togochi's men.

"If he takes Yinchuan, you could lose the support of more tribes," Commander Alayitung said. "This is all the more reason to stop him first."

Mandukhai suppressed her irritation. Togochi had appointed Commander Alayitung before they set up this camp. He was one of the few Borjigin commanders with extensive battle experience—particularly against the Oirat. Mandukhai valued Alayitung's expertise, and he had given his oath to her and Dayan, but her patience could only stretch so far.

"Commander, I appreciate your concern, but Dayan Khan is your royal heir," Mandukhai said firmly. "The spirits of past Khans chose him, and by the High Heavens by his own divine right. Bigirsen's mission is folly, and soon enough his followers will know that as well. Right now, we need to concern ourselves with the danger that has always lurked on our threshold. The Oirat."

Yaqui, one of Togochi's chosen commanders, snorted at this declaration.

Mandukhai threw a sharp glare at him. "Do you disagree, Commander Yaqui?"

Togochi stiffened, watching Yaqui's reaction with apparent disapproval.

Yaqui shifted in his seat under Togochi and Mandukhai's scrutiny. "I just ... have heard the men talking, my Khatun."

"Please, share." Mandukhai sat back and folded her hands in front of her.

"They suspected you would choose the Oirat as your first target," Yaqui explained. "Since ... well, since Paisahan khan sent men after you."

Mandukhai tensed. She had worked so hard to banish memories of that horrible ordeal, instead focusing on teaching Dayan to be a strong and wise leader, and on making him Khan. While vengeance certainly burned in her heart, Mandukhai's reason for choosing the Oirat first had been much more practical.

"I see." Mandukhai paused, letting the men gathered squirm as she pondered her next words. They had to hold the right weight. "I cannot fault a man for his ambition. It's in a man's nature to prove his strength as a warrior and leader, to seize power in whatever way he can. My reasons for choosing the Oirat are not so vengeful."

Mandukhai rose from her seat and glided slowly down the wide steps of the dais. The eyes of all the men followed her—along with Dayan's.

"Alayitung, you have fought the Oirat in the past, correct?" Mandukhai asked.

"Yes, my Khatun," Alayitung said.

Mandukhai nodded. She already knew as much. "What is the most valuable asset the Oirat control, in your experience?"

Togochi fought off a smirk as he watched Mandukhai. She tried not to show her pride at this. He knew where she was headed already.

"Horses," Alayitung answered.

"And controlling the horses also allows the Oirat to control food and transportation across the steppe," Mandukhai agreed.

Understanding dawned on the other men now, and Mandukhai raised her chin as she paced back up the dais steps.

"If we conquer the Oirat first, not only will we no longer have a massive enemy to our west, but we will also take control of the largest herds of horses in the empire," she said.

"We cannot attack them directly, Mandukhai," Togochi added. "Even with our combined forces, they vastly outnumber us."

Mandukhai turned to face the men, standing in front of her throne. A smile spread across her face. "I agree, Togochi. The key will be how we choose our ground. Then, we will lure the Oirat out in smaller forces and pick them off. Your job, *orlok*, is to work with Alayitung to determine how we will manage this. We must take the Zavkhan plateau and force the Oirat khan to kneel before the Great Khan, Dayan. I have not set your camp near the northern mountains for nothing. Take the rest of the winter, scout the passes, and create a strategy. When the thaw comes, we will ride into Oirat territory and complete what Dayan Khan's predecessors could not."

"You will declare war on the Oirat," Togochi said, as if seeking confirmation.

Mandukhai shook her head. "No, Togochi. Declaring war implies they are not subjects of Dayan Khan. We will ride in, and they will have the same opportunity as all other tribe leaders. To give their oath. If they choose not to accept their Great Khan, then we declare war on enemies of the Mongol Nation."

Mandukhai dismissed the men to carry out her orders. As they drifted toward the exit, heads together and already deep in conversation, Togochi strode toward the bottom of the dais.

"This is a bold move, Mandukhai," he said once the others were near the door and out of earshot. "The Oirat have not answered to a Great Khan in at least a hundred years. They split from us as far back as the feud between Kublai and Qaidu. If you fail, the vulturous Lords will pick apart the boy's bones."

"All the more reason for you to succeed, Togochi," Mandukhai said. She understood the risks. And without Unebolod around to rescue her again, she could not only lose the boy, but her own life. At some point, Mandukhai knew she had to put her faith in the High Heavens to guide her on the right path.

"I'm not Unebolod," Togochi said.

For the first time, Mandukhai noticed the uncertainty on his face. Had her faith in him been misplaced? *I cannot let him see my doubt.* Mandukhai descended and placed her hand on his shoulder. "I did not entrust this task to him. He has another path to walk. You, Togochi, were chosen for this."

Togochi pulled his shoulders back and gave a small nod. "Issama controls those lands. You understand that?"

Mandukhai nodded. "But he is far south with Bigirsen and cannot reach the Oirat in time to make a difference. Our plan must be quick so he cannot come to their aid. And when we win, we will cut off the Uyghur from some of their Oirat supply lines. I sent a spy, Seguse, behind enemy lines almost a year ago. I have heard nothing from him since, but I can hope that he still lives and that with his help we can surprise the Oirat from all sides."

"And if he does not live?"

Mandukhai raised her chin. "Then pray the High Heavens bless our white road, Togochi."

Though the months of travel back to Huoshai's territory had been brutal as winter hammered against their caravan, Esige reveled in the adventure. She had never been so far south in her life. Every day offered something new to discover, and every night as well—though in the ger's privacy. Married life suited Esige just fine.

The doubt she had about his true feelings for her had vanished completely. Now, every time he looked at her, she wondered how she had even considered his doubt.

This morning, Esige dressed in all the layers of fur she would allow Huoshai to drape over her growing body. She then pulled on her riding gloves, tightening them over her hands by lacing her fingers together and pressing into the spaces between her fingers. Huoshai's best friend, Ormeger, eased her horse down closer to the ground.

"I can handle mounting," she said for the hundredth time.

"I saw you struggling to dismount yesterday," Ormeger replied, glancing at her belly. "Better safe than not."

Esige huffed and climbed into the saddle, silently hating how hard it was to swing her leg over the mare's back now. By the time they returned to the main Urainkhai camp, Huoshai would not only be returning with a wife, but a newborn child as well. Esige had never imagined herself as a mother, but now found she looked forward to it.

"I still think you should ride in the cart now, for your own safety," Huoshai said as he easily mounted.

Esige glared at him, hating how easy it had been for him to climb into the saddle. There had been a time when she had been faster than him. "I will not be coddled or treated like an invalid."

Huoshai rolled his eyes, but the corner of his mouth curled up in a smirk that made heat race through Esige's core.

Ormeger guided her horse up to its feet again, then handed over the reins. "You picked a spunky one, Huoshai."

Esige lifted her chin proudly. She would rather be spunky than docile.

The caravan broke away from their camp and resumed the ride south. As always these days, Huoshai remained close to her side.

"How much further?" she asked after an hour. She hated how the saddle made her thighs hurt. That was new.

A dark shadow passed over Huoshai's face. "We should cross over in another week. Then another two months before we reach my father's camp." Tension drew his shoulder blades closer together. For most of this trip, his spirits had lifted and he joked with everyone. The closer they rode to his father, the less she saw of that lighthearted man she had fallen so in love with.

Mandukhai's mission weighed heavily on him.

And the judgment would be upon him soon.

CHAPTER THIRTY-FOUR

Saddleborn

ORDOS BASIN – LATE WINTER 1471

The camp was silent in the dead of night. Only a handful of people moved around Issama as he stood with Siker near her ger. He had chosen this night carefully. The men on watch were loyal to him. They would look the other way, see nothing.

After Bigirsen had cast Issama away from him, he had also planted a spy to watch Issama and send reports of suspicious activity to Bigirsen—who now rode with three *tumens* into the Gansu Corridor, far from Issama's camp in the Ordos Basin. If Bigirsen learned the truth of what Issama was up to, he would surely take Issama's head.

Unfortunately for Bigirsen, Issama had uncovered the spy almost immediately. Lord Guden had a deeply seeded and well-disguised hatred for Bigirsen. That hatred had allowed Issama to easily convince Guden to send false reports—reports Issama drafted himself—until they could finish Bigirsen for good. Issama was not currently in a position to kill him. But he could take away as many of Bigirsen's methods of control as possible. First had been Guden. Next would be Siker.

"I don't want to do this," Siker murmured, clutching their infant son, Burani, in the sling against her chest beneath her fur deel. "He will kill you and find me, anyway."

"Maybe." Issama pulled Siker closer. She didn't cry. Siker rarely ever cried. Mastery of her emotions was one thing he loved most about her. He pressed his forehead to hers. "If he kills me, go north. Find Mandukhai."

She shook her head.

"You must, Siker. Promise me. As mother of the Khan, she will protect you."

"Let's just kill him and be done with this," she whispered, glancing at four men moving around them. These men would be her escort. They would protect her until she could return to him. Or until he came to find her.

"I can't." Issama kissed her cheek. "Not yet. He is too far from my reach. I need to push the pieces into place first." He wrapped his arms around her and his son, holding the two of them against him. It was entirely possible he would never see either again.

For several minutes, they held each other, cradling the infant between them. Siker pressed her forehead into his neck. Issama stroked her back. This agony was a new sensation to him, further proof that he truly did love Siker. And Burani was his only son. He had to get them as far from Bigirsen as he could in case anything went wrong.

"We are ready, my Lord," one man said from a few steps away.

Siker and Issama broke apart. He cradled her face in his hands, memorizing it in the moonlight. "Trust no one. Only go to Mandukhai if you hear of my death. I will send for you once this is over."

Siker nodded.

Issama pressed one last, tender kiss to her lips, then withdrew completely to help her onto her horse with the infant.

A minute later, the two rode away with their four guards around them. Until this was over, Siker and Burani would be safely hidden at a small Gobi oasis, far from any of Bigirsen's eyes and ears.

Issama watched until Siker disappeared into the darkness, then slipped into Uingen's ger. If all of his wives disappeared, there would be no hiding Siker's absence, so Issama had to keep Uingen, Qolotai, and his infant daughter with him. Bigirsen could kill them instead, but it was a risk Issama had to take.

Uingen sat up straight as he entered, watching him with worry in her eyes. "She is gone, then?"

Issama nodded as he shrugged out of his fur and slipped off his boots. "You are certain Bigirsen's wife will say nothing?"

Uingen nodded. She and Siker had been having tea with one of Bigirsen's wives for months preparing for this day. Thankfully, her sympathy for Siker's plight outweighed her love for her husband. Bigirsen had tasked his wives with monitoring Siker, and two of them were deeply bitter about what he had done to Borogchin. If he would murder his favorite wife, what made either of them safe? Fear was a powerful motivator and Issama had capitalized on it. If anything happened to Bigirsen, Issama would have to be sure to care for his wives. It was the least he could do.

"Good." Issama laid back on the bed and pulled a fur blanket over him to ward off the winter chill clinging to the air.

Ongud-Urainkhai Border – Late Winter 1471

Esige tugged her fur-lined cloak tighter around her body as wind whipped past the Urainkhai caravan. Her horse snorted and bobbed his head. She would have patted his neck, but another wave of pain seized her abdomen. Gritting her teeth, Esige dug her gloved fingers into the front cantle until the pain passed. Wind hammered into her back, sending a chill down her spine that did nothing to help with her extreme discomfort.

It was only midday. The sky above was gray, threatening coming snow. *We are only a week away at this pace*, Esige reassured herself. She could hand the saddle for another week.

Something warm rushed down her legs. It took a moment for her to realize her clothing was now wet and fluid trickled into her boots. She glanced at Huoshai, who was huddled tight against the wind on his mare. *We cannot stop now. It's too early in the day. We need to press on until sunset.*

Esige said nothing about her water breaking. Not as her toes went dumb. Not as her legs froze to the saddle. Not as the waves of contractions hit her. Each time, Esige gritted her teeth and waited for the pain to pass. Then she counted the seconds in rhythm with the clop of hooves against the hard earth. A few times, a groan escaped her, but the howling of the wind swallowed her agony whole.

Miles passed. The pain became intensely more frequent and excruciating. *I cannot ride much longer*, she thought between agonizing contractions.

As if to punctuate her thought, another contraction slammed into her. Esige was certain all of her insides were trying to rip free from her body. Despite her best efforts to hold her pain in, a shriek of agony ripped from her throat. She leaned forward in the saddle, clutching her stomach with one hand and her cantle with the other. Sweat beaded and froze on her forehead. Esige tried to focus on her breathing, but the wind continuously knocked the air from her lungs.

"Esige, what's wrong?" Huoshai asked, edging his mare closer to her mount.

When she ripped her chapped lips apart to respond, another wail escaped instead.

"Halt!" Huoshai shouted back over his shoulder.

"No," she breathed, loathing how weak her voice sounded. "We need … to keep … going." The words came out broken by measured breaths.

He ignored her completely, dismounting. "I need a ger now!"

Esige blinked as the pain subsided, surprised by the tears freezing to her cheeks. "Huoshai, we can keep going."

In a flash, he had used his reins to hobble his horse, then turned to take her reins away. Esige had gripped them so tight for so long her fingers refused to release their grip. Huoshai rubbed his hands over Esige's, warming them, then helped ease the reins away. It still made her fingers ache as she uncurled them.

"I'm not an invalid," she said, but the weakness in her voice betrayed her words.

"No, you aren't," Huoshai agreed as he hobbled her horse. "But you are in labor."

"No, I'm n—" Her protest cut off with a sharp intake of breath as another contraction seized her abdomen.

A team of men and women rushed around in tandem, constructing a ger in remarkably quick order. Esige hardly had time for her contraction to pass before the lattice walls and roof lathes were already in place.

"Up you go," Huoshai said, helping her bring one leg over the horse's neck.

Esige cried out in alarm as her trousers peeled away, breaking and ripping where they had frozen to the saddle.

Abject horror drained the color from Huoshai's face. "Esige, how long ago did your water break?"

"About ten miles back."

"Ten ..." Huoshai gaped. Anger like she had never witnessed in him crossed his face. He called out over his shoulder. "Get the midwife! We will be lucky to have time to build a fire!"

Nemeku scrambled away to carry out the order. Huoshai slid one arm under Esige's legs and wrapped the other around her back. Esige held on as he pulled her from the saddle, then strode into the ger as teams of men and women worked to secure the felt roofing and walls.

ONGUD-KHORLOD BORDER – LATE WINTER 1471

Unebolod had tried not to think of his fling with Altan too much. It brought on a wave of guilt he knew he did not need to feel. Mandukhai had bound herself for a different path than him, and he knew the odds of them being married now were almost at zero. Still, he clung to the *almost* instead of the *zero*.

The hunt for the *sulde* of Genghis had brought Unebolod along the eastern edge of the Gobi over the winter months. The Jalair camp had come up empty—as had the Kharchin, Tabun, and various other lesser tribes. Unebolod grew more concerned the further south he traveled. If the sacred banner ended up in the hands of the Ongud—or worse, a southern tribe—Mandukhai and Dayan Khan would have a hard road to unity ahead of them.

To his surprise, many of the eastern Lords had been more than happy to follow him when he visited their camps. Now, he had the banners of the Tabun, Kharchin, and Asud fluttering beside the Khorchin. None of them had given their oaths to the Great Khan—that could only be done before Dayan and Mandukhai. But each had expressed an interest in following him on this mission to find the *sulde*. Unebolod worried they thought he still intended to take the title for himself once he found the banner.

Chapter Thirty-Five

Homecoming

Winter had passed swiftly after Esige had given birth, as if the weather had been determined to undermine her pregnancy at every turn. But once she was no longer with child, the sun broke out, melting the freshly fallen snow and turning the ground to mush. Perhaps it was actually a small mercy to prevent the infant from freezing.

The baby boy cooed in his sling against Esige's chest as they rode. She glanced down, brushing her fingers over his soft cheeks. One year ago, she had been mourning the loss of her uncle and preparing for the venture to Mount Burkhan Khaldun. So much had changed.

Emeeltorson squirmed, rooting for food. Esige shifted in the saddle, then adjusted the sling to feed. She and Huoshai had agreed to name their son for what he was, saddleborn. What greater omen could a man ask for his son than to be born in the saddle?

The infant latched on and began feeding, and Esige lifted her gaze to the horizon as the horse plodded alongside Huoshai's mount. They crested a hilltop.

Esige's breath caught.

Nestled among the rolling hills and dense forests, hundreds of Urainkhai gers clustered in family groups. While Esige had seen more gers together than this, the backdrop of blooming cherry trees crowded around a waterway made it one of the most remarkable things she had ever seen in nature.

"Cool," Nemeku breathed as his eyes widened from his saddle beside Esige. He had handled this trip far better than Esige had expected, riding nearly the entire day without complaint.

The Urainkhai warriors and families who had journeyed with Huoshai cheered and hooted in happiness to see their home again. *My home, now,* Esige told herself.

The awe and excitement of the moment evaporated as she gazed at Huoshai. He sat stiffly in his saddle, staring at the camp with a clenched jaw. No one else knew what this homecoming meant to him—what he would have to face. She reached out and placed her hand on his arm.

"Remember. This is not a bad thing. We will play to his traditional side."

Huoshai could only nod. Then he kicked his mare forward, descending the hill.

WESTERN ORDOS BASIN – SPRING 1471

Over the winter months, Bigirsen had abandoned Issama's strategy in the Gansu Corridor to sweep from the south up toward the north. Instead, he had pressed his advances on Yinchuan too soon. But the city was too vast, and Bigirsen hadn't led enough men to breach the gates. When that had failed, Bigirsen commanded Issama to press back the Ming in the Ordos Basin and cut off the supply lines from Xian.

Meanwhile, Bigirsen turned his forces deeper into the Gansu Corridor to cut off the Ming in Yinchuan from their resources. He raided small caravans. Sometimes the Ming won. Sometimes Bigirsen won. But throughout the winter months, the Mongol army could not enter Yinchuan. *Because Bigirsen abandoned my strategy. If he had just followed through, he would already be well beyond Yinchuan by now.*

One bonus had emerged, though. Men began doubting Bigirsen's ability to carry out Genghis Khan's vision.

Doubt had created an opportunity for Issama. Bigirsen's own vanity once more had left him vulnerable.

After a brutal loss near the gates of Yinchuan, the Urainkhai had abandoned Bigirsen.

Now, Issama watched as the lines of Urainkhai warriors returned to their homeland. Between their losses against the Ming and the rumors that

Tolokan khan's son had returned, the Urainkhai no longer had an interest in Bigirsen's war.

He is losing men and power, Issama thought as he sat on his mount and gazed across the valley where the Urainkhai disappeared into the distance. *Soon, I will make my move against him.*

"Lord Issama!"

He turned his mount north as one of his men rode toward him with a cart trailing along. Issama squinted, trying to place this man. Then he remembered.

His spy from Mandukhai's camp.

"I brought something for you," the spy said as he reined in beside Issama, then waved toward the cart.

Curious, Issama trotted toward the cart and pulled back the ties and felt.

Pure joy burst through him, an elation like he had never experienced before. He reached a trembling hand out and brushed his fingers tenderly over the horsehairs.

Tengri smiles upon me, Issama thought. *Soon I will defeat Bigirsen with the* sulde *of Genghis in my grasp. Then no one will question my right to rule.*

URAINKHAI CAMP – SPRING 1471

As their home was constructed, Esige and Huoshai marched toward his father's ger. She left Nemeku behind to oversee construction and help move their belonging inside. It had thrilled the boy to have a purpose.

Esige glanced at Huoshai, whose stiff strides made his anxiety obvious. She knew better than to reach out to him. He would not want reassurance right now, and touching him could make him appear weaker—or feel weaker. Esige understood the need for strength in this moment.

Emeeltorson slumbered in Esige's arms, now swathed in silks and freshly cleaned—something she also wished she could be. What did she look like right now? *I hope his father doesn't hate me.* Esige did not regret her choice of husband. Huoshai had proven to be exactly the man she wanted. Strong, intelligent, capable, and passionate. In a lot of ways, he reminded her of Unebolod.

The moment Esige ducked into the ger behind Huoshai, heat slammed against her, knocking the breath from her lungs. The air reeked of incense and smoke from the stove. Brilliant colors of red, jade, and yellow slashed across the open space. A handful of men sat on pillows and furs on the floor to her left. The space was not nearly as large as a gathering tent, but as gers went, it certainly was grand.

A man who appeared to be close to Manduul's age sat on the floor among the others, but he straightened as he saw Huoshai. *That must be his father*, she deduced. He was no more intimidating than any other man. Esige wondered if she could best him in combat, as she had so many others.

Tolokan brightened as he studied Huoshai. "How is it a messenger could arrive with news of a new Khan before you returned?"

"A messenger alone can travel much faster than a thousand warriors and their families," Huoshai replied. "Especially through the winter. Besides, we were slightly delayed."

Tolokan rose and approached the two of them, embracing his son. "It's good to have you back, Huoshai. We are surely going to need you and your men soon." He glanced at Esige, and something about his gaze made her uncomfortable, but she would never dare show him. "I see your mission was a success. And a child already?"

Huoshai turned slightly crimson. "I wouldn't call it a mission."

"Those were your exact words," Tolokan said in amusement. "I hope this was a matter of choice and not convenience." His gaze dropped to the infant, making the implication clear. He worried Huoshai had only married her because he had gotten her pregnant.

"What he chose was to jump off the highest cliff," Esige said. "Your son does like a challenge, my Lord."

Tolokan barked out a laugh. "That he does."

"Father, this is Esige," Huoshai said, stepping closer to her and sliding his arm around her waist to pull her closer. "And this," he brushed the baby's forehead, "is our son, Emeeltorson. Barely two weeks old now."

Tolokan ignored the infant. His dark eyes drilled into Esige and the corners of his mouth turned downward. "*Princess* Esige?"

Huoshai frowned. "Yes."

Tolokan's expression darkened, and he strode toward the back of the ger to pour himself a drink. "Huoshai, tell me you haven't sworn yourself to this new Great Khan."

Esige's breath hitched. The way Tolokan made that statement left little to be discerned. He did not support Mandukhai's decision. Esige glanced at Huoshai, worry shining in her eyes. The red that had flushed his cheeks a few minutes ago completely drained away. Huoshai's back was ramrod straight. His arms hung at his sides with his hands clenched into fists.

Tolokan downed his drink, then turned and frowned when he saw the state of his son. Esige wanted to intervene but was terrified that she would only make matters worse. She did not know Huoshai's father well enough to determine what the best words might be to smooth this over.

"Everyone out," Tolokan said. The calmness of his tone sent a chill down Esige's spine.

The men stood and left the ger.

Tolokan glared at Esige. "I said everyone."

Esige turned, watching Huoshai before making her move. He gave a subtle nod of his head, and she left him alone with his father.

But Esige was a master at hiding in plain sight.

The moment the door closed, Esige adjusted her deel, hiding the sleeping infant against her as best she could, then edged around the ger as she watched for shadows and passersby. Sneaking was much harder now that she had a child strapped to her body, but Esige found a place to sit near the wall of the ger so she could listen. Whenever someone passed by, she gave a small nod and acted as if she were simply there with her child. No one gave her a second glance.

Esige steadied her breathing to steady her hammering heart, then leaned cautiously closer to the felt walls of the ger.

"—give an oath to them," Tolokan roared. "Do you have any idea what you have done?"

"Yes, Father, in fact I do."

Esige smiled a little at the confident tone in Huoshai's voice. She had worried he would crumble under pressure from his father.

"I married a Borjigin princess and now have a son with her," Huoshai continued. "Dayan Khan is the heir of Genghis."

"Please." Derision dripped from Tolokan's tone. "You probably have as much Borjigin royal blood as that boy Khan does."

The statement made Esige's heart seize. The Urainkhai had been loyal to Kublai Khan, Genghis Khan's grandson. Was it possible that Huoshai could be descended from that line somehow? *No. The Ming killed Kublai's descendants long ago.*

"He has the eyes of Genghis, Father! I have seen it myself."

"Issama was right." Tolokan lowered his voice. Esige had to struggle to hear what he said next. "He said some power between a woman's legs would sway you. I made other arrangements for you. Better ones."

"Better than a Borjigin princess?" Huoshai's voice raised a pitch. "It's done. She is my wife. We have a son. I gave my oath to the rightful Great Khan, just like you will."

"I will not bend my knee to a child."

Huoshai's desperation came across crystal clear to Esige. "Please. I beg you. Reconsider."

"You will meet Ibarai's daughter."

"No, I won't. But you need to offer your allegiance to the Great Khan."

Will he do it? Will he carry out Mandukhai's order to kill his father?

"Get out of my sight," Tolokan snapped.

Esige rushed to her feet and glided away as casually as she could, taking a roundabout route to her ger.

Nemeku had busied himself inside, getting everything situated. When Esige entered, he puffed up proudly. "Almost done."

"You have done wonderfully, Nemeku," Esige said with a smile. "Can you go fetch us some water so I can clean Emeeltorson properly?"

Nemeku darted for the bucket and out the door in excitement.

Only a minute after he disappeared, she heard Huoshai's voice outside and edged toward the door to listen.

"You cannot do this, Huoshai," Ormeger hissed so softly Esige had to press her ear to the edge of the door to hear through the crack. "Your father—"

"I know." Huoshai cut him off sharply. "But I have no choice. I gave the oath, Ormeger. What can I do?"

"Blood protects blood," Ormeger replied.

The baby squawked. Esige glanced at him bundled on the bed, but he couldn't move swaddled in blankets as he was.

"What happens when he finds out what she asked me to do?" Huoshai asked Ormeger. "I have a wife and child to protect now."

Silence settled outside for so long Esige worried she should move away from the door before Huoshai caught her listening.

"I just need to know I have your support, Ormeger," Huoshai said at last. "No matter what happens."

"Do you really think you need to ask, cousin? Of course you have my support. I just like having my testicles attached is all."

Huoshai chuckled. "Good. I have an idea, but we need to proceed with caution. Meet me in the morning at our usual place. Bring along only those you trust with your life."

Boots scuffed the ground. Esige darted away from the door to the butcher's block on the opposite side of the ger and busied herself carving up chunks of meat as the door opened. Huoshai ducked in and strode up behind her, sliding his arm around her waist as he pressed against her back.

"I'm sorry, Esige," he murmured against her neck. "I don't know what I thought would happen, but that wasn't it."

"Is everything okay?" she asked. "Is he so lost that we cannot sway him?"

He sighed and pulled away. Esige turned as he sat beside their son. His shoulders sagged, but a small smile of joy curled the corners of his mouth. "It will be."

Huoshai had shared his plan with Esige, and she did not like it much, but she understood his logic. Starting with only men he trusted, Huoshai had begun secretly spreading stories about the Great Khan and Khatun, about their rightful place. He played on tradition and the legitimacy of Genghis to supplicate frayed nerves. Those men would then spread the same stories to only men they trusted. By the end of the first week, Huoshai was certain he had at least half of the tribe supporting the decision to follow the new Great Khan. Yet his father still did not. Nor did he know what Huoshai was up to.

The plan carried serious risk. If even one of those men decided Huoshai was wrong, or was loyal instead to his father, Huoshai faced treason charges and the two would have no choice but to face off against one another.

Esige knew she had to intervene as well. Men listened to their wives. While he worked on gathering support, she met with his mother, Chimgee, several times for tea. Chimgee then introduced Esige to other women, boasting proudly of her son's Borjigin wife. Knowing what would happen to Tolokan if he refused to follow Dayan Khan, Esige felt bad for Chimgee. She was a sweet woman—not at all as devious as women like Satai. Esige grew to like her mother-in-law.

Using the ears of the women, Esige did exactly as she told Mandukhai she would do. Women asked endless questions about this powerful new queen, and Esige cast Mandukhai in an array of bold colors. She told stories of Mandukhai's challenges; her dedication to Manduul Khan and his faith in her wisdom; her grand love for Unebolod and the sacrifice of that love she made for the good of the nation, the sake of tradition, and the legacy of Genghis. The image Esige painted was carefully crafted to make

Mandukhai appear both strong and wise, as well as womanly and demure. Such stories would carry weight when these wives told their husbands.

Even Nemeku picked up on the task, though whether or not by coincidence, Esige could not be certain. He played with kids, talked about the Khan's cool eyes and how Mandukhai had a strong spirit.

After two weeks, Esige bid farewell to Huoshai when he left in the morning to meet with his father. Every time he met Tolokan, she worried it would be the day.

Lunch came and left, but she still had not seen Huoshai. Nemeku had begged to go play with some of his new friends, and Esige had allowed it, but cautioned him about danger. He flippantly accepted her warning as he darted out.

As dinner approached, Esige worried that something had gone wrong. If he left for a hunt, he would have told her first.

Just when she was certain their plans were uncovered, the earth trembled. Esige knew that sensation. An army. Her heart sank into her stomach, and she scooped up the baby and rushed out the door. Huoshai would not attack his father openly, would he?

As Esige rounded Tolokan's ger, a group of guards seized her. It was all Esige could do to hold on to her son. She pulled as much as she could with a baby in her arms, attempting to break free.

"Let go! I am Lord Huoshai's wife and this will not go unpunished!" She shifted the boy to one arm and slipped a knife into her palm from up her sleeve. She didn't want to kill anyone, but she would fight to protect her son. *Where is Nemeku?* she wondered in a panic.

Tolokan stepped out of his ger and stretched his arms high above his head. "Be sure Chimgee stays inside," he ordered the guard near his door.

"My Lord khan! Tell these men they have made a mistake!" Esige jerked in their grasp but could not break free with the baby in her arms.

Tolokan marched toward them, and hope bloomed in Esige's chest. But instead of calling off his men, Tolokan took the baby from Esige's arms.

"What are you doing?" she asked, hoping, praying that there was some mistake, or that this was far more innocent than it felt. Esige knew it was a feeble hope, but she could not help clinging to it. "Give me back my son!"

"You think you can undermine me in my camp, among *my* people," Tolokan said coldly.

Esige's heart sank. Had she pushed too far?

"I don't know what witchy power you have over my son, but the only way to free him from your spell is to kill you. As for the boy Nemeku, I think Bigirsen might be interested to know where he is now."

Esige blinked. Everything slowed down. Her heartbeat steadied. She stopped struggling. Had Tolokan already sent word to Bigirsen? *Where is Nemeku?* she worried again.

Just as distressing was the realization that she had given Huoshai an heir, and if he fought back after her death, his father would still have an heir. Terribly cruel reality hammered down on her. Tolokan had no intention of kneeling to Dayan Khan. And he would make his defiance clearly known.

Three men. One on each arm. The third lingering nearby for reinforcement. Esige flipped the knife out and sliced the wrist of the first guard holding one arm. She swept her leg out to bring down the second guard. His grip didn't break, though, and the two of them tumbled to the ground. Esige tucked and twisted her arm around as they fell, forcing him to break his hold or break his arm. Dust kicked up and coated her mouth. The third grabbed Esige by the braid and yanked her back. For a moment, she cried out and kicked before remembering Unebolod's training.

Tolokan turned as if bored by the altercation and strode away with her son in his arms. Fury burned in Esige's stomach. *What will he do with Emeeltorson?* "What have you done with Huoshai?" she shouted after him.

Tolokan didn't acknowledge her question, but she had expected as much. Esige had been hoping someone nearby would worry about Huoshai and come to her aid. Nothing happened.

Desperate, Esige tucked her knife back in the belt, then reached back. Her finger scratched and dug at the guard's fingers wrapped around her braid. Using all the strength she could summon, Esige ripped the fingers away from her braid—and each other. The man screamed, releasing his grip as his fingers broke.

The first guard swung out with a sword. Esige tucked and rolled to avoid the blade. As she came out of the roll, she swiped out with her knife against the back of his heel, bringing him to the ground. Even as his knees hit the earth, she rammed her knife into his neck.

Tolokan was getting away with her son!

Esige spit dirt on the ground as the second guard had recovered, throwing his fist into Esige's jaw. She stumbled and hit the ground, stunned by the blow. Hot pain shot up through her head. He loomed over her. His grinning face blurred momentarily. His boot ground into her knife hand, pinning the weapon to the ground. They would knock her out or kill her now.

I'm out of time. Esige balled her free hand into a fist and threw a punch between his legs as hard as she could. He doubled over, and as he did, she spotted the sword on his hip. Esige yanked it free from his belt and rammed it through his stomach. *Twist to ensure the kill,* Unebolod had taught her. Esige jerked the hilt of the blade around.

A boot hammered against the side of her head, and Esige blacked out.

The wailing of her son pulled Esige out of her groggy slumber. She sat atop a horse, hands bound to the saddle and legs tied to the stirrups. A hundred armed Urainkhai warriors surrounded her, with Tolokan only two yards away holding Emeeltorson in his arm. Urainkhai banners fluttered behind him.

Esige blinked the dizziness away, focused on her surroundings. *How can I get my son back?*

"You spend your days telling lies around my camp," Tolokan called out, his deep voice riding across the sky like thunder. It took Esige a moment to realize he was not talking to her. "You tell people we must follow this false Khan or face his justice—a boy!—and leave your bride and baby alone as you undermine me. I thought I raised you to be smarter!"

Esige squinted against the dying sun to the west. Hundreds of mounted warriors sat like dark silhouettes against the blazing sunset. Banners fluttered behind one rider. Esige's heart sank. She recognized Huoshai's form anywhere. She had spent months committing it to memory.

"Leaving them to my will was your biggest mistake," Tolokan continued. "Stand down now, Huoshai, and I will forgive you and return your son to you."

Esige tugged at her bonds, attempting to edge her mount subtly closer to Tolokan. *I just need to get my son from him.*

"But the witch must die to break the spell she has over you!"

"Harm either of them and I will put an arrow through your eye!" Huoshai called from across the battlefield. His shadowy form shifted, and Esige recognized the movement as the draw of a bowstring. "Release them now and give your allegiance to the Great Khan, rightful heir of Genghis."

Not yet, Huoshai, Esige thought desperately as she edged closer to Tolokan. If he fired at his father, the baby would fall. Esige had to get close enough to catch him. And she had to find a way to break her bonds. Esige worked one finger at a time, trying to shift it out of the ropes. The warrior beside her grabbed Esige's head and yanked it back, placing a knife against her throat.

"Under the Eternal Blue Sky, by divine authority of the rightful heir of Genghis, the Great Khan, Dayan, and his queen, Mandukhai, the Urainkhai will serve the Great Khan!" Huoshai shouted. His voice rolled off the surrounding hills.

She closed her eyes, hating the sense of hopelessness that crept into her chest. *I cannot die like this.*

"I won't ask again," Huoshai said.

"Kill me and she dies anyway!" Tolokan shouted back as he noticed the knife on Esige's throat.

The arrow soared fast and powerful through the air. Tolokan ducked. The knifeman beside Esige moved so fast she was certain her life was over. Instinctively, she reached up to her throat before realizing he had not cut her open, but had instead cut her ropes. The warriors around her returned fire toward Huoshai's line. She rubbed at her wrists, then reached over to grab her son before Tolokan could realize she had been freed.

Tolokan yanked the baby back, startled by the sudden release of her bonds. He reached for her braid—why did men always see her braid as a sign of weakness?—and she wrapped her arm around his own, forcing him to lean back in the saddle as she threw a punch into his throat. Tolokan's grip released. Esige snatched Emeeltorson and glanced over her shoulder to see the guard who had freed her bonds bleeding to death with an arrow in his stomach on the ground.

Esige kicked her mount into action, racing toward Huoshai. She guided the mount in an uneven line, like a winding river, to avoid an arrow in her back.

A charge began on both sides of the battlefield as chaos broke out. Arrows flew across the sky as the two lines raced toward one another, with Esige yards ahead of the men she had escaped. The distance was not so much, but it seemed monstrously long as she raced to her husband and his men. An arrow narrowly missed her head as she shifted course. Esige dared a glance back again at the charging line of Tolokan's men. Fifteen yards separated her from them, but the gap grew as her mount picked up speed.

A shout arose from the distance behind her. "The khan is dead!" It carried everywhere, repeated all around the battlefield.

But neither line stopped. Huoshai's men continued to charge at Tolokan's. Only fifty yards separated the two lines now. *No. This cannot happen. The Urainkhai will destroy themselves in this fight!*

Esige took a deep breath and yanked her mount to a halt. She had to stop this.

The horses continued to charge. Arrows continued to zip across the sky—though none were directed at her any longer.

Esige dismounted, clutching the baby to her chest.

Forty yards between them.

The wind kicked up around her, making the deel swirl around her legs. Esige planted her feet and held up her hand as if she could halt the charge by sheer force of will.

Though her heart hammered in her chest more wildly than it had since her race with Huoshai months ago, Esige did her best to mimic Mandukhai's air of mystical authority.

The sun sent blazing rays across her body.

Please stop. They could trample her down easily. *Please stop.*

In the blink of an eye, both sides stopped within feet of Esige, staring at her like some strange, mythical thing. *This probably doesn't help the claim that I'm a witch*, she thought. *What would Mandukhai say now?*

"By the High Heavens," she began, throwing her voice out as loud and clear as she could. "We are *one* tribe. *One* nation. This division is exactly what men like Bigirsen want from us! Mandukhai Khatun and Dayan Khan will not allow further division. They seek to reunite the strength of the Mongol Nation. To become one, as Genghis taught."

She turned slowly, eyeing each of them. Huoshai remained close in his saddle, bow in hand, as if expecting someone to strike out at her.

"Your arrows are broken!" Esige continued. She paused, allowing the words to sink in. Her words implied they forgot the lessons of Genghis, that one arrow is weak and breakable, but many are strong. "Lord Huoshai understood this. And he has chosen the vision of Genghis! Will you do the same, or would you allow discord to continue breaking the arrows until there is nothing left but broken sticks?"

Huoshai dismounted and marched toward her, glaring at the opposing men as if daring them to act.

"You are not heathens," Esige said. "You are brave, powerful Urainkhai warriors, guardians of the borders. Men of the mountains. And you carry with you the flame of our once-great empire. Today, at this very moment, you choose what to do with that flame. Will you allow it to burn out? Or will you fan the flames until all the world can see our might?"

Huoshai slid his arm around Esige and she nearly melted back against him as her strength waned. He must have sensed her weakened state, because he slid the infant from her arms.

"Where is Nemeku?" she whispered.

"I think he is with my cousin's wife," Huoshai replied.

Esige relaxed a little more.

The two of them stood together in the center of a looming storm. She held her breath, waiting to see what would happen, praying these men would see reason and not draw swords.

Slowly, warriors dismounted outward like a great ripple.

All of them kneeled to Huoshai. Khan of the Urainkhai.

CHAPTER THIRTY-SIX

Shifting Alliances

ONGUD TERRITORY – SPRING 1471

As he camped near the edge of the Xilin River, Unebolod waited for the Ongud khan as he had two years ago. This man was stubborn, and Unebolod's patience for Korgiz was at an end. Just this morning, he had gathered up a thousand of his warriors, along with the lesser khans who followed him now. They mounted and rode toward the Ongud camp. Korgiz would either give up his stubborn endeavors, or Unebolod would exact the Khan's justice just as Huoshai had been sent to do among his own tribe.

The land in this part of the empire was remarkably flat and green, with only a few trees breaking up the horizon here or there. The river was long and winding, with several oxbows nearly folding back against each other in places. The grassland offered fertile ground for grazing.

A contingent of warriors and leaders rode toward the Ongud camp with Unebolod.

"I recognize those lines on your face, Unebolod," Albeq said.

Albeq had quickly followed Unebolod's banner. *What would Mandukhai think of my strength of support? Hopefully she will understand that I follow her. If these men follow me, they follow her as well.* Years ago, Unebolod and Albeq fought together against the Oirat and Uyghur forces. Albeq owed Unebolod a debt, and he had come to collect in the bitter winds of winter.

"These are Mandukhai Khatun's people," Albeq reminded him. "She will not thank you for attacking them."

"I will not attack," Unebolod snapped. He straightened his back. "I will give Korgiz the same choice all others were given. He can either accept his Khan, or he will face the Khan's justice." Mandukhai would understand that, surely.

Albeq sighed. "War is inevitable. You know that. Even if she unites the northern and eastern tribes, the southern tribes still follow Bigirsen. Perhaps more than ever before."

Unebolod felt an itch between his shoulders at this reminder. He could amass these tribes following him and attack Bigirsen head-on. If he raised the black banner against Bigirsen, he would have tens of thousands of men at his side. They could sweep across the south and force Bigirsen out of their lands for good. *Except he is deep in Ming territory, and I am not prepared for that battle*, he reminded himself.

They reached the edge of the Ongud camp, where Korgiz sat atop his mount with a thousand warriors at his back. The red banner of the Ongud fluttered in the air, lonely and defiant against a field of Unebolod's own multicolored banners. For the first time, he realized he had the support of all colors and none—just as Genghis had. This realization had him straightening in the saddle.

"I am uncertain you realize the position you have put me in, Lord Unebolod," Korgiz called to him. "Do you understand what is happening just at our backs?"

Unebolod glanced past Korgiz, which drew a snort of disgust from the Ongud khan.

"Not at my back, man, at all of our backs, to the south," Korgiz snapped, waving south as if they could see exactly what he meant.

Instead, Unebolod only saw flat grasslands.

Korgiz nodded. "You have not heard what Bigirsen has done these past months. What your Khatun has set ablaze among the Urainkhai. And now, with you in front of us and Bigirsen behind, I am trapped between two immovable objects."

Unebolod heard the stomp of impatient hooves behind him. The Lords riding with him all lined up at his sides. Bigirsen was not an immovable object. He was a stubborn old mule.

"While Mandukhai hosted a festival and catered to our base desires, Bigirsen conquered the Ordos and Chakhar, and forged a tenuous alliance with the Urainkhai," Korgiz explained. "Were we not in the north at the festival, he would have swept us up as well. Once he had the southern tribes—and stolen their leadership titles for himself—Bigirsen forced them all into Ming territory. It's only a matter of time before he turns around and comes after us. By then, he will have defeated the Ming and fulfilled Genghis Khan's vision. Our Khatun will not stand a chance against him then."

Had Bigirsen truly stolen titles from the tribe leaders? Could he do that without being Great Khan? *Korgiz must be toying with me. No man is foolish enough to think he can steal titles!* Unebolod's hatred of the Uyghur warlord bubbled up. A wave of heat washed over him.

"He is a starving dog, desperate for a bone," Unebolod said evenly. "She is a dragon with the wrath of a Khan. You would do well to remember that. She is a daughter of the Ongud."

"I will not follow you, Unebolod," Korgiz said.

"I'm not asking."

Korgiz nodded, satisfied. "Good."

"I'm not asking because it is not a choice, Lord Korgiz," Unebolod corrected, pleased with the way Korgiz's face reddened in anger. "Dayan Khan is your Great Khan. You will follow his chosen leaders or suffer the Khan's justice for your treason."

Korgiz fumed. "I gave no oath—"

"The Great Khan requires no oath to be your Great Khan. He simply is. He was chosen, installed upon sacred oaths to the High Heavens, blessed that same day by the Eternal Blue Sky." Unebolod had practiced this speech. The Lords riding with him had heard it as well. "I saw this for myself, when the clouds parted and the sun shone down on Him. If I am helpless to the will of the gods, who are you?"

Korgiz's jaw bobbed up and down as he attempted working out some form of argument. Unebolod edged his mount closer to Korgiz's horse, fingering the yellow ribbon still tied to his hilt.

"Do you see this yellow ribbon, Lord Korgiz?" Unebolod tilted his sword so Korgiz could clearly see it. Unebolod's hand wrapped around the hilt, prepared to draw. He could strike in a moment, then his men would launch into action—and hopefully, he would not end up with an arrow in the eye.

Korgiz's gaze locked on the yellow ribbon.

"I climbed the sacred mountain and prayed to Lord Tengri and the High Heavens," Unebolod explained, keeping his voice elevated enough for the men behind Korgiz to hear him as well. "I offered them a choice, an impossible choice for me, a mortal man, to make. Two ribbons, one fate. With one, I would do what you Lords wanted me to do, take the title and rule. With the other, I would fight for her and her chosen Khan, as my queen, until my dying breath. Which do you suppose the gods chose for me?"

Korgiz swallowed hard, still staring at the ribbon as if waiting for it to strike him. Unebolod understood that feeling. The ribbon often felt like a rope around his own neck.

"If I refuse, I will end as Tolokan khan did, won't I?" Korgiz said, his voice small.

Unebolod frowned. "Tolokan is dead?" The Urainkhai khan's death could not be a coincidence. Mandukhai had sent Huoshai to align his father—or kill him. Or perhaps Bigirsen had gotten to Tolokan first.

"I heard of his death just days ago," Korgiz said. "He followed Bigirsen and refused to follow Dayan Khan." Korgiz tore his gaze away from the ribbon and Unebolod saw the fear in the other man's eyes. "Huoshai khan rules over the Urainkhai now. He killed his father and put his head on a pole at the edge of their territory so that any who dare to challenge him will know better. She sent him, didn't she? His young wife was once in Mandukhai's care. It is obvious where his allegiance lies."

Unebolod felt a wave of relief at this news. Huoshai's father had refused the Khan, so Huoshai had carried out his promise. Unebolod no longer worried about Huoshai's allegiance to Mandukhai.

"We are not subjects of the Uyghur, Lord Korgiz," Unebolod said. "We are subjects of the Great Khan. All of us. And he will need us soon. The question is, will you follow your Khan and Khatun, knowing she has sent me on the same path she sent Huoshai upon?"

Korgiz grimaced and glanced south, as if he could see Bigirsen riding in at that moment. "I will do what I have always done." He met Unebolod's gaze, unflinching. "What is best for my people."

The Urainkhai abandonment had further enraged Bigirsen. It caused a division among the Ordos and Uyghur under Issama's command. Issama swept in on those men like a carrion bird over a carcass, capitalizing on their doubt to gain more followers. As those commanders and Lords realized Bigirsen intended to press forward with his plan to recklessly take the Ming on head-first—Issama met with the Lords and commanders individually.

By spring, only the *tumens* in the west, directly under Bigirsen's command, remained unfailingly loyal to Bigirsen. The rest either harbored doubts or agreed with Issama. And Issama possessed the one thing that would further his position among the tribal leaders.

The *sulde* of Genghis Khan himself.

Issama's spy had stolen it at the first opportunity, then fled Mount Burkhan Khaldun immediately and rode south to deliver it. For now, Issama hid it away. Later, when the right moment arrived, he would show the banner to the men, strip Bigirsen of his control, and rally the whole of the Mongol forces into Ming territory to complete what no one else had completed for centuries: rule over the entire empire.

Today, with the banner tucked safely away, Bigirsen hundreds of miles away with his own forces, and the support of a *tumen* of Uyghur, Chakhar, and Ordos warriors around his flanks, Issama felt the light of certain victory as surely as the spring sunshine on his back. His mount snorted, then pawed at the ground to dig up roots for grazing as Issama studied the landscape around his *tumen*.

Bigirsen believed he had stripped Issama of his power, then left him behind under watchful eyes. Instead, he had left behind a man capable of rallying the angry Mongols to his side.

"Are you certain this will work?" Nahai asked from his saddle beside Issama. He also fixed his gaze on the distance.

The corners of Issama's mouth curled into a vicious grin. "It has to. I've done the calculations. The arrogant Ming emperor thinks he has enough men. He thinks this Commander Wang Yue can hold us back. With Bigirsen preparing for a surprise attack at Zhongwei, the Ming forces are stretched too thin to protect the length of the border. Wang Yue only has about forty thousand men to cover over three hundred miles of border. He will concentrate most of them around the more populated areas."

Issama shifted in the saddle, squinting to the east where Lord Legusi and his warriors would draw out the local Ming soldiers. He could not see the Ordos warriors from here, but his scouts could send a message to him in a matter of seconds with arrows along the lines.

"When they draw out the Ming, we will close in around them on all sides and crush them," Issama said confidently.

Choosing the right path for the three different Mongol armies to travel without notice had been a particular challenge when so much of the Ordos basin comprised smooth plateaus and jagged rocky ledges feeding into waterways. Ten thousand men against perhaps half as many Ming. This should be easy. The idea was to draw out the Ming troops with a properly timed raid. Issama knew what he was doing. This Ming camp was a training ground. They would poorly prepare the troops here compared to thousands of mounted Mongols.

A signal arrow thumped against the ground fifty yards in front of Issama's men. It was time. He grinned and kicked his mount into action. The thunder of thousands of hooves against the earth shook the very ground as they crossed and echoed across the basin. Dust kicked up in a great cloud at their back.

By the time Issama's men had reached the Ming camp, the Ordos warriors had already set everything aflame. Tents burned bright and high. Horses screeched and darted without riders, wild-eyed, right into the thundering approach of Mongol warriors. Ming warriors raised halberds, swords, shields. But the footmen were no match for the Mongols, who formed a ring around the camp. Issama's Uyghur warriors closed in from the west. Guden's Chakhar warriors from the east. Each of them swung around to meet in the south as the Ordos warriors continued forward from the north.

The strategy was similar to men on a hunt. Form a circle, close in, and pick off everything trapped within. It could hardly be called a great battle. Ming cavalry had mounted, but with the ring of Mongols kicking up dust and raining arrows in from all directions, the cavalry had only one option. Head straight south to punch a hole through the roiling Mongol mass. Issama expected this strategy. It was the same reason he had guarded the southern flank instead of heading the northern charge. The Ming would attempt fleeing, creating a hole in the line so that the footmen could escape—a feeble effort since they could not outrun the superior riding skills of the Mongols. There would be no survivors.

As expected, the calvary formed ranks with lances and bows, then charged at the southern edge of the Mongol ring. Issama bared his teeth and raised his bow with the signal arrow. He did not have enough lancers himself, but the element of surprise was his friend. The calvary closed the gap between the lines. Mongol arrows knocked Ming riders from their horses as they drew near. Riderless horses ran wild in all directions, enhancing the chaos and trampling foot soldiers. Still, Issama held the arrow steady on the bowstring, not pulling it back yet. Timing was critical.

Nearly a thousand mounted Ming calvary drew tighter together. Their bowmen fired at the endlessly churning mass of Mongol horsemen, but only unseated a few dozen. Mongol movements were expert in their efficiency, creating a storm of moving targets. It forced the Ming to fire at random and pray the arrows would strike someone. Mongols, however, did not have the same challenge.

The thousand Ming cavalry quickly dwindled as the ranks rode closer. At their backs, the screams of footmen's deaths broke through the thunder of thousands of endlessly moving hooves. Flags of various colors fluttered all around the Mongol ring, signaling maneuvers at rapid speed, and warriors changed course in seconds, as directed.

The Mongol bowmen had picked apart the calvary.

Fifty yards. Issama raised his bow and pulled back the string tight. Fewer than three hundred calvary remained.

Twenty yards. He released the bowstring.

His signal arched high into the sky.

The forward lines of Mongols broke apart around the edges of the calvary. Behind them, a hundred of Issama's men raised their lances before the Ming reined back. The horses crashed into each other. Lances broke. Men flew from saddles.

Then the Mongols closed around the calvary and picked off the remaining riders. Issama fired arrows in rapid succession, easily hitting targets up close. One of the Ming riders knocked the bow from Issama's grasp. It flew across the battlefield, trampled into the earth by hooves.

Issama yanked out his sword and ducked as a Ming soldier took a swing at him. Issama thrust his sword up across the man's neck, just under the helmet. Blood sprayed from his throat as he slid from the saddle. Issama did not stop even as the blood hit his face. Instead, he spun his mount and charged the next rider.

In a matter of minutes, they had crushed the Ming calvary beneath the force of the Mongols. Issama's armor was coated with slick blood, and the scent of death mingled with the burning of the tents in the camp. Whoops of victory resounded from all directions, drawing a smile across Issama's face. His chest swelled with pride. He had done it. And now, his men would be bolstered by this crushing victory, and it would lift their spirits as they rode deeper into Ming territory.

Issama reined in near the edge of the Ming camp, heedless of the mountain of bodies all around. Before him, the fires died down.

Lord Legusi rode up beside Issama, grinning through his own layers of blood. They wrapped a bandage around a deep cut in his arm, but that did not hinder Legusi's excitement. "This is a glorious victory, Issama," Legusi said. "There were more men here than we expected."

"How many?" Issama asked, staring at the flames.

"Fifteen thousand maybe?" Legusi said. "Reinforcements likely meant to drive us out of the Ordos basin. That's nearly half of what you estimated their full force to be for the full length of the wall."

"Did it seem too easy to you?" Issama asked, gazing at the horizon.

"Maybe. Isn't that a good thing?" Legusi sagged a little, gazing toward the west. "Do you think my sister is safe?"

Issama did not answer. There was no way to know what Bigirsen would do with Legusi's sister. He used her as a bargaining chip against the Ordos Lord. *That will backfire on him as well*, Issama thought.

He turned his mount and called out so all commanders nearby could hear him. "Take only what you can carry. Burn the rest."

He would leave nothing behind for the Ming to salvage. All they would find in this place would be a heap of ash and bones to mark their passing. Perhaps it was a good thing that this battle had been easy, but something about it did not settle well with Issama. His warriors had won, but the resistance had been weak.

And Commander Wang Yue was not here. Where had he gone? Issama needed answers.

This victory meant Issama could push even deeper into Ming territory. Hopefully, Wang Yue was not waiting for him. There must have been a trap waiting somewhere. With any luck, Issama would meet Bigirsen on the other side of Yinchuan, holding the black *sulde* of Genghis Khan.

And then nothing would stop him again.

CHAPTER THIRTY-SEVEN

Trappings of War

Issama pressed his knuckles against the tabletop in Legusi's command tent. Scouts could not pinpoint the exact number of men the Ming had moving along the borders, but they had assessed where the greatest concentration of them were stationed. Now, as Issama waited for word from Bigirsen's messengers, he moved the pieces around on the map, then analyzed the strategy.

Most of the Ming hid along the Great Wall, only sending out small detachments to push the Mongols back. It was never enough. Issama crept south through the Ordos basin like a great wheel.

Guden huffed as Issama pursed his lips and gazed at the Chakhar forces marked on the map, then moved one piece further east. Issama ignored him. Bigirsen only kept Issama in this position because of his battle strategy. Once they beat the Ming, Bigirsen no doubt intended to turn Issama's brilliance against Unebolod to finally crush his strength—something Bigirsen had never accomplished on his own. *I live as long as I'm useful.*

Once more, Guden huffed.

Issama grimaced and stood upright. "Do you have something to say, Lord Guden?"

Guden scowled. "I find it convenient that the bulk of *my* forces are being moved toward the most heavily concentrated section of the wall."

Issama cocked his head. Why would Guden find that convenient? "Do you doubt my trust in you?"

The two glared at one another. Guden was nearly twice Issama's age and often thought himself clever when, in fact, his strategies were hazardous. How had the Chakhar thrived with him as their leader?

Guden opened his mouth at last, but before he could utter a word, Lord Legusi stormed in, waving a message in his hand. For one so young, he was easily irritable.

"Bigirsen has taken Zhongwei and heads north toward Wuzhong," Legusi proclaimed, slapping the message down on the table. A few of the Uyghur force markers with Bigirsen bounced and toppled. "We are running out of time, Issama. He still has my sister."

Yes, little Orghana. The girl was Legusi's only sister, and only six. Bigirsen used her as a bargaining chip against Legusi. Issama had needed to be careful when recruiting Legusi's trust. He worried over his little sister far too much. But Legusi had witnessed Issama's brilliant strategies in battle repeatedly. The moment Legusi began singing Issama's praises, Issama pounced. In exchange for Legusi's allegiance, Issama promised to use his battle prowess against Bigirsen to get back little Orghana—and kill Bigirsen. Legusi had quickly agreed.

Guden glanced at the map and smirked. Issama wanted to slap the smirk off Guden's face. Bigirsen's victory meant changing Issama's strategy with the Chakhar. *It seems Guden will get what he wants after all.* Issama snatched the Chakhar marker he had just moved east and shifted it west—away from the heavily concentrated section of the wall.

"No, Lord Legusi, we are right on schedule," Issama replied. "We will move toward Yinchuan to greet him. But we need to keep the families close." He dropped his gaze back to the map.

The Great Wall proved a burden. Issama would have to focus on taking one fort to the west now so that the Ming would not surprise his forces as he prepared to face off against Bigirsen. Yinchuan would be the most ideal location, but it was too close to Wuzhong. Bigirsen would be on top of them before Issama could regroup after fighting the Ming.

He stabbed a finger at the map. "Here. The Red Lake. The families can camp there and will still be within riding distance, but far enough back to avoid the Ming and Bigirsen's forces."

Before anyone could argue, Issama quickly moved markers around on the map: Bigirsen's forces along the western border from Zhongwei, tracking up toward Wuzhong; the families along the red salt lake; the Chakhar covering the eastern flank; the Ordos covering the western flank; and Issama's meager supply of Uyghur bringing up the center. All of them surrounded Yinchuan. Once Bigirsen took the city, they would trap him with the deadly currents of the Huang Ho River at his back. They would crush him easily as long as he didn't see through their plans.

"This is it, my Lords," Issama announced, grinning at the two tribe leaders. "This summer we will meet up with Bigirsen's forces and crush him at last. Then we can turn our attention to Mandukhai in the north."

These Lords who had been sent to spy on Issama were now his greatest assets in taking down Bigirsen. *He delivered them right into my hands. The old fool.*

"Yes," Guden said, staring at the map and stroking his beard. "I am curious to see this boy Khan for myself."

Issama dared a sideways glance at Guden. Could he trust the Chakhar khan once Bigirsen was dead? The boy was of Chakhar blood and Borjigin bone. Guden could easily turn against Issama in favor of Mandukhai and Dayan Khan. Especially if it benefited him.

I will have to put someone in a position to eliminate Guden at the slightest sign of betrayal, Issama decided. But first, he would appeal to Guden's practical side. Issama married Siker, who was the mother of this boy Khan. That had to be worth something.

Men hustled around the remains of the camp with purpose. Everyone had a job to do, and Mandukhai had to trust they would carry out their part. Whatever happened after this day would change the course of history—whether she lived to see it or died on the battlefield. Spring was in full swing, and scouts reported the passes through the Khangai Mountains were clear for crossing.

Mandukhai stood outside her ger, breathing the cool spring air and watching the bustle of activity as inside the ger, Tuya fitted and dressed Dayan Khan for the road ahead. Mandukhai's destiny hung on the tip of an arrow. A bad breeze could blow her in the wrong direction. A poor shot could destroy everything.

Three days ago, Mandukhai had ordered the families to pack up camp and head west—into Oirat territory. She sent only infantry to guard the families and supplies. The bulk of her forces remained with her for the invasion. By sending the families ahead, it gave them time to start the trek. The warriors would catch up and even pass the families in a matter of time, but it meant they would have families nearby to return to once the battle was won … or lost. It also allowed Mandukhai to establish her own camp within Oirat territory should she win. If she lost, the Oirat would swallow those families.

She heard the whispers of the men around her. They respected her decision to send the families and supplies ahead. Some even sounded surprised that *she*—a woman—could think of such a strategy. This move showed her warriors that Mandukhai had no intention of launching raids. The movement of the entire camp and the strategy of guarding the supplies and families showed them she meant to conquer. It was an old tactic that had not been used much in recent years.

Boke stood sentry outside her door, as he always did. Today, Mandukhai could sense the excitement and fear rolling off of him. She wished she could share his sentiments, but her nerves were a wreck. The men were used to battle. She was not.

"Are your men ready to protect their Khan?" Mandukhai asked for what must have been the hundredth time.

"To the death, my Khatun," Boke answered.

"And you have organized them appropriately?" she asked, knowing she did not need to ask this question. Boke was young, but skilled with organization.

"Yes, I will command the men around Dayan Khan," Boke confirmed, watching the movements of the men near her ger. "Torgus will command the men surrounding you."

"Then we are in excellent hands." Mandukhai placed a hand on his shoulder before turning to her door and stepping inside.

She had commanded a few servants to remain with the ger, take it down when the army rode out, and bring it to the rest of the tribe. Mandukhai feared sleeping in the open with Dayan. While his illness seemed mostly gone, he occasionally still fell into a fit of wheezing that concerned her. One night in the cold air could undo all of her hard work. But he was Great Khan. The men would need to follow him, to see him alongside her if they were to have any chance of showing their unified strength.

On this campaign, Mandukhai would have no change of clothes with her, nothing to freshen up her face. She would live and breathe the same as her men. She would have to. Divine right had gathered men at her back, but to hold them, she would have to show her strength.

Mandukhai closed her door behind her, gazing at the golden eyes of Dayan staring at her from beneath the protective helmet too big for his head, despite the custom make. Tuya fussed with the helmet to get it to remain steady and not fall over his eyes.

"Pad the inside with felt to hold it, Tuya," Mandukhai suggested as she turned to her own armor.

The silk deel Mandukhai wore was thick, designed to act as a final protective barrier to any arrows that might penetrate her armor. She knew that in the summer heat she would loath these layers, but they were necessary for her protection. Mandukhai lifted the skirted layer of lamellar armor. The craftsmen had created this for her over the winter, and the material was lighter than she had expected. The skirt comprised small, hardened, bleached leather rectangles stitched tightly together with thick cords of golden silk and backed by a layer of silk as an extra barrier. Mandukhai wrapped the skirt around her waist and buckled it in place. It hung perfectly to the tops of her boots and would provide ample cover over her legs.

The armor she wore over her chest was much like a deel, but without sleeves. Mandukhai slipped her arms through the openings, marveling at how flexible the material was. This top layer had also been custom-crafted for Mandukhai with the same lamellar style, but instead of leather, the top layer comprised plates of iron in pockets of the leather and laced together with the same thick golden silk. The straps on the side of the armor buckled together securely. Mandukhai fastened them herself, then unfastened them as swiftly as she could, just to test how quickly it could be removed.

Over her chest, a decorative strip of blue-dyed iron curved perfectly over her form. And across the metal, a golden dragon that matched her saddle and bow. Mandukhai twisted her body around, pretending to draw an arrow back with nothing but air. The metal plate shifted with her, flexing around her body and making the dragon come to life.

Satisfied, Mandukhai picked up the belt and fastened it in place. A series of metal disks housed multicolored stones—a representation of the multicolored horse and banner, the craftsman had explained. The belt had a clip for the sword loop. It would clasp the sword in place without making it difficult to draw.

Mandukhai unfastened her *boqta*, gathered the jewels in her hands, and lifted the crown off her head, setting it in the waiting box that would travel away from her. Such a crown was suitable for the court, but it would do her no good in battle. The symbolism of removing her crown was not lost on Mandukhai. It was all that separated her from the men.

If I fail in this, or die, the Oirat will rip Dayan apart. Everything I have sacrificed will be for nothing. She took a measured breath to steady her nerves.

The next piece was a brilliant gold and blue neck covering that draped around her neck and shoulders and down her arms. Mandukhai fumbled with the buckles for this lamellar creation, only able to use one hand on each to secure the armguards in place. She rolled her shoulders, moved her arms in all directions, and was once more satisfied with the range of motion.

Mandukhai shook her hair loose from the knot it usually remained in beneath the *boqta*, then began pulling it back into a weave of intricate braids. Tuya took over from there, creating a thick weave of braids that would keep her hair from her face, yet elaborate enough to show her rank. Tuya tied off the ends of the braids and tethered them together with threads of golden silk that matched the gold of Mandukhai's armor.

Mandukhai stared at the last piece of her armor—the helmet—for several long minutes as she slid the forearm guards into place.

The helmet shined in the light. The silver piece rose nearly a foot to a point where long streams of white horsehair hung down. The same golden dragons danced around the lip, and a layer of silver chain-mail was fastened with even smaller rings of gold. This protective layer would drape down her head and cover her neck, leaving her face the only visible target. Mandukhai traced a finger along the dragons, remembering the first time she had seen that dragon on the saddle and bow together. Unebolod had meant it as a symbol of her power, or so he had said. *A queen should put something like that on display.* Those had been his words.

And here I am, doing exactly that, Mandukhai thought.

She lifted the helmet, tucking it under her arm as she turned to Dayan.

The boy's armor covered his entire body, leaving no easy targets for a stray arrow. The pieces had to be created just for him, and the craftsmen had complained about how difficult it was to create something so small. Dayan certainly was small for his age. Nemeku was taller and broader, and nearly two years younger.

Thinking of Nemeku created another ache in Mandukhai's heart. Esige and Huoshai had insisted on taking the boy with them, raising him as their own son. Mandukhai hated giving the boy up, but she had little choice. Nemeku belonged with Esige. Hopefully, Bigirsen would not learn that his son was so close to him now.

Dayan waddled toward Mandukhai, moving awkwardly in his too-big armor. When he tipped his head back to look at her, the helmet slipped a little and covered one of his eyes. Mandukhai smiled at him and adjusted it.

"Our future begins today, Dayan Khan," she whispered. "The Mongols think we are weak. We need to put on our bravest faces and show them just how wrong they are. Stay close to me, Dayan. Stay close to Boke."

Dayan said nothing. Mandukhai could only hope he understood as she opened the door.

Dayan stepped out first, sticking close to Boke as Mandukhai had instructed.

Dozens of men waited outside for the Khatun and Khan to emerge. Mandukhai remained in the doorway, a shadow illuminated by the outside light. She slipped her helmet on, adjusted the chain-mail, fastened the strap, then reached for her quiver and bow where all the men could see her.

Dayan could have picked up the bow and quiver and strapped them on as a symbolic gesture. It would have shown the army that he meant to lead them. But Mandukhai knew she needed to command respect. It had to be her to retrieve the weapons of war. Until Dayan was old enough to make these decisions for himself, Mandukhai would be their leader.

A ripple of murmurs outside satisfied Mandukhai as she strapped on the quiver, then marched toward the door. Another box of arrows would already wait on her horse.

When Mandukhai had entered the ger earlier, the men would have seen her as a woman and a queen. Now, Mandukhai emerged dressed as any of the men prepared for war. The shock and awe on their faces pleased Mandukhai. Today, she showed the men who she was. She wore all the trappings of war. If she won this battle against the Oirat, Mandukhai would become more powerful than Toregene, Khutulun, and every other queen and female warrior before her.

Mandukhai guided Dayan to a horse that currently lay on the ground. One of Dayan's guards held the mount's bit to keep it in place. She had enlisted numerous skilled craftsmen over the winter months to design and build a saddle that would protect the young Khan and keep him on his horse. The saddle was a unique construction, designed to keep him in the saddle at all costs. The contraption resembled a box more than a saddle, made from thick, hardened leather woven together, just like their armor, over the horse's back and down the sides. Dayan could not ride with her forever. For this campaign, he would have to ride alone. The mare was well-trained, though, and she would follow where Boke's men guided her without Dayan needing to direct the horse.

Mandukhai offered her hand to assist Dayan as he climbed on, straddling the horse's back.

As Mandukhai fastened the leather wraps around Dayan's leg, Boke worked on the other side, securing Dayan in place while still giving him the ability to guide the horse in an emergency. The back of the saddle rose nearly all the way up Dayan's back, and a belt fastened around his waist to the saddle. The front of the saddle rose past his waist with a long pommel he could use to keep his balance. On either side of the saddle, an iron rod attached to a chain fastened above the waist. The entire contraption would keep him from falling out of the saddle. But if his horse fell, nothing could save him. Mandukhai prayed that would not be an issue.

Once Dayan was secured in place, Mandukhai mounted Dust. They had adorned her own white stallion with armor, just as Dayan's horse had been. The woven armor would protect the horse's entire body, leaving only the legs exposed. Dust's armor matched Mandukhai's own. A head guard had been placed over his face, leaving his eyes and mouth exposed but protecting him everywhere else. Mandukhai had braided Dust's mane and wove golden silk ribbons through the braids so that the hair would not get caught in the armor.

More men gathered around the Khan and Khatun since she had emerged from her ger. Mandukhai turned Dust to face them, gazing out at the awed and anxious faces.

"Warriors of the Mongol Nation," Mandukhai said, raising her voice high for all to hear. "The Oirat have challenged our right to rule for too long. Saddle up. Today, we ride out to show them who they serve. In the name of Dayan Khan!"

Cheers erupted and bows raised in the air. In minutes, the men had scattered and mounted, and Mandukhai's tiny army rode west with the Khan and Khatun in the center of the line.

CHAPTER THIRTY-EIGHT

Horse Sickness

Mandukhai tipped her head back, her helmet shifting slightly at the movement, and she basked in the warmth of the late-spring sunshine from her saddle with Dayan at her side. Her warriors had passed the caravan of families and supplies a week ago after they slipped through the pass in the Khangai Mountains and deeper into Oirat territory. Togochi's warriors would join them from the pass about twenty miles to the north, allowing Mandukhai to take the Oirat by surprise.

She had almost forgotten how green the lands here were, how fertile the grass, and so lush! It was no wonder this expanse of land made for fantastic herding. She had only been five when her tribe abandoned the Oirat territory and moved south, to their old homeland. Now, the Ongud were so far from here—months of travel around the Gobi.

"Here they come," General Alayitung said, shifting in his saddle beside her. "Are you sure you are ready for this, Mandukhai Khatun?"

Mandukhai dropped her face from the sunlight and glared at Alayitung. He was a good man and a traditional Borjigin loyalist. Manduul had trusted Alayitung as Vice Chancellor near the end of his life. Mandukhai had to trust that judgment. Togochi had sworn by Alayitung's dedication to the empire.

Alayitung looked away, uncomfortable with her scrutiny. "I don't mean to question you. I only mean to advise and protect, as promised."

"I trust Seguse," she said, watching the approaching line of Oirat horsemen. A thousand. Not nearly as many as she had, but still a formidable force without Togochi's knowledgeable hand to guide her men. He would join her later.

Last night, Mandukhai had received a message from Seguse. A year ago, she had sent Seguse, her trusted Uyghur spy, into Oirat territory to infiltrate the Oirat tribes. He had sent her nothing for so long she worried he had been discovered and killed. *The High Heavens smile upon my objective to send him exactly when I needed this*, she thought.

According to Seguse, General Toghon, commander of the Oirat in the east, nearest the border, requested to negotiate peacefully. Mandukhai had no reason to doubt Seguse. He would not have set up this meeting had he doubted Toghon's intentions.

Seguse reported that Paisahan khan's attack on Mongke Bulag and subsequent defeat, his failure to capture the queen, had been met with scrutiny among the Oirat subtribes. This forced Paisahan to retreat deeper into the Zavkhan River Valley to lick his wounds. It also made those lesser khans question Paisahan's own goals.

"Seguse is Uyghur," Alayitung said, then spit at the ground and glared at the horizon.

Uyghur had quickly become synonymous with Bigirsen, and none of the Mongols following her were keen on Bigirsen.

"He has more reasons to hate Bigirsen than you do, Alayitung," Mandukhai said.

Movement to her left drew Mandukhai's attention to Dayan. So far, the boy had stayed in his saddle, but for this meeting, she had removed all but the belt around his waist to give him more of an appearance of strength. It would not do for Toghon to see Dayan Khan as weak. The saddle was still too tall in the front and too high in the back to be normal, but she could do nothing about that without risking Dayan's safety.

The Oirat drew closer, and flashes of her captivity plagued her. Mandukhai had to resist the urge to rub at her wrists—long since healed but still bearing scars of the event. Her stomach twisted in sickening knots. Boke's men formed a protective arc around Mandukhai, Dayan, and her commanders. The rest of her army waited two hundred yards back—far enough not to seem threatening, but close enough to fire a shot, should the need arise. *Let us hope that never happens*, she thought as she spotted Seguse.

The Uyghur rode beside a young Oirat man decked out in his own battle gear. The horsehair streaming from his helmet marked him out as the general. *Toghon. He is younger than I expected,* Mandukhai realized.

Toghon's men studied Mandukhai's honor guard, but Toghon himself gazed past them at the wings of Borjigin warriors. It comprised the full force of her army, except for those protecting the families, but she would never admit that to Toghon. As far as he knew, this was just her honor guard and the bulk of her forces were not present.

"General Toghon," Mandukhai said, shattering the tense silence. "I was led to believe you come to broker peace with us."

Toghon's gaze snapped to Mandukhai, studying her. Mandukhai noticed how the corner of his mouth tipped up slightly. He assumed her weak, like most men. He would learn, like all men.

"I am here to negotiate," Toghon said, "on behalf of those of us who do not follow Paisahan khan."

Mandukhai raised her chin slightly and stared down at him as Dust bobbed his head. "We cannot negotiate."

Toghon's lips thinned, and his broad shoulders sloped dangerously. It reminded Mandukhai of Manduul's shoulders when he was in a violent mood. She had not backed down from Manduul when alone. She would not back down from Toghon with an army at her back.

"To negotiate would be to admit that your Khan is your equal, and that you are not subject to the laws and rule of the Great Khan," Mandukhai said, using the smoothest voice she could to make it clear she meant business but had no intention of starting an attack. "Dayan Khan does not negotiate for peace with those who are subjects under his divine rule. We have agreed to this meeting so that you can give him your binding oath, as you would any other Great Khan."

Toghon's lips parted ever so slightly as his face lifted into shock. The men around him shifted uncomfortably but said nothing. All eyes locked on Dayan Khan—a boy in all the trappings of manhood who eyed them like a curious wolf cub. Mandukhai could see the calculation in Toghon's eyes, churning like mare's milk is churned into *airag*. He couldn't be but five years older than she was. Did he remember what had happened to Esen when he attempted seizing control? How Esen's lust for power over Borjigin supremacy had shattered the empire and subjugated the Oirat under men like Bigirsen?

Toghon licked his lips before speaking, as if suddenly parched. "He is a boy—"

"He is your Khan," Mandukhai corrected.

"My lady Khatun," Toghon said, choosing his words with careful deliberation. "Dayan Khan's grandmother was a woman of the Oirat, as was your mother. He comes from the bone of Genghis and the blood of Oirat royalty. We do not question his right, only his ability."

Mandukhai's expression darkened. Dust snorted as if sensing her rising anger. "Was Genghis not a boy when he first showed his power?"

Toghon calculated her response, then snorted and chuckled. "Seguse was right about you."

Mandukhai glanced at Seguse, but the man gave nothing away.

Toghon dismounted. Her guards tensed, bows ready, but Mandukhai held up a hand to stop them from drawing. She would not have Toghon's acceptance of Dayan Khan appear to happen under duress. He glared at the guards for so long she wondered if he would change his mind. Toghon's own men tensed, ready to draw their own weapons. He held up a fist as he eyed Mandukhai and Dayan. She held her breath, waiting to see what would happen. At last, he raised a finger and spun it around.

"We came to broker peace," Toghon told Mandukhai as his men dismounted with a creak of saddle leather. "As children of the Oirat, your right to rule has no challenge here."

Toghon sank to a knee, and his men did as well. "We give our oaths of our own free will to follow the Khan and Khatun with salt, gers, horses, and blood as we should have done long ago."

Mandukhai's heart swelled with pride, but they did not win the battle. More Oirat remained in opposition to their Khan, and she would have to face them all.

The Borjigin families joined the Oirat camp at Mandukhai's command. By mixing with the locals, Mandukhai hoped Paisahan would not notice how far she had come into his territory. The tension between the two tribes was thicker than blood. Only a year ago, the Oirat had attacked Mongke Bulag, where the Borjigin had lived. They could not easily set aside such bad blood. Alayitung had clearly been uncomfortable leaving his family behind among the Oirat while he rode off at Dayan Khan's side. Yet, he had not protested either. Instead, he rode in sullen silence.

Seguse had gone west with Toghon and his men, but not before Toghon had lamented how few men Mandukhai had brought with her. Perhaps he had regretted bending to her will so quickly. Before he left, she had firmly reminded him that his oath to the Great Khan was superior to any other. That included Paisahan.

Toghon's task was simple. Warn the Oirat khan that she was coming. Misconstrue her numbers on the low end to give Paisahan false confidence. She could not afford to clash with the full force of the Oirat in one epic battle. He had to believe she was weak, but not so weak he could walk right over her.

On the battlefield, Togochi's warriors would sweep in. But if Paisahan pressed his full forces against her, she would be vastly outnumbered, even with Togochi's men. She hoped that Paisahan would see her as weak enough to send smaller *mingghans* at her instead of full *tumens*.

Mandukhai had to choose her ground and lure out smaller chunks of Paisahan's forces until he had nothing left to defend himself with. She would use the strategy wolves used to lure out a stallion from the herd. When wolves attacked a herd of horses, the foals would be pressed into the middle of a ring of mares. The mares would kick and kill the wolves, never breaking their circle. The stallion, however, had little to do with the fight—much like Paisahan khan. The wolves would lure the stallion away with a false sense of confidence. Then, when the stallion was isolated, the wolves would close in for the kill.

Mandukhai was the Queen of the Wolves now. Paisahan was a stallion that would need to be isolated. And by doing so, she would also further isolate the power Bigirsen had over the Mongols.

Dayan sneezed and swayed in his saddle beside Mandukhai. She cast a worried glance at him. This sneezing was new and had become a regular occurrence for him. By the end of the day, his eyes would be red and swollen, and he would itch at them endlessly. Each night, Mandukhai worried about what was happening to him, but each morning he would be bright and clear-eyed once more.

Alayitung mumbled under his breath. "He is ill, Mandukhai Khatun. We need to find someone to heal him, or he could die."

"The Khan is fine, General," Mandukhai said with a level of calm she certainly did not feel. If the men knew she worried the same thing, she could lose her tenuous grasp over the Nation.

Dayan scrubbed his sleeve over his nose, then rubbed a fist into his eyes. *Lord Tengri help us all*, Mandukhai prayed. *Genghis would not have chosen him if he would die. I must have faith.* But it was also Mandukhai's job to care for Dayan. Getei had been sure to point out that Dayan's fate would be tethered to her attentive care. Genghis had put this boy's fate in her hands. She could not fail. She would not fail.

Alayitung's glance at Dayan made it clear he did not believe her. Nor should he. But she could not show her own uncertainty.

Dayan sneezed three more times in rapid order. Mandukhai didn't flinch, but she knew they had to stop riding. She needed to consult with Getei. Thankfully, the man was never far from her. Mandukhai called the men to a halt for rest—not that any of them needed it; they all knew it was for the little Khan—and she helped Dayan off his horse.

As if knowing she would summon him, Getei appeared beside the two of them. He sized up Dayan's condition. The red eyes were puffier than normal at this time of day. The symptoms were getting worse.

Mandukhai commanded her guards to keep the men back so she could consult with Getei privately. Boke and his men dutifully formed a ring and pressed outward to give the three of them space.

Getei kneeled in front of Dayan, inspecting his eyes and looking up his nose. The boy sniffled and squinted. Mandukhai could tell he fought off another urge to rub at his eyes.

"It's the horse," Getei said, keeping his voice low enough so only she could hear.

"What?" Mandukhai's heart plummeted into the pit of her stomach. The horse made Dayan sick? "I don't understand."

"The condition is rare, but it happens from time to time," Getei explained. "Horse sickness."

"There must be something we can do!" A Khan who could not ride would not inspire confidence in his men.

Getei stroked his chin as he rose. "Perhaps. It depends on how far along the sickness has come. There is an herbal mix I learned from a Ming healer years ago. If we can get the herbs, we can administer them, but if this is too far advanced, it will not help him. Riding could kill him."

The world tilted beneath Mandukhai's feet. She wrapped her arm around Dayan's shoulders as if she could shelter him from this fate. *No. This cannot happen. Not so deep in Oirat territory. Not when my plans are in action.*

"Bring that mix to Dayan Khan, Getei," Mandukhai commanded, hearing how her voice pitched higher, frantic. She took a deep breath. "Above all else, find me that remedy."

Getei nodded and hustled away. What if he couldn't find it in time? What if Dayan's sickness was too far along and he died? Mandukhai smoothed her hands over her armor and cleared her mind, focusing on centering herself. After a few moments of careful breaths, she looked down at Dayan.

"You are Khan," she said, unable to decide this for herself and knowing it was unfair to ask an eight-year-old boy. But this was his fate as much as her own. "Can you ride?"

Perhaps it was some innate ability to sense her fears, or perhaps he simply did not understand how dire his situation was, but Dayan nodded. She wanted to refuse, to force the men to make camp, but it was too early in the day, and they needed to reach their destination before Paisahan's men. She needed to set her trap.

"Mount up!" she called out.

Boke brought Dayan's horse to the boy and hoisted him into the saddle. Dayan sat straight, blinking furiously but not touching his face. Still, he sniffled far too much for Mandukhai's comfort as she swung into her own saddle.

High Heavens, protect your precious son, she prayed as she guided the wings of horsemen across the valley floor.

Paisahan sent five thousand Oirat to attack Mandukhai's meager camp of only a thousand. As Alayitung had predicted, the Oirat rode straight at her camp in wing formation and curled around the edges.

But Mandukhai's men waited, ready. The bulk of her forces hid just on the other side of the rocky cliffs surrounding her camp. Mandukhai had ordered caltrops placed around the perimeter of the camp to slow the Oirat charge. As they closed around the camp, Mandukhai and the thousand men she kept in the camp rushed into action, racing to horses and riding toward a gap in the caltrops to pass safely through without harm. It gave the impression of fleeing as the Oirat fell into the trap.

Mandukhai quickly checked Dayan's saddle straps before leaping onto Dust's back. The guards closed in around them.

"Retreat through the lines!" Mandukhai hollered to her men. The commanders understood what the order truly meant.

Oirat raced forward, closing in around the camp as she had expected. Half of her camp warriors broke rode through the gap left for safe passage as the other half turned to cover their supposed retreat. The moment the Oirat entered the trap, her hiding warriors raced down the cliff and closed around the Oirat like the jaws of a wolf. Horses squealed behind her as they stumbled over the caltrops. Oirat screamed in agony or shouted orders to turn back.

Dust huffed out breaths as he raced out across the Zavkhan valley floor. Mandukhai held her bow and guided the horse with her knees, just as Unebolod had taught her. A quiver of a hundred arrows bounced at her leg. Heat pressed against the leather and iron armor, baking her alive. But the chase was exhilarating.

Dayan rode beside Mandukhai, securely locked in his saddle. Still, he pressed himself into the back of the saddle and held on to the front bars for dear life. His horse was well-trained to follow where Boke led. Mandukhai had directed trainers to work with the horse all winter and spring to prepare for this fight. Still, she wished she could just tie the reins to Dust so she did not have to worry constantly about Dayan and his little bouncing head.

As the last of Mandukhai's *mingghan* left the caltrop ring, they dropped more of the iron spikes on the ground to close the loop for any Oirat who infiltrated the camp. The spikes sealed them in for now. As they had planned, her *mingghan* turned like a great swirling mass, rounding back on the Oirat.

By this time, the men Alayitung commanded on the left wing circled around toward the western side of camp. The Oirat who had avoided the caltrop trap had turned back only to meet the full force of Alayitung's two thousand bowmen. Mandukhai could only watch for a moment before the dust from the battle and mass of heads and horses obscured her line of sight.

Mandukhai's heart hammered in her chest so hard she was certain it would explode. She could feel her pulse in her throat. Arrows sailed past her, but instead of worrying about herself, Mandukhai glanced at Dayan again. He had ducked behind the shield fitted to the front of his horse. The boy had a sword for emergencies—with limited knowledge of how to use it—but Boke's job was to ensure that would never be necessary. His men formed a tight ring around Dayan more effective than any shield. Nothing would get through.

An Oirat horse launched over the caltrops, escaping the ringed trap. Mandukhai's eyes widened.

"Get Dayan out past Togochi's forces," Mandukhai ordered Boke.

He nodded and led Dayan's guard north, away from the battlefield.

Be like Khutulun, she thought, feebly attempting to calm her racing pulse. *Khutulun, the heroine. Khutulun, the warrior princess.*

Mandukhai, the warrior queen.

She released an arrow as Unebolod had taught her, waiting for the moment the hooves left the ground in unison and relaxing her arm as her thumb released. The arrow planted in the warrior's armpit, but hardly slowed him down. A mask of determination set on his face. It was all Mandukhai could see as he raced directly at her. He raised his own bow as Mandukhai fumbled to retrieve her shield, barely getting it up in time to block the arrow.

As she ducked out from behind the shield a second later, she watched Torgus release an arrow that embedded in the Oirat's eye. He tumbled from the saddle, dead in an instant, but his horse continued the charge with wild determination. It veered wide of Mandukhai's knot of guards and raced away.

Thousands of Oirat remained trapped by all but her right wing. Instead of fleeing, they pressed their advance, clearly hoping to win the battle. Mandukhai spotted the Oirat command arrows with their colorful signal ribbons, but she struggled to follow what was happening. She had not properly trained for this. Someone would have to teach her what all the colors and horn blasts meant.

"For the Khan!" Mandukhai called, pulling another arrow from her quiver and deftly placing it against the string. With the right pressure from her thighs, Dust surged toward the oncoming storm.

An arrow scraped across her armguard, but the thick leather lamellar armor efficiently did its job. Mandukhai nudged her elbows down, remembering the hit she had struck against the Oirat's armpit, then released the arrow as the oncoming surge of Oirat pressed ever closer.

"To the Queen!" A call rang out distantly behind her.

Mandukhai charged forward, heart hammering like thunder, matching the thunder of the hooves against the earth. She released arrow after arrow in a blur of motion. Some hit the mark. A few flew past, but by fortune took out a mount behind her target instead. More glanced off her own armor. One lodged into her shoulder, throwing off her shot. Mandukhai cried out in alarm, nearly dropping the bow out of shock. Her shoulder screamed in burning agony. Her arms ached from firing so many arrows. Mandukhai blinked sweat from her eyes and realized her mistake when she glanced back.

None of her warriors were anywhere near her. She had charged forward on her own too aggressively, like an arrow flying across the battlefield.

But she could not turn back. It would expose her retreat.

Her cry of pain transformed into a fierce battle cry. Mandukhai stuffed down the pain and released another shot. It struck her target in the eye, throwing his head back before he tumbled from his horse, trampled to death beneath a hundred hooves.

Men closed in around her.

An arrow whistled through the air. Mandukhai gasped as a sword grazed the armor over her leg. A torrent of Oirat had surrounded her.

Mandukhai knew she was too close to use arrows, but her sword skills were severely lacking. She could not hope to survive with her sword in hand. The shield protected her right leg, but the left remained exposed. One man attempted yanking her from the saddle, grabbing the back of her armor, but she shifted her grip and reared Dust back on his hind legs. Instead of unseating her, the jerking motion unseated him. Dust's hooves connected with the men in front of her, who attempted gathering the reins.

The memory of Oirat surrounding her in the Orkhon Valley, of what they had done to her there, surged to the surface.

This is it, she thought, firing a shot through the hand of the man on her left as Dust's hooves settled back on the ground again. *I will die here.*

Another arrow screamed over the battlefield, signaling something she didn't understand. Mandukhai danced Dust in a circle, always moving but unable to advance or retreat, firing as many shots as she could to hold off the hands grasping at her. *Is Dayan safe? Did he make it past Togochi's wing?*

Togochi rode in the center of his five *mingghans* of Khorlod warriors toward the hilltop. The clash of steel, screams of men in battle, and whinnies of horses echoed off the valley walls. *Am I too late?*

A small knot of men raced over the hilltop straight toward him. Togochi tensed, signaling for his men to hold their fire as he squinted at the approaching warriors. At the head of the group, he recognized the grim face of Boke. No doubt the little Khan rode at the center of that ring of guards.

"Protect the Khan!" he called.

The horsemen kicked their horses into a gallop, quickly overtaking Boke.

He paused to confer with Boke as his men rushed past. "Where is Mandukhai?"

"Holding the Oirat back with her men," Boke replied.

Togochi grunted in irritation and whipped his mare into action.

As he crested the hill, worried that she had died and uncertain what he would do with Dayan if she did, Togochi yanked his mare to a halt and gaped at the chaos below.

They had pressed the Oirat into the trap in camp, just as Mandukhai had planned, but many of them seemed to have since escaped the trap. Alayitung commanded two thousand warriors who had closed in around the southern and western flanks of the battlefield, while Mandukhai's thousand warriors barred the path east. A gap in the line had opened up to the north, where Togochi's men now crashed down the hillside to finish the battle.

A single rider broke away from Mandukhai's *mingghan* and galloped at reckless speed toward the Oirat lines. Togochi cursed as he recognized the tails flying from the helmet. *Mandukhai, are you trying to get yourself killed?* he thought gruffly. But he admired her courage.

He raised his bow and bellowed, kicking his mare down the hill. "To the queen!"

No matter how many arrows his men released, he could not stop the Oirat from closing in around Mandukhai's mad charge across the field alone. By the time he reached the bottom of the hill, he could no longer see her. The Oirat had engulfed her.

Arrows took out a few of the Oirat around her as Mandukhai's warriors attempted to rescue her. A flash of colorful flags to the right. Another whistling arrow.

Suddenly, the Oirat abandoned their prey. Mandukhai continued dancing Dust around, wondering what had happened as her attackers broke away and fled.

Torgus stopped beside Mandukhai, fretting over her. "How deep is that arrow?"

But she was focused on the horizon as a thousand of the Oirat slipped through a gap before Togochi's line could collapse on them. The Khorlod warriors crashed down the hill like a wave, destroying anything in their way. A *mingghan* broke off on Alayitung's western flank and chased down the escaping Oirat as the rest of Togochi's warriors trapped the unlucky Oirat who remained. They began picking off the trapped Oirat one by one.

Mandukhai swatted Torgus's hand away. With a cluck and kick, Dust lurched into action after the fleeing Oirat. None could live. She needed to send a clear message. She would not be trifled with.

Torgus and the rest of her guards surged forward after her, firing arrows faster than her, taking out one Oirat after the other.

And soon, none remained.

The stench of blood and excrement suddenly slammed into Mandukhai's mouth and nose. She gagged and raised her arm to cover her face, only to scream as the arrow embedded in her shoulder sent a wave of burning pain through her arm and down her back.

Togochi sounded the horn as the battle ended. Thousands of dead Oirat littered the valley. Hundreds—perhaps even a thousand—of her own men joined them. Mandukhai scanned the gruesome sight as Torgus inspected the arrow in her shoulder.

Men without limbs and heads. Warriors with arrows that penetrated their armor. Others with arrows protruding from their faces. *So much death*. Mandukhai had not expected so much death. It was a waste of men.

"It didn't penetrate deep," Torgus reported. "The armor stopped the arrow, and the silk knotted it up. I can get it out, but it won't feel nice. We will need to bandage it right away."

Mandukhai nodded absently, still in shock by the bodies. Torgus removed the straps on her armguard and flipped it back to find the arrowhead.

"Mandukhai?" Togochi trotted up beside her. "What in the name of Tengri were you thinking charging in alone like that?"

The thump of hooves and arrows echoed in her ears as if the battle still raged. The sound muffled Togochi's voice. He continued to reprimand her for her behavior, but she heard none of it. The blood and bodies dominated her sight. She could not glance away as tears blurred her vision.

Togochi edged in her line of view, blocking the battlefield. His lips set in a grim line. "It gets easier."

"I don't want it to get eas—"

Torgus twisted the arrowhead in the silk to pull it from her shoulder, making her scream in alarm. Were it not for his firm grip on her arm, she would have jerked away from him. The arrow hung from her armor, stuck between the pieces of lamellar. Torgus prodded at the wound. White-hot pain seared her from the wound all the way to the pit of her stomach. He ripped a strip of cloth with his teeth, then held it there as he pulled silver from a pouch in his belt. Gently, Torgus peeled back the shoulder of her silk deel to patch the wound. Mandukhai hissed, but the cold silver felt like a salve.

"Dayan?" Mandukhai's heart leaped into her throat as she glanced around, only to find the boy watching her with wide eyes, still protected by his ring of guards.

"He is unharmed, my Khatun," Boke reported.

"You won your first battle, Mandukhai," Togochi said. A ghost of a smile crept across his face. "And with far more bravery than your late husband ever showed."

"This was only the first, Togochi," Mandukhai said, pressing her hand against the bandaged wound. "More Oirat will come."

"And we will be ready," he agreed.

Mandukhai wanted to feel a great swelling of pride at this victory. But seeing all the death that it brought left her empty inside. Her mission was clear. Unite the Mongols under one banner as they had been under Genghis.

But she could not afford to lose so many men to do it.

Dayan sneezed, drawing Mandukhai's awareness back to him. Over the sounds of horses plodding across the battlefield and men laughing, calling to each other, and talking, she heard a sound she prayed she would never hear again.

Dayan wheezed rattling, deep breaths. Each more of a struggle than the last.

"Get him off the horse!" Mandukhai shouted, leaping from her own saddle to rush to Dayan's side.

But the weariness from riding in battle made her knees give out before she could take a step.

Dayan slumped forward in the saddle.

The urgency of Dayan's condition created some doubt among the men, and Mandukhai had done her best to shield him. Once he had been removed from the horse and taken away from the mounts crowding around, Dayan's breathing had slowly steadied, but it had taken hours. Mandukhai had brushed cold water over his lips, careful not to get any in his mouth and choke him while keeping his mouth and nose open and unobstructed so he could breathe. He remained unconscious, and she prayed he only slept after the excitement of the battle.

Getei had arrived nearly two hours after Dayan's initial collapse, carrying a pungent salve that he immediately rubbed over the boy's chest. He had found the herbs to treat the horse sickness but feared it was too late given Dayan's condition. They could not administer the first dose until Dayan had woken up.

When he woke, Dayan hadn't questioned Mandukhai as she'd mixed the herbs into his water and cradled his head to help him drink. And then they waited.

The men moved around the battlefield, scavenging for supplies or anything valuable they could carry with them, but as the hours passed and it became clear there was nothing more to do, all eyes turned to the young Khan.

"We should take him back to the camp," Getei said with hushed urgency. "He will need rest and weeks of treatment if he is to have any chance."

"We cannot give up this ground," Mandukhai replied, glancing at the men lingering nearby.

Alayitung and Togochi hovered near Boke, watching Mandukhai and Getei care for Dayan.

"If we retreat to camp, the men might question us," Mandukhai said, terrified that it was already too late. "They might question our right to rule them and lead them. We have come too far to allow that to happen." Her gaze shifted down to Dayan. "Let me speak to the Khan alone."

Getei grimaced, but he did not protest as he stood and strode away.

Mandukhai gazed at Dayan, whose head rested in her lap. What had Siker and Bayan been thinking leaving this boy to die? How much of his condition was their fault for abandoning him? She stroked his cheek affectionately. The redness and puffiness in his eyes had abated somewhat but had not gone away.

"My sweet little Khan," Mandukhai murmured. "What have I done to you?"

Dayan wrapped his arms around just one of hers, hugging her arm against his chest. The small gesture filled her with compassion. Somehow, this little boy had stolen her heart. And she had failed him.

"If we turn back, you will get the rest you need to recover," she whispered. "But we could lose the support of our men. We could lose everything, Dayan. If we continue riding deeper across the plains, we could finally defeat the Oirat and bring them under your banner. No one would question our right to lead. But you could die." A tear slipped from her eye and rolled down her cheek, then dripped onto his cheek.

"Ride," he said meekly.

Mandukhai's heart stilled. It was the first word he had spoken since that night in her ger months ago. "Dayan—"

He unraveled his grip from her arm and rolled out of her lap. Mandukhai reached out to stop him, but she could not deter him.

Dayan Khan, so small and frail, rose awkwardly to his feet, gazing at her expectantly. The way he squared his shoulders so confidently made him look more like a Khan and less like a frail boy. Mandukhai watched him in awe as he awkwardly marched toward his horse.

She remained there on the ground, gazing after Dayan as Boke hoisted the boy into his saddle and strapped him in.

Getei materialized at Mandukhai's side. "Mandukhai ..."

She brushed her hands off and rose. "The Khan has spoken!" She called to the men. "We ride!"

Getei grabbed Mandukhai's arm as she started toward Dust, jerking her to a halt. "He will die."

Mandukhai yanked her arm away. "Touch me like that again, Getei, and I will take your hand off myself. You only need one to cast your bones."

Getei bowed his head in shame and stepped backward.

Mandukhai climbed onto Dust's back with the golden eyes of the Khan staring into her soul.

Chapter Thirty-Nine

Smoke in the Sky

Unebolod slapped another bug from the back of his neck and grimaced. The pesky things were everywhere, and they made him itch until he bled. The air was so thick his lungs weren't sure if he was breathing or drowning. He hated this place more than any other place he had ever been. Unebolod would rather spend a year in the Gobi than another day in this bug-infested, suffocating marshland.

After finishing his investigation among the Ongud, Unebolod had begun to worry. None of the northern or eastern tribes had the *sulde* of Genghis. That only left the southern tribes. The Urainkhai could be ruled out, but Unebolod could not ignore the Three Guards to the west of the Urainkhai. Nor could he ignore the Chakhar or Ordos. And if it had fallen in their hands, Bigirsen likely had it as well.

As his men had ventured deeper into Chakhar territory, it had shocked Unebolod to learn the bulk of the Chakhar forces were in the Ordos basin fighting with Bigirsen and Issama against the Ming. He had set up camp north of the Huang Ho River and sent more than a dozen of his best scouts into the basin to search for signs of the *sulde*.

Just a week ago, he had received a message that the Khatun and Khan led their forces into Oirat territory. And he was stuck in this stinking cesspool of wetland around the Huang Ho River.

He worried about Mandukhai's fate. She wouldn't be foolish enough to ride into battle herself, would she? *She would. That tenacious woman is too stubborn to stay behind.* He sneered at a nearby red bird as if it were the reason for his misery.

Unebolod's men lingered outside the edge of the forest that banked the river. They had chosen this location because the waterway was most narrow here, making for easier transportation of horses across on a small raft.

His scouts had reported a massive Mongol camp just over forty miles inland on the other side. A few scouts had gone ahead to search the camp, and he returned to the riverbank each day, pacing and swatting away bugs as he waited for word.

Had they discovered his scout? If Bigirsen controlled the Ordos tribes, and that was an Ordos camp, would Bigirsen have his men killed? It was likely. Highly likely. And then Bigirsen would attack him. *He can't attack,* Unebolod told himself again. *He is too far south.*

Yet he wanted Bigirsen to strike. From where Unebolod stood, it would appear to Bigirsen as if he only had a thousand men with him, but thousands more waited just to the north. Near enough that they could launch a full-scale battle. Oh, he itched to be the one to take Bigirsen's head.

Twigs snapped in the distance. Unebolod rested his hand on the bow as he stood beside his horse. A moment later, his scout rounded a cluster of trees, smacking a bug from his face. The raft waited to carry the scout to his side of the river. He tethered his mount to one of the tree branches before stepping onto the raft.

"Well?" Unebolod asked, trying to temper his waning patience. It was not the scout's fault he hated this place.

The scout reached his side of the river and glanced back over his shoulder as if he expected to be followed. "The camp is a massive conglomeration, my Lord," the scout answered. "Not just Ordos, but Uyghur, Chakhar, and a few Three Guards banners as well. It's like a small city."

"And the men?"

"Few. Just enough to protect the camp. We could raid, steal their wives, daughters, valuables, and they could never stop your superior force."

Unebolod hesitated. He could raid. He would win while Bigirsen's forces had their backs turned to the south, to the Ming. But without the Khatun's permission, he risked judgment. She would not want him to start a war with Bigirsen before the time was right. He huffed and slid his hand off his bow.

"No." Unebolod frowned as he mounted. "What about the *sulde*?"

"I have a lead." The scout shifted and glanced across the water again. "A woman who claims to know where the *sulde* is. She said she will bring it to me."

"Do you believe her?"

The scout sighed. "It's hard to say. I asked her why she would help us, and she told me she heard about our Khatun's courage, and she wanted to help her. She says her husband is hiding it and intends to use it against Bigirsen. Who can say with women what to trust?"

Unebolod frowned. "Did she say who her husband is?"

"No. Just that he is in charge of the battle strategy of the *tumens* in the basin."

That information narrowed it down but did not tell Unebolod the identity. Especially with so many tribes congregated together.

"Arrange the exchange with her," Unebolod commanded. "If she truly can get us the *sulde*, we will give her whatever she wants in exchange. But the *sulde* is the top priority. Nothing else comes before bringing that back here. No matter the cost."

The scout nodded and climbed back on the raft.

Unebolod watched him ride the raft across. In minutes, he was mounted and riding deeper into the Ordos basin once more.

More waiting, he thought bitterly. Unebolod hated this place. But if this woman told the truth, he could be headed north soon.

ORDOS BASIN – 70 MILES NORTHEAST OF YINCHUAN – SUMMER 1471

Issama rose with the wolf dawn and stretched his back, working his fists into a knot in his muscles. Sleeping on the ground was not something he enjoyed, even if he had grown used to it. The unforgiving land still made his back ache.

For the last few weeks, everything had gone according to plan. Issama, Legusi, and Guden led their forces deeper into the Ordos basin, clearing out more Ming camps along the way. Bigirsen moved his own Uyghur toward Yinchuan.

Tomorrow, Bigirsen planned to finish his attack on Yinchuan. Then, he would meet Legusi and Guden on the other side ... with Issama leading the charge against him.

Today, Issama would send Nahai to retrieve the *sulde* of Genghis Khan from the family camp thirty miles to the north. Issama could not wait to see the look on Bigirsen's face the moment he realized his mistake. *He should have killed me.*

Issama tipped his head back and closed his eyes, smiling to himself. His reign would dawn tomorrow.

He opened his eyes to bask in the deep blue-gray sky of the wolf dawn, then frowned at the wisps of gray puffing up in the northeast. He squinted. Those looked like smoke from fires. Hundreds of fires. Thousands. Too many to be campfires.

Calling out to the men sleeping around him, Issama nudged Nahai with the toe of his boot.

"What is that?" Issama snapped at his second in command. "I want men out immediately to investigate!"

Nahai staggered to his feet and peered at the horizon.

"Now!" Issama shouted.

The ground beneath his feet seemed to shudder. It took a moment to realize it was not his own disorientation, but the thunder of hooves. Issama's heart leaped into his throat. Horses. Had the Ming circled around his camp in the night? *They are attacking!* Issama thought in a panic.

Nahai was already gone when Issama turned around to retrieve his horse.

Ordos banners fluttered as horsemen rode toward the Uyghur section of camp. Had Legusi betrayed him to save his sister from Bigirsen? Issama rushed up to greet them on his own mount. The grim set of Legusi's face set Issama's teeth on edge. The Ordos Lords around Legusi were clearly stunned and angry about something.

"The family camp is burning," Legusi snapped. "At the red salt lake."

"What?" Issama's frown deepened. His heart plummeted. "How?" He turned his gaze toward the billowing smoke in the distance. It couldn't be the camp. How could he see the smoke from thirty miles away? *Those fires must be immense!*

"The Ming attacked the women and children," Legusi reported. His voice grew thicker, and grief made his youthful features wrinkle. "A few of my men escaped the camp to fetch reinforcements. The Chakhar warriors are already on the way to lend aid."

"No," Issama muttered as denial set firmly in his bones. Everything he had worked so hard for was lost! If the Ming set the camp ablaze, *everyone* would lose their families. Uingen and Qolotai were there with his infant daughter! As were Bigirsen's wives and children.

Then Issama realized what he had left behind with his wives. "The banner!" He kicked his mount toward the burning camp.

Legusi and his men began riding southwest.

Issama reined in and turned. "Where are you going?"

"I sent more than enough men to help secure what remains of our families," Legusi said. "But my sister is still in Bigirsen's care. If I don't rescue her before he finds out, he might kill her."

Issama raced to catch up to Legusi, riding beside him as Legusi's men glared at his back. "You can't go to Bigirsen. If you do, we will not beat him. This is our chance."

"Your plan is burning on the horizon, Issama," Legusi snapped, waving behind him. His face reddened in anger. "My men will do their best to secure what remains. But if we want to rebuild, we need him."

"No!"

Legusi yanked the reins of his mount and spun to face Issama. "You do whatever you wish, Issama. I no longer care. Right now, the only thing that matters to me is saving my sister." He kicked his mount into a canter and turned toward Yinchuan, then called over his shoulder, "Any way I can."

Issama's gaze darted around him, seeking support from any of the men nearby, but their camp was already barren as everyone rode north toward the burning gers. His limbs were too stiff to move.

Unebolod's sleep was broken by strange noises in the night. They carried on the sky like the rumblings of angry gods. He tossed and turned on the ground, swatting away bugs, certain his dreams had transferred to his awake mind. Somewhere distant he heard hooves. Unebolod rose, unable to shake the sense that something had gone terribly wrong.

Were those screams? The sounds were so distant it was as if they slid in and out of reality. Unebolod drifted to the riverbank once more. Far in the distance, dim light flickered across the horizon, a strange red-black pulsing light.

A rider raced toward him from the other side of the river. Unebolod prepared an arrow and took aim, keeping his breathing steady.

A second rider. A third another. Fourth.

He could fire fast, but he was not sure if he would be fast enough to take out a dozen men before they fired back at him.

The first man broke through the trees, holding something black, shadowed by the darkness.

"Ready the raft!" they shouted from the other side of the river.

All of Unebolod's scouts, more than a dozen of them, broke through the trees at dangerous speed. And in the hand of one man, the black *sulde* of Genghis Khan.

Unebolod dropped his bow and rushed to the river's edge, calling back to the camp for help. In moments, he had ten men with him, pulling the raft toward the shore to retrieve the scouts. The moment they hit the shore, the riders darted up the riverbank, and they sent the raft back for the rest.

The bannerman stood in front of Unebolod, his eyes wild with panicked fear.

"What happened?" Unebolod asked, reaching for the *sulde* pole. The scout relinquished it as if relieved.

"The woman brought the banner, as promised," he reported in a rush. "When we offered her safe passage with us, she insisted on going back for her daughter." He swallowed. "Just as she left, the Ming attacked their camp." The scout shuddered, his chest heaving with anxious breaths. "It was a massacre, my Lord. We would have helped, but your orders were clear. Bring back the *sulde* at any cost. If we had helped, we might not have made it back with the *sulde*. The Ming closed around the camp as quiet as could be. Then everything burned."

He brushed sweat from his brow, and Unebolod noticed the layers of soot covering the scout's face. They had gone close enough to the action to encounter smoke, at least. Close enough to be certain of their report.

Unebolod considered riding to the Mongols' aid. *Imagine riding in and rescuing the families*. The tides would turn on Bigirsen for certain, and they could capture the Uyghur women. "How many Ming?"

"It was hard to tell," another scout reported, leaning forward with his hands against his knees as if he had run the whole way and not ridden. "Our primary focus was on the *sulde*."

Unebolod's fist tightened around the pole. "Was it a thousand? More than our men?"

The scouts exchanged glances as the raft returned to the shore with the rest of the men.

"What?" Unebolod snapped.

One man licked his lips nervously. "By the time we could get the *tumens* across the river, it would be too late. The Ming were terribly efficient, and there weren't nearly enough men guarding the camp to put up a good fight."

"We should leave," another scout said. "If they saw us flee with the banner, they will come this way next."

It tempted Unebolod to let them come. He could have the river lined with bowmen before dawn, and they would butcher the Ming before they could cross.

Instead, he gazed up at the black banner, cloaked in darkness, and felt his duty pull him away from the river.

He had gotten what he came for. There would be no saving the camp, but he could help save the Nation. "The woman?"

They shook their heads. "We had to leave her there when she went back for her daughter. It was her or the *sulde*, my Lord."

Agony over turning his men away from a battle that could bring the Ordos and Chakhar firmly in Mandukhai's grasp clutched Unebolod's chest as he marched toward his own camp.

If he fought the Ming, he risked losing the *sulde*. He couldn't do it. He would return the banner to its rightful place, and he would return to Mandukhai.

Issama reached the remains of their main camp beside the red salt lake as the sun reached its zenith. The fires had burned out, but smoke continued billowing into the sky. Bodies littered the ground. Burned or butchered. Men, women, children.

As he rode cautiously through the maze of rubble, ash, and bodies, an emptiness filled his gut. Had *anyone* survived?

Somber silence filled the air. None of the men spoke as they sifted through the wreckage for survivors. None of them cried out in shock or horror. Every man was too stunned to make a sound.

This loss was Issama's fault. He had been so focused on defeating Bigirsen that he had missed some vital clue as to the Ming strategy. The failure made his bones heavy.

The longer he plodded along through the remains of the camp, the more he spotted signs of life. A few women and children had survived the attack, though not nearly as many as he would have hoped. Men milled around, helping these remnants find healing or family.

He passed the section of camp where Bigirsen's wives and children had lived. Bigirsen had not bothered taking them with him on his campaign, afraid they would be a burden or distraction from his ultimate goals. He had also believed his wives made good spies against Issama's family. Sadly, he had been mistaken in that assumption.

Now they were all dead. Nothing remained in their place but smoldering ashes. *He will kill me for this, for certain*, Issama realized. Everything he had worked for, all of his plans, had gone up in smoke. The alliance was broken. Tribes would scatter to lick their wounds or exact their own vengeance.

He watched a child pull the bleeding, burned corpse of his mother from the ashes of a ger and his heart ached in ways he had never known possible. The absolute agony within him made everything seem simultaneously folded and hammered like iron in a forge, as well as hollow.

Generations. All the families who had traveled close to the men fighting for Bigirsen—for him. Only a handful survived. How could they ever rebuild after this loss?

Issama jerked his mount to a halt as his own homes came into view. Everything was gone but the twisted, misshapen pipes of the stove. All had been reduced to rubble and ash.

The cart that had hidden the *sulde* now laid in a charred heap. If it survived, it would be unrecognizable now. Tears pricked the corners of his eyes. Issama blinked them back. The destruction of the sacred *sulde* of Genghis Khan would forever be linked to his name. The shame weighed in his gut like stone.

Uingen's ger was a mound beside Qolotai's. On the soot-covered ground beside her ger, Qolotai sat clutching a bundle to her chest. Her mouth remained open in a silent cry of grief as tears poured down her cheeks, leaving streaks of pale skin on her soot-covered face. Blood flowed from a wound in her head, and her clothing was covered in dirt and ash. Issama slid from his saddle, his movements involuntary as if someone else controlled his body. He shuffled stiffly toward her.

Qolotai's gaze lifted to the sky, and a strangled sob escaped her open mouth, but she quickly choked it off. Issama sank to his knees in front of her, unable to stand a moment longer as the reality of this heinous crime weighed him down. The baby girl in her arms didn't make a sound. Didn't move. He reached a trembling hand toward his daughter. Her skin was ice cold.

Everything inside of him shattered. Issama pulled Qolotai into his arms as she silently wept against his chest. His own eyes clouded with tears as he stared past them at Uingen's ger. He didn't have to investigate to know she was dead as well.

All around him, men sank to their knees or lost their stomachs as they realized the disheartening truth. Their families had not survived. Had Issama not sent Siker and Burani away from Bigirsen's grasp, they would be dead as well.

Commander Wang Yue is a coward, Issama thought as a fire of pure hate ignited in his core. He wanted to rally all the warriors and chase down the Ming, then wipe them off the face of the earth. *Tomorrow, I will try to rally them. This anger burning in me must be in them as well, and I will use it to burn the Ming to the ground in retribution. But today, the men will need their grief.*

Issama would no longer be safe anywhere. Bigirsen would use this as an excuse to take his head for certain. Any attacks he planned against the Ming, he needed to watch his back. Unless Issama could use this tragedy to turn Mongol bloodlust to its purest form, he would not have enough men to face the Ming and Bigirsen both. And there was every chance, based on Legusi's reaction to this tragedy, that the southern tribes would either flock to Bigirsen or Mandukhai now.

Issama would exact his revenge on the Ming, but then he needed to disappear long enough to avoid Bigirsen's wrath. Or kill him.

But today, he would bury his first wife and only daughter.

CHAPTER FORTY

Knives and Knees

Mandukhai's awe at Dayan's resilience increased with each passing day. Dayan rode beside Mandukhai without complaint, only sneezing or sniffling occasionally. The herbal mixture seemed to work. Mandukhai could still see the telltale signs of Dayan's illness—red eyes, sneezing, sniffling—but his breathing had become less of a problem. His stamina for riding decreased, but instead of forcing himself on, Dayan would force the men to stop by doing nothing more than halting his own horse. Boke would help him down, and Dayan would walk with his guards away from the horses, staring at the horizon as if he had some supernatural sense of the world.

The men who had doubted Dayan Khan in private before now openly exchanged stories about the Khan's gifts. Dayan's frequent breaks and distant gazes instilled a divine confidence Mandukhai never could have created herself. Doubts dissolved, replaced by admiration.

As the spring faded and the heat of summer came into full swing, the attitude of the army changed as well. Mandukhai, Togochi, and Alayitung created strategies to hunt down Oirat camps with too few men to defend them. She would then send in a group of warriors to stalk the camp, catch the attention of the Oirat warriors within, and lure them out into an open space where her army waited to close in around them. She met little opposition, and the size of her army grew with each victorious skirmish. It also weakened Paisahan's hold on the Oirat—and Bigirsen's.

A few of the Oirat commanders raced toward her army, only to surrender the moment they saw the banners of the Khan and Khatun flying high at Mandukhai's back. Week after week, Mandukhai would pick her target, her men would stalk and lure, then attack. None of the battles were large. She spread her forces across the Zavkhan plains for miles, sweeping Oirat under them in one skirmish after the next. They spared the men who gave their oath to their Great Khan. They killed the Lords who commanded them into battle for treason against the Khan and Khatun.

When she entered Oirat territory, Mandukhai had only commanded eight *mingghans* of a thousand warriors. Now, she controlled nearly four full *tumens* of ten thousand each.

Dayan always rode near Mandukhai, and always surrounded by his wall of guards. No enemy warriors could get close to the little Khan.

Despite her many victories, Mandukhai had still not rooted out Paisahan khan. As they made camp for the night, Mandukhai paced the grassy hill overlooking the camp. Dayan sat nearby, chewing on a long strand of grass and watching her. Occasionally, he would drink his herb-infused water.

Boke and Torgus commanded a ring of guards around the hilltop.

Paisahan's determination to avoid confrontation irritated Mandukhai. He would never kneel to the Khan or to her. Nor would he engage with her directly now that she had absorbed three *tumens* of his Oirat. His stubborn refusal to accept the inevitable drove Mandukhai mad.

The rumble of approaching hooves drew Mandukhai from her pacing and contemplation. She turned to face the incoming riders as her guards formed a protective arc.

Upon seeing Togochi, the guards relaxed. But Togochi was not alone. He rode with a handful of other men. And one woman.

Lady Altan.

Mandukhai motioned for Dayan to move beside her.

Togochi, Altan, and the other commanders dismounted before the guards. Togochi bowed deeply. His face was flushed and his eyes shone with excitement. Mandukhai's heart leaped.

"What is it?" Mandukhai asked, her gaze sweeping over Altan.

The other woman looked softer than Mandukhai remembered. The sling across her chest filled Mandukhai with a flash of envy as it squirmed. Altan adjusted the sling, stroking the infant inside absent-mindedly.

"Altan has come to us with good news," Togochi announced.

Mandukhai raised a brow.

Altan nodded. "I have found the Oirat khan's camp, my Khatun," she said. "We passed it about seventy miles northwest of here."

"Near the lake," Mandukhai breathed.

Altan grinned. "He has nowhere to run but through the mountains."

A thrill raced down Mandukhai's spine. *At last!*

"We will ride first thing in the morning," Mandukhai said. "Togochi, I leave it to you to organize the *tumens*."

He nodded, then mounted and left to prepare the men.

Mandukhai stepped closer to Altan, peering at the infant slung against the other woman's chest. "I did not know you married. And after so firmly refusing my suggestion."

Altan shrugged. "The heart works in mysterious ways. It happened quickly. This is Bagasun, my son."

Mandukhai's heart melted as she saw the infant's face. Would she ever have children? Esige had been the closest thing she had known to a child so far, and Mandukhai had refused to see Dayan as her child, considering the oath she had made to bind herself to him. One day, she might have to act as a wife when he grew old enough. Seeing him as her child would make that impossible. He was her ward, her responsibility, her future. But *not* her child.

"He is so tiny."

"He is only a week, and early, at that." Altan beamed down at the squirming baby as it rooted for food. "I was not due for weeks yet. But he is strong, like his father. He will make a good little Lord one day." She stroked Bagasun's cheek.

"Your husband must be so pleased to have a son," Mandukhai said. An ache opened in her stomach, remembering the child she and Unebolod had lost years ago. How she longed for a child!

"He is happy," Altan agreed.

Mandukhai stepped back, trying not to allow the infant to distract her. It surprised her to find Dayan standing beside her, craning his neck to see the baby.

"Who ended up being the lucky man to win your heart?" Mandukhai asked.

"One of my commanders. It was a long time coming, I think." Altan turned her attention to Dayan, and Mandukhai realized this woman and her tribe had not given their oaths. "Unebolod ordered my men this way back in the early winter. I am sorry it took us so long, but I had a hard ride."

"I imagine."

Altan shifted her sling, then kneeled in front of the two of them. "My lord Khan. My lady Khatun. You have proven your divine right."

Mandukhai arched an eyebrow. "Was that ever in question?"

"That is always in question, as you must know." Altan didn't flinch. Instead, she bowed her head as far as she could with an infant strapped across her chest. "To Mandukhai Khatun and Dayan Khan, the Jalair promise to always follow where the Great Khan and his descendants command. We offer salt, horses, ger, and blood."

Another victory. This oath added another five thousand warriors to Mandukhai's forces. If Unebolod maintained command of the eastern tribes as his most recent message indicated, and the Jalair to the far north bowed to her, once Mandukhai conquered the Oirat, she would only have the southern tribes to contend with ... *And Bigirsen.*

She held out her hand to Altan. Dayan cocked his head curiously, then held up the hand with the crescent moon ring. Mandukhai had needed to wrap threads around the band so it stayed on his little finger.

Altan kissed their rings.

"Rise, *Commander* Altan," Mandukhai said. "You are now a member of the Great Khan's empire. And in the morning, we ride to conquer the Oirat."

Paisahan's camp was nestled close to the edge of the lake, into which all the rivers out of the Khangai and Altai Mountains fed fresh water each spring. Mandukhai had commanded a *tumen* ahead of the bulk of her forces to catch Paisahan's attention and draw him out. While she wanted to conquer the Oirat, she had no desire to kill women or children. He commanded twice that many warriors, which would give him a false sense of confidence to attack. Or so she hoped.

General Alayitung and Togochi together had carefully selected the battleground, insisting the open space would allow them to ride in on the Oirat from all sides and collapse around them, forcing their foes to either submit or die. Even if the warriors following Paisahan submitted to Mandukhai, Paisahan's surrender would never be accepted.

Dust snorted, bobbing his head as Mandukhai watched the rising cloud of dust approaching. "Have we received a response from Toghon or Seguse?" she asked Altan.

The other woman had refused to stay behind, saying she wouldn't allow Mandukhai all the glory. Altan's infant son had been left in the care of other women so she could fight uninhibited.

Alayitung commanded the left wing of her forces, now far out of sight. Togochi commanded the right. Both would wait for the Oirat to come—for Paisahan to come—each with a *tumen* of eager warriors.

"Toghon said his men are ready to carry out your command," Altan reported with a nod. "They should be in position soon at the rear of Paisahan's forces. You are smarter than I gave you credit for, Mandukhai Khatun."

Mandukhai smiled at that, glancing at Dayan. She took great pride in usurping expectations.

Colored flags rose and fell up and down Mandukhai's lines as the Oirat rode into view, kicking up a great cloud of dust in their wake. The lines of Oirat enemies spanned out across the battlefield as they raced forward in a mass of horsemen.

"Your best guess?" she asked Altan.

"Ten thousand," Altan reported as she squinted into the distance. "Maybe more."

Not all the remaining Oirat enemies, then, she thought. Mandukhai grasped her bow and grinned at Altan. "Try to keep up." Then she kicked Dust into action.

The stallion leaped forward, and with him, all the warriors along her lines surged forward as well, racing head-on toward the oncoming storm still half a mile away. Altan whooped and joined Mandukhai. Dayan rode alongside them as well, hiding behind his wall of guards.

Paisahan's Oirat outnumbered the Jalair and Oirat warriors Mandukhai had already conquered and commanded nearly two to one. This had been a careful calculation on Togochi's part, dividing the queen's forces so that it would lull the enemy Oirat into a false sense of security. He and Alayitung rode out hours ahead of her own *tumen* to circle around wide enough to avoid detection.

Now, as her lines raced toward the enemy Oirat, Mandukhai spotted Paisahan's scouts racing away from the left and right wings, straight toward where the rest of her force waited in hiding. Arrows from her hidden force cut down several of the scouts. And in moments, the command flags of the Oirat began waving.

"They spotted our wings," Mandukhai hissed to herself.

As if to confirm this, two thousand of the Oirat broke off from the main line, each headed in opposite directions. One toward Togochi's waiting *tumen*. One toward Alayitung's waiting *tumen*. If the Oirat stalled those two men and their warriors long enough, the remaining Oirat could sweep through her own *tumen*.

Arrows arched toward her line as they raced toward the oncoming Oirat. Mandukhai ducked low against Dust's neck, then released her own arrow the moment the sky cleared. A glance toward Dayan reassured her that his wall of warriors remained in place.

Command arrows whistled toward her waiting left and right wings, giving the signal to Togochi and Alayitung to ride in early. If they did not meet on the battlefield together, her strategy could fall apart.

Mandukhai's *mingghan* shifted into an arrowhead formation, with the lancers at the tip to break through the Oirat line. She continued firing arrows, keeping her breath as steady as possible. The heat of the sun baked her helmet, and sweat dripped down her nose and temples. Adrenaline pumped through her veins. The first battle against the Oirat had shocked Mandukhai to her core. Now, with several skirmishes under her belt, she swiftly grew accustomed to the rigors and brutality.

The two forces crashed into one another, but the arrowhead formation had not worked as Mandukhai had hoped. Instead of breaking through the line to circle back on the Oirat rear, her lancers created a gap her bowmen and swordsmen rode into, but the Oirat split off and closed around them.

"Dayan!" Mandukhai called as panic gripped her. She could not see over the heads of so many men. Was that Boke's helmet a few yards away?

Togochi's *tumen* raced over the hilltop on the right as Alayitung's *tumen* closed in on the left, but the two thousand Oirat who broke off slowed her generals and their *tumens* down. The Oirat around her tightened their ring and attempted forcing her to race away with them.

Adrenaline transformed into terror as Mandukhai and her warriors were slowly herded away from the battlefield. *Paisahan is trying to capture me again!* Memories of what happened the last time the Oirat captured her surged to the surface. Mandukhai struggled to breathe, distracted as her head swam. *Where are Toghon and Seguse's rearguard? Have they betrayed me?* Her limbs trembled. She fumbled with her bow.

Altan shouted a command. Mandukhai could not make out Altan's words as blood thumped in Mandukhai's ears. In seconds, the Jalair warriors shifted into a horn formation. The Oirat broke into smaller groups. Mandukhai became lost in the churning mass of horses and dust. The dust coated her mouth. *Breath through the nose*, Togochi taught her. Messengers fought their way through the lines to reach Mandukhai. Arrows killed several of them before they could reach her.

"Torgus!" Mandukhai barked. "Send men to break a line for those scouts!"

In moments, the command was being carried out.

Mandukhai blinked sweat from her eyes as the Oirat became indistinguishable from her own warriors. Who was she to kill?

A horn sounded. The enemy Oirat recognized the command. In seconds, they turned away as Togochi and Alayitung continued cutting a path close to them, retreating toward the rear hill.

Mandukhai huffed, blowing a stray hair from her face as her panic abated. A glance revealed Boke's warrior wall remained tight around Dayan.

A second Oirat *tumen* rode over the hill. And with it, the fluttering banners of the Oirat khan.

A messenger who had been struggling through the mass finally reached Mandukhai. "They have more," he reported.

"I see that," Mandukhai snapped.

Altan raced to Mandukhai's side, standing in the stirrups and gazing across the battlefield. She let out a low whistle.

Another *tumen* rode in behind Paisahan's reinforcements. Mandukhai's stomach clenched. *Have I miscalculated Paisahan's forces?* She had been told he only had two *tumens* in total. Where had this third come from? *Have the Oirat lied to me?* Doubt crippled Mandukhai.

"That's Toghon's banner!" Altan exclaimed, pointing at the second *tumen* riding in behind Paisahan a quarter mile back.

Mandukhai released a breath she had not realized she held, then relaxed in her saddle. *This is it, then.* They would find out for certain if these new Oirat allies could be trusted.

Togochi's warriors on the right wing broke into a pinwheel of lines. Mandukhai watched as the men smoothly rode into formation, then the *tumen* raced toward the oncoming Oirat like a great spoked wheel, turning, churning out arrows.

Toghon's Oirat warriors moved into bow formation, reading Togochi's strategy in a way Mandukhai could not discern.

Altan whooped and grinned, then gave the command to her flagmen. In moments, the Jalair warriors raced forward like a great arrow, leaving Mandukhai behind with only five thousand of her own warriors.

Altan's warriors flew across the battlefield as Toghon's men curved around the oncoming Oirat warriors. He had cut off their option to retreat. Togochi's men continued churning like a wheel of death through the trapped Oirat. Alayitung's horn sounded and his men circled away, feigning retreat. A great, chaotic machine of death milled through the battlefield.

Mandukhai shook out her trembling hands, then grabbed her bow from the saddle hook and kicked Dust toward the action.

Altan's arrow formation pierced the Oirat line and shot through Toghon's bow formation.

Arrows fell from the sky like rain. Boke's warrior shield was peppered with arrows attempting to pick off the Khan. Mandukhai fired back until her quiver was empty, then she hooked her bow to the saddle and drew her sword.

An arrow slammed into Mandukhai's helmet, throwing her back. Had she not been holding the reins, the impact would have tossed her from the saddle. It was by fortune that she had just set down the bow and freed up a hand to hold on.

But her helmet slipped. The strap broke. The helmet tumbled to the ground. Swords flashed around her as her guards fought off the nearby Oirat.

Paisahan's flags waved in the distance, continuing their slow advance through the churning mass of her own *tumens*.

Mandukhai's heart leaped into her throat as the helmet disappeared beneath the mass of stomping hooves. If she dismounted to collect the helmet, horses would trample her to death in seconds. Without her helmet, Mandukhai was an open target for stray arrows.

"The Queen has no helmet!" someone shouted.

Mandukhai's panic increased as she swung her sword to block a swing at her neck. Would her men abandon her now?

"Bring another!" Someone else shouted.

Mandukhai glanced over to see Boke breaking formation from Dayan's guard. "No!"

But it was too late. Boke raced toward Mandukhai, killing Oirat with terrible efficiency. He ripped off his helmet as he broke through beside her, then smacked it down on her head.

"Stay with the Khan!" Mandukhai ordered.

A barrage of arrows and swords hacked away at the weakened wall around Dayan Khan. Panic gripped her, making her slower to react with her sword.

The battle seemed to slow as her warriors watched their Khatun to see what she would do. Mandukhai knew her next move would be critical. She could not hesitate a moment longer.

With a fierce cry, Mandukhai raised her sword in the air and charged toward the final enemy line.

The enemy Oirat had heard the cry and charged at her line like a pack of wolves eager for the kill.

And in the center of the Oirat, Paisahan raced straight toward her.

Mandukhai broke away from her warriors, headed straight for him.

Togochi lowered his sword and turned his mare in a circle as he assessed the battlefield. The Oirat were nearly finished, but he had not yet seen their khan. He kicked away from the mass of horsemen to a nearby hill to get a better view of the fray.

Several thousand enemy Oirat remained, but Mandukhai's *tumens* were making quick work of them. He scanned the field until he saw Paisahan's banners.

The khan raced ahead of them.

And charging straight at him, a warrior on a white horse. It took Togochi a moment to recognize it as Mandukhai. *What happened to her helmet?*

Oirat arrows rained down all around Mandukhai, but not a single one struck. Togochi gaped, awestruck. Rays of sunlight broke through the clouds, streaming ribbons of light on Mandukhai's path. He had witnessed nothing so magnificent in his life. The sight of her riding alone, without an arrow striking her armor or her horse, was a fearsome to behold. So much so that several of the remaining enemy Oirat abandoned their positions to flee. A few threw down their weapons.

Inspired by her confidence, Mandukhai's warriors released a fierce battle cry and raced after her. But by the time they began their charge, she was well ahead of them.

As Mandukhai and Paisahan raced toward one another, everyone else fell away.

The rest of the battle stopped as all eyes turned to the Khatun and Oirat khan

Togochi smiled as Mandukhai held her sword as he had taught her. *She never ceases to amaze me.*

Paisahan glared at Mandukhai, barking commands at his men.

But the men abandoned him.

He sneered, baring blackened teeth, then drew his sword.

Mandukhai's heart hammered hard enough in her chest to make her teeth feel it.

He raced close to her. Mandukhai glanced past him to see the rest of the Oirat had fallen away, giving up the fight.

Our success now rests on my ability to defeat Paisahan, she thought. If she failed, he would kill her and the men would likely turn against Dayan.

Mandukhai held her sword as Togochi had taught her, ready to take the impact of Paisahan's superior strength.

They drew closer.

She calmed her racing heart.

Closer.

She tightened her grip on the sword and leaned into Dust's neck.

Closer.

She steadied her breathing.

Paisahan's sword arced downward at her neck. Mandukhai held the sword steady in her hand, forcing his blow away as she predicted the motion. The impact jarred her arm, vibrating through her bones and into her skull. Mandukhai gritted her teeth and spun Dust around for the return attack.

As she predicted, Paisahan attempted the same attack a second time. Mandukhai waited, holding her sword steady. At the last moment, she edged Dust to the side and yanked back on the reins. The stallion kicked his hooves high into the air, taking an alarmed Paisahan in the chin, just under the lip of his helmet. He fell from the saddle.

The surrounding battlefield stilled. No one else rode within yards of their confrontation.

As Dust's hooves came down to the earth, Paisahan's horse raced away. Mandukhai leaped from the saddle. She strode toward him as she imagined Altan would. Confident. Certain of herself.

Paisahan scrambled away on his back, reaching for the sword he had dropped on the ground. Mandukhai placed her boot firmly against his crotch. He froze.

"You have proven yourself," Paisahan said instantly. "We submit."

"No." Mandukhai shook her head. She held the sword casually at her side.

Generals and commanders from both sides of the fray formed a ring around the two of them. Mandukhai knew she could not show him mercy. It would make her appear weak.

"These are not your people to give, Paisahan," she said. "They are, as they have always been, a part of the Great Khan's empire. But you, my Lord, have committed treason against your Khan by attacking his *tumens*."

Paisahan's gaze darted around the ring, clearly seeking an ally. Mandukhai swelled with pride as she realized the truth.

He had no allies left. His men had already surrendered.

Dayan marched in his too-big boots toward Mandukhai and Paisahan, as if he understood he needed to be present at this moment. *Boke must have helped him out of the saddle.*

"You cannot spill noble blood," Paisahan said.

"True," Mandukhai admitted. "But you gave up your nobility when you attacked your Khan."

Toghon stepped forward, kneeling beside Paisahan, facing Dayan.

"You are a traitor," Paisahan hissed.

"No, you are," Toghon said, then bowed his head and offered a horse blanket to Dayan.

Mandukhai held her breath. She didn't want Dayan touching a horse blanket. Especially not at this moment. What if it inflamed his illness?

Dayan simply peered into Paisahan's eyes in that soulful way only he could. The gaze unnerved Paisahan. He squirmed beneath Mandukhai's boot. Dayan nodded to Toghon.

"Honor your Great Khan and cover Paisahan's black face," Mandukhai commanded.

Toghon rose.

Paisahan remained prone on his back, with Mandukhai's boot firmly pressing against his crotch. Toghon laid the blanket over Paisahan's head and chest.

"No!" The blanket muffled the khan's protests.

Mandukhai stepped back as Toghon, Seguse, and Togochi rolled the blanket around the Oirat khan.

Paisahan called out to his son. Mandukhai's gaze swept across the men gathered around her, seeking the guilty party. A young man tried to slip backward into the crowd.

Mandukhai stabbed a finger in his direction. "Stop!"

The young Oirat lordling fell to his knees, trembling as he realized the horror of his situation. "I only followed his commands," he said in a rush. "I will serve. Khatun, please. I offer you ger, salt, horses, and blood."

Mandukhai stopped in front of him. He was so young. Perhaps close to her own age. "Prove it."

He peered up at her, terror in his eyes. "How?"

"Mount."

His face turned ashen, and his gaze flicked past her at the bundle that was his father. Paisahan continued to thrash in his blanket, but it was pointless. There would be no escaping his fate.

Mandukhai did not appreciate how this lordling hesitated. She hardened her tone. "Ride, son of Paisahan. Lead the charge."

He flinched, but nodded in agreement. What choice did he have? If he did not ride, he likely knew he would end up bound alongside his father.

Paisahan's son rose and edged toward a horse.

"You will lead your commanders in this charge, son of Paisahan," she called after him.

Her own commanders and generals backed up to give the Oirat lordling and his men space to ride. Many of her men nodded in approval of Mandukhai's decision.

The Oirat lordling mounted with his commanders. He stared at the thrashing blanket for a moment. His shoulders rose and fell with what she assumed was an attempt to calm himself. At last, he turned hardened eyes toward Mandukhai. She nudged Dayan out of the way, then placed a hand on the young Khan's shoulder.

"It is Lord Asha, Mandukhai Khatun," he clarified.

"Asha," she said, pointedly avoiding calling him Lord. "Prove your allegiance and we will see about the Lord part."

Asha grimaced, then kicked his mount into motion. His commanders followed his lead, their faces set in a stony mask that would have made Unebolod proud. With Asha leading the charge, they raced toward the struggling, bundled body. Upon the first pass over Paisahan's body, the khan screamed through the blanket, but he ceased his thrashing. After the second pass, he fell silent. By the third pass, blood poured out from the rolled-up blanket. Where Paisahan's head had been, now only a hoof indentation remained. For good measure, Asha led one last charge over his father's body.

"Sons do not forget such things," Togochi murmured to Mandukhai so no one else would hear him. "He will harbor resentment toward you the moment you leave."

"He will no longer command until I am certain of his loyalty," Mandukhai said. "None of the Oirat will." She turned and called Alayitung and Seguse forward.

The two men kneeled before their Queen.

"I give you Lords control of these lands," Mandukhai announced loud enough for everyone to hear. "You will carry out the Great Khan's will and judgment from this day until either myself or your Great Khan relieve you."

Alayitung and Seguse lifted stunned faces toward her.

"Your first order will be to implement the following new Oirat laws," Mandukhai said, loud and clear. "No Oirat may bear a crest longer than two fingers." The crest on a helmet displayed the rank of a wearer, and two fingers would be absurdly short for all Oirat, no matter their rank. "When in the presence of their Khan and Khatun, all Oirat must be on their knees at all times." It would be harder to attack if they were in such a position.

Mandukhai's gaze flicked around the ring. Several Oirat carried out the command and immediately dropped to their knees. The motion rippled outward like a great wave from the ring as she stood inside.

"Oirat will no longer carry knives in the presence of their Khan, Khatun, or his appointed leaders without explicit permission from those leaders." Removing Oirat knives in the presence of Alayitung and Seguse would help protect the two of them.

Several knives thumped against the ground.

Mandukhai smiled, then turned away from the ring, guiding Dayan along with her toward Dust.

This had been a glorious victory for the two of them. Even if Bigirsen defeated the Ming, he could not contend with the power and divine right Mandukhai and Dayan had put on display these past months. Soon enough, he would know it, too.

Togochi joined Mandukhai as they mounted and rode away from the battlefield. "Unebolod will be jealous of me," he said, grinning. His grin slipped as he glanced at her. "Now what shall we do, Mandukhai?"

"I will take Dayan back to the Ongi camp," Mandukhai said, glancing at the boy as he stared east. "Our little Khan will learn and grow stronger.

Then, once we have the *sulde* and enough support, we will conquer the southern tribes and reunite this fractured empire for good."

For now, Mandukhai would dedicate her time to teaching Dayan everything he needed to know about politics and fighting. She would have the best warriors train him for battle when he grew strong enough.

CHAPTER FORTY-ONE

Noyan

ONGI RIVER – LATE SUMMER 1472

Heat from the Gobi to the south blew against the small camp of the Great Khan. Unebolod had ridden a year to return with the *sulde*. Along the way, many of the Lords who had followed him had returned to their homeland as his *tumens* had passed through. They would return, when the time was right, to give their oaths to the Great Khan.

Tales of Mandukhai's successful campaign against the Oirat had reached him along the way. The taming of the Oirat, the men called it. Unebolod knew Mandukhai could be terribly fierce when she dug in her heels, but he had a hard time picturing her as the stories depicted. Blazing with divine light, fighting without a helmet, charging alone across a battlefield of thousands to take on the Oirat khan. Defeating him in one-on-one combat. While the stories strengthened her position, Unebolod just couldn't believe they were all true.

Two years he had been away, searching for the sacred black *sulde* of Genghis Khan—the spirit of the Khan himself.

Today, Unebolod rode into the camp with the butt of the *sulde* pole resting in his stirrup beside his boot. The black horsehairs fluttered above his head on the scorching breeze.

Men halted in their tasks when they saw him approach, whispering to each other about the *sulde*. Women and children scrambled out of the way.

The children stared at the banner in wide-eyed awe, their jaws hanging open.

Togochi rode up beside Unebolod. "It's a relief to see you back, brother."

"It's good to be back," Unebolod said, though he was uncertain that was true. Soon, he would have to see Mandukhai. Two years had dulled the pain of their breakup, but it had not kept his heart safe. He still loved her. He always would. "Where is she?"

"This way."

Togochi guided Unebolod toward the center of camp, where a massive gathering tent rested on a giant wooden cart. He examined the mobile tent with intense curiosity. It shone bright white in the sunshine, a beacon on the horizon of the camp. Blue wolves had been stitched all around roof and along the doorframe. The set of red wooden doors were closed. Unebolod eyed the blue wolves, green eagles, and yellow dragon carved and painted on the red. A white crescent moon and flame connected with the doors closed. He smirked and shook his head.

To the side of the giant cart, Togochi dismounted. Unebolod followed his lead.

He turned with the *sulde* in his hand to find Mandukhai beneath a white canopy, shielding her eyes and staring straight at him. Her face was unreadable.

A few feet away, sitting with his legs crossed on the ground, the boy used a stick to draw in the dirt beneath him. Unebolod pressed down a wave of resentment and marched toward Dayan, not daring to glance at Mandukhai until this was over with.

As he drew closer, Mandukhai rose from her seat but did not interrupt.

Unebolod's approach with the *sulde* drew attention from men, women, and children nearby. A small crowd gathered.

He stopped a few feet from Dayan, thrust the pole of the *sulde* into the dirt, and kneeled with his head bowed, hand wrapped around the banner post to be sure it didn't fall.

Dayan rolled to the side and stood, staring up at the banner. Several painfully long seconds passed. Unebolod was uncertain if the boy understood what was happening.

A swish of skirts drew Unebolod's gaze toward Dayan. Mandukhai kneeled at the boy's shoulder, whispering in his ear. The tenderness in the way she touched Dayan's shoulder created a lump in Unebolod's throat. He glanced away.

Dayan stepped toward Unebolod and placed his hand on Unebolod's shoulder.

"He has accepted your position as steward of the *sulde*, Lord Unebolod," Mandukhai explained. Unebolod hated how the sound of her voice made his heart skip. "Do you accept your Great Khan's honor?"

Unebolod swallowed the lump in his throat. "I do."

"Rise, then, Unebolod Noyan, *orlok* of the eastern *tumens*, Lord of the Khorchin," she said formally.

Noyan. Despite himself, Unebolod fought off a few tears, forcing them back. This new title placed Unebolod above all others in her new Mongol Empire—except for herself and the Great Khan. It was a high honor to be given this title. None had truly born the title in any real fashion since the days of Genghis Khan's empire.

"You honor me," he said as he stood. "You should know what returning this *sulde* has cost."

She folded her hands together in front of her, waiting patiently for him to continue.

"We discovered the *sulde* in a Uyghur-Ordos camp in the Ordos basin," Unebolod explained.

He relayed the details his scouts had given him regarding the massacre, and the terrible choice he had to make when he turned his back on the women and children to save the *sulde* from Ming hands—or destruction. Mandukhai listened to the story wearing a serene mask, but tears welled in her eyes as he told her about the ultimate cost and loss of life.

When he finished, a hush had fallen over the gathering. Mandukhai eyed the boy Khan—now nine-years-old and filling out much better now that he had time to heal.

"It is a tragedy we will never forget," Mandukhai said at last, her voice thick with grief. "But you are released from the burden of this horrible choice, Unebolod. You did as instructed."

"Make their sacrifice worthwhile, Mandukhai," Unebolod said. "Put Dayan Khan in front of the *sulde* and make his installment final."

Mandukhai's eyes darted around the open space. "Togochi, Unebolod, please join Dayan Khan and myself in the gathering tent."

She didn't wait to see if they would obey. Mandukhai simply took Dayan's hand and climbed the steps with him, expecting that they would follow.

And they did. Because something in Mandukhai had changed while he had been away.

She carried with her an aura of wisdom and power that he was certain would bring the world to its knees.

Mandukhai's heart was racing with grief, but also excitement. She had not realized how much she missed Unebolod's presence until he returned. Now she could not get enough of the details and lines of his face.

The guards closed the door, leaving the four of them completely alone inside the gathering tent.

Dayan marched to his throne and seated himself. Mandukhai did not join him. Instead, she turned to face Togochi and Unebolod. They needed to understand her position clearly, and where that would lead them in the years to come.

"I will not call *kurultai* again so soon," Mandukhai said, knowing this would not be what either of her *orloks* wanted to hear. "We need to be certain he stands a chance of winning this time."

"Mandukhai, we need to strike while the iron is hot!" Unebolod said. "Install him officially in front of the *sulde*, then we can attack Bigirsen while he is weak."

"Is he weak?" Mandukhai asked. She was not so certain.

"The families are vulnerable," Unebolod explained. "The forces are scattered. He is isolated and throwing himself at the Ming like a mad dog. Yes. He is weak."

Of one thing, Mandukhai could always be certain. Unebolod would never be satisfied as long as Bigirsen continued breathing. But she would not attack him when she did not have enough support in the south. She would lose.

"It would be foolish to assume that a mad animal caught in a trap would not gnaw off its leg to find freedom." Mandukhai shook her head. She had more to worry about than Bigirsen. "If he truly is weak, we have time to regroup, restructure, and plan a proper course that will ensure his defeat. With enough time, we may get others to come to Dayan on their own."

Unebolod crossed his arms in a huff. "You can't be serious. You cut the Uyghur off from their Oirat alliance! That means he has also lost a major source of his supplies. He will have to send men as far as Turfan now."

"I *have* taken the Oirat from him," Mandukhai said, her voice heating as her anger rose. "And for now, that will have to be good enough. Once the other tribes learn that we have the goods they want to trade, they will turn away from him and toward us."

"Or he will regroup and attack," Unebolod snapped.

Togochi cleared his throat. "I agree with Mandukhai."

Unebolod threw his hands in the air and turned. "Of course." He spun back around. "Fine. So what are we planning to do with our time?"

Mandukhai smiled. "Prepare. Teach. We have a young Khan who needs training, and I can think of no two better men. He needs to learn what it means to rule and when it's best to fight."

She edged toward Unebolod, placing a calming hand on his arm. His muscles twitched under her hand. "Much like a broken bone, we must take time to heal. Then we can grow stronger together."

The time is coming, Genghis. I will finish what you started.

Curious to know how Bayan escaped Lord Bolunai? Scan the code to download the free prequel, Prosperous Eternity.

Ready for the next book? Read on after the Glossary for a sneak peek at Chapter One of Empress of the Jade Realm.

If you enjoyed the book, please leave a review! Reviews can help influence other potential readers' buying decisions, which is critical for indie authors like me.

Historical Notes

Before we dive too far in, I wanted to make a note on pronunciations: Many of the name pronunciations in this novel have been simplified to make it easier for American readers. For example, Genghis is actually pronounced Chinggis. There are also many more tribes and characters in the true story than I have included in the book. To make it easier for readers to digest without being overwhelmed by hundreds of names and dozens of tribes, I compressed some characters/tribes into only a few key figures, as much as possible, throughout the epic tale.

The Oirat did not actually attack Mongke Bulag or capture Mandukhai. The connection between Mandukhai and Unebolod had become such a strong, unbreakable thing throughout the course of the books that I had to write something that would force a little distance between the two of them. Otherwise, what came next for the two of them would not have been as easy for readers to accept.

According to history, Esige's role was pretty small, but as I wrote these books, she developed such a forceful personality that I could not put her in the background like her sister had been. Esige was married off to Huoshai of the Urainkhai (or perhaps of the Three Guards). The exact timing of that marriage is somewhat murky. In a few texts, it makes it sound early in Mandukhai's reign. In other texts, it takes several more years, and that marriage cemented the alliance between Dayan and some of the southern tribes.

The disappearance of the *sulde* of Genghis Khan is a noted part of history. Where it went is still unknown. It disappeared, then one day reappeared just when Dayan needed it most. I took a few creative liberties with this. After all, as cunning as Issama was, I found it easy to believe he would have had a hand in the disappearance somehow. Having Unebolod find it and return it was not part of the history, but as duty-bound as he is written in these books, he would have stopped at nothing to find it and bring it to Mandukhai.

As news of Manduul Khan's death spread through the Mongol Empire, Mandukhai began receiving offers from Mongol Lords seeking the position of Great Khan. Without a legitimate heir to the title, any man who could win her favor had a chance to win the title. Issama sent Mandukhai an offer to live a pampered, spoiled life in warmer climates south of the Gobi. The Ming offered her a position in their court if she fled her land and entered China. This would have effectively given the Ming superiority over the Mongols. She had but to surrender to the Ming publicly and then she could live a life of luxury and ease for the rest of her days.

Unebolod's vow to "light your fire" for Mandukhai was recorded by historian Altan Tobci. According to the records, Unebolod and Mandukhai passed a series of letters to one another. He promised to light her fire and point out pastures, thus swearing to love her, give her children, and protect her. Together, they would start a new dynasty. Mandukhai wrote back the comment about the tent flap and threshold, finishing with "I will not go to you." Her words effectively reinforced that she would not share his ger, live with him, or marry him. I didn't think having letters passed back and forth would make for very engaging reading, though. These two have such a strong bond that I felt for others to accept this exchange, it had to be public and face-to-face. Plus, that just makes for more tense and emotional reading.

Mandukhai's refusal to accept Unebolod's proposal inspired a lot of resistance. Many of the Mongol Lords respected Unebolod and saw him as the most practical choice for Great Khan. Many of them tried to sway her to change her mind. She did, in fact, ask others for their advice. One woman advised her to accept Unebolod because "his word is good" and Mandukhai might find happiness. Another woman told Mandukhai plainly that she would have a good husband who would take care of her and cherish her, but her road would grow dark. She would lose the title she held and lose the respect of some of the people. But if she refused him and devoted herself to the service of the people, she would make her name famous and walk the road of enlightenment.

It played out much as it did in this book. Mandukhai lost her temper and threw a cup of hot tea at the first woman. Another record states that she poured it over the woman's head instead. Regardless, the message was the same. Mandukhai knew she was not just a woman, but a force to be reckoned with. She knew she had the power to finish what Genghis could not.

Batu's condition had been recorded as dire. He had been abandoned, neglected, and possibly abused. He was sickly. He had a "hunchback-like growth." According to the *Mongol Chronicle Altan Tobci* and *Erdeni-yin Tobci*, a healer used silver and the ancient art of *bariach*—a form of therapeutic massage and bone setting—to straighten the boy's spine and fix him. By the time he reached Mandukhai, he suffered from pneumonia after falling into a creek and being unable to save himself from the water. Mandukhai took him under her wing, protected him, healed him, and basically sheltered him from everyone. Though history does not record him as having allergies to horses, it was easy to believe that a boy as weak as he was, with such a compromised immune system, would have been susceptible to allergies as well.

Without the *sulde* of Genghis Khan, or the support of the Mongol Lords, Mandukhai faced an uphill battle to name the boy Great Khan, even with his lineage. According to the laws of Genghis, a candidate for the khanship had to gain the support of the majority of tribes to validate the claim. Without that support, anyone not attending could deny the Great Khan's legitimacy. This was how Kublai and his brother Ariq ended up in civil war. Mandukhai likely wanted to avoid such a war again, which meant she needed the claim to be as unbreakable as possible until she could make the installation official. Without the *sulde*, she needed strong spiritual and religious support.

It's hard to explain in a few words the significance of the choice Mandukhai made to install Batu at the Shrine of the First Queen. In fact, without this moment, the shrine would have been lost to history. It represented the womb of the earth mother and brought worshippers to honor the female spirit. Many saw this decision as Mandukhai's attempt at restoring the balance between the male and female spiritualism for the first time since the era of Genghis.

The entire scene was detailed in a few different historical documents, but most notably in *The Jewel Translucent Sutra: Altan Khan and the Mongols in the Sixteenth Century*, as well as *Rashid al-Din's Rashiduddin Fazullah's Jami'u't-Tawarikh*. Mandukhai approached the shrine and delivered her plea to the First Queen as I wrote it in the book, though I made a few adjustments to the flow of the sentences to make it easier for English readers to follow. Everything written in the scene follows these historical records, right down to Batu and his too-big boots. With the vows made at the shrine, Mandukhai essentially married herself to Batu—now Dayan Khan—and only he could release her from that marriage. They did not actually have an intimate relationship. It was more like a promise to dedicate her life to him and his cause. It also meant she could not be with Unebolod unless Dayan released her from the vows when he grew of age, or he died.

However, the way Mandukhai worded her vow was brilliant. It left no doubt that, should Dayan die and he not have heirs, she would have no choice but to marry Unebolod and support him as Great Khan. While cutting him off at that moment in time, she had left the door open to possibilities. Also, if Mandukhai died before Dayan became a man, Unebolod would then take up the position as Regent.

When Mandukhai launched her attack against the Oirat, she did so for precisely the reasons she mentioned in this book. Not only would it cripple Bigirsen and Issama's control over the flow of goods, but it gave her those goods instead. She had almost no army to speak of, save the few who stuck around to support her after installing Dayan—not nearly enough for a war. But that did not stop her. She organized the men and used politics when possible, but small skirmishes when necessary, until nothing remained to resist her rule. It was noted as brilliantly executed. And yes, she rode into battle with Dayan, though records indicate Dayan was "in a box" when he rode into battle. What exactly that box was had not been described.

In battle, Mandukhai did, in fact, lose her helmet. According to Mongol custom and belief, losing a helmet could indicate the loss of her divine right. Mandukhai knew she had to act quickly. Not only could an enemy fire an arrow at her head, but her men could desert her. So Mandukhai charged forward fearlessly. According to Altan Tobci, Mandukhai destroyed them entirely. She took prisoners and killed those who were disloyal to her.

In the chapter Knives and Knees, Mandukhai lays out several laws for the Oirat after their defeat. These laws were accurate according to the *Yellow Chronicle of the Oirat*.

I wanted to discuss the massacre at the red salt lake. The incident actually happened in 1472, but I bumped it up a year, to 1471, to advance the timeline a little so it could fit better into the story. According to the *History of the Eastern Mongols During the Ming Dynasty from 1368-1634*, Ming Commander, Wang Yue, understood he didn't stand a chance against Bigirsen's impressive forces. However, he could not get the reinforcements he needed. He had 40,000 soldiers but would need at least 150,000 to defeat Bigirsen's army. Since the emperor refused to send help, Wang Yue devised a new tactic. He snuck his army around the Mongols and attacked the families camped at the red salt lake. His army captured or killed without mercy. They herded the animals and burned the gers, then they set up an ambush for the Mongol reinforcements that would inevitably come. It was a terrible loss that scattered the Mongols in all directions, and Bigirsen disappeared briefly back to his homeland, licking the wounds.

At this point, Mandukhai decided to use this time to gather new allies and raise Dayan to be the Great Khan the Mongol Empire would need. Not much happens for a few years...

Fun fact. Only thirteen of the over seventy named characters in this book are completely fictional. The rest are in historical records, though the role they play may differ slightly from what was written in history, and a few of the names were shortened to make reading easier for English readers.

If you would like to learn more about the Mongols and some of the customs and battles I describe in this book, you can visit me online at starrzdavies.com.

Acknowledgments

This book was particularly hard to write. Partly because I knew it would ruffle a few feathers. For those of you who didn't put the book down and storm away, thank you! I promise the last book will not disappoint you and I hope it will be worth all this heartache. Writing such an epic love story knowing that this fate was coming certainly ran me through the emotional ringer.

To those who are interested, I wanted to acknowledge the Mongolian ballad written about Mandukhai and Unebolod titled, "Manduhai hatan guitar." It's a brief, two-and-a-half-minute video clip of music from a Mongolian symphony written in her honor. You can watch the video on Youtube. The video is of her as an old woman looking back on her life, and she was not thinking about the battles or the great things she did. She was thinking of the man whom she gave up in order to do her duty.

First, I want to thank my husband, Tazz, for giving me the space and time to write. Without him, I'm not sure I would be able to do this. I also wanted to thank my kids for their endless patience as I lost mine working through this book. Even if they have not read the stories, their interest in the Mongol culture and history has helped me talk through some of my story issues (even if they didn't know it).

Once more, thank you to Jack Weatherford for bringing Mandukhai's story to the world. Your research and work (as well as encouragement) have helped me bring this series to life. I hope I have helped further her legacy.

As always, I owe a debt of gratitude to my fellow authors in the SPWG—Dennis, Mike I, Mike P, Gail, Jennifer, and Danielle. You continue to show incredible patience as I push these books through the group as quickly as possible.

To my Advanced Reader Team: Your dedication to my books is nothing short of a miracle. And to my Patreon patron, Tyson, thank you for your endless support over the years! If you want to see your name in the acknowledgments, be sure to join me on Patreon. It will also give you access to my discord server to discuss the books and connect with my community.

And of course, my readers. Without you, what would even be the point of writing? I sincerely hope you enjoy her story as much as I loved writing it. Spread the word. Word of mouth is much more effective for authors than any other form of marketing, so if you enjoyed the book, tell others about the Fractured Empire Saga! Also, please leave an honest review on Goodreads and with the bookseller you purchased the book from. For indie authors, reviews are the fuel that keeps us going! Not only does it help spread the word about our books, but it helps validate our writing to other readers who may not have heard of us before. Thank you!

Empress of the Jade Realm
Chapter One: A Long Time Coming

The summer sun burned hot and high in the sky. Not even the cool breeze blowing down off the Khentii Mountains relieved the infernal heat. Mandukhai sat on a cushioned chair beneath a white canopy, reviewing the day's reports while sipping honey wine chilled with snow from the mountains. Sweat beaded on her brow and she used a cloth to wipe it away before it could drop on the reports and smudge the ink. Not that wiping the sweat did much good. A minute later, more rose to the surface.

The hollow thumps of sword fighting from the practice yard ten yards away carried toward her. Mandukhai lowered the reports and watched the sparring match.

Unebolod had gathered a half dozen fighters to join him. The six men formed a ring around the small, wiry form of Dayan Khan. At thirteen, he was not yet as big as the men, but not a small boy any longer. The fighters danced around him like a pack of wolves preparing for the kill. Dayan watched each of them twisting to fend off blows when any of them lunged forward. But each strike still pushed him back.

Every day, Unebolod or Togochi would teach Dayan how to fight. Sometimes with bows or swords on horseback—which Dayan had fallen off of more than once, thankfully to no serious injury—and sometimes with swords one-on-one. Recently, Unebolod had begun surprising Dayan with an uneven match. And Unebolod never made it easy for Dayan, pushing him to become stronger, better.

But Dayan was still only a boy and sparring matches like this one today were hardly fair: six grown, experienced men against one boy. Dayan had yet to win a single match. She worried how this would impact his confidence.

One warrior struck out, catching Dayan's side. He cried out as the wooden practice sword hit him. Before he could recover, Unebolod used the moment of weakness to finish the fight. His movements were graceful, smooth. Mandukhai could not help admiring the way the sun shone off his muscular arms and shoulders in his sleeveless *deel*.

Dayan blocked Unebolod's blow, but the force of it was enough to make Dayan trip over his own feet. He fell on his back. In seconds, Unebolod had the practice sword poised over Dayan's throat.

Mandukhai grimaced as Dayan used his hand to knock the sword away.

"This was not a fair fight!" Dayan protested. His face turned red with anger as he pushed himself to his feet sullenly.

Unebolod response was calm. "Learn to use all of your senses, Dayan. Men who wish to kill you will not fight fair. Especially once they have you alone. You need to learn how to defend yourself."

Dayan brushed the dirt off his deel gruffly. "But I won't be alone, will I? Boke and my guards will be there." His golden gaze darted to the guards waiting beside the sparring space as if to prove his point. He threw his wooden sword on the ground. "We are done."

Mandukhai sighed as Dayan stormed off. As Dayan had predicted, his guards closed in around him like a shield.

"My lady Khatun," Togochi said, drawing her back to her own task.

Togochi had returned late last night from a mission to bring his own Khorlod tribe fully under the banner of the Great Khan. The journey had been exhausting, so she had given him the night to recover before giving her his report. It would not change anything in one night.

Mandukhai wanted to console Dayan, but she knew that this was more important than soothing Dayan's moody angst. Hopefully he would grow out of that soon.

Unebolod strolled over to join them, his mouth set in a grim line. She knew he thought she was too soft on Dayan. He said nothing as he stopped at the edge of the canopy, leaning against the post with the casual grace of a wild cat.

"Togochi, I hope you had a good night of rest to recover," Mandukhai said.

Togochi rubbed his neck, chagrined. "I would like to say I did, but my wives were happy to see me return."

Mandukhai smiled. Jaghan had been sick with worry most of the time he had been gone. The women had tea every other day—a ritual Mandukhai was too busy for, but one she knew was necessary as well. The women needed to feel as if they had a voice with her.

Togochi cleared his throat and adopted a more serious expression. "It went well, Mandukhai. Mendu khan is a bit of an old soul, and stuck in the old ways. Between the young Khan's legitimacy and my position here, Mendu was more than willing to give his support. He says when you are ready to ride south, the Khorlod tribe will join your ranks."

Relief washed over Mandukhai. Togochi's position in the Great Khan's budding empire was one of the highest ranks a man could achieve—*orlok* of the northern *tumens*—and only a lesser khan had a higher position, and only over his own tribe. Mendu khan would have known that, if he had refused to follow Mandukhai and Dayan, Togochi could have killed him and taken over control of the tribe fully. Mandukhai aimed for as few deaths as possible. Killing khans and nobles would impose her strength, but it would also ruffle feathers. She hoped to make this reunification smooth and peaceful—and only fight when absolutely necessary.

She would have to fight one day against the Uyghur. Mandukhai had hoped that the Ming would, as Unebolod stated it, remove the Uyghur boot from their throats so she would not have to worry about it. If the Ming had killed Bigirsen for her, Mandukhai would have more easily unified the southern tribes. But nothing was ever so easy.

"That is a relief then," Mandukhai said sincerely. "Alayitung just sent a report this morning that one of the Oirat Lords attempted a revolt. Thankfully, it was put down almost as swiftly as it began. Chari now leads that branch of Oirat. Asha khan had the other Lord executed." She sighed, gazing at the reports in her lap. "Each of these deaths is necessary, I know, but it feels like such a waste."

Unebolod snorted. "That Lord was probably loyal to Bigirsen. We need to deal with him soon, Mandukhai. Before he gathers strength again."

"The Ordos Lords have abandoned him," Mandukhai replied. "That massacre at the red salt lake lost him all of his support in the south."

"But for how long?" Unebolod asked, crossing his arms over his barrel chest. Mandukhai tried not to stare. It would do neither of them any good. "The Ming built a wall to block him out of Zhongwei and Wuzhong, but if he finds even an inch he will be like a dog with a bone. All it takes is one right move to position himself again. This fight against him has been a long time coming."

The bloodlust Unebolod had for Bigirsen was unhealthy. Mandukhai wanted the Uyghur warlord dead as well, but she had to be careful how she went about it. Bigirsen may have lost control of the southern tribes, but he could still be dangerous even with only the Uyghur. Her foothold over the Oirat was more important now than ever.

Unebolod had returned to her with the *sulde*, found in Bigirsen's camp, and told her all about the massacre. The women and children killed by the Ming. The loss had crippled the southern tribes, and Unebolod had pressed her to move in and assert the Great Khan's authority over the area before they recovered. She had refused. She would not use such a horrific tragedy to gain her own power. It was a move for the weak.

After the massacre, the south had become unmanageable terrain. The tribes constantly fought with each other with one clear purpose: kidnapping women and girls in an effort to rebuild. Females had become a commodity that the men constantly pillaged for. Another reason she had no desire to ride south yet. She would not put herself or any of the women under her protection in such a dangerous place. Not yet.

Mandukhai simply did not have enough warriors to launch the attack in the south. While she had garnered the loyalty of six subtribes—and the Oirat—six others remained between her and the south. And that did not include the twenty tribes and subtribes in the south. Instead, she had focused these past few years on teaching Dayan and making as many allies in the north as she could. It was tedious work—these lesser khans all seemed to want something from her—and she had only gathered oaths from three of them. *Four, now, with Mendu khan*, she thought.

She set her reports in her red lacquer box and closed the lid. "Bigirsen will have to wait a little longer, Unebolod. We are just far too outnumbered to run the risk."

Unebolod's jaw twitched. The two of them had this argument several times, and he had always insisted he could easily sweep Bigirsen off the map with their warriors, especially if he rode through Oirat territory to get to Bigirsen's men. But Bigirsen was not a fool. He kept his warriors on the move. They could not pinpoint his location since the massacre at the red salt lake.

"I agree with Mandukhai," Togochi said. "Until we know where he is and have more warriors to ensure victory, we cannot launch an attack. It would leave us vulnerable to the southern tribes. And if the Oirat are attempting revolts—even as brief as they are—we risk exposing ourselves to them as well, which would put us right back where we started."

Unebolod took an urgent step closer, waving his hand toward the gathering tent in the distance. "Put that boy in front of the *sulde*, and it will bring the rest of the eastern tribes to us," Unebolod said tersely. "Perhaps even some of the southern tribes."

Mandukhai raised a brow in his direction. "*That boy* needs more men behind him first. This is a matter of numbers, not blood. Right now, we don't even have half the tribes under our banner. Without securing the majority, we risk his life. I won't do it."

"You can't shield him forever," Unebolod retorted.

"Watch me!" Mandukhai surged to her feet and marched away.

Unebolod's impatience was precisely what had kept her from naming him Great Khan instantly after Manduul's death. He had displayed such impatience before, when Manduul had left him in charge as he rode off to fight with Bayan. With each passing year, she grew more certain that her vision with Genghis, where the horizon burned, would have certainly been their fate if Unebolod was in charge.

Mandukhai, however, took a more patient, practical approach. *Who is he to tell me I cannot shield Dayan forever? I can, and I will.*

FRACTURED EMPIRE SAGA

A MONGOLIAN HISTORICAL ROMANCE

A ROMANTIC HISTORICAL FICTION SERIES
BASED ON TRUE EVENTS AND FEATURING
EMOTIONALLY RICH CHARACTERS,
POLITICAL POWER PLAYS, BRUTAL WARFARE,
DYNAMIC RELATIONSHIPS, AND FORBIDDEN ROMANCE

WWW.STARRZDAVIES.COM/FRACTURED-EMPIRE-SAGA

BOOKS BY STARR Z. DAVIES

<u>Divica Stormborn Chronicles</u>
Stormvalor
Stormveil
Stormcrown
<u>Divica War of Two Crowns</u>
Volume 1: Darkness Falls
<u>Powers Series</u>
Ordinary
Unique
(extra)ordinary
Superior
<u>Powers Origins</u>
Miller: Origin
Enid: Origin
Celeste: Origin
<u>Powers Legacy</u>
Powers Legacy: The Prequel
Desolation
Infiltration
Insurrection
Invasion
<u>Fractured Empire Saga</u>
Daughter of the Yellow Dragon
Lords of the Black Banner
Mother of the Blue Wolf
Empress of the Jade Realm
Prosperous Eternity
<u>Stand-Alone Stories</u>
Stones: A Steampunk Short Story

About Starr Z. Davies

 STARR Z. DAVIES is an award-winning author of over 20 tales that span dystopian realms, epic fantasies, and echoes of forgotten histories. Dubbed the "Character Assassin," she weaves stories where heroes are tested by fire—both emotional and physical.

From her woodland home in northern Wisconsin, she crafts worlds while surrounded by her greatest allies: a supportive husband, two imaginative children, and a curious menagerie of robotic pets. When not conjuring new adventures, she dabbles in home enchantments, swims like a siren, battles through video game quests, and devours books like ancient tomes of power.

If you want to become friends with Starr, dark chocolate, Doctor Who, Parks & Rec, The Office, and the MCU are all fantastic ways into her heart. That or a love for fantasy books by indie authors.

Learn more about Starr and her books.

Keep up with Starr by signing up for her newsletter.

Want to be part of her community? Follow Starr on social media.

facebook.com/szdavies
instagram.com/s.z.davies
threads.com/s.z.davies
tiktok.com/starrzdavies